DAVID LAKE

Tears of Glass

The Pioneering Paranoia California Thriller - The Sunday Times

First published by Edwards and Partners 2019

This novel is entirely a work of fiction. The names, characters and incidents portrayed in it are the work of the author's imagination. Any resemblance to actual persons, living or dead, events or localities is entirely coincidental.

David Lake asserts the moral right to be identified as the author of this work.

David Lake has no responsibility for the persistence or accuracy of URLs for external or third-party Internet Websites referred to in this publication and does not guarantee that any content on such Websites is, or will remain, accurate or appropriate.

Designations used by companies to distinguish their products are often claimed as trademarks. All brand names and product names used in this book and on its cover are trade names, service marks, trademarks and registered trademarks of their respective owners. The publishers and the book are not associated with any product or vendor mentioned in this book. None of the companies referenced within the book have endorsed the book.

British Library Catalog Publication Data -

A Catalog Record for this book is available on request from The British Library.

Third edition

ISBN: 9781973462149

This book was professionally typeset on Reedsy.
Find out more at reedsy.com

Contents

1

Acknowlegements / Music Link

For Sally
  Carys, Macsen, Rhiannon, Auryn and Alexis
  And for
  Paul
  Tears of Glass Website http://www.tearsofglass.co.uk ***Alex Drillsma –***
Praxima
  www.praxima.co.uk
  Cover **Spiffing Covers**
  Music **Paul Millns**
  www.paulmillns.com
  'Superb Singer/Songwriter' **Time Out**
  'A voice burning with emotion' **Edinburgh Evening News**
  'A charismatic performer, deeply involved and impeccably phrased.'
  Daily Telegraph
  THE MUSIC 14 tracks - 14 Chapters
  Many are the Artist's original Demos
  https://soundcloud.com/tears-of-glass-1
  Since the mid-seventies, the songs of **Paul Millns** have been a source of
pleasure and inspiration. This book is a direct result of my regard for him
and his talent.
  David Lake. **Audiobook and Paperback now available.**

*The Pioneering, Paranoia , California Thriller. – **Sunday Times***

*A wonderful, scintillating package in which words and music speak to the heart and mind about the importance of Truth and of Love and of Honesty. - **BBC TV - The Slate / Late Show***

*Superb – **Time Out***

*Lake's timeless masterpiece – **Hush Hush Hollywood Biz Entertainment News***

*A Roller-Coaster Thriller laced with delicious moments of dark humour - but lyrical, even in the midst of mayhem. - **BBC Radio***

*If the central premise is correct, I'm heading for the hills. - **BBC Radio***

*Three parts Big Sleep to two parts Wilt. - **The Independent***

*Like tasting a particularly nice fruit and smelling it at the same time – **BBC TV – The Slate***

*It is a metaphor for our times. **I WANT TO MAKE THIS MOVIE . - Irvin Kershner, Director - Empire Strikes Back***
*An exceptional novel that entertains on multiple levels, Tears Of Glass is a must read for the year ahead and is recommended without reservation. - **BookViral***

2

Prologue

8.02 pm. Oval Office, White House. March 23rd 1983
President Ronald Reagan speaks to the Nation on Television and Radio.
Extracts from;
ADDRESS TO THE NATION ON DEFENCE AND NATIONAL SECURITY
My fellow Americans, thank you for sharing your time with me tonight.

The subject I want to discuss with you, peace and national security, is both timely and important. Timely, because I have reached a decision which offers new hope for our children in the 21st Century........

........I am directing a comprehensive and intensive effort to define a long-term research and development programme to begin to achieve our ultimate goal of eliminating the threat posed by Strategic Nuclear Missiles.

..........My fellow Americans, tonight we are launching and effort which holds the promise of changing the course of human history.

Thank you, goodnight and God Bless you.

Ten Years Later...
Ronald Wilson Reagan
Good morning. It's a pleasure to be able to speak to you today on this tenth anniversary of the announcement of the Strategic Defence Initiative.......

As you know, however, critics of SDI from the very beginning have been all too eager to denounce the program........The threats have not disappeared – many new threats, in fact, are rapidly emerging .

Thank you again. God bless you, and may God bless America.

One Year later ... 1994

A battered Mustang left the track and headed for the City, leaving in its wake the smell of bourbon and the sounds of Neil Young and Crazy Horse.

Young picked the guts out of 'Cowgirl in the sand' with a rusty nail and hung them with precision on electric strings of barbed-wire.

3

Tears of glass

Los Angeles - Foothills

The car moved fast against the rain. It pitched and rolled and dipped hard at the hairpins. It had seen better days, but then so had the driver. The thunderstorm had moved on and the squalls were tiring. Soon the heat would come.

He reeled in the silver road, one hand on the wheel, one around a can of beer. The cigarette had almost burned to the filter when he spat it out. The wind carried it away.

The wipers smeared the last of the rain into neat arcs, the drops on the periphery remained static and the air stank of it.

The Mustang hissed onwards, down through low hills and all alone. He lit another cigarette, slowed slightly and lobbed the can into a roadside bin; straight in, it didn't touch the sides. The Mustang moved off at speed, the hood was down and the driver was wet.

He didn't seem to care.

Los Angeles - Central

Beneath a tangle of Freeways a rat-faced individual squeezed himself into a phone-box and listened intently to his master.

'Take her out.' The metallic voice clipped the words neatly and spat them down the line. The rat-faced recipient mumbled a reply which was lost in the rumble from the overhead freeway. 'Yes,' the first voice concurred. 'The man too ... No loose ends.' The receivers were carefully replaced.

Los Angeles - Laurel Canyon

In a more acceptable part of town, a wasted young lady was also completing a call. Speaking to an answering machine she ended her excuses and moved over to the dresser.

Just the lips to do and she'd be finished. She'd missed him, but the message she'd left would probably bring him around at some time during the evening and she wanted everything to be perfect.

Other men appreciated the effort, but he seemed happy enough in her company whatever the circumstances. He had a touch of naiveté, a childlike quality that took everything as he found it. He was easy to please. He also pleased her.

She brushed the long hair straight to the waist. It was so pale as to be almost steel. Her head was on one side, like a bird studying a crack in a tree. The fierce brush strokes tugged at it; the resulting rhythmic jerking enhancing the impression of the bird trying to figure where the insect was. Her eyes fixed straight ahead, sightless, while her mind was elsewhere.

She was thinking about him too much. Men didn't usually get to her like this, although most would have liked to get to her any way they could.

He was starting to change the situation quite dramatically. She was, for the first time, losing absolute control over an affair. He was oblivious to this, sensitivity not being his strong point.

She gave herself a mental slap and turned to more practical matters in the mirror. She chose the dark purple lipstick and worked it expertly, turning her upper lip into a sharp bow. When its companion was finished, she pursed and puckered them together, sat back and admired the result.

Outside her window the storm had left a dirty lemon light, turning the hills' sandy shale to burnt umber. Rain was rare, especially at this time of year and she missed the seasons of Europe and the melancholy of the temperate.

Climate and habitat dictate the characteristics of a population, or perhaps people are attracted to areas that reflect their personality. Here, the shrub clung tenaciously to sandy rock and individual plants and scrub, spiky, tough and bitter, survived in isolation; fiercely competitive, never achieving an easy integration. No homogeneous swathes of vegetation graced the landscape and the animal life, mainly reptiles, survived in a state of permanent mutual suspicion.

It was a land of extremes, especially inland away from the coast. The furnace of the day and the cold of the night; over millions of years the stress cracking the rock to sand.

The natural plant and animal life was directly descended from the time when dinosaurs had no enemies except each other. The present inhabitants shared similar characteristics in that they would devour anyone at the first sign of weakness, but the stresses imposed by just *being* were enough to crack many of the new arrivals.

Los Angeles - Laurel Canyon

The black sedan moved smoothly with quiet intent. 'Take it easy, we've plenty of time.' The rat-faced passenger peered through the rain spattered windshield and started to ease his fingers into black leather gloves. His companion at the wheel was already fixed up.

The Rat retrieved a Beretta semiautomatic from the glove-box and carefully screwed the silencer in place. It was only a .22, but a head shot would do the job and with no messy exit-wounds to hinder the Cleaners.

'We won't be needing that,' said his companion.

'Insurance,' said the Rat.

Towards the coastline the cooling breezes off the Pacific evened things out a little and the permanent smog over the urban sprawl induced a womb-like feeling of stability. The natural colours under this umbrella were more muted than those on the inland side of the Sierras, but the colours created by the population were primary, often with a neon core to shout their presence. The individuals were the same.

The vegetation near the coast grew thicker and closer. This led to friction. The vegetation became as dry, brittle and combustible as the personalities of the inhabitants. Like a Hollywood rumour, needing just a spark to set it off, it would spread; a wild fire, out of control and all the way to the sea.

She picked up her third coffee of the morning, but it wasn't doing any good. Spending the whole of the night trying to have a good time had only resulted in a morning of depression. She was feeling rough ... and bad about not seeing him. She'd make up for it tonight.

She went back to the brush and on to automatic, picking up the remote and finding some sounds on the radio. The rock station was blasting out some golden oldies and between brush strokes she croaked along with the track, 'I want it painted black.'

Los Angeles - West Hollywood

The front of the Mustang dived to touch the tarmac. The back twitched and the worn tyres sacrificed a little more of themselves. The driver threw open the door and eased himself out.

Tickets attesting to a variety of traffic violations spilled onto the sidewalk, the wind taking some and pasting them to a drug-store window.

He was over six foot tall, wide shoulders, but slim and almost athletic. The latter a legacy of younger days. He moved with a slightly rolling gait not unlike a B-Movie gunslinger, the hands hanging loosely over what would have been the holsters. This impression was accentuated by the high-heeled leather boots worn under the jeans. A set of spurs would not have been out of place. He could have been early thirties, maybe older.

Water was still sliding off the scuffed leather jacket and his denim shirt was stretched tight and wet across his chest. He strode purposefully along the damp and purpling sidewalk, stopping at a heavy wooden door. He swept the dark hair off his tanned face with the fingers of a strong hand and entered the bar. Eat your heart out, Eastwood.

Los Angeles. - Laurel Canyon

THE BLONDE

She pressed the remote again and the house echoed to the sound of silence. Her father's friends had disappeared first thing and at least she wouldn't have to face them. It had been a heavy night. Her silk robe was black, piped thinly with red. She wore it like a sheath. Only a body-bag would have touched in more places. Where it did touch it stretched the fabric as well as the bounds of credibility. She was tall, but tight, working out regularly with weights as well as her instructor.

Her overstated charms had never left her short of male attention and she had more than indulged herself. She could have been a 'Lady who Lunched,' but didn't have the restraint required. She was a red meat eater and wasn't yet ready to be put out to grass. There were no more charities left to support and her youth didn't help her sit well with her elders. She found herself falling short of her father's requirements and spent her time between the lines. White ones.

The problem with being both desirable and available was that her threshold of boredom was low. She had compensated by experimenting sexually and with narcotics, usually together, but like all drugs the hit was less intense and less satisfying with every event and her activities were becoming more extreme.

This guy she had just met was giving her a shot of something else. He had most of the required physical attributes, but didn't flaunt them. He didn't dress well, didn't make a show. His jeans had passed their fade-by date and his shirts had been on his back for too long.

He was the original Marlboro Man, but although strong, wasn't silent. His hair usually needed a wash and covered his collar at the back. He smoked too much and drank the liquor of the grain, often to excess.

Despite this he had something she hadn't come into contact with very often in her short life ... a childlike innocence and a naive sense of right and wrong. Maybe his belief in natural justice was a result of a lack of exposure to the seedy side of life. Balls! That wasn't true. He *had* been exposed to it. It just didn't register. *THE DARK SIDE*

Perhaps he filtered it. Like his smokes most of the crap was trapped close to the point of ingestion. In *his* case the filter seemed to be a wry humour, rye whisky and a degree of intelligence.

She had risen late. The back of her throat felt like it had been scrubbed with a wire brush. The dehydrating effect of too much alcohol seemed to have shrunk the skin around her skull and the pressure produced a throbbing pain. Her sinuses were on fire and her nose needed blowing at regular intervals. She had used half a box of tissues since she crawled out of bed and no amount of cream or make-up could completely mask the reddening nostrils. She cursed her supplier. Christ knows what he'd been cutting the coke with. She'd have to get another dealer.

Virginia

On the other side on the country a man in a very white shirt was trying to sound confidant. 'We've got a confirmation on that sir ... no doubt about it.' The metallic voice sounded pleased with itself. 'Yes I agree sir; he'll have to go too.

It's unfortunate, but he may cause us a problem. We've logged all the other units and we'll leave them in place ... if we bust them they'll only find replacements ... It's being attended to right now sir ...Thank you sir.' Simoncons The metalman's smile was smug as he clipped the phone snug into its cradle.

Los Angeles - Laurel Canyon

The Blonde with the coke habit was really pissed. Her friends had stayed far too late. Three or four in the morning and she had wanted him today.

They should have stayed up in Topanga. People were expected to go wild up there. There must have been eight or nine of them and they'd all pushed it too far ... she must remember to tell Maria to get more booze in.

Her fathers' friends had not been amused and this righteous brotherhood was sure to pass on the details of her indiscretions. Father would be furious, at least on the surface, but the anger would pass as it always did. True anger only exists when you care enough about something. She looked in the mirror and didn't like what she saw. She wasn't ready for him. Sleep, coffee and showers; lots of them.

These friends of her father had hung around longer than she'd wanted. They were usually in bed by midnight, but last night they stretched their chorus of disapproval way past this hour.

At least they only came for two or three days at a time and then two or three months could pass before they returned. She saw more of them than of her father. — *AT LEAST THEY KEPT THE AIRCON*

'Sod Europe, he spent too much time there, especially since mother left ... perhaps that's *why* she left.' She shrugged and sneezed again and snatched at the box of tissues. ~~She tried to take one, but they're designed to come out by the handful. She cursed quietly. Keeping the redness at bay was going to be impossible.~~

'Why couldn't they stay in a hotel? Jesus ... hanging around this place, never going out. Couldn't they stay with her father's partners over in Fairfax? At least they'd be closer to the Downtown action.'

Up here off Laurel Canyon they just hung around getting under her feet. ~~But being his technical people, they did make themselves useful around the house.~~ The filtration plant was always playing up and the air-conditioning was fragile. They seemed happy to check these over whenever they turned up. Putting her make-up on was a bad idea. She'd run a bath, very hot. She didn't have the energy to stand in the shower.

East Los Angeles

'Miss Jackie didn't want nobody around today.' Maria was talking to her youngest and carefully unpacking the contents of the brown paper bag,

11

placing them in considered heaps on the table.

Most of what she was saying was rhetorical as Ricci was only fourteen and the focus of his attention was divided between the new trainers his father had bought him and the lady in the kitchen of the house next door.

She was younger than his mom, and walked around the place in her underwear most of the time. She looked up from her sink and looked straight at him. Quite a lot he thought. He was certain she was looking at him. He ducked his eyes when she caught them with hers. He didn't know why ... why he felt so ... He didn't know what he felt.

She *was* a nice lady. His father had said that. He had said it when he had just finished talking to her over the wooden fence his face reddening under the swarthy skin. She had told Ricci that he was big for his age. She *was* a nice lady.

Their living-room was small and cluttered. A shrine to *Our Lady*, competing with a bronze Jesus, two television sets and a litter of armchairs too big for the room. She laid out the Yerba Buena - the dried mint; two cuts of meat, bags of rice, fat chilies and packs of beer.

'She's heading for trouble, looked real ill. Mr. Curtis should do something 'bout that girl.'

The TV came to life when a reporter announced a news flash. A White SUV was moving at a steady pace along a Freeway. Police cars and a cavalcade of motorists following it at a respectful distance. Choppers floated in and out of shot...'

'Remarkable scenes here today .. O.J. Simpson is said to be in The Bronco ... Earlier, his ex- wife, Nicole, was found stabbed to death along with her friend Ron Goldman. ...This double slaying .....'

Maria switched it off and glanced at her son. ' Oh Dear Jesus. My oh my...'

Ricci wasn't listening. The lady was looking at him again and smiling a knowing smile, but he didn't know why.

Los Angeles - Laurel Canyon

The door bell chimed. Twice. The Blonde hesitated, cursing her decision to send the maid home. Hispanics were cheap and with no Green-Card, devoted. Just never around when you wanted them. It chimed again.

She rose, pulling her robe around her protectively. She moved to the top of the staircase and descended, fingers working the stray locks of hair off her face and eyes checking the hallway mirrors for anything out of place. She slid the bolts, turned the lock and cursed quietly as she realised the chain was not hooked up.

The two men were not particularly well built and not bulky, but they had a presence; an authority, a stillness and economy of movement found only in very powerful men.

'Miss Curtis? ... Miss Jackie Curtis? ... Police.'

They smiled firmly and two leather wallets enclosing a flash of metallic silver opened and shut quickly. They were very courteous, their movements almost oriental in their dignity. 'Just a few words miss,' said one, and they were through the door.

She had almost taken them for insurance, or real-estate agents, but they didn't have that nervous quality. These two had the massive calm of people at ease in their profession and who did not have to convince others to be at ease with *them*.

'What is it officer, err ... detect ...?' Her voice trailed off as she closed the door and followed them into the lounge. This was spacious, and displayed a vulgar opulence. Lots of Louis the something, curves and scrolls, white and gold. Versace would have been lost in the background.

'Nothing to be alarmed about miss.' Said the smaller of the two. He had turned around and she was facing him now. The other man had disappeared. The one addressing her put both his hands deep into his overcoat.

It was a very expensive one, dark blue, pure wool and cut by old hands. Like his partner's, his shirt was very white. The black shoes were very slim, very Italian and not very Policeman. He stopped smiling and looked straight through her. He gave a slight nod.

Los Angeles - West Hollywood

'I ... am a very human being.'

The man had been drinking, but not that much. He had come out of the storm wet and warmly smiling and had sat at the bar for about an hour. He had a good face, blue, or were they grey, eyes hooded by slanting lids and a strong mouth above a chiseled chin.

' She told me that the first time we met. Don't know whar she meant, but I took it as a compliment.' He pushed his glass towards the barmaid as he spoke and raised one finger. She assumed he wanted another.

'Bourbon?'

The finger went up again and he nodded.

He was focused on the middle distance and didn't seem to be aware of her anyway, except when she tried to put ice in his drink. His hand moved like a snake-strike to cover the glass.

'Sorry,' she snapped.

'My fault,' he smiled quickly, 'should have reminded you.'

The tension created was out of all proportion to the incident. He diffused it by speaking directly to her.

'She's not coming ... I know that. I knew that half an hour ago... and probably knew it yesterday when I rang her.'

The barmaid appeared to relax. She picked up a cloth from under the bar and pretended to clean up the counter around his elbows.

'Strange creatures, women. When asked a question requiring a yes or no answer ... whatever the reply, there's only a fifty percent chance they mean it.'

She started angrily scrubbing at one particular spot thinking what a drag it was that all the good-looking guys turned out to be assholes.

'They have no sense of time, no sense of direction,' then quieter to himself, 'but a wonderful sense of self-preservation.'

She threw the cloth into the sink and stalked away down the bar.

Los Angeles - Laurel Canyon

The Angels

Her head jerked back as something bit deep into her neck. Her eyeballs were straining to escape and her lungs were burning. The knee in her back seemed to be pushing her tongue to the ceiling, but it didn't last for long. Her world became very dark and eventually, very peaceful.

The taller of the two men lowered her gently to the floor and carefully unwound the black silk scarf.

'That'll have to go back on later,' said the other.

'Yes, sorry about that ... force of habit.' He folded the scarf neatly and slid it into a pocket.

Together they lifted her and moved through into the hall. The tall one took her under the armpits and was first to the stairs. Dead bodies are not very co-operative before rigor sets in and lifting a sack of jello may have been easier. They took her up head first, the man holding the legs having difficulty pinning the smooth, waxed limbs tight between his arms and his side. After four steps and losing his grip twice, he resorted to draping her long legs over his shoulders.

The radio was playing 'Stairway to Heaven' as they proceeded up the curved staircase in this slightly surreal fashion. Her backside bumping rhythmically on each stair and her pelvis thrusting into the smaller man's face. Almost the scenario she had planned for that evening, but not quite. She had reached Heaven anyway, albeit by a different route than originally anticipated. Death imitating Art.

Los Angeles - West Hollywood

The man at the bar seemed to have resigned himself to the fact that his date wasn't coming. He was focusing on the interior now and not through the window. She eyed him with brief sideways glances, stolen when she thought he wasn't looking. She flicked loose strands of ~~dyed blonde~~ hair back over her ears and removed her gum, squeezing it under the bar-top, just by the Miller-Lite drip tray where she would be sure to find it later.

She was certain he was looking at her and seemed to like what he was seeing ... unless it was what he was hearing. She had just put on a Springsteen tape.

He struck a match on the sole of his boot and lit up.

'That'll kill you.' She was making conversation.

'The only thing that causes death is *life*,' he replied with a smile.

His finger was raised again. Funny, he only had to twist his hand and the gesture would have been quite obscene. He wasn't the type.

'Black-Bushmills please ... just a shot.'

'Pardon, Sir?'

'Irish whiskey, it's up there.' He pointed at a sealed bottle on the very top shelf.

She looked around for an open equivalent at ground level, without success.

She murmured 'Shit' under her breath.

'Want a hand?' He was trying to be helpful.

'It's OK. I can get it.' And she went off, the clack of her heels keeping time with her pendulum motion. He watched her return with a small aluminium stepladder and kept watching as she carefully mounted it. She couldn't quite reach, but he spent a few moments encouraging her from his position below her short hemline.

She knew exactly what he was up to, but her butt was good and he was kind and kinda cute.

She was hardly aware of it, but he had suddenly sprung up onto the bar and was reaching above her, bracing himself with one hand on the wall and the other plucking the bottle off the shelf. He was now leaning heavily against her from behind and didn't seem in a hurry to get down. She twisted her head towards his and said dryly.

'Thanks for the hand.'

'I think you'll find it's not my hand.'

Her body doubled up, propelling him backwards with her rear. He fell back, braking his fall on the bar top before hitting the floor. The bottle rolled six feet along the polished wood then fell off. He had recovered and caught it with one hand before it shattered.

He threw his head back on the floor, shut his eyes and gasped. He opened them again when the water hit his face.

She was standing in a dark plastic Mac streaked with wet electric light. Dark hair plastered close to her head framed a white slim face. It wasn't the face he'd come here to meet, but it would do very well. She had been standing there kicking her boots off. His shoulder was wet and water was hitting his neck, running on over his nipple. He slapped his shirt quickly and a flush rose on his face.

'It's wet' she said.

'Yes,' he said. 'It's the water.'

Los Angeles - Laurel Canyon

The tall one kicked open her bedroom door donkey-fashion and staggered backwards into the room. They threw her on the bed and straightened themselves up.

Her bedroom was almost sterile and starkly furnished. Black and grey with a hint of scarlet and plenty of chrome.

The smaller man's sharp features creased to stretch his thin lips into a tight wire.

'Let's go to it.' He squeezed the words out.

They worked in silence, competently, like a pair of surgeons who had performed an operation a dozen times. Her dressing-gown was removed and placed on a chair, then her panties joined them. The bed was large with chrome-work at the ends. They stripped off the black leather cover and laid her in the middle of the silk sheet, which was also black. The tall one opened a mirrored wardrobe and selected from various items of leather and vinyl clothing. He threw them to his companion and turned his attention to the dressing-table, opening the drawers one by one and eventually producing four lengths of black silk.

'This colour-combination's lacking imagination,' said the small rat-faced one as he eased her fingers into elbow-length gloves. These were followed by zippered panties, a Basque made up entirely of straps; stockings, suspenders, cut-away bra and outrageously high stilettos.

They stretched her arms and legs to meet the corners of the bed and proceeded to tie wrists and ankles to the chrome using the silk strips. When they had finished they stepped back to admire their work.

The Rat went over to the wardrobe and parted the hanging clothes. He knew just where to look. He selected a short leather strap attached to a handle, and practiced a few sharp wristy strokes in the air. He nodded to his colleague who lifted and twisted her bottom, offering her flank. The Rat slashed three times, producing reddening wheals on the exposed area of buttock. As he tossed the strap casually on the floor, the other one busied himself replacing the scarf around her neck and giving it a final tug.

Los Angeles - West Hollywood

'Coffee?' she addressed the barmaid who was putting the steps away.

'Sure.'

The lady in the Mac sat on a stool and threw her handbag on the bar. Keys, diary and a packet of cigarettes spilled out. He got to his feet and placed the bottle of whiskey next to them. He was still looking embarrassed and various displacement activities came into play. Wiping of hands on his jeans, mopping at the bar with a pile of paper napkins, running his fingers through his hair and fumbling around in his pockets. He eventually produced a crumpled pack of cigarettes, sat on a stool and brandished one in her general direction.

'A dying breed.'

'Literally,' she replied.

'Sharp lady,' he thought. Now that she had walked onto his stage he was in no hurry to make an exit. He theatrically groped for a light.

'May I?' indicating his need by making flicking gestures with his thumb, raising his eyebrows and leaning towards her. She didn't reply, but a pair of green headlights flashed, then dipped. She threw the heavy gold lighter on the bar and turned away.

He picked it up and jabbed at the mechanism four or five times before giving up. 'A lighter made to fail,' he said to her.

She extended a slim arm and snapped it open. The overlong flame ruined his performance as he stooped close, singeing his hair and burning his nose.

'Shit!' He turned quickly as the ceiling flew away. It wasn't his day.

The girl appeared not to notice his discomfort. That, or she was a very good poker player.

She smiled briefly at the barmaid then buried her head in her handbag effectively banning further communication. The man was not to be put off.

'I'm Morgan. Do you come here often?' The sentence sounded like an apology.

'That the best you can do?'

He tried again.

'I could not speak ... for amazement at your beauty.'

She looked up, staring at him with wide unbelieving eyes and a mouth quivering between amusement and incredulity. Her lips tried to form a suitable response, but seemed to fail miserably. She was saved from trying to bring this suspended moment to earth by the scrape of the bar door opening, this distraction pulling all three sets of eyes towards the door.

A stocky man, early thirties and very smart, entered the room and walked towards the bar. He could have been a financier or maybe a lawyer. Whatever he was he was a stranger to *this* bar; eyes glancing and head jerking whilst he found his bearings. He was about to order a drink when the electric Mac lady's face suddenly cut from darkly feline to delighted pussycat. Two rows of bright whites filled her face and the green searchlights flooded the newcomer.

'Charles!'

'Sara! What a wonderful surprise ... what the hell are *you* doing here?' The man, claiming his territory, placed himself directly in front of her and the curtain came down.

Outside, the rain fell vertically, working its way under the leather jacket and his wet shirt echoed his dampened spirits. His girl had not turned up and the girl who *had* turned up, turned him down. The Mustang was full of water.

'Give me that you fuck!' Three kids were fighting over a football. The biggest sitting on top of the smallest and trying to yank the oval object of desire from skinny fingers covered in blood and dirt. Morgan grabbed a collar and pulled them apart.

'Easy son, do your fighting on the field, OK?

'Fuck YOU, faggot.'

'Nice.' Morgan picked up the ball and looked around. Forty yards away and one story up, a small 'Pepsi' sign neoned its message against the darkening sky. He stared at it hard.

'In your dreams'

Morgan squeezed the ball in one hand, weighed it up and launched it with a lot of wrist and a little shoulder. Four pairs of eyes followed it to the target and three widened as the sign exploded in a shower of glass and sparks. Three little people stood in silence and the big guy turned away.

'Never did like neon'

'Shit ... who the hell are *you?*'

'Good question,' said Morgan to himself and walked on.

Virginia

The room was dark and the desk, telephone and face of the man who held it was striped with light from thin horizontal blinds. The face was tight and pale, the hair cropped close to the head the only distinguishing feature on which being steel-framed glasses. He wore a white button-down shirt, dark tie and the trousers of a dark suit. The man was speaking in clipped metallic tones.

'It's Siemonsen ... Have the Cleaners gone in ...? Good. Any feedback from the cops ....? Good, so no problems ...? Excellent! What ... !?' The stripes of light across his face did a passable imitation of a Munch lithograph.

'Are you serious ...!? YOU THOUGHT HE'D BE THERE ...? So you only took out the GIRL ...? Shit ... Just DO IT ...! as soon as you can ... Yes he IS important, VERY FUCKING IMPORTANT ...! The people upstairs want everything CLEAN. Do it NOW ...! But careful ... Ever so, ever so careful. It must look ... It must look ... RIGHT ...! GOT IT!'

He slammed the 'phone down.

Los Angeles - West Hollywood

Morgan threw a long leg over the door, the other followed it and he splashed down behind the wheel. He pushed the cassette and lighter buttons and let his mind slip into neutral. The Mustang's nose jerked out into the traffic and he slid into the stream of cars moving out of town, the exhaust leaving a trail of smoke on the water.

The rain was still falling as the Mustang sailed in the freeway stream. He headed north-east towards the San Gabriel foothills. He had driven from the west side of the city via the Santa Monica freeway and was now turning left off Glendale and on to Foothill. He'd soon be climbing the quieter roads north of Tujunga.

About a year earlier and just after the divorce he had acquired what was no more than a large wooden shed on the extremity of a sizeable estate off Mt.Gleason Ave.

One of the Ram's shareholders owned it and had offered him this place out of sympathy and maybe loyalty. He had converted it more or less by himself into a reasonable living space. Being an architect helped.

The cabin gave him the sense of freedom he had not experienced since leaving the hills of his childhood and the prison of his marriage. The union had produced no children and for that he was grateful. He was probably a little sad at the same time, but nobody got close enough to be that sure. The divorce had left him short of cash as he had left everything he had with her. He let her take the house and what remained of his bank balance, although any neutral opinion would have concluded *he* was the injured party. Maybe too injured to care. When your wife shacks up with your best friend the wounds go pretty deep. The ones in the back take longer to heal.

He fished in his pocket and pulled out a tape. It had been given to him by an old college friend and now a drinking friend.

This friend, Charlie, had dropped out of his embryonic academic career just before they threw him out for excessive use of cannabis and alcohol.

21

Women and Rock Music were the other impostors in both their lives at that time and nothing seemed to have changed much.

Charlie had talked his way into Atlantic records and risen to a position of reasonable status in the A and R department. Assholes and Rubbish, or was it Artists and Repertoire. This term was left over from the days of Tin-Pan Alley when record companies would take on writers independently of their artists and would develop both using a natural symbiosis.

Elton John and Bernie Taupin were one of the last great examples of this system of development, which was now regarded as tedious and inefficient.

The Majors now wanted to buy finished product, their accountants insisting on knowing what they were getting from the outset. Budgeting was simplified, cost over-runs unlikely and the whole process, including image, packaging and videos, could be supplied by independent management and production companies. This made things very neat and. tidy for the label executives. The net result was the creation of product for the executives and not music for the people. The modern artist and his product were highly polished, well produced, beautifully filmed and sterile. Predictability was another by-product. As nothing should be left to chance, the new technology allowed sampling of existing backing tracks, often from already successful records. They were all starting to sound alike.

Charlie and he would argue for hours over the relative merits of past and present bands, never agreeing to differ.

They and their parents typified a generation. The post-war bulge, influenced by the sixties-seventies and now having influence.

They had remained in contact through a mutual interest in women and. football. Charlie watched and Morgan played.

John Morgan had gone to UCLA on a sports scholarship like most of his team-mates and he had walked into the first team thanks to a good eye, quick feet and a fast arm.

At one time he thought he was going to make it as a pro, but the best he could manage was third string for the Rams, which in most people's eyes was pretty damn good. Morgan had done just enough academic work at college to get the qualifications necessary to enter his architectural practice.

Which was just as well, he was never going to hack it in a big way on the field.

Lack of discipline was his big problem. He was too much of a rebel for the highly technical methods employed by the big football teams - or he was just stupid. He wanted to play things off the cuff and the modern, almost military, tactics just didn't allow for that. He didn't last.

Morgan's interest in music had gradually faded over the years. He now felt the stuff coming over the airwaves at him was totally alien. It was computerised Crap, or was it Rap ... something like that... the Artists; their term, not his, all had letters instead of names ... 'Hi, I'm M.C. and this S.H.I.T.!'

He was getting bitter, or was it old. Probably both. Why did music arouse such passion? Jesus, it was only three minutes of disposable memories. Unless it came out of that unique moment in time, that moment when man caught his breath for the first time after the war and had the time to think. The moment when values were questioned, when 'Alternative' was a state of mind, not a decision to be made, when the streams of Blues, Soul, Folk and Pop, fused into the river of Rock, which then became a flood. Red-hot, it flowed unopposed through our consciousness, and then society.

This rambling mental diarrhoea continued ...

Crosby, Stills, Nash and Young, the ultimate; Van Morrison ... The Doors, Janis Joplin, Jimi Hendrix, Fleetwood Mac, Joni Mitchell, Carole King , Tapestry, the Stones ... Ruby Tuesday, the memories flowed ... Dylan, God how we needed Dylan then, Cocker, Paul Simon, Beefheart, Tubular Bells ... Bell and Arc ... now there was a band, only two albums, or was it one. 'She's got everything she needs, she's an artist, she don't look back' ... He thought of his wife ... ex-wife ... the line summed it up perfectly.

Morgan had missed the birth of this creative explosion, but had caught up.

The music from the tape player was getting through to him. He was rocking in his seat. The rhythm induced by the track had permeated his mind, then his body. The wipers seemed to have latched onto it. His hands were going now.

He broke off and punched out the tape. PAUL MILLS or was it ... he wiped the drops of water off ... MINT.... no MILLNS, that was it MILLNS. He slapped it back in. He liked it.

'What did Charlie say? ... Demo too rough, dated ... guy's too old. Just up your street Morgan. Take it, I can't use it.'

The freeway traffic was sliding along. Five lanes of reticulate movement and the wipers were moving to the beat.

Bet you didn't know where this road was leading

When your heart broke ranks, you made your move too soon

Every little thorn of conscience left you bleeding

And every little tumble left you bruised, and howling at the moon

The car in front braked suddenly, jerking Morgan out of his rhythm and as the rain doubled his braking distance he only just stopped himself from hitting the car in front.

These tears are made of glass. They fall down to the ground, and they break at last

Morgan was back into the music. It wasn't studio quality, probably a home-based four-track tape recorder, but it was OK. The singer sounded like he'd been sleeping on a park bench for a week.

Tears of glass, Can I get a reason

Why breaking hearts is back in season

He wound it back and took in the opening lines again.

I bet you didn't know where this road was leading

But when your heart broke rank, you made your move to soon

Every little thorn of conscience left you bleeding

And every little tumble left you bruised and howling at the moon

These tears are made of glass

They fall down to the ground

And they break at last

Can I get a reason why breaking hearts is back in season?

Tears of glass, fall so Tears fast, Break at last, Tears of glass

Like diamonds on the ground

Tears of glass

Oh they all broke down
That little secret look that you save for strangers
As you brush the crumbs of passion from your breast
Even learned to forgo love and all its dangers
To change the rules of the game, we both play them best
These tears are made of glass
They fall down to the ground
And they break at last
Can I find a reason?
Why breaking hearts is back in season
Tears of glass, Fall so fast, Break at last, Tears of glass
Like diamonds on the ground
Tears of glass
Oh they all broke down
These tears made of glass
They fall down to the ground
And break at last
Can I find a reason?
Why breaking hearts is back in season
Tears of glass, Fall so fast, Break at last, Tears of glass

The Mustang took the link road off the freeway as yet another belt of rain came over. The wipers were on again and the heavens were crying. The tears on the windshield moved laterally and spilt into the wind. He narrowed his eyes and squinted through the glass, but his vision was blurred.

The divorce had left him short of cash and he had been lucky to get the deposit on this place. The Rams' president had been more than helpful in putting the squeeze on his bank manager.

'Hey do you think I'm a schmuck? When you want anything ... I mean *anything* ... You only gotta ask.' Morgan's shoulders were smacked heartily. 'After all we've been through?' Morgan's cynically raised eyebrow must have registered at this point. 'OK ... OK ... I hated your guts sometimes, but we were a team ... Yeah? ... We did some great things ... Yeah?'

Morgan exploded. 'I was IN the team ... Remember?' I was out there ...

25

Doing it!'

'Only sometimes, you were strictly third- string. You've got a fast arm boy, but you ain't got no bulk – you're just a skinny runt.'

Morgan was getting a little heated. 'Coach and I ... WE were the team ... You were just assing around on the outside ... Until you thought YOU were a coach. YOU fucked up?'

'I ... Fucked up ...! Jesus Morgan, YOU lost us the chance of a place in the Superbowl!'

There was awesome silence; it went on for some time. Then the explosion.

'I nearly GOT you there! ... And if you hadn't interfered with coach, I'd have WON it for you ... For ME! You had no right... I knew what I was doing ... I ... Oh shit ... You would never understand what I was doing out there.'

'Now look Morgan.'

'You had no right! ...We had it worked out. We couldn't have taken them on playing our usual game! They knew it inside out! This had to be different. We were into something really special. You just had to stick your big ass into a seat that didn't fit.'

'Look Morgan, we've been over this a hundred times'

'And you still don't listen! ... This team is not going to get through another season. Anaheim will never see you again. Where's coach now? ... Sitting on his butt in a downtown bar telling stories about what might have been ... He's never had a job since. After what you did. The humiliation was like something out of *Carrie!*'

The silence went on for longer than they both wanted. Morgan spoke first, 'Is this why you're helping me ... Guilt money?'

'If you want the loan you'll get your finger out of my chest.'

Morgan, unusually for him, bowed to expediency and got the loan and thus the cabin.

The Mustang bumped up the narrow lane leading to his new home. The track was just about wide enough, except when Morgan had spent too much time in the bar. The red paintwork had experienced a pretty tough time over the past year and rust was appearing in fine horizontal lines where stone and shrub had come in contact with it.

Up here, his back to the great mountainous bulwark nature had provided between the coast and the desert, he could face westward, down on Los Angeles and into his problems.

Morgan splattered up to his porch and kicked open the door. It wasn't locked. He didn't see the need. If someone wanted to break in, then not much would stop them out here. There was nothing worth stealing anyway.

The interior was a fair imitation of a student bedsit ... the morning after an end of term party. Clothes were scattered over chairs and floor, dirty dishes filled the sink and draining board, shelves were piled with books, tapes and magazines. Any available flat surface had two or three objects fighting the will of gravity. Cardboard boxes of empty bottles, books on the Impressionists, expressing his need to impress? Probably not, they were tucked away in the darkest corners.

He walked past the strategically placed oval football, neatly hiding the wedding 'photo. Out of sight, but not yet ready to be out of his life. The drawing-board, the architectural stool, the finely drawn office blocks, some enhanced by fantasy turrets freely drawn in magic marker and never to see the light of day. The same could be said for the scuffed bag of battered golf-clubs which had not seen daylight for over a year.

Morgan yanked open the fridge and neatly side-stepped a six-pack of beer. He ripped a can off the pack and threw the rest back in. He repeated this process a few times as the cans seemed to be breeding in there.

He crashed backwards into a low sofa and splayed his legs long. The ring pull was off the can with a loud hiss before his ass touched down and he had flicked it twelve feet into the room's only basket in the same movement. It took him three gulps to finish the beer. He squeezed the empty can flat with one hand and sent it after the ring-pull.

He belched loudly, stretched a long arm over his head and touched a button on the answering-machine.

After the usual whirring and clicking, a strong black voice which should have been signed up by Motown, boomed out?

'Are we ever goin' to see you again man? ... Get yore ass down here and get in shape!'

Morgan smiled. More clicks.

'Morgan? ... Mr Brewster here ... I'm a little worried. The last set of drawings you did on the Snelling Building ... err ... Frank's not at all happy ... Could you come into my office first thing? I'm sure we can sort it out. Thank you.'

More clicks. Morgan belched theatrically.

Two more females left terse invitations to get in touch, but he was already twisting the neck on a bottle of Jack Daniel's and didn't register too much interest.

He was pouring two fingers down his throat when another female voice, husky and inviting, floated through the ether.

'Hello Morgan ... Sorry about today, something ... came up ... Why don't you come over tonight, late as you like ... Bye Morgan.'

He leapt off his chair and smacked the overhead beam. 'YES!' His shoes were kicked off and his belt unbuckled in one movement. By the time he reached the bathroom door he was naked, a trail of clothes in his wake.

Both bath taps were turned on full and he emptied any bottle of bath oil, salts, shampoo and even aftershave he could find into the water. He then jumped into the steaming broth. He had forgotten one sock and this was duly dispatched over his right shoulder, sticking briefly to the bathroom wall before sliding to the floor.

Morgan stuffed a towel behind his head and closed his eyes. After a few seconds one eye opened and fixed on a half-empty, or half-full, as Morgan the optimist would have viewed it, bottle of Jim Beam. This was almost hidden by the curtain, but the eagle eye had got a bead on it. He reached up, took it by the neck and got reacquainted.

Outside, the night was falling like a weight upon his mind and black upon the desert, except where the sun's orange rim touched me earth. There, it was quick and flashed with red. Night never fell along the urban coastline; it was held at bay by necklaces of diamond-bright light, strewn over the hills and piled into heaps in the valleys between. Inside his mind, there was nothing to hold back the night.

It was some time later, when Morgan surfaced, literally, from the most sensual, near-death experience of his life. He didn't know it, but he would have quite a few of these over the coming weeks.

When Morgan opened his eyes, the bathwater was almost cold and his skin was crimped and wrinkled. He pulled himself out, wrapping as many towels as he could find around his body. Moving into the living area he crashed onto the sofa. When his eyes closed this time it was with a joint resolve not to re-open unless the world was coming to an end ... and not even then.

'Oh shit! ...' Morgan wasn't a happy man. He peered at the watch he had just rescued from underneath the pile of junk strewn around his living space.

'Oh Jesus ...' He banged it on his thigh and put it to his ear. He looked at it again, and eventually got it into focus. It didn't reassure him. He threw it across the room and picked up the 'phone. Her line was ringing. Ringing and ringing and ringing. 'Why doesn't the stupid girl answer?' He sat down heavily and slammed the 'phone on the hook just before he passed out again.

Los Angeles - Laurel Canyon

Maria Meja stepped off the orange bus and eyed the four lanes of traffic with justifiable suspicion. She made this journey most weekdays and crossing this stretch of road didn't get any easier. She was perspiring freely as the air-conditioning on the bus had broken down yet again and the journey-time seemed to be getting longer. The Rapid Transport District buses belied their name and the number of passengers they carried was continuing to fall.

She was carrying too much weight. The first two kids had produced no effect on what was a pretty good body, at least that's what her husband claimed, but the third and unplanned one had done the damage. Still, compared with some of their fellow countrymen the Mejas had little to complain about. Robert had a part-time warehouse job at the docks over in

San Pedro and this cleaning work covered the little extras. The Feds had left them alone for some time and would probably not bother them too much again. Respectable people, the Mejas ... they'd all tell you that.

East Los Angeles, where she had a small apartment with Robert and the two boys who were still at home had no coastal breezes to dissipate the smog. It was criss-crossed with freeways which added to the pollution. Whittier Boulevard is its main artery, where the polished low-riders performed their courtship ritual at the weekends and her place was two blocks off it. On the periphery of society the Hispanics turned inwards with dignity not hopelessness like the blacks in Watts. At least that's what she told herself.

Establishing a presence in the east side of the city they made their contribution to its character and also its split personality. Mexican American, Latino, Latin Am, Spanish Am, Hispanic, La Raza, the Race, all these terms had been used since the first influx from south of the border at the turn of the century. The next wave came after World War II, but the seventies saw a massive influx. Indian in blood and soul, Spanish in language and civilisation, these people were a growing influence on the city.

There were nearly twenty million illegals in states and nearly half the population of L.A. was Hispanic. Crossing the border was no problem, it only took a few minutes. Some could even cross the Rio Grande using stepping-stones from the shantytown fringes of Juarez which was only two hundred yards from the El Paso detention centre.

The Cholos were becoming more assertive. These young men who joined the gangs had started out spraying Chicano graffiti and murals demanding perceived rights, but this soon encompassed extortion, stealing and killing for honour or revenge.

They were getting like the gutter rats down in Watts, with their drugs and guns and macho swaggers. They were no better when they were at home. Crossing the border didn't change them, just gave them the opportunity to develop their natural inclinations, whether dark or of good intent. The land of opportunity was just that. Being a criminal north of the border was more rewarding than being one in the south. Stealing chickens or dealing drugs, it was the same process, The rewards were different, exaggerated and in this town, extreme.

Sophisticated Mex-Ams were now accountants, lawyers, owners of corporations and city officials. They had originally been tolerated as most immigrants usually are, because the indigenous population didn't want the menial jobs. Now with almost the highest birth-rate in world the tensions in the city were mounting. The Catholic churches couldn't help as fewer and fewer immigrants were attending.

The Blacks, as well as those of European origin, were getting worried. The flow from south of the border was not abating and the myth of the melting pot, part of the American dream, was becoming a nightmare in this part of the States. By the turn of the century, the white population of L.A. would be in the minority. Maria kept herself to herself and took care of her family, did her work well and made sure her boys kept out of trouble.

She had negotiated the main road and turned down an avenue of large villas washed pink and white and cream. Each cowered privately behind large trees and manicured shrubs. Unlike their parallels in Beverly Hills which were deliberately built to be as visual as possible, skirting the roadside in loud and lewd lumps of icing masking the fruit cakes within.

Here, the long driveways were protected from the main thoroughfare by substantial metal gates and these were protected in turn by electronics and cameras.

At the fifth house on the right she turned towards the gates and automatically raised her finger to the video bell-push. It took her a moment or two before she realised the gates were open.

'Now I didn't think Mr. Curtis would be back for at least two weeks.' She spoke out loud assuming that his daughter, alone in the house, would never have left the gates open even for a few minutes. She crunched up the gravel driveway taking in the scent from the rose-bushes and noting with satisfaction the mathematical precision of the lawns.

She looked around and up towards the house. It was in traditional Spanish-Colonial style and featured heavy terracotta curved tiles on the roof, the white walls punctuated by curves and arches above the doors and windows.

'I'm gonna have a word with that young lady, them gates had better be closed and quick. Can't take any chances, even 'round here.'

She had reached the house. It was quiet. Maybe there should have been some background noise, a tape playing, a radio ... something. The sprinklers, dealing out a deck of water, they weren't on. She always did that first thing in the morning. It had rained heavily the day before, but she still felt uneasy. Mr Curtis' big Buick wasn't there ... could have been in the garage, but he usually left it outside. Even the cars of the house-guests had gone.

The quiet weighed down, together with the morning sun. She pressed the bell knowing she wouldn't get an answer then banged the large brass knocker and started to walk around the house, peering in at every window and finding nothing out of place and nobody in sight. After two circuits she gazed up at Jackie's bedroom window. The curtains were pulled back. Her mistress was not asleep and was not answering the door. She bit her lip thoughtfully. She didn't feel good about this.

Maria came to a decision and waddled off towards the garden shed at the back of the house, eventually returning with a heavy wooden ladder. By the time she had dragged it around the front she was sweating and cursing in equal amounts. She picked up one end of the ladder and lifted it onto her shoulders. She staggered towards the wall and placed one end against it as high as she was able. Maria then went down on her hands and knees and pushed the grounded end towards the wall. She alternated these two procedures a number of times until the top of her ladder was at rest just below the bedroom window. She suddenly felt very guilty. If the house had been visible from the road this act would have been regarded as more than a little suspicious. If it *had* been visible she would have not even contemplated this action, acute embarrassment wouldn't have let her.

Her anxiety was heightened by the fact that the ladder had left black scuff marks at various points up the immaculate white paintwork and Maria was now wishing she had never got into this. She was suddenly very angry with herself, as well as worried. She had visions of court cases, accusations of breaking and entry, damage to property and the threat of deportation. What the hell would Robert say?

It was too late now and she forced herself to mount the first rung.

4

Man overboard

Los Angeles - Laurel Canyon

'Sorry,' said the officer, 'Ain't no one allowed in there.'

The previous day's storm had cleared the smog and the sun beat down, unfiltered through the clarified air. The colours were bright and sharp and up here the beautiful and the lucky felt good to be alive.

A small crowd had gathered at the gate, mainly newspaper men, some locals and a few passing drivers that had just stopped and pulled over. Occasionally one would break off and try to get something out of one of L.A.'s finest dressed in the almost-black uniform and flat, blacked, peaked caps so unsuitable for the climate. The gun, baton and shades being in the absolute black that is defined by the total absence of light. Only the white vest, just visible above the top button of the jacket, gave any contrast, together with the large oval silver badge. His, needed a polish.

Two black-and-whites were parked on the roadway just outside the gates, their engines dead.

'Can you tell us what's happening?' said one of the newsmen.

'Sorry again,' said the officer, 'I don't know. Just be patient you guys, I'm sure they'll be making a statement soon.'

'Is she dead?'

'C'mon,' said the officer, gradually losing patience. 'Give a guy a chance. I'm just standing here. I've just got my job to do.'

'Is Robbery-Homicide in on this?'

'Maybe.'

'Is there an ambulance in there?'

'Look, you can see just as well as I can. Sure there's an ambulance down there. Now I can't say any more, I don't know any more and quite frankly I don't care anymore.'

They gathered in a scrum and seemed to come to a decision. One of them started to walk off down the road and around the outer perimeter walls.

The officer suspected they were looking for some way to scale them, but he shrugged his metaphorical shoulders. It wasn't his job anyway. What did he care. These guys were on twice his salary. He was told to stand there - he was going to stand there.

A gaggle of officials were coming back down from the house. Three in uniform, two in lightweight suits. One of the suits was a big man wearing a cream coloured one, cut too tight and slightly too short; the shiny bulges emphasising the raw power of the body which was also reflected in the man's bull-featured red face.

The big man leaned against the metal gates and spoke to him.

'I want to give these guys something. NOW! Can you get hold of them?'

The officer shouted up the road, 'Hey fellas ...! Feeding time.' They came running. In fact they seemed to increase in numbers. The press pressed forward. There must have been eight of them outside now, including two photographers.

The big man took a wad of gum out of his mouth and was about to throw it away, but seemed intimidated by the almost antiseptic surroundings. Even the shrubs looked as if they'd been polished that morning, leaf by leaf.

He popped the gum back and in, swallowed it, then shouted through the metal bars with all the grace of a bad-tempered gorilla. 'There has been a death in this house. We are investigating if there are any suspicious circumstances. When we know more, we will supply further details ...

Thank you gentlemen, that's all I have to say for now.'

This caused a mild storm of protest from the assembled crowd.

'Hey John, was she murdered'

'How many of them dead?'

'Any of them still alive?'

'When did it happen?'

'You gotta give us something.'

The stretched suit turned 'round and took a few strides towards the gate.

'We will be issuing another statement in about five hours gentlemen... and that's it.'

The entourage trudged back to the house. They were led by the big man. He weighed two hundred and forty-five pounds. That was confirmed by a standard police physical he had gone through about ten years earlier. Thereafter, he was known as 'Big John,' although his name was Nick.

'John!' said the smaller man in a suit. 'What's the next move?'

The big man growled, 'Doc here yet?'

'On the way,' said the smaller man. 'It's Blake.'

'We do nothing, absolutely nothing till I get those guys in there. If it's Blake they mean business.' *They're serious*

The entourage was silent. They didn't normally argue with Big John.

'What have you got on the girl?'

The smaller suit flicked through a small notebook and read out loud to the rhythm of their marching feet. 'Jacqueline Monique Curtis, age twenty-eight, couple of convictions for possession, only cannabis ... no other form. She didn't work, lived at home ... this address.'

'Parents?'

'Lived with her father. Parents divorced four years ago, mother believed to be in Miami.'

'She would be.'

'Father owns a trading company ... heavy plant and machinery, seems successful. Import-export. Mostly Europe. He came over after the war. Lithuanian by birth ... changed his name from Kuchinsky. He's clean.'

'Mother?'

'American ...We've nothing on her.'

'Anything else?'

'That's it. Nice ordinary family.'

'No such thing.' said John.

Nobody said a word as they trooped on in formation, the phalanx led by the two suits.

After a while the big man broke the silence. 'I've had the heat on me on this one. I do nothing, absolutely nothing, until the medics get here.'

'What's so special about this one?' said the small suit.

'I don't know,' said John. 'The guy was rich, but not that rich. The house is big, but not that big.'

'Maybe she was screwing the Commissioner,' said a uniform. The name of the officer wearing it was Fernandez.

One look from Big John brought a red face and more silence. When the little group had crunched their way up to the house the big man stopped them.

'I'm going back inside. Bring the doc up when he arrives, meanwhile you can check the whole place over, look for signs of forced entry, and get statements from the neighbours and staff ... get as much background on the girl as you can, friends, lifestyle, any work she may have done ... Been on to her parents yet?...You've got the diary right?' His henchman nodded continuously.

'Get on it. Oh yeah, and be discreet ... Got it! ... Mustn't go upsetting anybody.'

He entered the bedroom, slumped down into a leather chair and gazed around the room. He felt uncomfortable. The clinical surroundings were so much at odds with his personality. The body on the bed did not seem human. It seemed part of a ritual tableau, the centre - piece at a contemporary art museum.

The body, white against black, was sculptured and inanimate. He was a blunt man maybe even simple, but sitting in this dark and chrome tomb the awesome finality of death needed this peace into which he tried not to let his breathing intrude.

She was quite beautiful, high cheek bones, delicate nose, white, white skin and, as always in death, the face was empty of all earthly pain, quite unreal. The peace was broken by a knock on the door.

'Yeah, who is it?' The door was opened quietly.

'Excuse me, Lieutenant.' The young officer spoke softly ... 'Doctor Blake.'

The big man shook himself out of this unaccustomed period of self-absorption and deliberately roared, 'Hi Doc!'

Blake was the opposite of the big man, small, thin-featured, neat and meticulous in his movements.

'Hello John ... what's with this tread-carefully stuff?'

The big man shuffled over to the bed and gazed down on the body.

'Do you know something Blake? If this had happened in Watts we would have had no crowd, no reporters, no nothing. Up here, we get a gaggle of reptiles at the gate, cameramen ... and *you*.' Blake's eyebrows rose, just a fraction.

'I got a priority call. I was told to talk to no one, to be discreet and above all, to be accurate.'

'It's all yours Blake,' said the big man.

Doctor Blake moved quietly around the bed, staying about three feet away from it during the circuit. Nothing broke the stillness for the next three or four minutes. Blake neither touched, nor moved anything. He then moved nearer.

After peering intently at the body from various angles, Blake nodded to the big man, who then shouted through the door.

'Ok you guys, in you come.'

A cameraman, a detective and another doctor came in through the door and took up positions around the bed.

She lay like a perfectly placed starfish, wide open, sightless eyes fixed on the ceiling. Head, legs and arms formed a tightly-stretched pentangle, the white limbs forming the ultimate contrast with the surface on which she rested. Strips of black silk held her ankles and wrists and the silk scarf around her neck had choked the life out of her. Whether by accident or design Blake couldn't say.

38

They stood in silence for a few moments, gazing down at the body. The cameraman erected the tripod and started blazing away.

'I want everything,' said John. 'All angles, the room, everything. I don't want nothing left out. Then take it back down the stairs, out through the house and through the garden. I want every damn blade of grass in this place covered.'

A second medic entered the room and was opening his bag. Thermometers came out, and were inserted into every available orifice. Blake was gently easing the black silk scarf from around the neck and gazing intently at what lay below.

The big man left the room .He stood at the top of the staircase and looked down at the print men studiously dusting. He was angry at being summoned by his Captain and briefed as to the delicate nature of the investigation, but not *why*. He was then told to say nothing to anyone.

'I want this kept under wraps John. Everything comes back to me.'

This kind of thing happened from time to time, but he was usually told *why*. What the hell, he didn't even know a crime had been committed yet. The door opened behind him and Blake was beckoning. Back in the bedroom Big John was thoughtful. 'Well? Am I looking at a homicide?'

'I don't know, I honestly don't know,' replied Blake. The two men had been doing their jobs for the best part of two decades and had the mutual respect of two cynics. 'I'd like to point you in the right direction, but I honestly don't know. It's an unusually *clean* death. She was strangled all right, but perhaps it wasn't intentional.'

'What the hell do you mean?' said the big man. 'She was strangled,' he lifted his shoulders. 'She was strangled. That's Murder in my book'

'John,' said Blake sighing. 'You know as well as I do ... she was strangled, she didn't do it to herself, OK ... but just look at what this lady was into.' He pointed to the strap on the floor and threw open the wardrobe door, sweeping his arm along the racks of exotica. 'She got a kick out of taking things to the edge, and maybe this time a lover just went that bit too far'

'Lover? What's this got to do with love?' The big man prowled around the bed shaking his head. All this was beyond him. He was happy to just get laid and that was getting harder as the years crept up on him. Cops were a bad bet and old ones were especially to be avoided. They knew too much and had seen too much, making it almost impossible to enter into a normal relationship.

A meaningful partnership must possess an element of mystery, a road of discovery for both participants. Cops knew there *was* no mystery, just an ongoing fight to retain sanity in a world that rewarded only an excess of the basic instincts.

'I'll know more when I get her on the table.'

'Semen?'

'No,' said Blake, 'no semen, but that means nothing' Blake looked around the room. 'Nice place, some classy designer ... Some bucks!'

'Yes,' said John, 'you could say that. A designer death.'

The room was quiet. John broke this silence by calling in the dusting team. When they'd finished, he went through the room, opening drawers and checking the contents of wardrobes and cabinets. The big man paced the dark cage, inwardly fighting the confines of his brief and the restriction imposed by the lack of clarity present in the evidence. He turned to Blake.

'There was talk of the Feds coming in on this one. The chief told them to butt out. Now I've got to come up big.'

'Why the Feds?'

'Search me, maybe a narcotics connection ... or maybe the pressure's coming from somewhere higher ... there could be a political angle ... maybe Clinton's in town.'

Blake smiled briefly, acknowledging the irony in John's voice. The big man pushed one side of the small coffee table Bake pocketed a set of leather handcuffs. and a small drawer appeared on the opposite side. He removed a small plastic sachet and tipped a little of the inevitable white powder on the back of a large hand. He sniffed and licked it.

'Coke, average stuff, nothing dramatic. It would have been a surprise if I hadn't found any.' He fingered a number of mildly pornographic magazines also found in the drawer, which he shut after first palming the coke into his jacket pocket. Blake raised an eyebrow, but said nothing. He'd seen the big man do this before.

'What the hell,' he thought. 'Whatever turns you on.' He looked at the lady again whilst pocketing a set of leather handcuffs. He looked at the wardrobe and pondered on her party clothes. He was still thinking about them as he walked away from the house, the barking of Big John's orders receding behind him.

Morgan, like a great many other Angelinos, only used the freeways when he wanted time to think and this morning was definitely not one of those times. There was no direct route from his place to hers up in the Santa Monica mountains, and the four freeways in between all ran from the north-west to the south-east and therefore at right angles to the flight of the crow.

His motorbike was the ideal way to get around fast and he had worked out a good route through Sun Valley and North Hollywood.

The BMW's front wheel bounced and slid to the right. Morgan tugged at the handlebars and tightened his grip with his knees. The wind was working under this jacket and was trying to pull him off the bike. He didn't reduce speed as he weaved his way through the traffic, but he was just about in control and pressed on, the throttle open as much as he dared. He was only about twelve hours late and his head was throbbing. The wind helped.

'Oh Christ' he shouted to himself. 'She'll kill me.' Little did he know. The bike was a divorce present to himself, the Easy Rider generation having got there before him. He was making up for lost time.

The L.A. traffic didn't get any easier to negotiate, but he was making good time. After an hour, he whipped into her avenue and throttled back severely. He focused on the small group of people at her gate and the police cars. He idled cautiously to the edge of the group and switched off.

Morgan looked through the gates, just as the ambulance doors were swung open to allow the gurney to be wheeled into the back of it.

Cops and medics moved purposefully around the body, like roadies at a final sound check. It looked like a final check for the person being slid into the back of the ambulance; like a baking-tray into an oven.

'Who the hell is that,' thought Morgan, then out louder, and with a hint of panic in his voice, 'Who is she, officer?' *Body Bag* [handwritten margin note]

The words died on his lips as the blanket slipped briefly to expose a length of exotically clad thigh and leg. The officer's eyes narrowed as he made his way towards Morgan. 'How do you know it's a She? ... and who the hell are *you*?'

Morgan froze, and panicked inwardly. He was confused and found himself remounting his steely steed and wheeling back the way he'd come. The officer cursed loudly, squinting at the dirty plate and not getting it. He shrugged. 'What the hell, just a punk. Not the sort of guy this family would know ... forget it.'

The big man would have had quite a lot to say to this officer had he been aware of this exchange.

Morgan was aware of some neighbourly remarks as he took off.

'Always knew something would happen to that woman, all silk and leather, *belts + straps* [handwritten margin note] a bad combination'

'All that, just to get your end away.'

Morgan's end was well away by now, he was moving much too fast. His eyes were streaming, wind or tears, it was hard to tell. Morgan's thoughts were also moving fast and not in any particular order. 'What the hell happened, is she dead? ... Yeah, she's dead.' Nothing tangible, the attitude of the people around the gurney; resigned, matter of fact, remote from the body. No one was in her space. No one stooping to tuck in the blanket, or drop a word of comfort. Remote. All the players were remote. 'Even I was remote,' he shouted. The slipstream carried the words away.

Even sex with her was more of a mechanical operation than he would have liked. She had led him through routines which pleased her, with absolute precision and dispassion, insisting on wearing an assortment of leather and rubber creations which must have cost more than Morgan's loan repayments. This circus embarrassed him more than he cared to admit, but that scene being performed outside the house had shown him that this particular show was over.

'Overdose? Illness? ... Do they know about me? We only just met, only been to bed twice ... they can't know about me. Not possible ... They can't know I was coming round, can they?' He braked suddenly and slid to a halt. 'Jesus Christ, Morgan, hell's the matter with you? ... The girl's *dead* !'

He hated himself then; and wiped away another tear. Hard tears, tears of emotion or frustration ? Bittersweet or crocodile? Real or resentful?

He shook his head slowly and moved off again.

Virginia

Back in the darkened, light-striped office, Siemonsen was on the 'phone. The earnest voice at the other end was trying to sound competent. 'Well sir, that's quite right. We could do without these articles; the Brits were always a bit leaky. I don't believe there's anything to connect them ...'

'Can you do something about it?' said Siemonsen, interrupting sharply.

'We are taking care of that right now sir, but to be quite frank, I don't think anyone is likely to put two and two together ... The reports are scattered over lots of journals, and over quite a period of time. The odd suicide in sensitive areas of research, the occasional scandal regarding plutonium accounting, or lack of it; Congress moaning about budgets and Clinton planning to resurrect SDI ... All newsworthy, but not anything that could reach critical mass.'

'Put water on the fire ... then blow away the smoke.' Siemonsen said, picking up the silver frame sitting at the right hand corner of his desk which held the twin photographs of his parents. He was looking at them thoughtfully.   *Bonum well - graffiti*

'Got it, sir. No problem ... Thank you sir.'

Siemonsen wrote carefully with his fountain pen, the one his mother had bought him all those years ago, A HARD RAIN'S GONNA FALL.

Los Angeles - Laurel Canyon

'Excuse me sir, but I think you should take a look downstairs.' Officer Fernandez was young and very keen.

'Been through it, what did I miss?' The big man was irritable.

'I mean RIGHT downstairs, there's a cellar.'

'Cellar?'

'Yes sir ... door off the kitchen. Looked like a storage unit.'

'Why didn't anyone pick up on this?' John snarled angrily.

'We just did sir.' The reply was too cocky.

The officer was yanked off his feet as John grabbed his tunic between the clavicles with one big paw and lifted. He slammed the startled officer against the wall at the stop of the staircase and held him there.

'Listen son, if you want to stay in one piece you'll keep your fucking mouth shut until you got something to say ... GOT ME?'

The officer's face was getting as red as John's and his heels were scraping for purchase on the wall. In the hallway below them half a dozen pairs of eyes watched and wondered what to do. John saved them from making a decision by letting go. The young man doubled up, holding his throat.

'Hey Lieutenant.' The voice had just joined the eyes in the hall and had missed the action. 'You'd better come down here.'

John went through the motions of straightening out his sleeves although they were too short ever to look right and walked with deliberate dignity down the stairs.

'Look at this John, there's a small utility area off the rear of the kitchen. It has a narrow staircase leading up to a small landing outside her bedroom, a sort of back-passage.'

'And there's brand new door been installed right next to the rear kitchen door in the utility area. It had been screened off by this full-height wall cabinet. It's not locked and there are stairs down to a cellar.'

When the lights were on it was very well lit - for a cellar. A harsh light was provided by high intensity lamps, but it was cool, a vibrating hum testified to the efficiency of the air-con. This basement was big and empty.

'Well?' growled the big man.

'Take a look at the floor sir, it looks like there was a large piece of equipment bolted to the floor along that wall ... and again here, in the centre.' Fernandez had recovered and spoke with a careful humility. He pointed to outlines of dust caught in a light film of grease mapping original positions of rectangular objects. 'Some must have been pretty heavy, look; the tiles are cracked ... and over here, crushed!'

The big man paced the room staring at the floor. 'Looks like they were dragged across the cellar towards the door.'

'And up the steps and out through the hall,' replied the conscientious young man. 'The scratches go right through.'

'Any other way into this room?' said John. 'Cellar-flaps?'

'No sir.'

'Strange.' John stalked the room again and looked at the walls. 'They dismantled whatever was here and stacked the pieces against this section of wall, then took it out piece by piece. Get forensic down here; I want to know when this stuff was moved.'

Morgan was leaning into the wind, standing bolt-upright on the footrests. The bike was tearing over the blasted rock and dirt, sometimes on the surface of the road, often in the scrub. Arms in crucifixion he offered himself; a manic sacrificial scarecrow howling at the moon, but there were no takers. He was returning in the evening light, washed-up and ghost-like. 'Was she dead? ... Or some mistake? A dream?'

Morgan bumped up his dirt track and parked the bike against the side of the cabin. He kicked open the door and a half bottle of rye later he lay on the bed, gazing at the ceiling and mumbling to himself, misquoting.

'Beneath the bare light-bulb the plaster did crack.' Was he cracking? In the screaming battleground of his mind the conflicting emotions ebbed and flowed. Guilt ... 'If I'd been there this wouldn't have happened. Remorse ... 'She had so much life, all to live for.' Anger ... 'How could anyone give themselves the right to take a life? ... and what about the right not to die?' Frustration ...'Why? For what reason?' He took another slug. The frustration was also sexual, but he dismissed that thought quickly, feeling a flash of contempt for himself. The square bottle was flung with great force against the wall, shattering over the wooden floorboards and showering the Native Indian rugs with glass splinters. The fragments glistered yellow in the light of the evening sun.

Fear was moving from the back of his brain to the front. He was going to get implicated in this. Brewster would go mad and he wouldn't find another job ... The cash would dry up and his ex would have a field-day.

'I knew there was something wrong with you, Morgan ... Seems like 1 got out just in time.'

He twisted and turned, rolled over and reached into a bedside drawer to pick up the cassette. Staring at it didn't produce the right effect and he didn't have the energy to move into his living-room. He rolled to the edge of the bed and reached into the drawers of a pine chest. After scrabbling about under dirty underwear he found a tape-machine.

He popped the cassette into the portable tape-deck, the batteries were OK. He lay back and waited.

I still walk down to the river; still go leaning in the wind
Returning in the evening, never knowing where I've been
Passing other strangers, out on their own high wire
The washed-up of the water, along with the dead bird and tyre
You left your timetable open; I had to sneak a glance
Seems the early morning train is much your better chance
And I won't be home tomorrow, got to see a good friend of mine
So leave the keys in the kitchen and don't forget your books this time
Man overboard, throw him a reason, throw him a line
Man overboard, it's just a season, happens all the time
His heart's on hold, there's ice his soul
He's twisting and turning
He's learning to roll with the tide
Well I'm almost life-like, I'm almost quite real
Even the ghost of Banquo, would surely know the way I feel
And I've been hacking up some ladders, mostly slipping down those snakes
Don't pass go, collect no dough, surely there must be some mistake
We thought we were flying so high, and looping all the loops
We were only lions in a cage, and jumping through those hoops
And a strange kind of quiet, falls upon these days

Even my neighbour across the hall, seems to know you'd go away
I don't know how she knows
Man overboard, throw him a reason, throw him a line
Man overboard, it's just the season, happens all the time
His heart's on hold, there's ice in his soul
He's twisting and turning He's learning to roll with the tide
Man overboard, throw him a reason, throw him a line
Man overboard, it's just the season, happens all the time
His heart's on hold, there's ice in the soul
He's twisting and turning
He's learning to roll with the tide

He cradled the cassette case to his chest, played the track a few more times, drank a lot and waited for the call or the knock on the door. It didn't come.

$\longrightarrow$

Los Angeles - Downtown

'Morning Mr Morgan.' The girl at the desk flicked back her dark hair and gave him a sideways glance, together with what she regarded as an enigmatic smile. Morgan was bustling past, his one and only suit flapping fashionably and a large bundle of newspapers under one arm. The bundle attracted more than a few stares from his fellow passengers in the lift. Morgan got out at the sixth floor and marched into his office, kicking open the door as both his arms were occupied in cradling the bundle of newsprint. Some of his colleagues were laughing at him through the glass partition.

Two of Morgan's phones were ringing. He ignored them and crashed through the newspapers, skipping briskly through the broadsheets and more carefully through the smaller local tabloids. After twenty minutes his office housed a mountain of papers scattered over the floor and desktop. He was peering intently two inches above the columns when, at last, he seemed to have found what he was looking for. His head and fingers stopped jerking and he gazed intently at a small column at the foot of an inside page.

'DEATH IN THE CANYON!' was the headline. The account that followed was less lurid and not very instructive.

The body of a young woman, Jacqueline Curtis, twenty-eight, of Laurel Canyon was discovered yesterday morning by her maid.

Miss Curtis, who was home alone at the time, was found in her bedroom. Police cannot yet verify if there were any suspicious circumstances. Next-of-kin have been informed.'

'No suspicious circumstances, Jesus Christ!' shouted Morgan. 'What the hell is going on?'

He made a movement to pick up the telephone. His immediate thoughts were to ring the police, or maybe the coroner's office. He thought again, left the telephone, sat back and gazed at the wall.

There was a sharp knock on his office door which opened before he could react. One of the secretaries put her head around it, stared at Morgan, the office floor, then back at Morgan with eyebrows raised.

'Mr Brewster would like to see you Morgan ... straight away.'

'Sure, sure,' he said, not making a move.

'It seems pretty urgent, Morgan.'

He stared at the ceiling.

'You been a naughty boy again? ... Now if you really want to be naughty?' She licked her lips slowly.

'Give me a break.'

'Where?' She snapped and slammed the door.

The 'phone was ringing angrily. Morgan picked it up. 'Yes sir. Yes sir ... Yes Mr Brewster, right away.' Morgan pulled a face, then pulled his jacket off the back of a chair and headed down the corridor.

'Could be anything, John.' The man was sitting opposite the big man and spoke the words with implied technical knowledge hoping his superior would infer diligent investigation. He was wrong.

'It was not ANYTHING! ... It was SOMETHING! ... and I want to know what it WAS!'

They were squeezed into the thinly partitioned office at Parker Centre. Privacy was not a priority in the world of law-enforcement. John continued.

48

'There were two main units and three or four smaller ones. They weighed a lot more than a household freezer and they were recently removed ...' John went on ...'Neighbours see anything?'

The small suit shifted on the hard wooden visitor's chair. 'One van seen at the end of road ... just after eleven. Two witnesses saw a large grey van. No markings. Sat low in the road. Could be it, but we're having trouble getting a make ... nobody got the plates.'

John was leafing through a sheaf of papers on his cracked laminate desktop. 'They've come up with the van's tyre tracks in the gravel driveway. Most had been brushed over, but they were careless. Traces of going in light, coming out heavy ... very heavy ... must have had modified suspension.'

'Yeah, it looked like a normal Ford ... pity it was so private ... no sight-lines from the main drag.'

'Anything else?'

'That new door. Fresh oil on the hinges. Very fresh. There were signs of old wiring that was probably a form of alarm system to the original door. The old door frame was still in place, but was splintered in places ... looked like somebody had tried to smash through it at some time.'

'What about the party people?' said John.

'Too stoned. She kept playing a tape they both liked. Over and over.'

'They?'

'New boyfriend.'

'Oh yeah?'

'Don't read too much into it. She was liberated ... in a big way.'

John scowled, 'Like Vietnam.'

'Same result ... both got fucked.'

'Where's the tape now?' said John.

'Wouldn't know which one. It can't be significant.'

'It may have a name on it, an address even.'

The small suit looked resigned to another wasted afternoon. 'I'll ask around those dope heads again.'

'Ask about *this* guy... and the tape ... What about the maid?'

'Talked to her ... she doesn't know anything. Confirmed there was nothing taken.'

'House-guests?'

'All from Europe. Mainly East and Central. Worked with the father ... some are engineers. Looked after his ship's engines and checked over the plant he was trading. He didn't charter all the ships ... he owned two. His business was mainly machine-exports to Eastern Europe. Goods imported in exchange. Some cargo went by plane.'

'Check him out for any sniff of narcotics ... shipments from South America.'

Morgan was far away, he was staring blindly through the big glass window at the building site adjacent. Diggers and cranes clawed at the earth and workmen spilled out of it. Yet another office-block was being constructed in this part of the town. The business district rose up like slabs of rock squeezed upwards by its surrounding continental plates, or maybe just continentals. A modern Stonehenge, built as a monument to L.A.'s victory over nature, the theft of water and as a place to worship the prophets of profit. — Fnan'.

The double-glazing muffled the sound of the vibrating power-hammers. It was a strangely hypnotic and reassuring rhythm, but Brewster's voice was quietly getting through to him. '... And another thing Morgan, your work is not improving. It is not even retaining its mediocrity. That desk you specified for Carlton Brown.' At this point Morgan raised his eyes to the ceiling. 'Yes, Carlton E. Brown,' went on Brewster deliberately. 'A man who has given this firm an enormous amount of work... and a man I especially wanted to be given the best, the very best, of our professional attention.'

Morgan was still gazing out of the window. The ball and chain was swinging hypnotically across the large plate-window and Morgan was wondering which Japanese company was funding this particular development. The Americans didn't seem to want to invest in their own cities anymore. The American business, the American economy, was tired. Morgan was tired.

Brewster was rambling on. He was approaching sixty and had silver grey hair. He was wearing a dark grey suit over a slate grey waistcoat; stretched tightly over an expanding paunch. His light-grey tie was made of silk, the matching handkerchief spilling like a hanging garden out of his top pocket. His socks and shoes were hidden by the desk, but if Morgan had been able to see them he would not have been surprised at their colour. He was a grey man, but he spoke in sepia tones.

'That desk ... that desk came in one solid piece ... ONE SOLID PIECE! Sure, you did a wonderful job with the manufacturer. The grain was a perfect match. The inlay was some of the best work Frank had ever seen ... and the colour match with the panelling couldn't have been faulted, but ...' At this point he screamed ... 'WE COULDN'T GET IT THROUGH THE FUCKING DOOR!' He went on with a menacing quietness, 'We had to get a crane, take it up three stories, take out his window and half his WALL!' He resumed shouting ... 'DO YOU KNOW WHAT THAT COST?' Brewster mopped his brow with a handkerchief. 'What is going on in your head? No, don't tell me, a child of three couldn't have made a mistake like that.'

Morgan appeared unruffled. 'I guess I got carried away. It *was* a nice piece of work.'

Brewster nearly had apoplexy at this point. 'You guess, GUESS! Don't guess anymore ... use a TAPE! Carried away! ... That's exactly what's going to happen to you, Morgan if I've got anything to do with it.' Brewster swallowed two pills and half a glass of water. It seemed to calm him down a little.

'Your problem, Morgan, is that you never grew up. There's a real world out there,' and then very loudly, 'AND IT'S MEASURED IN FEET AND INCHES! You're a dreamer!'

'Let you be in my dream, if I can be in yours,' retorted Morgan. At this point Brewster went raving mad.

'This is my dream Morgan ... I dream that you are going to walk out of here ... no run. You are going to keep running till you are either out on the sidewalk or Security catches up with you.' He started dialling, 'Two minutes should do it, either way'

Morgan turned and sauntered out, stopped at the door and looked back at Brewster, 'So a raise is out of the question?'

Morgan slammed the door behind him leaving Brewster shaking with rage and started to walk quickly down the corridor back to his office.

He was more worried than his outward appearance suggested. He needed this job, but it looked as if it had just disappeared.

His thoughts were cut dramatically short by a loud bang. His office door came to meet him. The lights went out, everything went black and a sharp hammering reverberated between his eardrums and his skull. He felt as if he had been sacked by the whole Raiders' defence.

The lights started to come on in Morgan's brain and when he opened his eyes he was aware of a murky light from the outside world. He staggered to his feet, put one arm against the wall and stared at what used to be the door of his office.

What remained of it was swinging gently on two hinges. Clouds of dust billowed out through the doorway and bits of the ceiling started to fall to the floor. Morgan brushed splinters of wood from his suit and made his way gingerly towards his now smoking office. Two of Morgan's colleagues had arrived at the doorway simultaneously. One remarked, 'Jesus,' and the other, 'Christ.'

Lying on the floor of the office and surrounded by debris, bits of desk, crushed filing-cabinets and broken ceiling-tiles, was a large iron ball attached to two chains. These snaked out of what remained of the office wall and window. As Morgan groped over the wreckage and peered into the outside world he saw the chains reaching up and up, gently swaying over the adjacent building-site. They swept on up to the summit of the tallest crane.

The wail of the siren was fading, but the strobes kept stroking the back of his retina. He was vaguely aware of someone in a black uniform thrusting a cigarette between his fingers, pushing his hand up to his mouth and a light appearing at the end. He sucked in deeply.

'He's in shock,' came a voice.

'And the blow on the head from the light-fitting didn't help,' came another.

Morgan became aware of two police cars, one ambulance and a fire- truck.

He was also aware of a cop talking to him and Brewster pacing up and down in the background. The crane driver was talking to another cop.

'I only went for a leak. Two minutes, maybe three. When you gotta go, you gotta go.'

Morgan stood up shakily, 'I'm not ready to go.'

Brewster grabbed Morgan's arm, pulled him to one side and said quietly 'You're a vandal Morgan, I want you out of here ... and fast.'

Morgan took hold of Brewster by the throat with his free arm. 'You can't think I had anything to do with this? You're crazy, I was almost killed.' Brewster wasn't listening. He was walking away muttering threats and holding his throat.

The cop turned to Morgan. 'Kids ... KIDS! You can't turn your back.' They both looked up together at the hole in the side of the building. 'Ain't no respect. Do your best for them.' Morgan's jaw dropped and he started to open his mouth, but shut it, shrugged his shoulders and turned away.

The cop was busy scribbling. Morgan glanced at it as he turned. The officer had taken out his notebook and was ostentatiously writing in thick black non-regulation felt-tip, 'KIDS'.

Los Angeles - Ram's Training facilities

The smell of liniment and stale sweat made him feel at home, together with the metallic clang of the locker doors. The splashing of water in the showers and the excited bragging and banter gave him a feeling of belonging. He had no feeling in his body except the pain of the draining of all energy. It was a familiar feeling and he started to feel quite good about life although by his appearance anyone would be forgiven for thinking life didn't feel too good about *him*.

A large black shape towered over him, 'I shouldn't have got you down here man, it just ain't there no more.'

Another large shadow walked past, 'Hey Aaron. Was it ever?'

The original black shape shouted, 'Before your time brother, it was there all right.'

Morgan was slumped in a corner, still in his kit. He was trying to pull a ring on a can of beer, but didn't have the strength. The black athlete squatted down in front of him, removed the can with over-deliberate gentleness and did it for him.

Morgan remained slumped and swallowed greedily from the can. 'Seriously man, I appreciate you trying to help, but you should pack it in. These training nights will kill you. It ain't as if you're going to make the team again. Who needs a quarterback who can't lift his arm?'

Morgan raised his can in mock salute and agreement.

'Ain't seen you down here for a while. Who is she? She really must have got to you.'

Morgan mumbled quietly into his beer, 'Somebody got to *her*.'

The black footballer sat down. 'What's that?'

'Nothing. Let's have a drink.'

The changing-room door opened and a man put his head around it. He was short and stocky with greased-back hair. He had a bar-tenders waistcoat on and the bar till-roll in one hand.

'Morgan! It's Freddy on the phone ... he wants to borrow your bike. Some broad he wants to scare the pants off. He should be so lucky.'

'Randy little sod. Tell him the keys are in the usual place,' said Morgan, 'but I want it back in the morning ... all of it.'

Morgan struggled to his feet, put his arm around his friend and they both headed for the bar, Aaron picking up a ball on the way out.

At the other end of the locker room a player was getting a whisper from a team-mate.

'Don't disrespect. That guy was timed at sixty seven.'

Not impressed, the player shouts, ' Hey kid, how good *were* you?'

Morgan and Aaron exchanged glances. Morgan whipped the ball from Aaron, spun and sent the ball hard into the player's gut, smacking him back into the wall. He slid down and sat, legs straight out and the ball buried somewhere in the hunched body. For a second the only movement was a dribble of vomit from the stricken player. Quickly followed by cheers and whoops of laughter.

At Parker Centre, the headquarters of the LAPD, the small suit who went by the name of Weller was strutting through the open-plan banks of desks, ringing telephones and small argumentative groups towards the office of Nick Steadman or Big John as he was known to his enemies. He didn't have any friends. The two were part of the seventy five strong Robbery-Homicide Division. Every cop's aspiration. John and Weller's section was 'Special Investigation.'

Safely inside on the command 'Come!' he slid the cassette across the desk on the command 'Well!' and smirked, although it started off as a confident smile.

'That's it, that's the tape, John, but I can't see what good it'll do us. No ID, no address, but they told me that she called her guy, Morgan.'

John fingered it and slipped it out of its case. He fingered it some more. 'Who's this Paul Mills.'

'MILLNS.'

'Well?'

'The artist ... the guy who wrote the stuff. Look it's nothing, just a demo tape. She had tapes everywhere ... nothing as rough as this though.'

'How do you know it's the right one?'

'What right one? ... There is no RIGHT one. It's just a tape for Chrissake.'

'How do you know?' The big man wasn't letting go.

'Talked to the deadbeats at the party. She played it non-stop. Drove everyone mad.'

'That bad?'

'No, it's OK ... I'd like to hear the studio version, this is too raw.'

'Really?' said the big man, pocketing the tape, 'And you'd be an expert on that?' Weller shrugged and left.

And so it was later, as both companions were telling tales and still sitting on bar-stools, that Morgan was mellowing out. He was now looking reasonably presentable, having showered and changed, however, inside he was deteriorating fast due to some very serious drinking.

'Come on Aaron,' he addressed his black companion, 'Get them in.'

'I think you should cut it out, Morgan.' Aaron's huge white teeth flashed in a wide grin. 'I'll call you a cab.'

'No don't worry, I'm fine.'

'Are you crazy?' said Aaron. 'And you should definitely pack in these training nights. This'll kill you.'

'Looks like I'm gonna be killed anyway.'

'What's that?' but Morgan had slurred this words so quietly he couldn't pick it up. Morgan just shook his head and said nothing.

Aaron went on, 'Still coaching those kids?'

'Twice a week.'

'Wasting your time. They may be deprived, but *if* they grow up, they'll be depriving *you*, probably at the point of a knife'

'They just need a little help.'

'Are you going soft?'

'Soft in the head. Anyway, those kids are the only guys I can look good against these days.'

'That's the first sensible thing you've said all evening.'

Morgan's car lurched to a halt at the bottom of his driveway. He had difficulty in getting out. Looking a little worse for wear he stumbled towards the cabin. He picked up pieces of dried earth and hurled them over the stone wall as he staggered. He threw large chunks into the air and tried to catch them. By the time he was half way up his track he was covered in soil.

Morgan was reliving past glories, hurling chunks of soil through the air and remembering when Aaron was on the end of them. Good days.

Morgan stooped to pick up a piece about the size of a football. He was about to kick it when he suddenly looked at it very intently, as only drunks can. Realisation was slow in coming as he swayed there silently, but when it did, he was holding a human head.

The moon was full and by its light the whole scene looked like something out of a Corman movie. Morgan still held the head at full stretch in his arms, the words formed on his lips, 'Freddy?' The head didn't respond.

A look of horror, then disbelief, crossed Morgan's face. He screamed as he threw Freddy's head to the ground, then turned and ran and stumbled and tripped towards his cabin. He sprawled headlong over a large shape. It was the headless body. Covered in blood and rising, he started to run. Something snagged his face. He ran on towards his home. Bursting through the door and snatching at the 'phone. He dialled quickly and not very accurately. After three attempts somebody responded at the other end.

Morgan was leaning against the wall, the 'phone and his arm smeared with blood. Blood covered his clothes and his hair. A shaking and stirred Morgan burbled into the telephone.

'Police? ... I want to report a body ... and a head ... A HEAD!'

Morgan was leaning against the cabin doorpost, slapping his face to convince himself that he wasn't dreaming and trying to unscramble his brain. The feeling of déjà vu was strengthened by the manic strobe of two police cars and one Coronor's van.. The cop was stalking around and talking to Morgan from a couple of yards away. He was furiously writing notes. Morgan was dimly aware that it was the same cop that questioned him at his office the previous day. Other cops were moving around with tape-measures and talking in knowing tones. The officer eventually came into Morgan's space. He had a vaguely Irish accent.

'Name's Kelly, only transferred to this division today. You lucky at cards?' The cop looked around. 'Twice in one week.' He looked up at the stars, 'Someone up there likes you.'

'Someone down here doesn't,' retorted Morgan. He retched and then vomited.

Kelly skipped out of the way and looked with disdain at the mess on the ground. He walked back down Morgan's driveway, beckoning for him to follow.

The two made their way down, Morgan trailing in his wake. They stopped at a motorbike lying on the ground, gleaming in the moonlight. The cop shone his torch along a wire stretched across the track and twanged it with his index finger.

'Did you know him well?'

Morgan gazed intently at the wire. 'He was my best man.'

The cop twanged the wire again. 'You married?'

Morgan joined in this time and twanged the wire himself. 'Divorced.'

They were both now staring at the wire, their eyes about six inches from it. Kelly's finger glowed white in the light of the torch as it reached out and produced another twang. 'What happened?' Neither of them took their eyes off the wire.

'She went off with the best man.'

The cop's eyes remained unblinking as his finger reached out for the last time. 'I reckon you've got a head start on him now.' Twang.

Morgan raised his shoulders and kicked at a clump of earth, then suddenly jumped back, eyeing it suspiciously. The cop started taking notes again.

'Anybody take the bike regular?'

Morgan was tired. 'Now and again ... You know ... No, it wasn't regular. Most of my friends took it, now and again ... Nothing regular.'

Kelly shrugged, they turned and walked back to the cabin. He stopped and talked to some of his colleagues, leaving Morgan to trudge on and reach the cabin first. Morgan turned to wait for him just as the body bag was being lifted into the back of the van. He broke off and headed towards Morgan. 'Kids!' said the cop. Another look of disbelief flashed across Morgan's face. 'Kids been seen around here. Little bastards. Can't trust them. No respect. Do your best, make sacrifices. We don't own them you see, we only look after them for a while. Then they're off, gone, can't do nothing.' He looked sad.

'Kids?'

'Gone ... with her, don't come round no more.' The cop turned and walked away.

Morgan slumped on the porch. Mud and blood were drying. He was starting to feel the cold. After the surge of Adrenalin had died his body and mind were running on empty.

He looked up to see a uniform emerging from the darkness swinging what looked like a plastic shopping bag with a melon in it. When he was twenty yards away from the medics, the officer whirled the bag around his head and let fly. It was a good throw and an even better catch by one of the team.

He smiled in grim appreciation and clapped slowly. Freddy always regarded himself as a high flier.

Morgan shouted to the detectives around him, 'I'm bushed, I'm going to bed.'

'Yeah,' shouted one, 'Get your head down,' then immediately looked embarrassed, shrugged and walked over to him. 'This is a bad business, real bad. We'll sort it real quick. Kids around here are OK normally, bit of high spirits, real stupid, not vindictive, just stupid.'

Morgan stared at the detective with contempt written in capital letters on his face, uttered the word 'Bollocks,' and turned inside. He collapsed on the bed.

Virginia

Siemonsen's face was lit from below by the light from his desk-lamp. The phone was glued to his ear. He was looking very worried. He raised his voice a pitch and was trying to sound efficient.

'Yes Head, I'm sorry sir, no more cock-ups sir, you have my word. May I just say sir ... *sir*? ... Shit!' He replaced the telephone.

Los Angeles

'What time did you say your train was leavin?' The cab-driver was talking out of the side of his mouth. Morgan was gazing past the back of the driver's head to the road beyond.

'Ten ten,' replied Morgan absently, although the real time was ten fifty-five, and a few hours from then he'd be in Vegas.

'Right,' said the driver. 'Where did you say you was going?'

'I didn't.'

'Right, right ... Going far?'

Morgan's eyebrows twitched. 'Yes.'

'Right,' said the driver and gave up at this point. They drove on in silence while Morgan reflected on his decision to get as far away as possible in the shortest time. Plane travel was traceable and cars did not have the anonymity he was seeking. He wanted a crowd, but his instincts were to get over the mountains to the desert. There, he would have the time and certainly the space to work things out. ' Forty days and Forty nights should do it.' Events were conspiring against him. The train to Las Vegas was the answer, then back into the desert. He didn't care which one.

5

Drowning in the deep end

Los Angeles

The cab pulled up at Union Station. Morgan looked up at this Spanish Mission of a building and prayed that this was the gateway to his salvation. The clock, etched in black on the impossibly white tower told him he had time for a beer. Outside the station he took out a large canvas bag from the rear seat, looked at his watch and headed across the road to a bar. The cab driver looked at the meagre tip offered, mumbled something obscene and drove off.

Morgan pushed the bar door open with the bag, and squeezed through. Inside. It was almost black, dim red lights lighting up the perimeter at various intervals. He made his way over to the only other source of light in the place.

'Beer please. A cold one.'

'We're shut,' said the barmaid, scrubbing furiously at a glass. Morgan looked around slowly, then looked back at her.

'While you're standing there behind the bar, and I'm sitting *at* the bar, we could come to some arrangement ... like you pour a drink, and I drink it. Things tend to happen that way.'

She was about to say something very rude, but he got in first.

'Look, the door was open, I've got a ten-dollar bill in my hand, and I would like a beer ... please.'

'Like I told you, we're shut.'

'Aw come on for Christ-sake,' said Morgan. 'Do you want me to put some money in your till or not?'

'You can stuff it up your ass for all I care,' she said.

Morgan looked at her. 'Going for Business Woman of the Year, are we?'

She slammed a glass down and was about to say something when a voice floated out of the darkness. It seemed to surprise both of them. Low and husky, but full of warmth.

'I'll have a beer.'

Morgan's face brightened.

'Me too,' came another voice from the shadows.

'Yeah, line them up sister,' they chorused from the gloom.

The barmaid scowled, but started to slam the empty beer glasses on the bar. Out of the corners two or three shadows emerged and took on a human form. They shuffled and shambled over to the bar like the walking dead.

As Morgan's eyes became accustomed to the gloom, he also became aware of a couple of guitars, lots of electric leads, mike-stands and an electric piano. They lined up at the bar and nodded in the direction of the beer tap.

While the barmaid was pouring their drinks, the guy with the low husky voice said, 'Put it on the tab.'

'What tab?' came the reply.

'Well out of our gig money then.'

The barmaid shrugged, 'If you make any.'

The little group, including Morgan, downed their beers in silence. Eventually the low husky voice said, 'OK, let's check this sound.'

They ambled back to their dark corner and while Morgan was downing his second beer, they clicked and buzzed, hit keys and made the usual cluttered noises small bands had made since the dawn of the electric guitar. The husky voice played a little boogie-woogie on the electric piano. It was nice. Morgan settled back on his stool and ordered another beer.

'We really are shut you know,' said the barmaid, thawing out a little and looking at him from under long and fluttering false eyelashes, 'but as you're in, you're in.' She walked around the bar, up to the door and slammed the bolt.

'And keep that noise down,' she shouted towards the corner.

'We've got to do a sound check, Carla.'

'Just keep the sound in check,' she retorted, then turning to Morgan, 'Who the hell do these guys think they are? All these bands are the same. Ain't no one heard of them before and ain't no one gonna hear them again and when they get in any place, they take it over ... as if their next gig is gonna be Madison Square Garden.'

'Ever had a dream?'

'More like a fucking nightmare,' she replied.

'OK, let's do one,' said the husky voice. Morgan had started his fourth beer and felt more relaxed and a little safer. His bad dreams were fading in this beery womb. He wasn't really listening to the first few bars. Then the chorus hit him ...

Drowning in the deep end, please save me
I'm drowning in the deep end
Hold on tight this time
I'm drowning in the deep end
Going down, down, down, down, down, down, down,
For the last time babe

He attacked his beer again, drowning in the malted warmth.

Day by day, feeling you slip away
So slowly
Day by day, you don't know me
Can't go on now your heart has gone You don't call me.
Seems so long since you called me.
I know something's wrong
'Cos I'm drowning in the deep end
Please save me
I'm drowning in the deep end

63

Hold on tight this time
I'm drowning in the deep end
I'm going dawn, down, down, down, down
For the last time babe
The tides have turned
As far as love's concerned
You don't need it
The tides have turned and you're leaving
Taking two steps forward
Three steps back, I see it clearly now
You are far ahead
I call you back, but you don't hear me now
'Cos I'm drowning in the deep end
Please save me
I'm drowning in the deep end
Hold on tight this time
I'm drowning in the deep end
I'm going down, down, down, down, down
For the last time babe
'Cos I'm drowning in the deep end
Please save me
I'm drowning in the deep end
Hold on tight this time
I'm drowning in the deep end
I'm going down, down, down, down, down
For the last time babe.
I'm drowning - please save me - in the deep end

'Oh yes,' he could certainly relate to that. He could also relate to the voice. He could also relate to the whole thing. He had heard this before, not this song, but this man, this voice, the phrasing... Blues percolating through. Yes, oh yes, he knew who this was. The band played on.

When they'd finished Morgan advanced towards the keyboard player bearing two beers. He put one on the piano.

'Hi, my name's Morgan.'

The husky voice glanced up at him and took the beer without speaking. He looked as if he hadn't slept for a week, which happened to be true. Morgan and the keyboard player looked at each other in silence for a few seconds. When the player had downed half the beer he put it down on the piano. Morgan thought about leaving and looked at his watch. He had some time.

The piano-man said slowly, 'I'm Paul.'

'Yes I know,' said Morgan, 'Paul Mills.'

'Millns,' came the reply 'M I L L N S.' He spelt it out slowly. 'Millns.'

'Right, right.' said Morgan. The keyboard player looked at him again, sharper this time.

'How do you know me?' There was caution behind the eyes which were set in a sensitive face that most would describe as lived-in. Although unshaven and un-rested, this one looked more like a squat.

'Somebody gave me a tape of yours.'

'Oh, yeah.'

'Yeah, umm, some A and R guy.'

The pianist shrugged. 'That's one more record company not picking up an option'

Morgan carried on regardless. 'Not got a deal yet?'

The pianist replied. 'Lots of deals, no money, small labels, cheap production, no promotion,' then looking straight at Morgan. 'Tapes going to the wrong people.'

Morgan looked uncomfortable. 'You got a number?'

'Why?' replied Paul.

'I'd like to buy you a beer sometime.'

'Buy me one now if you like.' The two moved to the bar.

'Shit ... Gotta go ...Train.' He threw some money on the bar and looked at Paul. 'Best of luck, see you around. I hope.'

The husky-voiced pianist said nothing, just watched Morgan's back as he disappeared through the door. The canvas bag got stuck, but after some persuasion it followed shortly after him.

Morgan raced and slid over the marbled concourse, his heavy bag bouncing off his thigh. A number of people were bumped on the way before his eyes had adjusted to the soft darkness of the interior. He did pretty well, dodging most of the crowd. He was in a hurry. The main clock said 10.55 and he could just see the back of his train. It wasn't moving, but he knew it soon would be.

The great silver double-decker sporting its patriotic red, white and blue stripes, was starting to move. The two huge diesel engines at the front throbbing in unison as they overcame the inertia of the six coaches.

He was running towards the barrier and picking up speed. He'd not bought a ticket, but that was no problem he'd get one on board.

Morgan increased speed. The train started to pull out. As he arrived at the gate two men came together just in front of him and Morgan wasn't going to get through there in a hurry. He did a neat swerve around them and leapt the four-foot high barrier.

'Hey!' came the shout. 'What the hell's up with you, fella?' The words were lost to Morgan as he cleared the barrier and kept sprinting up the platform.

'Jesus Christ,' said one man to the other, 'Is that dude crazy or something.'

'He's maybe crazy, but he's pretty fit,' said the other.

They watched with arms folded, anticipating Morgan's failure to catch the train. The silver cigar-tube was picking up speed. He focused on the silver grab-handles on the doors. An attendant was waving his arms and shouting. He wasn't sure if he meant 'Come on,' or 'Get back.' He kept going and the man kept the door open. It was a nice arrangement.

The train was moving faster, Morgan's legs were pumping and the bag was bouncing even more. He got a hand to the last grab-handle and kept his legs going.

'Five dollars he's not going to make it,' said one.

'I'll take that,' said the other.

It would have been easier without the bag. Morgan just could not make that leap with the weight behind him. The train was accelerating now and so was Morgan. He managed to get abreast of the open door and slung his bag in first. He was free now to sprint, but he had to as the train was now really getting into its stride. Some of the passengers' heads were looking out of the windows and the small crowd were cheering on the platform. Morgan got both hands on the train, but his legs couldn't keep up. His boots were dragging along the platform doing them no good at all.

Morgan was cursing quietly to himself. There was only one option and he was exercising it. Purely by using the strength in his forearms, he dragged his body towards the open door, finally getting enough forward purchase to lift one knee into the doorway and against the frame of the door, twisting himself on board. The other leg followed. He fell on the floor of the corridor while the door was closed behind him. He got to his feet quickly.

'Well that's five dollars for me,' said one.

'It was worth it to watch that,' said the other.

Morgan gathered himself, brushed himself down, looked at the scuffed boots, cursed, looked at his bag, yep it was all there.

'You shouldn't have done that sir,' said the attendant. 'We ain't insured for that.'

'Thanks for keeping the door open for me,' Morgan said gratefully. He slung his bag over his shoulder and opened the first door. A number of heads turned as he made his way down the corridor. Some had seen the incident, others were just surprised that there should be anyone getting on the train so late. All the seats were taken. This was true of the third and fourth carriages.

There wasn't much room in the corridors either. They were full of cases. A lot of people were leaving the city, heading for Vegas and beyond and this was the only train of the day.

As he entered the fourth carriage he looked up to see one available seat in the designated smoking-area.

All the seats were in aircraft formation, facing forward. Amtrak was not a privately run service, Federal money ensured there was an alternative to the car and this service would take those who wished stress-free travel all the way to Chicago.

As the train gathered speed through the static lines of freight wagons he looked out at the tired track and faint air of neglect; not the rolling stock, the dusty areas between, at the birds on the wire, the dead birds and the tyres.

The only available seat was on the narrow side of the car, with just one lady sitting next to it. Morgan made his way towards this space, throwing his bag under the seat before he collapsed into it.

He held his breath and looked around him. Luckily it was the smoking section and there weren't many left in these unenlightened times. He fumbled in his pockets and pulled out a crumpled pack of Marlboro, lit up, leaned back and sighed gratefully.

He looked across at the occupant of the adjacent seat. She had her head buried in a magazine. Morgan stood up, got rid of his jacket in the overhead bin and slumped back down again. She looked up at the second slumping. Morgan stared at her intently for a few seconds, then recognition dawned. He hastily pulled out another cigarette and brandished it in her direction.

'Not your brand,' said Morgan.

She looked up in surprise. It was the girl he had met in the bar. The electric-mac lady.

'Oh, it's you,' she said tonelessly and without enthusiasm.

'Hi, I'm Morgan, and you are?' There was no response. She buried her head in the magazine again.

'Sara, isn't it?' The young lady smiled weakly, but still didn't reply.

Morgan was getting into his stride now and leaned over across the arm-rest.

'How far are you going?' There was still no response, just another page being shuffled viciously. 'I'm going all the way,' said Morgan in his most lecherous manner.

Sara scowled. 'Hope you enjoy the ride, asshole.'

This pleasant exchange was interrupted by an announcement that the bar was serving drinks. Morgan grinned widely and attracted the attention of the attendant. 'Do you mind getting us something?'

'What would you like sir?'

'A large beer please, and a gin and tonic for the lady.'

Sara turned to the attendant. 'No thank you, not for me.'

'Go on my dear, have one,' said Morgan conspiratorially, 'One little one won't hurt you at all darling. In fact, Doctor Egor says you're almost there.'

He turned to the attendant.

'Do you know, he said he's never seen anyone dry out so quickly.'

Sara exploded, or was about to. Her mouth opened, but before anything burst forth Morgan had pushed a cigarette into it... and lit up. Sara spluttered. Morgan raised himself and slapped her on the back then turned to the attendant.

'Better make that a large one.'

The attendant's expression was that of sympathy for the obviously long-suffering Mr Morgan. He poured the drinks and disappeared. When Sara had recovered, she pulled the cigarette from her mouth and crushed it viciously into the ashtray.

'You bastard, you bloody bastard.' A number of heads were turning in their direction.

'Shssh. Please my dear, control yourself.' Sara was white with anger. She picked up the large gin and tonic and slammed it down in one hit. Morgan looked on in surprise.

'Another?'

'A very large one.'

Morgan looked very pleased and waved to the attendant again. He returned, gave Morgan a pitying look and slapped a couple more drinks down on the table.

They were climbing slowly, up through Cajon Pass, that great slash through the southernmost reaches of the Sierras. The sky was light blue, its purity muted by the permanent golden haze above the city. As the train moved east the haze would fade.

The soup of the sprawling city soon gave way to the floodlit space of rust and blue. The rock glowed pink and gold, except for the exposed sections of the San Andreas Fault, as purple as dried blood and ready to weep again.

The train descended carefully down to the flat plain of the Mojave Desert.

Morgan was beginning to feel better. The alcohol had anaesthetised him sufficiently to dull the memory of the events of the previous night. 'We'll be back for a statement in the morning Mr Morgan.' They'll be lucky. One of these days there'll be no morning, for *him*.

To the north and west lay Edwards Air Force Base and across the border in Nevada, missile-testing facilities and underground nuclear test-sites. Death Valley, the hottest and lowest point in the western hemisphere was up that way, parts of it three hundred feet below sea level. Together with Zabriskie Point and the hellishly stunning landscape.

He was moving away from his fears and tears, towards the safe anonymity of Vegas. What the hell, he might get lucky.

Perhaps he always was lucky. He had scraped through college on the minimum of academic effort and the maximum of sport and lechery. He had glided through his football career on a prayer and Aaron's wing. His marriage had ended before kids had come along and the week had brought a couple of deaths and a demolished office without Morgan receiving so much as a scratch.

Should he be pleased with himself? When they died, they were the closest two people to him. Was that sad? Close to him physically, but in any other way? Was anybody ever? Did he really build those defences so high?

He knew her only in the biblical sense and however much he tried to grieve, he couldn't find that trigger in his heart. He had never cared enough for true remorse. Another reason to hate himself. Freddy had been his best friend, which only meant that he saw more of him than most other people.

They had joined the practice together, but Freddy had been the conservative one. Careful, never went out on a limb. Had a nice house and saved large chunks of his salary. His own wife had obviously fallen for these safe pastures. Freddy needed Morgan to give him the excitement and Morgan needed someone to show-off to.

They golfed at least once a week. Morgan was the most naturally gifted and Freddy always won. 'Only because you took fewer shots than I did ... but mine were the best.' Freddy didn't argue with that, just took the money with a smile.

'Why make it hard for yourself ... lay it up. Why go for it all the time? Play the percentage game.' Morgan could never do that. All or nothing... and he always came up with nothing. Sometimes he'd pull off an outrageous shot; over water, around trees, and move two strokes ahead. The next piece of extravagance would put him three shots back.

This week had exploded like a wild bunker shot. 'What the hell was going on? Three incidents, all revolving around *him*. What had he done? Upset someone who had been close to the girl? ... Jealous boyfriend? ... That was it, overreacting quite a bit though.

Mistaken identity? ... His wife? No ... She had the lot anyway.

He looked at his companion. Sara's head was drumming rhythmically on the window. Morgan reached over and moved her head away from the window to a more central position on her seat. They had been drinking for about two hours and Sara was fast asleep. The table was full of empty beer cans, glasses and two full ashtrays.

Morgan reached over, picked up the magazine she was reading and skipped idly through the pages. He gave up and went for a newspaper she had stuffed into her carry-bag. It was an English one, The Sunday Times and quite a few years old, After ten minutes of scanning one particular article caught his attention and had the word 'Britain' in the headline.

His father had come over from that country a generation ago, from a little piece of land stuck on the end of England called Wales. He had coloured Morgan's childhood with poetic descriptions of the landscape, music, character and passions of that dark and brooding Celtic country. The scenery, the bards, mystics, fables, and legends. Morgan listened, bright eyed at log fires. Memories of his mother's dark skin and the smell of broth.

His father had met his mother when he crossed the Atlantic to mine the coal in Pennsylvania. He moved west to the sunshine before he died. Morgan was an only child and loved accordingly. His mother was part Sioux. Fiercely Indian, she lived in the rhythm of the seasons and the rhyme of the land.

Both parents had regard for the natural laws and took strength from nature and its inevitability. The rain and the sun made all things live and in

California they were at least half alive. They had a respect for the balance of man and environment. Both had died at a reasonable age from natural causes.

'Do what is right, not what is the law of the land. True Rightness comes from within and the true law was made in heaven, not on earth.' Morgan smiled to himself at these remembered words of advice. 'The Ten Commandments weren't a bad foundation for moral behaviour, whatever your religion ... worship should not be confined to a building, or a time of year and beings were human, whatever their origin.' Morgan wasn't so sure.

The name of his father's village had more letters in it than houses with bathrooms, but that's about all he could remember.

They had made the trip over to the UK a couple of times. A short stay for two weeks in the north of England in his teens and earlier staying for a year in his father's home village in the Rhondda Valley, but that was a long time ago. Morgan was very young and his childhood memories were only in monochrome, or maybe that was the colour of the country. A soft rain fell continuously, but it dampened nothing. The warmth of the nation burned in each soul, and the mist was a veil, not a shroud.

Cocooned in this legend of grey, the people emitted a hot passion, evaporating all thoughts of despair, poverty or ill-feeling. The communities coalesced and formed constant threads through the mining valleys of the south and less linear groupings elsewhere. The collective strength being forged in the steelworks, mines and farms throughout this barely conquered and independent nation. The cement which bound the soul-forces was a mixture of water from the heavens, the fire in the belly... and the earth, so dramatic in its contrasts of granite and pasture and fashioned by the wind from its Celtic counterpart across the Irish Sea.

The coal-miner's son ploughed on through the article.

PENTAGON QUIZZES BRITAIN OVER TWENTY TWO DEATHS
Shouted the headline.

'Pentagon officials in Washington will this week seek an explanation from the British Government for the deaths of twenty-two British defence workers, some

72

of whom were involved in top secret projects. All the deaths took place in the UK, but the scientists were working on Star Wars projects for the USA, as well as other missile programmes.'

Morgan read on. It seemed that these people died over a two to three-year period by deaths that were deemed accidental. There were suicides, car crashes, burnings and various other accidents. The tone of the article was sceptical. The British Government seemed to be making out a case for acts of God to which the Americans seem to be raising one heavy eyebrow and saying, 'Oh yeah, pull the other one.' Morgan threw the paper down.

Sara was waking up.

She was a good-looking girl, but not in an obvious way. Something about the face. Wasn't it always? He didn't want that face to go away.

'Where are we? What time is it?'

'Pass, twice.'

Sara was looking at the debris on the table with horror. She looked at Morgan with that expression that said, 'What the hell did we do last night and did I do it with you? Oh my God, I'll never forgive myself.'

Morgan looked at her thoughtfully, 'Where are you going and what are you going to do when you get there?'

Sara turned her thoughts to the window and the desert beyond. 'In a month's time I'm going to Europe for two years. I want to spend a little time in a lot of space before I go. When we hit the desert, I hit the road.'

'Why Europe?'

'I'm doing post-grad studies in modern history and European languages and,' belligerently now, 'I'm twenty-seven, unmarried, couple of jobs, a couple of boyfriends, not serious, and a nice middle-class background. OK?' Morgan's hands went up in mock surrender.

'What about you?' asked Sara. 'Joining a circus?'

Morgan tried the brave grin. 'Changing jobs, just taking a break.'

She scowled and looked at him hard. 'What are you running from?'

Morgan suddenly looked guarded. 'What makes you think that?' He was looking around for the car attendant. The drinks were finished, and he couldn't face the walk to the bar.

'Your eyes,' she said. 'The haunted and hunted look. My mother used to have it.'

'Balls,' came the reply.

Sara ignored that and continued seamlessly. 'She ran off six years ago. I guess she waited until I was in college.'

Morgan picked up a magazine and continued to read. The attendant was pretending not to notice his raised arm. The arm came down as Morgan became engrossed in the Mag. After some time he looked up. 'This train doesn't stop in the desert, that's it out there. It doesn't stop till Vegas.'

'Is that where you're going?'

'For a while. I'm getting lost in the crowd.'

'Why?'

He stared at her, then looked at her as though he was trying to make up his mind about something, then blurted out, 'Somebody is trying to kill me.'

Sara was about to laugh, but stopped when she saw the expression on his face.

'You cannot be serious?'

'Only sometimes,' replied Morgan, 'and this is one of them. They killed a friend of mine last night by mistake. Cut his head off.'

Sara came back quickly, 'So some heel's got his head?'

Morgan relaxed now, getting back into form, 'And now I'm head-over-heels.'

Sara smiled. 'And for a moment there I was starting to believe you.'

He changed the subject. 'How are you getting from Vegas to the desert? Hiring a car?'

'Well I'm not walking. Anyway, I'm getting off before then.'

'Like I said, we don't stop before then.'

'I do, when we get to Jean.'

'Who's she?'

'It's a town, about thirty miles short of Vegas.'

'You going to jump?'

'Don't need to, I've made arrangements. Daddy's got connections with Amtrak.' Morgan smiled grimly to himself and changed the subject.

'By the way, who's the tall, dark stranger?'

Sara lit up another cigarette and puffed into the air, 'Just a friend.'

'A good one?'

'All my friends are good.'

'I'm good.'

'You're not a friend.'

'Yet.'

'Why don't you just piss off and get a life Morgan,' she snapped. 'You're a bloody dinosaur, which dark pit did you crawl out of?'

'One in a Welsh valley, at least my father did. He dug coal for a living, or a dying. He played a game called Rugby. It's like our Football, except they don't use armour. They sing a lot too.'

'If you love it so much, why don't you go back there?'

'Too wet, but I'm a real American. Only half my genes come from there and they're pretty repressed.'

'Mother?'

'A true native,' Morgan said with satisfaction, 'Part Native-American.'

'Jesus,' said Sara, 'No wonder you're a mess. The spirits of the ancients must be having a ball in your head. Who are you this week ... King Arthur or Sitting-Bull?'

Morgan went quiet, then, 'This week is more like General Custer.' They both looked out of the window. They both looked sad.

Los Angeles

Big John laid out the white powder in two neat lines on the face of the travelling shaving-mirror he'd bought for use on his vacations. He'd never taken it out of the condo on account of he never took a break.

He took a small penknife out of his jacket pocket, moved the can of beer to one side with its tip and started to chop and cut the powder. The scrape and screech was drowning out the ball-game commentary, but the satisfaction he derived from the constantly changing patterns he created almost made up for that. He turned the sound up and cracked a ten dollar bill flat, then

75

rolled it up into a tight tube. Placing a finger over one side of his noticeably broken nose, he sniffed up each of the four lines he had created, alternating nostrils between each sweep.

He licked the remains gathered on the tips of his fingers and swallowed it, along with the rest of his beer.

He replaced the knife in a different pocket and then his fingers reminded him of what he had put there. The cassette had little information on it. A handwritten scrawl testified to fourteen tracks and the name of the artist. That was it. Like Weller said ... 'So what?'

He picked up the phone and dialled a number from memory. Nobody answered. He thumbed through a dog-eared notebook and came up with two more blanks and one response. It was negative.

He heaved himself over to his music-centre and fumbled about for a while before he managed to get the right combination of buttons in the right order, turned down the volume on the set, then opened another beer and settled down.

Desert Town

'How about I come with you?'

 'Forget it.'

 'We can share the driving.'

 'No way! ... The whole point is to get away ... from idiots like you. I Vant to be alone ... Get it?'

 'You won't know I'm there.'

 'Shut it, Morgan.'

 'You'll miss me.'

 'You do your thing and I'll do mine, OK?'

 'I'll just get off with you anyway.'

 'You've been trying to get off with me since we met.'

 'Not doing too good am I?'

 'Nope.'

The train ground into a small-town station. The boards read JEAN. An announcement came over the speakers. 'We are stopping here for a few minutes. Please do not leave the train unless you're getting off.'

'Sounds reasonable,' came the comment from Morgan. He had followed her off and they both struggled with her luggage towards the platform exit. The air was drier and cleaner than they remembered when they had boarded the train, and the light was brighter and the colours sharper.

Jean was typical of most American small towns ... and America in general, in that it pushed as much as possible to the surface, or up in the air. The dirty washing of billboards and signage hung out to dry on a forest of poles and its cabling and wires were strung out in a tangle of tendons above the roadways and sidewalks. The skeleton of the town was outside the body, whereas European countries tended to bury theirs, then dig them up at the most inconvenient times.

Passers-by outside the station were aware of a heated argument in the heat. Sara was sounding off.

'Look Morgan, I'm staying one night in a cheap hotel and in the morning I'm off, on my own, to nowhere, OK? ... It's been nice knowing you Morgan, hope the cavalry arrive. Bye.'

Sara stalked out of the station and waved for a cab. He was running after her.

'No problem! Tonight we'll just have one last drink.'

She turned on him, 'With you, there's no such thing as a one last drink.'

'Let's do a movie.'

'Movie! ... This town hasn't even got running water.' A dusty cab pulled up. Sara opened the door and jumped in. Morgan looked as if he'd just lost a winning lottery ticket. The cab was just about to pull off, when she stuck her head out of the window. 'Pick me up at nine ... the White Lodge.'

The great monster with one metallic eye loomed out of the mist. It lumbered straight towards them. A voice rang out. *'The lasers! the lasers! Hit them with the lasers.'*

No sound broke the stillness, except the crunching of popcorn in Morgan's mouth. The remains of two other packets were being crunched on the floor, together with two or three empty beer cans. Everything flickered around them in black and white. The only other sound was the hiss of the sound track. Sara was looking bored stiff. She removed his arm for the second time from around her shoulders. She was annoyed. *'They came from Planet Krypton... great.'*

She folded her arms and closed her eyes. Morgan encouraged her to put her head on his shoulder, but she refused. He pulled a tab on yet another can. When that one was finished and crushed into the growing pile, he headed for the bathroom while Sara tried to sleep. There weren't many people in the cinema, but the heat was stifling. She was restless and took a long pull from a hip-flask. Sara had been hitting the hard stuff on the quiet for most of the evening. It was the only way she was going to get through this.

As Morgan disappeared through the toilet door, a well-dressed man started to walk down the aisle, slowly, to let his eyes become accustomed to the darkness. He looked around and spotted a pretty girl in the dim light. He looked around again slowly, then made his way over to her seat. When he arrived there he realised she was sleeping and sat down next to her, eyeing her sideways, taking off his glasses and giving them a wipe.

One of the kids from the town must have been in this seat before him, judging by the debris scattered on seat and floor. He raised himself slightly and brushed his expensive overcoat and sat back down again. This lady was worth sitting next to.

Sara started to move. Still half asleep she turned towards the stranger and put her head on his shoulder and her arm across his thighs. The stranger's face showed pleasant surprise. His hand started to wander towards Sara's knee, she didn't seem to object. He licked his lips nervously. His hands started to move up her thigh, a smile was starting to grow on Sara's face.

She slipped to a kneeling position and emerged between his legs. She pulled at her companion's zipper and dived in, her head bobbing enthusiastically, much to the delight of the stranger. The stranger's sweaty features took on an expression of surprised satisfaction; then complete surprise. His eyes opened wide and his head jerked back. Sara carried on with great determination, especially when the stranger's legs flew up over the front seats and started to thrash violently.

She stopped. 'You like that don't you?' she whispered fiercely, 'But keep the noise down.' The stranger was gurgling now and his hands were clawing at his neck. His legs continued to kick out over the seats as Sara ploughed on diligently. Suddenly, his head fell forward and the body followed, slumped over the seat in front. Sara extracted herself and slid back into her seat.

'You needed that.' She whispered sleepily, wiping her face, licking her lips and nestling her head on the stranger's arm.

Morgan came out of the bathroom and allowed a few seconds for his eyes to adjust and turned into the aisle. He stopped and stared. There was Sara, still half asleep and a strange man in Morgan's seat. His head was bent forward, a rope wound tight around his neck and a knife protruding from his back. His hand gripped Sara's stocking and she was nibbling the corpse's ear.

Los Angeles - Downtown

'Where the hell's Morgan today?' The man was about thirty and dressed in Rodeo Drive casual-smart. He sat down with the others picking at the green salad and sipping from glasses of white wine, opaque from their chill.

One of his colleagues, a frosted girl with looks to match, coolly flicked a glance at him.

'He's probably a little shaken up.'

'Yeah, but he's missed the last three days,' said the original voice.

'I heard he had a bit of trouble up at his cabin,' said another girl, with a bit more concern in her voice

'He's always in trouble,' said yet another.

'That just isn't so.' The one other male in the group spoke from the far end of the table. It was a window seat and although the restaurant was cool, the sun always got the better of the diners next to the glass. His jacket had been removed and the floral tie had been loosened to form a wide noose. He had a nice smile.

The nice young man spoke up for the missing man. 'The guy's OK. Sure he's a bit off the wall. He downright refused that Nomura job. Tt was there on a plate for him.'

'You're wrong there,' said a colleague. 'It was there on a plate for *us*. Morgan only stayed with the presentation because the client wanted him in on it. Morgan went right to the wire, but Brewster screwed it up.'

'Is that right?' said the aggressive Rodeo Drive one.

'Yep, in fact I know the guys at Nomura went behind Brewster's back and straight to Morgan, but you know something? The old sonofabitch, he wouldn't touch it.'

'What do you mean?' said the casual smart. 'They wanted to cut us out and go straight to Morgan?'

'Yep, that's about the size of it, but as I said, he felt he couldn't do that to his employer.'

'What's wrong with the guy?' said Mr Smarm. 'Anybody with any sense would grab an offer like that.'

'Like you said,' one of the girls piped up, the frosty one. 'He hasn't got any sense.'

'Maybe he's got something else,' said the nice young man and started to put the debris on a tray then took it back to the counter. When he returned the conversation came back to Morgan.

'Didn't he play some ball game?' said the girl with the smile.

'Yeah,' said the nice young man. 'He was a quarterback for the Rams.'

'No!' exclaimed smarmy one, 'I can't believe that.'

'Well it's true; quite a long time ago now. Morgan came out of UCLA with great references and joined the Rams as second or third string. They were going to bring him on over the next few seasons. As the story goes, their regular quarter back got crocked in the play offs and Morgan stepped in and apparently, um, screwed it up.'

'Well, I'll be,' said Mr Smarm.

'Yeah,' said the nice young man, 'they had a tremendous wide receiver at the time. Now what was his name? Aaron Cleveland. That's it. Really tall, athletic guy. Could move like the wind, better than even time for the hundred. Could catch the ball too. I reckon it was mainly him, rather than Morgan, that got them so far, but Morgan seemed to find him most times, Aaron just did the rest.'

'Morgan was the one who threw the ball?'

'Yeah, that's the one.'

The girl was impressed; she was obviously looking at Morgan in a new light.

'Don't those guys make a lot of money?'

'Oh sure, I know Morgan did ... problem was, he got hooked up, got married. When she left him she took him for every penny.'

'You're kidding. Wow! What did he *do*?'

'He didn't do anything,' said the nice young man, '*she* did it all.'

'Why the hell is he broke then?' said Miss Frost.

'He just gave it all away apparently. The lot. The house, money, car, everything. Just walked out.'

'I knew he was crazy.'

'It was a cleansing process I believe,' said the nice young man, 'getting rid of old baggage and all that.'

'Anyway, what happened during the play offs, why didn't they make it?'

'Yeah, we never heard anything about that.'

'Well, apparently Morgan screwed up,' said the nice young man.

'What did I tell you?' said the smarmy one in triumph.

'I don't know the details,' the nice one proceeded knowledgeably. 'The press had a field day. They were up against the 49-ers who were having a good season that year.'

'Don't they always?'

'The Rams were really very much second favourites. Out in the final quarter there wasn't much in it. Morgan had been feeding nice balls to Aaron. I guess the defence got wise and put everything on Aaron and Morgan had nowhere else to go. There was some talk that Morgan bottled it.'

'What do you mean?' said one of the girls.

'Well, apparently he had a chance of a touchdown with Aaron, but at that time the defence were really looking for that play, crowded Morgan, crowded Aaron. Morgan bottled it and threw wildly to another player. The pass didn't make it, the opposition took it and they went the length of the field and that was that.'

'Could happen to anyone,' said one of the girls.

'Well that wasn't how the president of the team saw it at the time,' said the nice one. 'Heads rolled, including Morgan's and the coach.'

'Spare the regrets please,' said Mr Flashy Smarm. 'That Aaron's not the guy who's still down at the Rams now ... ? I still see him about... in the papers sometimes, helps out in training. I've seen him hanging around the sides of the pitch.'

'Yep, that's him. He's doing OK, not wonderful, OK.'

'So how come Morgan ended up with us?' One of the girls asked.

'Well,' said the nice one, 'he was one of those guys, those college athletes, who didn't just waste his time on the academic side. He was an architect by right before he joined the Rams, although I suspect he didn't intend to use it ever again.'

'I still can't believe Nomura came in for him, especially after that other Jap fiasco!'

'You mean Sumitomo?'

'Right.'

'What happened?' said the smarmy one.

'Well you know how you try to bow at about the same height as them.'

'Well?'

'Morgan denies it, but I know he'd been having trouble with some Jap sonofabitch, didn't see eye to eye over the marble detailing.'

'Hard for Morgan to see eye to eye with him anyway, height-wise there was quite a difference.'

'They came to the bowing bit, just after Morgan was overruled by Brewster and funnily enough, they both bowed together. Morgan goes down faster and lower than normal and splat! ... The Jap gets butted right in the face. Went down like a kamikaze. Blood everywhere!'

'Accident of course, but nobody seemed to argue much with Morgan after that!'

'Well he'd better show up soon,' said the frosty lady, 'or they'll be giving the Snelling project to someone else.'

'I think it's too late,' said the flash, smarmy, Rodeo-slime guy, pulling out his gum and sticking it under the table. 'It's not even an issue now.'

'What do you mean?' queried the nice one.

'Well I heard Brewster's given him the chop.'

'Why?' said one of the girls.

'Oh, he's had it coming for a long time. I reckon that incident at the office was the last straw ... and the fact that he ain't showed for three days doesn't help.'

'What was that you were saying about another incident at the cabin?' said one of the girls.

'I don't know. Just something I overheard in the office. There was an accident involving a motorbike. I think somebody got killed. Not too sure.'

The group got up, left the table and filed out of the restaurant.

'Who's got the Snelling job now?'

'I have,' said the gum-chewer as he closed the door on his way out.

Desert Town

'Jilted! ... For a *corpse*.' Morgan had put on his bitter voice.

'Shut up,' Sara replied.

They were seated in the cinema manager's office, which was slightly better furnished than the flea-pit they had just been in. The local Sheriff was between them and the cinema manager.

Morgan continued whispering, 'Just like being stabbed in the back.'

She turned on him, 'You're an asshole, you know that?'

He was unperturbed. 'How did you explain the fact that the deceased had your lipstick on his collar ... and his zipper?'

The green eyes flashed. He turned away. 'The piece of stocking in his hand was harder.'

He smiled quickly. The Sheriff turned to the couple. 'Where you two staying tonight?'

He was the spitting image of Steiger's Sheriff in '*In the Heat of the Night*', Same clothes, same shades, same gun, same gum. Sara and Morgan glanced at each other. Sara looked at the sheriff and said firmly, 'The White Lodge.'

His eyes narrowed behind the dark glasses. 'Both of you?'

They both looked straight ahead, 'Yes,' she replied firmly.

Morgan tried to suppress a smile. They both stood up and faced the Sheriff.

'You can go now,' he said. 'I'll shoot 'round in the morning.'

Morgan and Sara turned to go. He called after them, 'So you didn't know him?' Sara flushed and looked embarrassed. 'Gill Roderick. Nice man, quiet, you know ... family man.'

Morgan and Sara walked through the door. Sara looked more than a little guilty. They clacked across the tiled foyer heading for the outside door. The voice of the Sheriff came after them. 'By the way, the kiosk in the foyer sells pantyhose.'

They looked at each other and left hurriedly.

Virginia

The room was large and dark grey. Dark grey men were seated around a large table. They all wore grey suits and college ties with white shirts. The room was lit from only one window. Strong parallel lines of light were thrown across the walls, table and faces of the group by horizontal blinds.

The men looked very serious. At the head of the table sat a man with a severe crew cut which gave the impression of him having a flat top to his head. This man was the immediate centre of attention. He turned to one of the listeners halfway down the table.

'Siemonsen, tell me why he's still alive?'

Siemonsen moved uncomfortably in his seat. 'I've had my best men on this,' he blurted. 'Best operators ... always produced results.' He looked around the table for confirmation and some of the other heads nodded in agreement. 'It's just bad luck. A random factor. The theory of chaos states

...' at this point he was interrupted by the head man.

'Chaos? ... This whole operation has been chaos. This man seems to generate it just by *being* there.' All the suits around the table looked uncomfortable. 'I don't need to stress the importance of a successful conclusion ... and this has to be fast.'

In silence they glanced furtively at each other. 'Do we know if Morgan is aware of the knowledge within his possession and more importantly, the significance of it?'

Siemonsen was furiously cleaning his glasses, 'We're working on that sir.'

'Don't bother, just terminate,' said Head.

Siemonsen made a note. Head went on, 'Gentlemen, some stories are already leaking to the press, here and in Europe, but although annoying, they don't exactly represent a threat to national security.' They all nodded in agreement. 'However,' he spoke with extreme gravitas, 'if someone like our friend made his knowledge public, then a whole string of connections could be made and that could be embarrassing. Very embarrassing indeed.' He turned again to the unfortunate Siemonsen. 'I'm getting you a little help.'

Siemonsen looked peeved.

'Things are getting messy. The people on the top floor are nervous. I believe we may even have to move the theatre of operation.' Head raised his hand to counter any objection.

'I can't afford to draw any more attention to our target. A balance must be struck between expediency and the need for total security. That's all.'

They all gathered papers, shuffled them and started to leave. He turned at the door, 'You will all receive written instructions by tonight.'

A couple of the suits smiled wryly, one even sniggered at Siemonsen's obvious discomfort.

6

When love comes calling

London

Late spring, early June, was a good time to be in London. The temperature was getting to an acceptable level and the rains had not yet started. In the parks the colours were diamond bright, framed and contained by the dark borders of rhododendron. The sun was bright enough to create crystal-hard shards of light shattering the olive darkness of the evergreens and scattered by waxed mirrors coating the stiff leaves. Behind the glinting sharpness all was light absorbing blue-black shadow.

Birds and ducks were turning up the volume, along with the walkmen and the flowers were vying for the attention of the bees. Optimism was in the air. Smiles were starting to form on the faces of long suffering Londoners. Yes, it was a good time.

A little way from St James Park, between Trafalgar Square and Big Ben, is a wide avenue known as Whitehall. The area housed establishments connected with the military might, or lack of it, of Great Britain.

Although clichéd, most of the locals seemed to be wearing pin-striped suits and carrying rolled-umbrellas. This really did happen in this area whatever the time of year, supposedly a mark of the stability of the British

Empire.

In truth, all three Services were being drastically reduced in size and had been ever since the end of the Second World War. The army had approximately three times as many pen-pushers as men capable of fighting and the navy's total number of fighting ships was just about to be reduced to thirty-nine. Nelson sat atop his column and turned a blind eye to all this.

The air force seemed to have suffered less than the other services, but it may have been because it had a higher profile, especially after the Falklands and Gulf Wars.

The third street down on the left off Whitehall retained a number of Victorian buildings and on the fourth floor of one a small, but beautifully formed office was vibrating to the antique ring of the Bakelite telephone's bell. It was a richly furnished room, high ceilinged and mahogany panelled. A full-length portrait of the Queen hung proud on the wall opposite the leather-inlaid desk. A distinguished gentleman with silvered locks and sporting a regimental tie, the origin of which was obscure, was pouring tea from a silver service. The Spode china saucers and cups rang slightly, echoing the telephone ring.

The brass letters on the rosewood background indicated that the distinguished gentleman was Sir Anthony McLean and he was carefully measuring out a spoonful of brown sugar and ignoring the telephone. When he was quite sure that the tea in his cup was assembled correctly he picked up the 'phone.

'McLean here ... Hello old boy! How are things in the land of the Free?... Ah yes Siemonsen, your head did mention it. When do think your... ah...*target* ... will be coming over?... Hmm, it would be nice if you could be a little more precise ... Yes I do see your problem.'

He took a sip, scraping the bottom of the cup on the rim of the saucer to catch any drips.

'We'll let him come into the country unhindered, then plan a really nice surprise. Lead him on to the punch so to speak. Of course *I* have a problem also ... He does have links with this country in terms of nationality... although it is only Wales and doesn't really count. If things do blow up I suppose I can placate the Welsh Secretary with a Jap factory making plastic rugby players ... It's a game! ... Like your football, but without the armour ...Yes it is bloody stupid. Cheerio!'

As the receiver was replaced there came three tentative knocks on the door.

'Come!'

The door opened and through it came a little old lady, smelling of furniture- polish and freshly baked scones. Her white hair was neatly pinned back and she held a brown paper bag in one hand.

'Shall I freshen the pot, Sir Anthony?'

'No thank you Doris, I think I'll take a stroll.'

He took out a pewter chain watch from his waistcoat pocket and glanced at it. He rose and moved over to the window. The glass behind the net curtains. 'Beautiful day.'

He walked around the desk, and chose a rolled umbrella from a choice of three on a stand.

She handed him the bag. 'For the ducks, Sir.'

'Ah! Thank you Doris. Organic?'

'White sliced Sir, I'm afraid. Couldn't put up with the queue ... Not the waiting sir, the SMELL ... It's the hot weather you see, and those open-toed sandals; that, and all the wool they wear ... Not healthy sir, no, not at all healthy.'

'Quite Doris, quite.' He took the bag and walked out. Doris took a duster out of a pocket of her floral pinafore and started to polish the desk.

The brass letters on the rosewood background indicated that the distinguished gentleman was Sir Anthony McLean, and he was carefully measuring out a spoonful of brown sugar and ignoring the telephone. When he was quite sure that the tea in his cup was assembled correctly he picked up the 'phone.

'McLean here ... Hello old boy! How are things in the land of the Free?... Ah yes Siemonsen, your head did mention it. When do think Your... ah...*target* ... will be coming over?... Hmm, it would be nice if You could be a little more precise ... Yes I do see your problem.'

He took a sip, scraping the bottom of the cup on the rim of the saucer to catch any drips.

'We'll let him come into the country unhindered, then plan a really nice surprise. Lead him on to the punch, so to speak. Of course *I* have a problem also ... He does have links with this country in terms of nationality... although it is only Wales and doesn't really count. If things do blow up, I suppose I can placate the Welsh Secretary with a Jap factory making plastic rugby players ... It's a game! ... Like your football, but without the armour ...Yes it is bloody stupid, Cheerio!'

As the receiver was replaced, there came three tentative knocks on the door.

'Come!

The door opened and through it came a little old lady smelling of furniture polish and freshly baked scones. Her white hair was neatly pinned back and she held a brown paper bag in one hand.

' Shall I freshen the pot , Sir Anthony?'

'No thank you Doris, I think I'll take a stroll.'

He took out a pewter chain watch from his waistcoat pocket and glanced at it. He rose and moved over to the window. The glass sparkled behind the net curtains.

' Beautiful day.'

He walked around the desk and chose a rolled umbrella from a choice of three on a stand.

She handed him a bag. ' For the ducks, Sir.'

'Ah, Thank you Doris. Organic?'

' White sliced Sir, I'm afraid. Couldn't put up with the queue... Not the waiting Sir... The SMELL...It's the hot weather you see, and those open-toed sandals. That, and all the wool they wear. Not healthy Sir, no...not at all healthy.'

'Quite, Doris...Quite.' He took the bag and walked out. Doris took a duster out of a pocket of her floral pinafore and started to polish the desk.

Virginia

'They're quite mad you know.'

The recipient of this remark put his chin into the palm of his hand and stared unblinking at the young man with the button-down shirt.

'What makes you think that?' The speaker was a comfortably large man with piercingly intelligent eyes. He was embedded in a winged leather armchair, the focal point of his den at the top of his secluded wooded home an hour or so outside Washington.

'Would you mobilise all your resources to eliminate one man?'

'Depends who he was ... and how important he was. Besides I'm sure it's not *all* Siemonsen's resources.'

'OK, maybe I'm exaggerating, but they're going right over the top and for what? Some bozo who may, or may not, know something?'

'What thing?'

He hesitated, 'I don't know, something that's got them all worked up ... Head's team, that is.'

'Confined to Head's team is it ... this panic?'

'Yes.'

The listener, senior to the young man, but not directly, was thoughtful. The young man was impatient to fill the silence. He had much to learn. 'And the methods they use! ... They don't go for a simple termination, oh no, it has to be dressed up, has to be ... well, *theatrical,* if you like, *dramatic.*'

'Perhaps he's making a statement,' said the listener, 'I seem to remember a number of, shall we say, *bizarre,* terminations originating in your department, if I recall correctly.'

'That's right, we get some weird directives. I think he's gone ape. I just thought you ought to know ... as your team is independent of ours. I don't know who else to talk to.'

London

The lake in St James' Park shimmered like a mirage in greens and turquoise. It was the first really hot day of the year and the sun had gone Monet-mad, vibrating the colours and the surfaces which bore them.

Sir Anthony fed a raucous group of ducks, casting his bread judiciously upon the waters and permitting himself the occasional smile of satisfaction.

One hundred and fifty yards beyond, a furtive individual, wearing a light coloured trench coat and brown trilby hat, was approaching Sir Anthony's silent communion in a manner not dissimilar to a yacht tacking up the Solent.

He eventually sidled up to Sir Anthony and stopped, looked around obviously and then leaned over and whispered, 'Got your message Sir.'

'You're a bloody idiot, Trench!' This was delivered in a broad East-End accent.

'Whatsat?'

'You 'erd me you stupid bastard.' Sir Anthony continued to feed the ducks. 'The press are startin' to wake up. You gotta be more careful. The Pentagon has got its knickers in a twist, which doesn't help. Got another little job for you. Not now, but later. Same as the others, *accidents*. But no cock-ups!'

'The Lady?'

'No. Not her, Not yet.'

'It'll go smooth Tony 'onest, I ...'

'An' another thing,' Sir Anthony, or Tony, as he had just become, turned on Trench. 'That 'orse you gave me ... 2.30 at Newmarket ... still runnin ...'

Sir Anthony pushed his finger into Trench's chest. 'If you fuck this one up, *you'll* still be runnin. Now get lost, an if I 'ear you've been 'anging round the Green Man of a weekend when my little Lizzie's behind the bar, I'll 'ave you so 'elp me.'

Trench retreated and Sir Anthony called after him.

'God save the Queen.'

'God save the Queen,' replied Trench, but with not quite the same enthusiasm.

Sir Anthony threw the remainder of the bread, still in its paper bag, over his shoulder and into the pond. This was greeted with an angry quack as he walked away.

Virginia

'Get hold of McLean and put him in the picture.' Head's voice burrowed into Siemonsen's brain like a drill. He wanted the pain to go away. 'I want nothing to happen to him on this side of the pond ... got that!' Siemonsen nodded silently, resenting and disagreeing, but complying. 'That's all, you may leave.'

Siemonsen understood the curt autocratic tones adopted by all bad teachers and recognised the uselessness of disagreement. Besides, he had already made contact. Siemonsen was always ahead of the game.

London

Sir Anthony McLean was an unusual man. Called to the service of his country not through the usual channels of Oxbridge and the Military, but through a passion for horses.

His interest was not in the breeding or the acquisition of them, or indeed of running them in competition. He liked to bet on them.

His background was rather more humble than that of his peer group, but nonetheless his devotion to duty was second to none, almost fanatical you might say.

He had met his present employer at Royal Ascot. Not in the areas reserved for VIPS and movers and shakers, but just outside the public toilets near the parade ring.

He had been remonstrating with a lout who had dared to criticise the Queen for occupying the best seats in the place and the best position in the country.

Sir Anthony had called the man's parentage into question and had then thrown him quite a distance. The poor man ended up inside the paddock just as the Queens horse, Easy Money, was being led past.

Sir Anthony had been collared by two uniformed policemen and was about to be led away when a white-haired old lady, her voice slurring slightly and a faint smell of juniper on her breath, intervened. She wore a blue floral print and a matching hat at a jolly angle. 'Officer may I have a word?' The policeman straightened up and tried to remove his helmet, but fumbled the chin-strap.

'Now then,' said the little old lady, 'you *have* been a naughty boy, haven't you? But I must say you were more than a little provoked. I should have done something myself if you hadn't stepped in.'

'Is the 'orse alright?' The arrested man seemed concerned, although he had one arm halfway up his back.

'Thank you yes, but I don't think he'll run.'

'Just as well.'

'Why do you say that?' She was studying him with a whimsical intent.

'Look at the coat, no shine ... temperature ... And the third favourite will take it ... Ground's too soft for 'im, and wrong jockey.'

'Officer, will you let this gentleman stay here awhile?' The policeman bowed awkwardly and stepped backwards.

'Eh!' The arrested man looked confused.

'It's my daughter's horse,' said the floral print, by way of explanation.

'But that's the Queen's 'orse.'

'Exactly.'

'Oh my good God ... MA'AM.' The light had eventually dawned.

'I didn't rec ... I ... I ...' He tried to go down on one knee.

'Don't be silly,' he was told firmly.

'Let's see if you're right, shall we?' She led him towards the rails, slipping a silver hip-flask into his hand. 'You look as if you need this.' The man took a large tot, but then seemed at a loss as to how to wipe the neck clean. He started with his sleeve, then back of his hand, groped without success for a handkerchief and was saved further embarrassment by the lady snatching it back and downing the remaining contents.

'What did you do in the war?'

'Had a gift for languages ... Ma'am ... an' ciphers ... worked on the Enigma Codes ... made sergeant.' He kept staring at her, not quite believing the situation he found himself in.

'And now?' As she spoke a number of discreetly large gentlemen crowded them, but before he could answer they all looked up as the horses thundered past and the announcement came over the Tannoy. 'Winner ... Lucky Break, second ...'

'Third favourite wasn't it?' She had turned to one of her escorts.

'Correct Ma'am ... third favourite indeed.'

She looked at him again and the eyebrows went up. He carried on. 'Foreman printer, Ma'am ... in Fleet Street ... Night shift mostly, but only part -time now, even with the move to Docklands. Do some moonlighting as a night-time security man.'

'Perfect,' came the odd response from the grand old lady. 'How would you like to work for my daughter?'

He was on his knees by now and wondering when he was going to wake up.

'What's your name?'

'Name? ... Tony, Ma'am.'

'Arise, Sir Anthony,' she said, waving a glass over both his shoulders and drinking back the contents in one hit. He was still kneeling and looking completely confused when she bent over him and whispered. 'Up you get, can't spend the rest of your life on your knees ... work to do.' She beckoned for a refill and another betting slip. When he was back on his feet she spoke briskly. 'What are your hobbies ?... How do you spend your time? ...Tell me more, then we'll look at the card together.' She offered him her arm, which he took after some prompting and as they strolled away he could be heard saying ...

'Amateur dramatics, Ma'am ... an' a bit of singin.'

Ten years later he was now walking from Whitehall up through Trafalgar Square, towards Chinatown and into the backstreets of Soho. He avoided the main thoroughfares, avoided the sun's spotlight and stuck to the narrow walk-throughs. Quiet in their neglect and illuminated gently by their secrets and memories and by the soft source-less light found only in the back rat-runs and alleyways of the capital.

England is one of the few countries to possess it. A timeless veil that black-and-white photographers would drop their Nikons for. This history of ancient light seeps from the brickwork pores. An ethereal translucent wash, common across whole swathes of the north, but in London only the more secretive parts of the city seemed to cradle it.

He stopped at a number of coffee shops, not always for a cup. He sometimes walked straight through, then out of some rear door. Sometimes he just sat and watched the street before moving on.

Emerging into Charing Cross Road he raised an umbrella, a gift incidentally from the KGB and not something to get stuck with. Ignoring the black cab which swerved quickly to his side, he jumped into the rear seat of the black, stretched cat behind it.

'Home,' was his only comment to the driver.

The Jaguar slid up Commercial Road eastwards, away from the City of London and turned south into what used to be the docklands; past the newly converted warehouses and toy-town houses which developers had optimistically built in the boom years before the recession bit deep and purred on into one of the more depressed parts of the East-End.

Its highly polished metal-work mirrored the drab Victorian two-up, two-down rows of small terraced houses. It then mirrored a neon oasis of takeaway Indian restaurants, fish-and-chip shops and mini-cab offices. It pulled up at a small used-car lot, defined on a piece of waste ground by wire and corrugated fencing.

The evening was closing in and when Sir Anthony emerged from the rear seat he looked very tired. He walked into the lot, ignoring the used cars and walked under a loud plastic banner proclaiming the bargains within, making his way without deviating to a toilet at the rear.

By the time he was halfway across the lot the Jaguar had moved off.

Before disappearing into the toilet, Sir Anthony gave the briefest of nods to his right where a battered Portacabin leaned against one wall.

In the doorway, a dubious-looking car salesman met the nod with a brief glance of recognition and acknowledgement. He was wearing a camel-haired brown overcoat and a greasy trilby hat, the brim of which shaded his eyes and emphasised the lower half of his face. The mouth was talking to a middle-aged couple, but the eyes, unseen, were everywhere else. He was addressing most of his patter to the wife.

'Onest love, one lady owner, just like yourself ... refined.'

The large-jowled lady tittered coyly and adjusted her heaving nylon bodice. Her husband's eyes were raised to the heavens.

'But I gotta tell yer,' he said earnestly, 'there's a geaser coming back in ten minutes with cash, an' he'll be mad if he finds that I've let it go. So if we can just get the paperwork out of the way ...' He beckoned both of them towards his grubby office.

'Hey wait a minute, 'ang about,' shouted the husband. 'We ain't decided yet.'

'Well at least let's make a start on the paperwork while you're making your mind up,' said the salesman. 'Where did you get that dress, lady? My wife is looking for just such a ...' This exchange was cut off as Sir Anthony entered the toilet door and shut it.

There were two cubicles in the toilet. He went to the end one which showed an engaged sign. He took a key out of his pocket, turned the lock and entered. The cubicle seemed larger inside than it was outside, which wasn't surprising as that was exactly what it was. It had been enlarged and contained a rack of coat-hangers, a wardrobe, a chest-of-drawers and a well-lit mirror. It did not have a loo.

Sir Anthony sat on small chair and loosened his tie, sighing as he did so. He unbuttoned his waistcoat, took his jacket off and the trousers soon followed. He hung them neatly. On went the collarless shirt and a pair of dungarees. His handmade shoes were laid neatly alongside two other pairs and were replaced by a pair of boots. The immaculate hair was brushed forward and scuffed up. A little tin containing a mixture of dirt and ash was taken out of a drawer and he dabbed his fingers into the mixture, applying it to his face along with a little oil. His finger nails were plunged into a separate tin of boot- polish, producing a nicely blackened result..

Twenty minutes later Sir Anthony, or more appropriately, Tony, emerged from the toilet, walked past the still arguing trio and sauntered down the road, stopping only at a small newsagent to pick up a copy of the Sun. He glanced briefly at the young lady on page three and walked on through a maze of small back streets arriving at a little terraced cottage.

It had a small front garden with a splendid display of rose bushes, although this looked a little incongruous in this drab East-End Street.

The only other touches of colour were provided by a small cluttered general store owned by a family from Bombay.

Sir Anthony took a key out of his dungaree pocket and entered his front door.

'Hello luv,' said his wife, giving him a peck on the cheek. 'How was your day?' She was a small plump lady with rose-coloured cheeks and a lot of floral patterns on her blouse, skirt and pinafore; they all clashed. She was, however, colour co-ordinated with the living-room, which also had flowered wallpaper, carpets and curtains. They all clashed with each other as well as with her. Flying docks, imitation copper and cheap prints abounded, but the room was dominated by a large portrait of the Queen, above the coal-effect gas fire.

Various photographs, large and small, of other members of the Royal Family, past and present, were displayed prominently. Tony returned the kiss and unravelled his newspaper. She removed his coat and plumped up a cushion in his armchair.

'Put your feet up dear, kettle's on.'

'Thanks luv,' he replied, as she removed his slippers from in front of the fire and put her hands inside them to test the temperature. Once satisfied, she eased them on his feet, removed his shoes and returned to the kitchen.

As Tony buried his head in the newspaper, his wife's voice floated from the kitchen, 'Ow's things at the plant luv? Elsie was saying there's a number that's being laid off.'

Tony continued reading in silence, although he did manage a faint grunt. His wife returned from the kitchen with a cup of tea and put it on the arm of the chair. She went back to the kitchen and returned with a basket of ironing, which she placed next to the permanently erected ironing-board and started to lay out various garments. As she got to work she carried on talking.

'Er 'Enry's worried, what with all those kids an' all.'

'Look luv, I can't go around sorting out lost causes, just 'cos some silly sod's got a willy for a brain.'

'And that eldest of theirs,' she went on, 'that Tracy.'

Tony wasn't deflected. 'He's a lazy bugger anyway, be glad to get rid of him.'

'If you ask me that weight she's putting on isn't due to beefburgers.' This parallel conversation continued.

'People these days gotta learn that hard graft is not just for mugs and donkeys.'

'Anyway,' said his wife finally, 'I said you'd put a word in for him.'

She put the iron down and started to fuss with various bits of washing in the kitchen. Her voice again came from that direction.

'Elsie was saying, the word is you're never about much these days. They don't see you for weeks sometimes.' She popped her head around the door looking at him quizzically.

He looked up over the top of his paper. 'I've told you before luv, I'm management now. Your average worker don't understand.'

'How do you mean?'

'I'm up there with the bosses, looking after the lads' interests, courses to attend.'

She looked suitably impressed and a little proud.

'Lots of seminars ... an' tests and workin' parties an' things. Clever People in striped shirts telling us how to get it right.'

She was bringing in another cup of tea. 'Was that one all right luv?'

'Yes thanks dear, and I haven't finished it yet.'

'Never mind,' she said. 'Here's your second.'

'Where do they come from? You know,' she said, 'these clever people.'

'Ah,' said Tony. 'Consultants, luv, consultants. When their own companies go bust, they can't find a job so they become consultants an' tell us how to do it.'

She nodded, then she thought, then she shook her head. The 'phone rang. She waddled over and answered it.

'Hello? Yes, he's here. ... Tony!' She put her hand over the mouthpiece and whispered conspiratorially. 'It's that barman from the Palace, you know ... Quentin. Sounds ever such a nice boy.'

Tony leapt up and walked over to the telephone. He took it from her hand. 'Hello Quent, what's up?'

Quentin was talking.

'When?'

Quentin was talking some more.

'Comin' over are they? Right, we'll be ready.' Tony's wife was giving him an inquiring look. He put the 'phone down and by way of explanation shouted through into the kitchen. 'Got tickets for the dogs ... being treated by the Gov'nor.'

'Oh,' she said 'they must think a lot of you in that boozer luv, always keeping in touch and giving you little treats and you being only part-time 'an all. You never take me there you know, don't even think I know where it is.'

'You know luv ... up West, not really a place for a lady.' The expression on his wife's face matched that of the prospective car buyer's.

'But the Gov'nor's all right,' he went on, looking fondly at the picture of the Queen. 'Dresses a bit flash, but 'eart of gold. Got problems with their kids too. The eldest 'as had a bit of wife trouble. She's been chattin' up the regulars, an' puttin 'im down, and 'e's taken to wandering around chatting to the grass, drivin' 'is missus mad.'

'Well you talk to your roses,' she said.

'That's different, init. Got to round 'ere, they need all the 'elp they can get.'

'Takes all sorts you know, luv.' She was trying to be reasonable. 'Live and let live I always say. Not as if they were running the country is it?'

Desert Town

Sara crashed on the bed, stared at the ceiling and closed her eyes. Morgan returned some time later, carrying a couple of screw-top bottles of wine and a six-pack of beer. Sara looked at him.

'Food?' she asked.

He triumphantly produced a couple of bags of crisps and peanuts. Sara's face fell.

'You really know how to treat a girl.'

'What do you expect from this place,' said Morgan. 'There's nothing open, and if there was, they wouldn't be selling anything.'

'Liar, you're cleaned out.' He didn't reply and therefore didn't deny it. They sat on the bed and picnicked on the crisps and booze.

'What the hell is going on, Morgan? I meet you on a train, we get off, we go out, I end up cuddling a dead body.'

'It's become a habit ... the dead bodies that is.' She looked at him.

'I think that's the third this week,' said Morgan, 'and my office was demolished.'

'I take it you're serious? I never really know with you.'

'Yes, I'm serious.'

'That knife was real enough I suppose,' she reflected.

'You should know, you were cuddling it.' She ignored this.

'What the hell are the cops doing about it all?'

'Accidents,' said Morgan. 'The first two were accidents. This one's a bit harder to explain. Maybe there's no connection, maybe it's just a bad dream, maybe I'm just unlucky.'

'Or maybe lucky.'

He took a swig from a bottle of red wine and wiped the rim with the sleeve of his shirt. He passed the bottle in her direction.

'I'll never get those stains off,' she said, taking hold of his denim cuffs and checking out the pink damp patches.

He looked slightly surprised at this sudden burst of domesticity, but returned to his thread. 'The whole thing is so unreal. I got out of L.A. to give myself some space - and time to think. Soon as I do, this happens.' Morgan took another slug.

'That won't help, you know,' said Sara.

'Oh yes it will.'

She moved across the room and fished into her bag. She produced a bottle of Jack Daniel's. Morgan's face lit up.

'This is better.'

'A girl after my own heart.'

'Purely medicinal purposes, sweetheart,' and passed it over to him.

'What's a nice girl like you, doing carrying around a nice bottle like this?'

'I don't sleep too good sometimes,' she replied.

'Now that's something I don't have a problem with,' said Morgan, unscrewing the bottle and taking a few gulps. He wiped the top with his hand this time and passed it back to Sara, who wiped it again with her hand and gulped some more. They had run out of things to talk about, no ... they had just run out of talk.

They lay back in silence for about half an hour, drinking steadily and occasionally crunching. Morgan moved around the bottles. Sara stuck mainly to the bourbon.

She swung her slim legs off the bed and wearily made her way to the shower, coming back in twenty minutes wrapped in white towels. Her long wet hair, dark with water, spilled over the whiteness. She jumped on the bed and crossed her legs Buddha fashion and poured herself another drink.

'Someone doesn't like you Morgan, who have you upset?' His answer came slower than normal, probably the drink, possibly his thoughts about the question.

'No one ... honest. I'm really freaked out by all this. It's like a bad dream.'

'What have you been up to lately?'

This made him belligerent, 'Sod all.'

'That I can believe, and that's about all you can do isn't it? Everybody's a body, not a person, just a piece of meat. No wonder she dumped you. Does she or doesn't she? Will she or won't she. Are they all numbers to you?'

'Why are you saying this?' He was getting angry and full of righteous indignation. 'You're going down the wrong road lady. Just because I tease you a little doesn't mean I'm a complete moron. Why should I pour my soul out to you anyway? Do you expect your men to be walking around with stickers on their chests proclaiming their mystical sensitivity?' "I am a new man. I am full of bullshit and I won't screw you until I've said something meaningful."

He gulped long and hard, then continued. 'What shall it be? We must have met in another life? ... I feel I've touched your soul before ... It's our karma ... How can something so good, be so wrong ... It's God's will ... Shall I go on?'

Sara grabbed the squat square bottle and drank greedily. It was nearly empty. 'You know ... it's a funny thing,' he was slurring now, 'but I actually believe in some of those things.'

She was nearly gone, but hanging on. 'If you think you can get me into bed with a line like that ... you must be dumber than you, you ...'

'Think' He helped her out.

She elbowed herself up against the bedhead and pointed a toe towards the floor. 'That's where you're sleeping boyo. Get down there where you belong.'

He didn't move. Probably couldn't. He kept talking. 'I don't see people in terms of male or female, or for that matter, black or white, rich or poor, right wing, left wing or broken wing. They are just people.'

'Balls.' she said, 'You don't really believe that. Every time you look at a woman, I see the piece-of-meat factor in your eyes.'

He tried to get her into focus.

'How are you going to cook this one, how much heat does this one require, and for how long? Do you let it smoulder for a while, what juices to add, or do you bring it to the boil quickly?'

'You're just projecting your prej ... predj ... predju ... ju ... juices. People often do that to oth ... other people ... some ... sometimes.' he replied. He pulled himself together remarkably well with another slug.

'Men chasing women is like men chasing careers, goals, touchdowns, success! But goddamn it, you can be interested in someone for all sorts of reasons besides sexual ones. Half the people in the world are either male or female and at some point in time they will have a relationship with a member of the opposite sex and it won't necessarily be with the aim to bed them.'

'Or the same sex,' she interrupted.

'Whatever ... I don't care what a man or woman is in terms of status, money, religion or anything else; I either like them or I don't like them. Either way I'll treat them with respect until they give me cause not to.' She thought about this for a while.

'If you are not bullshitting me, then maybe you *are* different.'

'There are plenty more like me where I come from.' He said.

'And where's that?'

'From right here ... we're all members of the human race ... we're all floating down the river of life.'

'What?'

'Life's a river. It flows from up there, to down there.' He pointed his long arms wildly in both directions. 'It only goes one way and it always ends in the same place.' He attacked what was left of the red. 'Ninety-five percent of people sit on the bank of the river of life and just dip their toes in. That's OK, that's fine.' The arms did a Jewish-Tailor impersonation. 'The sun shines sometimes, sometimes it rains. They get hot, they get cold, they don't do very much, things get done *to* them. It's a relatively safe and sane way to get through life. Occasionally they dip their toes in the water, paddle about a bit, then yank them out to dry. Eventually they just flop into the river and get carried to the sea.'

'What about the other five percent?' She reached out and snatched back the remains of the red.

'Well, they just stand on that bank getting a little bored. They look around, it's quite pleasant, but they want to know what's further down the river; they want to know what's round the next bend. So they dive in. They dive into the middle where the river's flowing fast and for a time it's great, the sun shines, they feel good, they're moving. And then whack, whack, they hit a rock... crash! They're under white water, they can't breathe, they're drowning, they panic, they scrabble to the bank and pull themselves up, out of breath.

They get their breath back; they vow never to go back in that water again. They sit there, put their toes in the water, they breathe deeply, and do you know what they feel? ... They'll give it one more shot. And in they go again.

And they hit more rocks, more waterfalls ... whirlpools. They'll scrabble back on that bank two or three times, or as many times as it takes them.

Both types of people get to the sea eventually, some arrive in a state of grace having gone quietly... others are taken there, bruised and battered, but maybe this second group of crazy people have learnt something, experienced something, have tried to do something, or done something.

All people get to the same place; they all reach the sea. The river of life only flows one way, there's no going back.'

She chewed this over for a while, then chewed on the end of the bottle. 'And what about reincarnation?'

He lit up and seemed to have sobered up. 'I don't have a problem with that,' he said, 'except I see it a little differently. I don't think we ever go away.'

'How do you mean'

'Like the water in the river, it hits the sea, it evaporates, it becomes a cloud ... it comes over the land and it falls down into the river again. Everything is cyclic. We are all on that treadmill. Sure, our atoms and molecules may get split up and re-distributed, but as Einstein stated, the total amount of matter in the universe is finite. I think we've all been buzzing around the universe since time began ... and probably before that.' He broke off for a quick pee, and carried on as before when he returned from the bathroom.

'Everything is made up of the same basic building material. A relatively small range of elements made up from atoms and molecules; these in turn are only differentiated by the way they accumulate from nuclei and electrons.

This applies to human beings, trees, rocks, water, air, everything. In fact everything is the same as everything else and if you accept the fact that one of the smallest of the building blocks is an atom, and that in turn is made up of a miniature solar system ... electrons flying around a nucleus in the centre, as we fly around our sun ... you will realise that, that is mostly *space*; charges between these constituent parts holding them in place.'

'Where did you get all this?'

'I *did* get an education too, remember, it's all pretty basic stuff.' He tried to get off the bed and nearly made it. When he had got to his feet, he stood there swaying and went into a professor sketch, his thumbs in what would have been his lapels, if he had any.

'You may therefore conclude that most things are made up of nothing, the bits that *are* something, are only electrical charges anyway.

It would seem, therefore, aside from the fact that nothing exists, or put another way,' and here he started singing, "Nothing is real," and all this unreality is revolving around everything else, then our universe might be an electron whizzing round the outer rim of another incredibly massive universe, which in turn could be spinning around an even greater one. Thus it goes on. Everything revolves around everything else, that, ladies and gentlemen, is the meaning of life.'

She took the bottle from his hand and looked at the label.

'I must get some more of this stuff.' She gave him a slow hand-clap.'

He wasn't finished. She groaned.

'If you throw a stone into a pond what do you get?'

'Wet?'

'Ripples,' he said, correcting her. 'And the further they get away from the stone, the weaker they become. They start to fade. The energy is being dissipated. Then, if you look closely you'll get a little eddy, a number of them in fact, a little swirl, a little mini whirlpool. Then it all fades.'

'So?'

He was getting excited. There was a manic gleam in the eye.

'It's as if the energy was trying to hang on to itself, it doesn't want to be dissipated. Structure means retention of energy. A tower has potential energy. If it falls, it loses that energy. I think the reason for life on earth in *all* its forms is simply another way of nature experimenting in retaining its energy and not dissipating it.

With all living things going through a life-cycle, reacting constantly with gases and foodstuffs all around them, eventually all life forms cannot maintain this running-on-the-spot. When death occurs all the constituents of all living things return to the environment around them. Ashes to ashes, dust to dust, molecules to atoms.'

They both looked 'round frantically for smokes and the last dregs from the bottle of White which was around there somewhere.

'That lot then reconstitutes itself, either as another human form, or even a tree, or grass, or bits of all sorts of things. The reproduction of all living things is an extension of this desperation to retain a structure and thereby, the *energy*. Long term of course it's a useless exercise. As we have an expanding universe, a point will be reached when all the bits of matter are too far away from each other to have any influence. That's when maximum entropy sets in and all energy eventually floats off into the ether.'

'God, how depressing,' she said. He missed the irony.

'Oh, I think it'll take a while yet,' he replied, 'and of course, the universe could start to condense back in on itself.'

'Perhaps we'll meet ourselves coming back the other way.' She was being facetious, but he was too pissed to notice.

'Maybe so,' he said, screwing up his mind to try to work that one out. She continued before he opened his mouth.

'That scenario doesn't place human beings in a very important place in the universe.'

'Exactly,' he retorted, 'and that makes me feel good.'

'Good?'

'If everyone realised how bloody unimportant they are, how all their little problems and worries and schemes and clothes and accessories and neighbours and status and money were all irrelevant in the long run, they might realise that *they're* also irrelevant in the short run. We'd all be a bit happier.'

'Are you saying we should all give up, Sit back and do nothing?'

'Not at all, we should strive for our own goals, but not get too hung up on them. We shouldn't miss the wider picture.'

'Women never do,' she said.

He took another pull on the bottle and offered her the last drop. She was out.

She was waking up.

'Nothing is real.'

'Oh, shit! What do you mean?' she said, holding her head.

'Everything is what you want it to be. A number of different scenarios can be wrought from the same set of facts. In fact, the inferences from just one statement can be as wide as your imagination.' She showed no interest, but he went on anyway.

'The best detective story ever written was called 'The Nine Mile Walk.' My father bought me a book of short crime stories when I was about ten, and this one has stayed with me. Can't remember the name of the author. Two guys were arguing about inferences and their accuracy. One asked the other to give him a sentence of about ten words. He came up with "A nine mile walk is no joke, especially in the rain." The first guy made only two assumptions; that the time and place of the statement were here and now. He inferred that the speaker was walking *towards* their town as those living outside know to the nearest mile the distance *to* the town and those living *in* it would say a village was about ten miles away. He also inferred that the walk took place between midnight and five in the morning, being the time when public transport finished and started up again; that the walk took place the previous evening, as it hadn't rained for weeks; that the walk took place along an isolated road, as the guy could have thumbed a lift; that he didn't live in the area as he would have made arrangements with his neighbours; that it was vital to make the walk ... nobody does that unless it was important; that he didn't have a car or he would have slept in it until the morning and that there were no telephones around as he could have called a cab.

They looked at a map of the locality and pinpointed a spot exactly nine miles outside the town where the last train from the town stopped for water. The road back from there was no more than a track. There'd be no cars and no telephone.

There was a lot more to it, but he deduced that the speaker had caught the last train, and had got off when it stopped for water, then walked back.

They then caught sight of a local paper announcing a dead body was found on *that* train the night before.

The guy who came up with the sentence remembered he heard it as they came into the coffee shop and recognised the man who said it. They called the cops and that was that.

That one sentence convicted someone, but was the inference right? What other tangents can we go off on?'

Sara didn't want to go anywhere. She just wanted him to shut up. The guy was a one-man debating society. She'd known similar cases. Something traumatic would happen to them and they'd go off into the recesses of their minds to find a meaning, instead of looking for it right out front. They usually came back to reality in the end, as that was where the answers were always to be found. Some never came back ... Maybe they were the contented ones. She was awake now and needed to sleep. He was still rambling.

'Like atoms, nothing is real, therefore we aren't either. All part of one great universe of the mind. Imagination can take you places your body can't follow ... so why not make more use of it. Bodies become redundant. And this may be a bad dream, the sequences held together by intangible forces...like magnetism or gravity ... maybe love is the magnet, pulling our thoughts hopes and fears around its black hole ... like heavenly bodies exerting an influence that cannot be seen and ...'

''How much have we had?' she slurred, taking advantage of a pause and looking at the empty glassware. There was no response; he was almost out of it.

Somewhere at the edge of town an owl hooted as Morgan reached out and fumbled pathetically in his jacket pocket, 'Just gotta listen to this ... just remembered it.' He shook her awake and she forced herself to respond.

'What is it?'

'It's a demo tape by a failed songwriter. He sings and plays piano and occasionally puts a band together.'

'Where did you get it?'

'A friend of mine gave it to me. I've been playing it quite a bit over the last couple of days, at least I've been trying to. Don't seem to be able to find the time. Now's as good a time as any.'

'What's so good about it?' She tried to close her eyes.

Morgan was taking the cassette out of its case and was trying to force it into his machine.

'There's just something about it. The voice maybe, soaked in blues, bit of soul, a voice from the recent past. It's just real music, not contrived, synthesized, or put together to hit any particular commercial market. It's just real music from a real guy.'

'Do you know him?'

'No, not really. I met him briefly. No I don't know him.'

He pressed the tape button and leaned back. They lay together, their heads resting on the same pillow.

When love comes calling, you'd better be at home
Nobody knows the pain of walking through this life alone
When love comes calling, open up your door
They say that those who love
Grow stronger than they ever did before
And I believe there's still time
To love somebody
Still time to hold someone
'Cos my life has been any empty story
Tossed and turned on every storm
But I pray there's time enough to find
The one, my heart is longing for
When love comes calling
When love comes calling, you'd better be around
'Cos love won't wait or hesitate, but leaves without a sound
And I believe there's still time to love somebody
Still time to hold someone
'Cos my life has been an empty story
Tossed and turned on every storm
But I pray there's time enough to find the one my heart is longing for
When love comes calling
Calling at your door
Comes calling at your door

Morgan was drifting away. Sara slipped off the bed and staggered across the room to fetch a blanket from the pile on the sofa and place it gently around him. She lay on the sofa herself, pulling another blanket over her. They both drifted away to the track.

The white owl was beating hard on the window. Sara awoke in the middle of the night and her eyes focused on this black and white negative. She was cold. She made out Morgan in the shaft of moonlight, asleep in the foetal position. She gathered her thin blanket around her and as quietly as she could, slipped into bed with him. She lay still and listened to her heart beat. Morgan stirred and turned over towards her. She tried to remain frozen as Morgan's arm came across her body. He was breathing softly, but regularly. She was bushed and started to sink.

Sara dreamed.

Waves were breaking gently on a beach, then bigger waves on rocks, then great gales and waves breaking on towering cliffs, finally the storm abated and she was back to the gentle surf sliding up the sand pushing the clichés ahead of it.

She woke as the weak early sunlight filled the room. She smiled dreamily and murmured 'Morgan, oh Morgan ... Morgan the Organ.' Then whispered, 'The man with the child in his eyes.' He was draped over her. They were both naked and Sara was holding him very tight.

Morgan's eyes opened and looked at her for a moment.

'Bit of a storm last night ... I think we're safe now my love.' They both drifted off to sleep.

7

Drive, she said

'Why did you want me anyway?'

The question was put to an aesthetic gentleman reclining in the mahogany and port recesses of a Washington club that didn't exist.

'I'm worried about the Ames situation, and what he could say about our group.'

'What about Ames? Are they going to pull him in soon?'

'Well, he's been a silly boy, flashing it about. I blame his South American tart. They've both blown it.'

'Wasn't he her controller?'

'Yes. Unfortunately we can't dispose of him now. You know how the boss insists on natural causes whenever possible. I suppose he could conveniently hang himself once inside, but that's a bit too obvious. The Intelligence Oversight Committee will be watching out for that one. We'll invent another mole and allow Ames to do a deal, and swing it that way. I'll finger someone, then either let them take the rap or they'll have to commit suicide.'

'Couldn't that happen to Ames?'

'No, we want the money in Panama. Only he knows where it is. Do you know there are fifty billion dollars sitting in the one hundred and fifty banks in Panama City? Most of it is drug money and a great deal of it is ours. They're getting a bit sensitive down there, and the secrecy is more stringent than Switzerland.

They want to hang on to it themselves, as the average life span of their depositors is fairly short. By the year two thousand the Panamanians want full control of the canal as well as their own destiny. This is a dangerous situation. Panama is the umbilical cord between the North American mother and the South American baby. The cord was cut by the Canal, but the baby never grew up. We've been the midwife, then the nanny ... now the teenager wants to leave home. The infrastructure Ames built up down there must be kept in place. It's not just the money, it's the control.' He twisted the pen tightly in his fingers.

'At least James Woolsey is having a field day pushing for bigger budgets. Pity he's straight. He's a good guy.'

'Yes, but I can't risk inviting him into the frame. Not sure how he'll react. It's bad form to be out front anyway. We get more done this way.'

'I don't think I can keep Ames out of jail, but he won't be in for long. Sure, he'll get life, but that can mean anything.'

'We'll probably arrange a swop and then use him as a double. If he doesn't co-operate, we'll take him out inside.'

'When did you recruit him?'

'1985, just after we sent Lee Howard to Moscow to dump on the CIA guys who had got wind of us. He didn't know what he was doing; we just fed him the information.'

The Soviets woke up after the failed coup by Kryuchkov ... Yeltsin was not a happy man.

'We made Ames head of Soviet Counter Intelligence, although he was working for us controlling South America. He had a couple of flats in Columbia ... Bogota. He attended the weekly meetings of division chiefs in this building ... Counter Narcotics. We sent him to Venezuela quite often. Technology and industrial espionage officially, but really it was back in the States that he came into his own... the Savannah material ... He sneaked it out from that plant beautifully. We also used his Soviet contacts to place our material in Moscow.

He got Sir Anthony to lift the M25 limits on embassy staff to make it easier to move money around ... We could get out to the banks on the UK Channel Islands. Ames was our courier, or financial controller, for most of the drug money from South America.

At least Noriega has played ball. He's been helpful, not like Escobar. He was big trouble.'

'Will Ames dump on us? ... Talk about our consortium?'

'No, he knows he'll be a dead man.'

'What's the situation with the runner?'

'Morgan? ... Not sure. It's this tape he guards closely, I got a track list. See what you can make of it. It's important ... I think. The girl's father was a big cog in the East-European wheel and knew everything about the Soviet side of the operation. She must have got wind of something. She was sitting on *TOP* of it, for Christ's sake.'

'Pity he went bad. How did you find out?'

'The father? ... Tried to do a deal with Ames. Wanted to take off to South America with the key to the Panama accounts ... and Ames' wife's contacts to help him disappear. The ace they were going to play would have been the exposure of our *special defence* arrangements, and of our other string-pulling activities.

Ames had to get his wrists slapped, although he would never have gone along with it.'

'What about Curtis?'

'His daughter was *our* responsibility. The Soviets are going to deal with Curtis themselves. Probably have already. Apparently he was involved with siphoning off their London money.'

'His colleagues were dealt with by the Sportsmen?'

'I believe so.'

'You think this Morgan is in on it?'

'Definitely not, but she might have said something to him ... pillow talk.'

'She didn't seem to use pillows very often.'

'We found this tape at her place. At least the LAPD did. The Commissioner got a copy to us. She gave it to him. He's obsessed with it. Keeps it close to him, must be important. It's just a demo by a bozo. Who'd be that interested in a bad recording by a failure? There must be more to it. Hasn't even got any backing singers.'

'Yeah, that does seem significant.'

'You taking the piss?'

'Wouldn't dream of it. Why don't we blow him away?'

'We'll frighten him a bit ... he might talk. Although it's probably too late for that. Some people in Head's department seem to be trying to wipe him out.'

'And that tape?'

'Work on it. Put it through the computers. Could be something there.'

'Message?'

'Almost certainly. Code numbers, 'phone numbers, account numbers, agents' names, addresses of placements ... Could contain anything.'

'The songwriter?'

'Leftie, nothing serious, but we think that tape is significant. Curtis or his daughter may have doctored it to contain information detrimental to our operation.'

'I'll get Siemonsen to direct Roberts to work on it. He's a musician too ... It might help.'

Desert Town

'Did you have a good night?' The Sheriff was still doing his Rod Steiger impersonation as he leaned against the bar and looked at the couple. The White Lodge in daylight was as seedy as it had appeared the day before.

The couple were sitting quite close together and said in unison, 'Yes, thank you, Sheriff.'

'Heat of the Night' smiled to himself knowingly. He cleared his throat and got down to more serious questions.

'Now it would seem that the only person with a motive in this case is you,

Mr Morgan.' Morgan looked offended. The Sheriff wasn't finished.

'You return to your seat, have a fit of jealousy, and before you know it ... WHAM!' The Sheriff thumped the table hard, bouncing a couple of glasses. When they had settled, he spoke in a softer voice. 'I don't think it happened that way. Besides, I never seen a Quarterback who carried a knife.' Then thoughtfully. ' But maybe that doesn't apply to *Running* Backs.' The Sheriff took a swig from a bottle of beer. 'Now that leaves me with two problems. One; Who the hell *did* do it? And two; Well, Gill was well-liked in this town. You two are strangers, and it strikes me that the best thing you can do is get out. Sooner than later.'

The Sheriff took another swig. As he did so, he looked out of the corner of his eye at Morgan and continued to develop his theme after wiping his lips, 'It did cross my mind that maybe that knife wasn't meant for Gill, you get my drift?'

Morgan and Sara answered in unison, 'We get your drift.'

'Umm ...you've been a little accident-prone lately, son. Take my advice, keep moving and don't turn your back.'

'May the wind be always at yours,' replied Morgan.

The sheriff grunted an acknowledgement, put his hands in his pocket and took something out. He held it out in the palm of his hand. It was a small capsule.

'By the way, is this yours?'

Morgan and Sara shook their heads and shrugged their shoulders, again in unison.

'It was found in the seat behind the deceased. I'll have it checked out. Maybe some fancy medication that will give us a lead. Maybe not.'

The sheriff started to leave. He stopped and turned, 'Just one more thing, I believe a statement is overdue ... back in the smoke.' Morgan made to say something. The Sheriff raised his hand to stop him.

'Before you leave, come and see me, we'll sort it out then ... and I'll want to know your next stop ... Bye.' He waved and walked out.

The couple finished their drinks; their mood was sombre.

'Do you want to wait a month before hitting Europe?' asked Morgan. After some thought, she replied, speaking quickly, 'No, we'll drive back to L.A. and get the first available flight. We'll drive through the desert ... if anyone is following us, we'll know it. We can see for ten miles in any direction.'

She pulled a wallet out of her bag and flicked it open.

'I've got my bits of plastic. I'll hire a car and meet you in the Sheriff's office in an hour.' Morgan's face expressed a delighted surprise at her efficiency. She wasn't finished. 'I don't know what you've done, but one day I'm gonna make you tell me.' Morgan just shrugged his shoulders and lifted his arms. 'Let's go,' she said.

Virginia

Siemonsen sat in his office, half a dozen acolytes around him. The 'phone was jammed in his ear.

'I'm having my balls chewed off,' said Siemonsen into the mouthpiece ... 'Yes, very lucky.' He held his arm up to still the sniggers ... 'Listen, if this isn't brought to a successful conclusion soon, then you can forget your pension. We'll take him out in Europe and this time it's got to be quiet.' His colleagues were nodding in silent agreement. Siemonsen was angry ... 'Using a knife was crazy AND a rope. Just a candlestick and you could have played Cluedo ...Yes I know it was nothing to do with you ...Your partner just doesn't think!' 'What's that? ... Oh Jesus, the *Last-Resort!*... Right, I'll sort it out ... Look, he's got to go. I don't care what he does or doesn't know, just make sure it goes *right* next time.' He slammed the 'phone down and looked at his colleagues.

'Rebellion?' said one.

Siemonsen replied, 'Our guy reckons Morgan isn't worth hitting.'

Another colleague leaned across, 'He should try telling that to the man upstairs.' The room was quiet for a moment.

Siemonsen was drumming his fingers on the polished desktop. Eventually, he spoke. 'There's another problem ... A capsule was dropped.'

Glances were exchanged between all those present. The looks were ones of concern.

'Yes, a Last-Resort capsule. Now that could be traceable to this organ-isation. I'll have to move quickly on that one.' He paused for thought. 'Gentlemen, I know we operate a strict compartmentalisation here and that is born of necessity.' He put his hands together in a praying mantis position, 'But I don't think it would do any harm for you to know certain things that others,' he raised his eyes, 'deem to be,' quietly now, 'most secret.'

He had their full attention. 'When we wish London to handle certain jobs for us; jobs that are unusually sensitive, we do not always use the... shall we say ... *normal* channels. There are rules when we are in London, as there are here ... But they can change with the situation.' He broke off and poured himself a glass of mineral water.

'Sir Anthony McLean heads up a very specialised section. He is an Establishment figure who is dedicated to upholding the more,' he thought for a moment, '*traditional* values of their society.'

He suddenly stood up. 'I think at this point, gentlemen, we should take a break. Tom, Simon and you Jeffrey, stay here. The rest of you can come back in fifteen minutes.' When the room had cleared, he resumed. 'In short gentlemen ... he works for the Royal Family.'

The three exchanged the usual sceptical glances. Unperturbed, Siemonsen carried on. 'The Royals have always held the real power in Europe, despite the introduction of elected government. They just have to wield it very discreetly. The same thing happens here of course, and the common bond is money ... mega-bucks. The people who control it are the effective rulers. This applies to any country in the world.

The control of the world order, it's trading policies, boundaries, popu-lation, principles, hopes and fears ...They are far too important to be left to politicians. Who are these guys anyway? Who do people vote for in a democracy? The present system can't work. Anyone who puts himself forward for election is a shit, almost by definition. The good guys are too busy doing things, making things, writing things, raising families with the right responsibilities. Now that means we chose from a list of shits, and pick the least shittiest, Right? The result is ... we get a government completely made up of various shades of the brown stuff. So what are we gonna get? ... Shat on! That's what.

Now, as these guys play their little democratic games once every five years, and not much else, we have had in place a team of people that does the real job for them, full time. We decide on crop yields, money supply, territorial rights, investment, employment levels, interest rates, and just about everything that's important enough.

This all takes money. We control more money than any one Government. We *are,* in effect, the *World* Government. We don't need a base, don't need elections. We identify the real power in a country, or put our own puppet in place ... Yes, even in the States.

We persuade from the shadows and the key to this almost unlimited power is the fact that we are a brotherhood, a consortium, a freemasonry, free to direct the politics of the planet for the maximum good of all. The Illuminati and Bilderberg groups are the relatively small and public faces of a much larger body.' He gave a wry smile. 'And they keep the Conspiracy Theorists occupied.'

We are helped, of course, by the fact that we have the ultimate *persuader.* It's worked for the last ten years.'   *THE PLACEMENTS*

Siemonsen paused to take on water. 'Look at the crazy spending on defence, ruining both superpowers. Now we have no problem. We delegate the nitty-gritty to the assholes. They make their buck ... we take the overview. 'Drug money? So what? Let the idiots who want to kill themselves do so. We can't feed them all. African states? Same damn thing every year; famine and mass deaths. Sure we can stop it, but why bother? ... There isn't enough room on this planet for all of us. It's a dirty job, but somebody's got to do it.'

He rose and paced the room.

'We are saving the world from itself. We control the nuclear arms race and all governments are aware that they cannot step out of line; at least, the people with *real* power in each country do. Security is vital. It is our strength. We need secrecy. In this instance, this particular problem that we have, then I think McLean's department is the one to handle it. He's not as kind of, umm ... *picky* as other departments they have over there ... and God knows they're not nearly picky enough.'

One of his colleagues poured himself another water. A few drops were spilt on to the polished surface. His finger idly traced connections between them. He spoke bluntly.

'Where does Morgan come into this?'

Siemonsen snapped, 'A minor irritant, but the knowledge he possesses, knowingly or not, could, if made public, enable people to piece a few things together; which would do a little more than just *embarrass* the Establishment. The fact that the most powerful countries in the world could be shown to have come to the certain cosy arrangement that some of us around this table are aware of, would have dire consequences. The *Governments* don't necessarily know about us, although we sometimes have to let them in on it. Certain elected representatives just need a stack of money to agree to keep their heads down. No, it's our people in secondary positions who call the shots.' Siemonsen gathered his papers together. 'I hope that clarifies the position gentlemen.' Siemonsen rose, indicating that the meeting was over.

As two of his team left, one said to the other ... 'I hope that clarifies the position, gentlemen ... Sure it does ... Easy.'

The other said nothing until they had moved a little way down the corridor. 'I think he said the super-rich stick it to the rest.'

His friend came back, 'Tell us something we didn't know.'

Desert Town

'Can I help you?' The couple looked lost and had a certain hesitancy about them, as all those who are starting to leave middle age possess.

'Why yes, Sheriff, it's about that murder ... in the cinema. We were there ...We were sat down right behind him.'

The Sheriff moved quickly to the door and shut it. 'Names?'

'Mr and Mrs Jackson ... We thought we'd better come and see you. We'd have come earlier, but we were out of town.'

'What did you see?'

'Well, nothing,' said Mrs Jackson. 'I'm afraid ... didn't see nothing. It was so dark, even dropped my asthma capsule ... couldn't find it anywhere.'

'Is this it?'

'Why, yes.'

Mrs Jackson reached out and took it gratefully from the Sheriff's outstretched hand while Mr Jackson moved around behind him.

'This it?' The car was a Ford of some kind and looked very tired.

'At least it's topless,' she said, with slight resentment in her voice. 'That's the way I thought you liked them.'

He sat in and switched on. It started. It was OK.

'Sheriffs' office is all closed up ... I don't want to hang around too long.'

'Let's go,' he agreed.

The town of Jean was more like twenty miles short of Vegas. They crossed route 15 and took the State Highway 161 to Goodsprings, then headed west to Sandy and crossed the Nevada State Line back into California. They continued due west to the Tecopa Pass which cut through the southernmost tip of the Nopah Range - which was about six thousand feet high in places. To the north lay Death Valley.

They sliced through the dusty waste rising like a sea on their flanks. Pale yellow sand, scrubbed white in places. Broken and scumbled with olive, it flowed past, swelling in the distance to bigger waves of pink, blue and purple.

It was one of the driest places on earth and the vegetation was sparse, being mainly made up of stubby cacti and creosote. After a rare shower of rain the earth would greedily suck the surface dry, but just below the surface, droplets of rainwater coated the small stones and the roots of the scattered creosote bushes searched for every last drop. They needed a vast root system to gather in as much as possible, thus preventing the survival of any other living plant in its sphere of influence. Multinational corporations employed the same tactics.

New stems formed near its base and the central part would die away, resulting in an ever expanding ring which could reach thirty yards in diameter. The original plant could be ten thousand years old and was the world's oldest living organism.

They were driving through mythical America.

The blue-domed sky, unbroken by cloud, was having problems holding up the sun. It bore down, throbbing with frustration at not being able to get at them. Instead, it reached out its fingers and scratched the earth's surface, raising its temperature to about 100°F. There was no humidity in this rustless place.

They pulled over and stretched their legs. The dry stillness and vast cathedral sky combined to lift their spirits and free-up tension. They stared in silence for a long time, breathing in the space.

' Good for the head' said Sara.

'And the soul.' He scanned the horizon. ' There are no fences facing.'

She nodded. ' Let's go.'

The car slewed back on the road, kicking up a white dust.

'What's a feminist?' Morgan's words were spoken through teeth clenching a cigarette. Sara looked at him, raising a pair of dark glasses as if to confirm his presence. He took the cigarette out and flicked it into the slip stream.

'What's a feminist?' he repeated.

'Why do you ask?'

'That's what you regard yourself as, isn't it?'

She looked straight ahead. 'If you *must* put labels on people.'

'I never put labels on anything ... I read them sometimes ... Are you going to tell me?'

'You're joking?'

'No.'

'You want me to tell you what a feminist is?'

'Yes.'

'Ok ... I believe that women are fully equal to men. In areas of business, politics, and any intellectual pursuit we are certainly the equal of men. Physically, we might lack a little, but we more than make up for that with our superior intellect. Men are linear thinkers; they have tunnel vision. They handle only one project at a time and carry things through in a single-minded fashion. Women have the ability to handle many different things at the same time, although we could be accused of not devoting ourselves one hundred percent to a particular project ... As I say, that is because we can *handle* more than one at a time. Women have the ability to stand back from a series of problems and see the whole, not missing the wood for the trees. Men frequently run up blind alleys, although I'll admit that they probably get up the alleys faster.' She stopped and looked at him. The heat wouldn't go away.

'So is that it?' said Morgan. She hesitated.

'Yes, I suppose that's it.'

'So what?' said Morgan.

'What do you mean, So what?'

'So what you've said is perfectly straightforward. Who on earth would disagree with that? You've summed up the differences between men and women quite neatly.'

'So what's the problem?'

'*There isn't one*, that's just the point. I presume you call yourself a feminist because you have a problem. People who stick labels on themselves are usually fighting something.'

'What's the *problem*?' she shouted. 'Jesus, you bastards are the problem.' She lit up. 'It's not the differences between men and women, but the way men have used those differences.' Sara wiped her brow with the back of her wrist. 'Look Morgan, men are single-minded, they're also more aggressive, or maybe they're more single-minded *and* more aggressive. Anyway ... men have used their aggression to achieve positions of power in the world of business, politics, the home, you name it. All the problems of the world have been created by men. Every war was started by a man, countries are run by men, governments are controlled by men, education is controlled by men, there is hardly a woman in a position of power anywhere in the world who has another woman to rely on to help her. Any woman who has got that far has had to adopt male attitudes and submerge the feminine side of her nature.'

'But all the great strides in civilisation have been made by men,' Morgan chipped in. 'All the great scientific discoveries, the great voyages, even the great movements in Art ... Go on ...' he said to her, 'reel me off five great female scientists and five great female artists ... I'll give you ten seconds.'

Sara wrestled with the wheel and pretended she hadn't heard. 'Men have abused their position of power to keep women in their place. They go out and have a good time; we stay at home with the kids. That's the way it's always been, and as far as I can see it, unless we do something about it, that's the way it always will be.' She lit up again.

'How many of these great scientists and explorers had to handle two or three kids, changing nappies, dressing them, taking them to school, cleaning the house, cooking?... "Hi, Mr Kennedy, come and give us your speech about booting Khrushchev out of Cuba, come and tell those Ruskies where to shove it."

"Sure, just a minute, I'm just changing this nappy, and then I've got to run down to the drug store; we're right out of baby powder ... and as soon as I've picked up the kids from school, I'll get onto that microphone and kick some ass."

'Oh come on,' said Morgan. 'It's just a natural division of labour; man the hunter, woman the maker of the nest. This pattern is repeated throughout nature. The female of the species usually decides on the nesting place and often builds the nest, while the male is foraging for food for the family. In fact the female of the species usually chooses a mate who is a good hunter or forager and someone who can protect her nest. Unless the male is a good provider he doesn't get chosen as a mate.'

'Some things never change, do they?' she replied. Morgan offered her a beer. She took it. 'This world needs more of a female influence.' She had got the bit between her teeth now. 'If people would stand back and look at our problems as a whole, instead of trying to sort out each individual one, then maybe we would get somewhere.'

They spent that night in the car. The stars crowded the blue-black heavens and Neil Young sang *Helpless* on the radio, so at least one other knew how they felt.

Los Angeles

'What happened in Jean.' The big man was trying to make sense of the telex.

'Two dead bodies ... and Morgan was there.'

'Right, let's get out there.' John had turned to Weller.

'Sorry John, no can do ... I can't let you go.' The chief was standing in the doorway and his voice was firm. 'Lay off the case for the time being ... I'm being leaned on from upstairs.'

'DA?'

'No.'

'Feds?'

'No.'

'How much further up the stairs do I have to go?'

'Call it political.'

'If it's drugs, screw it. The CIA lost a shipment worth two million dollars last week ... from under their noses!' John stormed out and Weller went after him.

'Why are we off the homicide?' Weller was looking for a reason.

'What homicide?' quipped the big man. 'There ain't no homicide.' He stopped and gazed out of the window. 'We'll go anyway.'

Desert

The white convertible was travelling through the spectacularly lunar landscape. Above the horizon everything was light blue, dark blue or violet. Below the horizon it was violet, orange and white. Morgan was driving and Sara was lying back in the passenger seat. 'We should have waited for the Sheriff,' she said.

'We did ... We couldn't have possibly left it any longer,' said Morgan. 'He's probably gone fishing.'

Morgan was driving in the centre of the road. There was no sign of another vehicle in front or behind them. The front of the convertible gobbled up the centre lines at the front and the tail spat them out the back. They disappeared behind the convertible, like tracer bullets, into the distance. It was incredibly hot. There was no shade save the convertible's hood, but they had decided to dispense with that.

Who would want to drive through almost John Wayne country with a roof? That was further to the east in Utah, but the only things missing were the rust-coloured buttes rising to the sky and the Indians. Scrub and sand were sliding past and the Indian raiding party was about to pounce on their uncovered wagon. Morgan had a cigarette in one hand, the usual can of beer between his knees and a cassette in the other, which he was pushing into the player. They both leaned back and went with the music.

Drive she said, take me away from here
I don't want to feel the birth of even one more tear
People breaking down, raking around in the dust
And if you hurt all the time, you can't tell the shine from the rust
Get these long white lines clear in our sights
Let's get these wheels turning, let 'em burn like a flame
Till the end of the night
Come on and drive, drive, she said
Come on and drive, drive, she said
Drive she said, take me away from this place
I'm tired of this town, I'm tired of the whole human race
Sometimes you just have to bend, in the end to the wind
When you're fighting those battles you know you never can win
You can lose your life waiting for your dreams to arrive
At least while we're moving we know that our souls are still half alive
Come on and drive, drive, she said Come on and drive, drive, she said
Well drive she said, don't stop till this highway ends
I don't care if I don't see those hard faces again
Turn my back on the ones, who never had the time
People change with their clothes, and who knows which face you will find
Get these long white lines clear in our sights
Let's get these wheels turning, let 'em burn like a flame

Till the end of the night
Drive she said
Till the end of the night.

This was a rhythmic rock track and the tracer bullets kept disappearing from the tail in time with the beat of the repetitive piano. By the time the track had finished they had covered almost five miles, and there was still no sign of Indians.

Morgan was taking in the space, and talking to it as well as to Sara.

'Solo songwriters tend to melancholy ... Dylan, Cohen, Hardin ... pure like a single malt, but often it takes a blend of two to get perspective. Lennon-McCartney, Jagger- Richards, John -Taupin, even Mike Oldfield's Tubular Bells needed the midwifery skills of fine old Tom Newman to deliver the baby.'

'You're an Anglophile.'

'I went back over to England when I was about fifteen. My father had relatives in Manchester. It was big and gritty city. We stayed for a week or two, but that was when I got hit by the music bug. I mean "Real Music." There was an old cinema around the corner from where we were staying and I was drawn to the posters pasted up outside. It had been converted to a rock music venue, but with the enthusiasm of the fanatic. The posters were crazy and like nothing I'd seen before. And the even names of the bands were from left-field. I've still got a flyer at the cabin somewhere. I can remember the odd name ... Groundhogs, Budgie, Vinegar Joe, Atomic Rooster. Even some US bands ... Commander Cody, Dr. Hook ... I passed this place daily when I went to fetch the milk!

The cathartic moment occurred when I sneaked out through my bedroom window and joined up with a bunch of regulars slipping in through an emergency exit. What hit me I shall never forget. The place was dark and cavernous and filled with weed. I was high within ten minutes just breathing it all in. Getting alcohol was no problem. I just grabbed half-full glasses from the tables. Their owners seem to be lying in heaps on the floor. "The Sensational Alex Harvey Band" were just that. I was hooked, and after climbing back into my room undetected, I resolved to repeat the experience.

I went back two or three times. Witnessed Hell's Angels helping pass drinks around, motorbikes being driven up the front steps, a car trying to park in the foyer, two or three bands a night, a stammering Scots DJ, a heavenly female vision moving to "Yours is no disgrace," musicians joining the crowd for a drink, regulars helping out in the cloakroom and the management not batting an eyelid. The atmosphere was pure ... Magic!'

He hit the bottle again. 'Can't remember the name of the place. Stone something ...or was it Stoned! Yeah, that was it *Stonedground!*'

'You're not really trans-atlantic,' she said, 'you're mid-atlantic. Stuck in the middle.

' With you.'

' Accounts for a lot.'

'The English bands were picking up on the progressive influences from the States and taking that forward. Led Zeppelin were iconic, Floyd were sublime. That era was life-changing, anything could happen. I even saw a poster in Manchester for Neil Young supported by *The Eagles.* Can you believe that! I now spend nights out on the hills under the stars listening to Tangerine Dream . It all came from that period over the pond.'

' Good taste, Mr.Morgan, but what about Classical? Don't you ever listen to Mozart?'

'Too many notes ... Bach could say twice as much with half as many.'

Her mouth opened in outrage, but Morgan got in before her. 'The last chorus of his Mathew Passion ... now *that* could rival Dark side of the Moon.'

Morgan was imagining a rock version. Plant on lead vocals, backed by Peter Gabriel and a chorus of Christie Hynde, Dusty Springfield, Emmylou Harris, Joni Mitchell and driven by great deep waves of Bonham's drums, Bruce's bass and Vangelis on Bosendorfer. The whole swelling crescendo taken to even greater heights by Page's guitar picking up the highs and lifting them to the heavens.

Sara shook her head sadly and stared into the blue.

Morgan flicked to the radio, which had been helpfully tuned into the local news station by the hire company and they came in halfway through a news bulletin.

The first item they heard had Morgan slowing down dramatically and Sara putting on the brakes. A bland mid-west voice announced ...

'Sheriff P. Garrett was found dead this afternoon. Shocked officers broke into his office and found the sheriff slumped in his chair. Cause of death seems to have been suicide. The remains of a cyanide capsule was found in his mouth. The community has suffered a great loss. We will be bringing you a full report in our next bulletin ... And now a word from our sponsor.'

Sara switched off. 'Poor guy,' she exclaimed. 'He just didn't seem the type.'

'Are you completely *stupid?*' Morgan exploded. 'Of course it wasn't suicide, and I don't think that capsule was a snack between meals. It must have been the one he found in the seat behind your boyfriend. The one he was going to check out. Now he's checked out.'

She turned on him. 'Happens to most of the people you meet, doesn't it?'

His eyes blazed. 'Too many, and what sort of people would walk around with cyanide capsules, either for themselves or for others.'

There was a long silence. Morgan started to accelerate. Sara was staring out at the desert. After some time she said softly, 'Secret services, spies, CIA ... people like that.'

He drove on. The desert was very big and they were extremely small.

Los Angeles

The man in the telephone-box seemed to be having trouble working out where to put his coins. He obviously wasn't used to it. His large black brief-case was restricting his movements, and when he turned his head, his steel- framed glasses smashed against the glass. He had to constantly readjust them.

Siemonsen was speaking in an agitated voice. 'I don't want the Brits getting the credit for this one. This is going to be dealt with by *my* department, and in *my* territory ... and you're going see that it happens. I do not need to tell you that if anything should go wrong, the order did not come from me. I should not have to remind you that your little habit would not be appreciated by those upstairs. Yes...,' and then smiled fondly, 'I *am* your guardian ... *angel.*' He replaced the 'phone gently and left the box.

Desert

Morgan changed the stick-shift down from fourth to third. The road was heading into a blind bend. Large pink and pale-orange boulders guarded the dark entrance. Midway through the rocky outcrop, Morgan changed down again and slammed his foot on the brake-pedal shortly after. He came up dusty in a squeal of brakes. Up ahead, a beat-up pickup almost blocked the road. It had slewed across it and struck a rock. A young woman appeared to be lying on the ground. A man was having trouble helping her to her feet. They were both bleeding and the man appeared to be in a state of shock. Morgan advanced the white convertible slowly. He was about to stop, when Sara screamed, 'Put your foot down!'

Morgan hesitated. 'You've seen too many movies.'

Sara was shouting, 'Get the hell out of here. Go!'

Morgan was confused, and compromised by driving slowly through the only gap available. The woman was halfway off the ground now and as Morgan came alongside her, she suddenly leapt across in front of the car and fell across his windshield, smearing it with blood.

'Shit!' exclaimed Morgan, and again the white convertible braked sharply, jerking the woman off the bonnet.

Sara seemed shocked by the sudden close-up of the lady's face pressed briefly to the windshield.

'Don't stop, don't stop!' urged Sara. 'Move, move!'

Morgan glared at her and pulled on the hand brake. They both jumped out of the car. The man was bending over the apparently lifeless body of the woman.

'Baby, baby, oh my poor baby.' He was shaking her shoulders. Grim-faced, Morgan approached them.

Sara was shouting and trying to grab his arm. Morgan shook it off, and moved forward.

'Come back!' she urged. 'Keep an arm's length away, give yourself space!'

A brief look of puzzlement crossed Morgan's face, but the moment passed and he walked on. When he reached the pair, the man looked up and shook his head.

'Get up,' said Morgan in a surprisingly crisp voice.

'Get up ... over there.'

The man responded, looking hurt and bewildered. Morgan knelt at the side of the woman, felt her weak pulse and loosened her collar. The silver chain holding a small silver cross was twisted tightly, chafing her neck. He loosened it gently. Almost immediately there was a loud thump behind him. He whirled around to find Sara lying prone. The man was not looking bewildered any more. He was standing over her and pointing a very large gun at Morgan's head.

'Get up ... over there,' he echoed.

Morgan rose slowly, cursing to himself. 'Dummy move, and I bought it.' Morgan's cheeks flushed with anger. He looked straight up and started to walk deliberately towards the man.

'Stop!' said the man, his voice rising in pitch. 'Right there!'

Morgan ignored this, and continued walking towards him.

'You stupid bastard,' exclaimed the gun-man and backed away slowly, wiping his nose on his sleeve as he did so. Morgan continued walking; the gun-man was still backing away, keeping his distance. Morgan kept on walking until he reached Sara, ignoring the gunman. She was coming to, rubbing the side of her neck. The man was screaming now.

'Get up! Get up, both of you!' He wiped his nose again.

Morgan dragged Sara to her feet. 'Are you all right?'

'You stupid bastard,' she said to him.

The gunman was slowly moving around the convertible. The woman was still lying on the ground. He switched on the engine with the car in neutral and beckoned the two of them towards him with the gun. With his free hand he took a piece of metal out of his pocket and wedged the accelerator down with it. He performed the operation with one hand and seemed incredibly professional and competent. The gun-hand was always pointed at the couple; it didn't move an inch. The gunman placed one leg on the clutch pedal, flicked the car into gear, then released the clutch. It leapt forward, crashing into the truck.

After the tearing noise, dust and smoke had settled, the gunman quietly motioned to the couple. 'Get in.'

They exchanged glances and got into the damaged car. The gunman walked round to the petrol cap and unscrewed it. He produced a rag, which he stuffed into the tank. Morgan looked at Sara.

'I'll always listen to you in future.'

'What future?'

The gunman took a lighter out of a breast pocket. Morgan put his hand on the door and the dash, tensing himself to spring out. The gunman flicked the lighter and almost immediately sneezed loudly, blowing out the flame. At that moment Morgan moved and in two strides had brought the gunman down in a flying tackle. They rolled over, fighting as they rolled, moving away from the car and truck.

Sara jumped out and stood watching. Morgan was desperately clawing for the gun handle. Once found, he brought it down with great force a number of times on the road.

This took two hands and although he succeeded in breaking the gunman's grip on the gun, it did not prevent the gunman's free hand descending on the back of his neck. The lights went out briefly. When they came on again, the gunman was standing over him, breathing heavily. He had retrieved the gun. It was a huge revolver and the chrome work was bright in the sunlight. It was the sort of thing you noticed when your head was about to be blown off. It was pointing directly between his eyes.

As Morgan was contemplating the damage it might do if it went off, a small red hole appeared in the middle of the gunman's head. A loud bark followed almost immediately, like the sound of heat-cracked rock, and the gunman fell as though his strings had been cut. The legs crumpled and he fell straight down into a tangled heap. Morgan was now kneeling right next to what was the gunman's head; his face was intact, there was just no back to his head.

The remains of that were scattered over about three square yards of the track. The spreading stain was a dark, almost black, red. Fragments of brain and bone threw up light at all angles. It was very still. Morgan rose shakily to his feet and looked around. Sara was running towards him. Behind her, the body of the woman still lying on the ground could be seen, but now a gun was in her outstretched hand. It was a nine millimetre semi-automatic and it was pointing in his direction.

'Oh my God,' sobbed Sara, and threw her arms around him. They both made their way over to the woman's still body. Morgan bent over her.

'Looks like she's fired her last shot.' He looked back at the dead gunman and remarked. 'Not a bad one either.'

'Her worst,' said Sara. 'She was aiming at *you*.'

Morgan went down on one knee and emptied the pockets of the woman. He found nothing unusual. He walked back to the man's body and did the same. He found a small packet of white powder, sniffed it and licked it ... 'Coke!'

'Bad habit,' said Sara.

'It was for *him*.' He emptied the contents into the palm of his hand and buried his face in it, breathing deeply. He licked his fingers, then wiped them on his thighs.

'It's a good thing we're not down to our last glass of water ... I wouldn't give much for my chances.' Sara remarked as she stooped over the fallen lady and removed the crucifix, shielding this act from Morgan.

The front of the convertible was embedded in the truck. Morgan kicked at the bumper, which came away, freeing the car. He jumped in and tried a few times to start the engine. On the fourth attempt it fired. He reversed, tearing off the remains of the bumper in the process.

Morgan picked up the revolver and checked the chambers. All six rounds were present and correct.

'Looks like a .44 Magnum.' Sara nodded towards the big gun. 'You could stop a truck with that.'

'Yep, it's a Colt Anaconda.' Said Morgan nonchalantly, admiring the stainless-steel finish.

'I'd be more impressed if you hadn't seen it written on the barrel. Which is the eight-inch model by the way.'

'Sure it is.' He said, placing it in his crutch and gripping the barrel.

'In your dreams.'

He left the automatic where it lay.

'Let's get out of here,' he shouted. She jumped in. They drove off in the wrecked car, hub-caps falling off and chrome strips flapping. Morgan was slugging back the Jack Daniel's. Sara was talking to him.

'Are you going to tell me what this is all about?'

'No,' he replied, 'because I haven't got a bloody clue.'

She seemed to believe him and after some thought and two cigarettes, she tried to straighten things out in her mind.

'Let's be logical about this. One; someone is out to kill you. Correction, a group of people are out to kill you. Two; this group has employees who carry cyanide capsules around with them.'

'The last two didn't.'

'Maybe they're learning. Too dangerous. If something went wrong. You know. Three; they know your movements pretty well. Four; they're trying to make it look like an accident ... except for the knife, that doesn't figure. Five; ... There isn't a five.'

They drove on in silence, consuming liberal quantities of liquor. Eventually Sara came up with, 'It seems governmental, not criminal.'

Morgan looked at her sharply. 'Why? ... The cyanide capsule?'

'Partly, but it's the incidents. All could be attempted murder; all could have been accidents ... in the eyes of the law that is. But all have been deemed accidental and in an *indecently short time*. It smells of institutionalised whitewash.'

'That's the student in you talking, you can't ignore that party back there on the road.'

'I can't, but *they* can. Did we hear anything about the stabbing on the news?'

Morgan's face clouded briefly.

'I bet we hear nothing of this.'

Morgan looked a little thoughtful. He lit another cigarette.

'I'm not letting you get involved any more than you already are,' he said. 'When you get on that plane, I'm staying.'

'Oh no,' said Sara groaning, 'not Bogart. You shouldn't mess with him ... he's sacred. Pull over.'

'Why?'

'You tried to pull me with Betjeman and dump me with Bogart.'

She turned to him with a slow, liquor-laden, sensual smile.

'I'm going to show you what Bergman *should* have done.'

The white convertible bumped back onto the road, leaving a trail of chrome and twisted metal through the scrub. The two occupants looked fairly relaxed and at peace with the world.

'We'll drive on to Silver Lake and fill up. We need water and gas. And more Jack'

'And I could do with a beer.'

Virginia

'We're getting something. Patterns, some definite blocks and sequences.'

'Isn't that called music? Isn't it supposed to be in repetitive groupings?'

'You're so sceptical. I know what I'm doing.'

'Do you know how many scientific experiments have been proved invalid in the last two years? It's been proved conclusively, especially in commercially-funded projects, that the researchers' prejudices have been colouring their results. Experiments have a tendency to come out in favour of the will of the researcher. Even well-intentioned research gives answers the researchers expect or want, even with double-blind placebos. The recent figures show an unintentional manipulation of results. Look at cold fusion. The figures were so marginally in favour they couldn't be reproduced. There's still debate; what's the betting they'll be proved invalid?'

'What are you suggesting?'

'There's a danger of you getting what you hoped for.'

'That's a serious accusation.'

'Only, Roberts ... if you can't tell the shine from the rust.'

8

Secret operations

Desert

Morgan was driving and hitting at yet another bottle that she'd had the good sense to stow. He alternated the slugs with draws on the cigarette.

'How do you do it? How do you just keep drinking that stuff, and in those quantities?'

'Practice.'

'You smoke too much.' She said this after blowing out a long stream herself.

'Yes I do.' She wasn't getting anywhere. She shut her eyes.

The road was long and straight, pointing ahead south-west and away from the desert core. In a couple of hours they'd meet up with the freeway and would turn west to L.A.

The air above the road ahead shimmered more than the air above the sand; the heat reflecting off its surface with more intensity than off the land. The mirages merged and separated; a constant dance of liquid veils.

His mind was dancing, not with the intensity of the air close to the ground, but flowing in harmony with the higher strata.

Images, soft and fading with age, mingled with harsher and blacker imprints. The recent recollections were the sharpest and most bleak. Even these softened when his mental focus shifted, moving them quickly to the edges of his memory. He saw the wife who wasn't, laughing and deriding, cold and biting, refusing to answer the unasked question ... Now she hung, forlorn over the grave ... a last flower thrown on the coffin ... then a second box, the finest marquetry, gleaming lacquer, the size of a hat box, no it was a plastic bag ... No, No ... he was wrong, only one casket, a long one. And she threw no flower, just turned to him with bitter accusation in her eyes ...'It wasn't me...it wasn't me ... It wasn't my fault!' He screamed at her ... Then the steel blonde hair wrapped around the scene, wiping it away, and replacing the cold with a white heat ... white on black ... white lines on black mirrors, and one black thin line, neat around the throat of a dove ...Tears, salt and wet ... In the wind and on his cheek .. .his mother wiping them away... and his wife's voice; 'Still childlike, still childlike ...' The watery tears became a flood ... He was drowning, clutching a tape to pull himself out ... reels and reels, and miles of tape, making music; he drew on it ... It wrapped itself around his body, enclosing and holding, tightening, then releasing ... He was driving on ... Drive she said. He *was* ... Faster and faster; the images were keeping up. He was on fast forward ... Give me a reason ... throw me a line ... Climb, I must climb. But the snake was waiting and he was slipping now ... going down, down ... hold on, hold on to love ... must hold on to love.

The wheel slipped through his watery hands.

The fire swept the image away, sharp with the bark from the dark round hole, turning its blackness to orange ... then red bright in the head and black on the ground ...Take me away from here ... The faces were changing in front of him as he drove through them ... smiling, crying, laughing, triumphant, beckoning, accusing, loving, swirling ... Who knows what face he would find ... How long would it stay?

It was a secret. A secret to which he held a key ... he couldn't see it. It was turned away from him. Turn out the light, turn it out ... Everything's going to be all right ...

The few tired hand-claps were punctuated by the odd jeer. The scattered pools of orange light around the periphery of the room highlighted bottles, hands and faces. There were more people sitting in the blue darkness than the clapping implied. What cuffs and arms did appear in the orange glow appeared to be clad in various colours of check, and large areas of denim. The heavy darkness and the smoke from a hundred cigarettes hung like a tented shroud and forced what little light there was to the level of the floor. A sad grey-white fluorescence dominated the left-hand side of the room and attracted the tanned and the grey-faced, non-sitting customers like flies to an electrostat. They stuck there with about the same amount of movement.

Sara and Morgan were two of them. Hot out of the desert and nearly out of his mind, the latter slaked his thirst.

As the lethargic stripper shambled off the small stage and down an unsteady wooden staircase, Morgan poured the remainder of his beer into a glass and downed the last of it. Sara seemed to be the only other female in the place except for the ladies on the stage and was attracting a few appreciative glances. Morgan attracted the odd leer. She peered through the blue soup.

'What a dump. Let's get out of here and get our heads down.'

'Have another beer,' said Morgan. 'There's another act on in a minute.' He didn't seem in a hurry to leave.

'Act!' exclaimed Sara. 'They haven't the energy to unhook their bras. You've hardly looked at the stage all night anyway.'

'I've been looking at the door,' came the reply.

'And that's another reason to go. We're exposed out here; at least we can lock the door at a motel.'

Morgan was gesticulating for more drinks. Sara was trying to pull him towards the door.

'Hang on,' Morgan held back. 'This is the best place we can be. The guys in here can *smell* trouble, just watch the customers and they'll watch out for us.'

She stopped pulling and looked at him thoughtfully.

'I'm occasionally reminded that you possess the odd brain cell. I stress the odd. It's more animal cunning, instinct rather than intelligence.' Morgan grinned and pulled the beers across the bar towards them.

'There were two skunks,' he spoke as if imparting vital information, 'twins, called In and Out. One day, In went out and was gone a long time. Mummy Skunk said to Out, 'Where's In?'

'In's gone out.' said Out. 'Well go out and find him.' said Mummy Skunk. After some time the two skunks came home together. 'Well done Out,' said Mummy Skunk. 'How did you find him?'

'Easy Mummy, said Out ... *Instinked!*'

Sara shook her head, and a number of the drinkers around the bar joined her. She took another swig and was looking at him again with that look. 'You move pretty fast when you have to.'

'I played a bit of football some time ago. Booze and women have slowed me up. It's not the affairs,' he added, by way of explanation, 'it's the divorces ... that's what gets to you.'

Behind them a pianist was striking up some blues on an old upright piano. He banged out a couple of minutes of quite passable honky-tonk. Some other musos appeared to be getting drum kit and guitars set up behind him. The blues stopped when one of the band started whistling into the microphone.

Secret operations moving through the night
Barricade the roads and draw the cordons tight
Wake up next morning to the sound of marching feet
A little local trouble, but your protection is complete
Secret operations, but no need to fear
The radio announcements say the roads have all been cleared.
The police are armed and doubled for our leader's re-election
The curfew is only for your own protection
And we 'll be fine, we 'll be fine, we 'll be fine
We'll all laugh about it when we meet next time
Turn out the lights, everything's all right
It's just secret operations in the night

Secret operations, rumbling through the streets
Several suspects taken, while the nation sleeps
It 'll be warm again tomorrow so the weatherman believes
If they open up the road- blocks we could go down to the beach
Secret operations, but we got nothing here to hide
And if you stop to think about it, those boys are really on our side
When times like these are tough, they've got to be a little rough
But if we stay out of trouble, we 'll be safe enough
And we'll be fine, we'll be fine, we'll be fine
We'll all laugh about it when we meet next time
Turn out the lights, everything's all right
It's just secret operations in the night
That's all, just secret operations in the night

The music was smoother than the beer and most of the people in the bar seemed to know the band, and the song. They joined in the choruses with a raucous enthusiasm. Morgan was staring at the pianist intently - and looked as white as death.

'What's the matter?' she said quickly.

'Well I'll be damned.' He mouthed the words slowly.

'What is it?'

'*Who* is it?' he replied. 'It's the guy who made the tape.'

'You're joking.'

'No, no ... that's him all right.' Morgan had lost his clarity, he sounded dazed.

'What the hell is he doing here?'

'Same as us,' replied Morgan with a little more resolve. 'Trying to survive.'

The words kept repeating in his head ...Turn out the light, everything's all right ... He had that thought in his head ... out there in the desert ... He wanted the sun turned off; he wanted all his bad dreams to stop their attack ... He wanted everything to be all right ... all right.

The band finished and the crowd, at last, showed some animation; they were on their feet, stamping.

'*The crowd cried out for more.*' Morgan spoke as he looked down into his drink.

The pianist raised a weary arm, then headed down the steps to the bar. As Paul was making his way through the crowd, a trucker who could have modelled for Michelin-Man, threw a huge arm around his shoulders and crushed him close to his sweaty tee-shirt.

'Nice one man,' said the heavy. 'Now one more for me, huh. All You Need Is Love. Do you know it?' Paul was having difficulty in backing away.

'Sorry man, I only do my own stuff, OK?'

'Sure,' said the heavy, still holding Paul's arm. 'Just one for me, *now*! All you need is fucking love. OK?'

Morgan made his way to this touching scene, but before he had covered half the distance, Paul had brought his knee up into the man's groin and twisted away out of his grasp. The main expression on the heavy's face was that of surprise, and before it turned to anger, Morgan had taken the last few strides and threw a right hand into the man's face. It didn't seem to produce any effect other than more surprise.

'Oh shit,' gasped Morgan, but he was saved from any further action when a chair was broken across the heavy's head. Surprise was now turning to irritation on the man's face. He bellowed and twisted around, holding his arms out as he did so. This scything motion accounted for at least three men before he had completed half a turn.

Morgan correctly decided this was time for a retreat. As he moved backwards towards the bar, he bumped into Sara coming in the other direction.

'I think it's time we left,' he said. 'Travel plans to make.'

They made their way to a dimly-lit exit behind the stage; the sound of breaking glass and screaming strippers following in their wake as the whole place erupted. Making their way down a small corridor behind the stage, they pushed their way past half-clad ladies and bouncers cowering. It sounded like a war going on behind them. They eventually burst through an emergency exit and out into a narrow dark alley. Morgan grabbed Sara's arm, and they started to run.

The alley-way was as black as a coal mine, but they ran as fast as they could to the soft glowing light at one end, to the sanctuary of the main street. As they neared the main drag, they became aware of a group of figures ahead of them. One was lying on the ground, and the other two were laying into this figure with fists and boots.

Morgan let go of Sara's arm and picked up speed. She shouted something after him, but he wasn't listening. One of the standing figures had lifted a trash-can above his head, and was about to bring it down on the unfortunate prone figure below, when he was caught in the small of his back by Morgan's shoulder charge.

The two crashed to the floor along with the trash-can. Morgan was up quickly. The guy he hit was still out. As Morgan rose he swung hopefully in the direction of the standing attacker's head. It was his lucky night. He felt his fist strike on something hard and brittle. He guessed his opponent would have to visit the dentist pretty soon. Morgan instinctively sucked up the pain across his knuckles and simultaneously felt pain across the back of his head. The alley temporarily became even darker as he crashed to the floor.

November the Fifth had come early in Morgan's head. This wasn't too bad compared with the two successive and painful blows to his ribs, which seemed to have been struck with a sledge-hammer. Morgan rolled to one side, catching a glimpse of Paul's face lying horizontally as he did so. He was dimly aware of two figures standing over him. The first must have recovered ... and then there was one.

The other went down in a scream of pain, followed by the tinkle of glass. He guessed somebody had hit the man over the head with a bottle; he guessed it could have only been Sara.

He shook his head and got up on one knee weaving instinctively, which was just as well, as the remaining assailant was still thrashing at this head with his feet. There was another crash of glass on skull, and the second man went down. Morgan got to his feet groggily and focused on Sara standing there holding two bottles in her hands, one was broken.

'We'd better move' she said.

They both bent down and helped Paul to his feet. He walked unsteadily between them for a few steps and then broke into a run with them, growling huskily, 'I'm all right.'

Sara ran into the main street and flagged down a passing cab. She bundled the two men into the back and jumped in after them.

'Stop here!' the big man shouted. He had spotted a sign outside a bar.

Tonight BLUES PIANO with PAUL MILLNS

'That's him, that's him! Good idea of mine to check out the What's-on-in-Wasteland ads.'

They ran across the road, avoiding the late-night manic drivers and prowling cabs. As they reached the door, someone was coming through the window. The glass-covered figure rolled over twice and lay still.

Inside, the fight was in full swing. A crashing blow from a huge right hand sent the first person to bar the big man's progress, to the ground. The second went the same way.

Weller was stumbling in John's footsteps and lashing out with varying degrees of success. In the centre of the room the Michelin-Man stood, circled neatly by prone and broken-headed bodies; his arms were still scything, although he had fewer takers now.

John walked up to him and ignoring the carnage, shouted to anyone fit enough to listen, 'Where's the piano player?'

'Somebody shot him!' said a voice, but John ignored this.

'You! ... You with the gut.'

The neolithic mountain squinted at him. Weller had moved around to his blind side.

'You seen him?'

'He let out a bellow and beat his chest. He obviously wasn't going to co-operate fully with the request made by the officers of the law, so Weller hit him. He used the leg of a broken table, but it didn't do the trick. It only annoyed the giant even more. John was a big man, but this one towered over him. They were going to have problems with this one. Weller tried to draw his gun, but that really got the heavy angry. As the revolver came up, the giant grabbed Welter's gun hand and stuck a finger down the barrel, then started to laugh.

'C'mon asshole, what you gonna do about it?'

Weller's hand was held tight; he was confused, as he didn't come across this situation very often. Big John stood back and drew his own gun. 'We're police officers!' This really got the giant mad. The rest of the fighting had subsided, and these three were the centre of attention.

'Just take it easy,' said John again. 'We're the police ... just step back.'

'Not until I've buried this runt.' The giant was definite about this. He turned his back on John and his attention to Weller. Weller didn't welcome this development.

John cocked the gun as noisily as he could. 'Get your finger out, fella!'

He was ignored.

The giant's fist on his spare arm was drawn back and everybody in the room who could still see waited for Welter's face to disappear, including Weller.

'Cut it out!' shouted John, but the last part was drowned out by the bark from Weller's .38, and the scream of pain from the giant. The monster crashed to the floor holding his shattered hand and the silence which descended was only broken by the whimpers from the now stilled, man-mountain.

John stared at the man. 'Don't stick your finger where it don't belong.'

Weller was still shaking as he and John walked to the bar with as much nonchalance as they could muster.

'You!' The beefy finger was pointing at a barman.

'Yes, sir, anything I can do for you gents?'

'Call an ambulance ... and we weren't here, OK?' He looked at the giant.

'He wouldn't say anything about an assault on two officers of the law would he?' The barman shook his head.

'The piano player ... where is he?'

'Gone mister... Err; officer ...Took off with a girl and a guy. Tall guy ... he moved fast.'

'Which way did they go?' The barman pointed in the direction of the rear exit. The big man and Weller stepped over the wreckage, ignoring the giant who was sitting up and practicing forming a fist without a full hand of fingers; he seemed happy enough.

Out in the alley, two figures were starting to come round.

'What happened to you two?' John spoke without sympathy.

'Nothing.'

'Who are you? ... I want your ID.' John wasn't polite. The big man leafed through a wallet offered ungraciously.

'The Rodent Termination Co. Inc ... Well now, this one looks a bit like a Rattus, don't you think Weller?'

'Sure do, sir.'

'The girl hit me.' The Rat spoke through clenched teeth. He was holding the side of his head.

'What girl?' Weller's interest was aroused.

'She was with them ... two guys ... they attacked us.'

'Oh yeah?' John did not look convinced. 'Book 'em,' he snapped at Weller.

'Where to lady?' asked the cab driver. They looked at each other.

'Bates' Motel.' Paul growled at the driver.

'Bates' Motel.' said Sara and Morgan in unison.

'Bates,' said Paul, and slumped back on the seat.

Twenty minutes later the cab bumped into the forecourt of a motel which could have done with a lick of paint ... or razing to the ground. The three shambled across an uneven patch of ground and made for the end cabin.

The room was lit by a low table-lamp. Two figures were stretched out on the bed with half their clothing removed. Two bowls of lukewarm water were on the side table, and towels were tied around heads and arms. The liquid in one of the bowls was a pale pink colour and darker patches of red were spreading on the towels. One figure eased himself half-upright and leaned back against the bedhead. He rubbed his ribs gingerly and felt around his teeth and gums. The sound of running water ceased abruptly, and Sara's voice floated from the shower- room.

'That was a bloody stupid thing to do.'

145

The figure against the bedhead turned his head slightly.

'You his minder?' Paul shouted back. 'You can work for me if you like.'

The recumbent figure on the bed spoke up. 'Let's get some sleep.'

'What did you hit them with.' said Paul.

Sara had padded into the room with a large bath towel wrapped tightly around her body. Her hair hung wet against the nape of her neck. She shook her head, fanning out the dark locks and snatched at a cigarette from its pack. Viciously. She snapped it alight, threw the lighter on the table, tossed her head back, and blew the smoke out of her nostrils.

'The barman's friend ... bottles of Galliano.'

Morgan raised one eye open, 'Where did you get them?'

'A skip of empty bottles.'

'You're lucky there's some heavy drinkers in there ... and with sophisticated taste,' opined Morgan.

Paul was stretching out his hands and flexing his fingers. He seemed satisfied with the result. Morgan turned to him, 'What you gonna do now Paul?'

'Well I'm booked in there until the end of the week, but somehow I don't think they'll want me back. It's a pity, I need the money.'

'I can help you out,' Morgan said.

'You two get into bed,' Sara said firmly. 'I'll stay here on the sofa.' They didn't argue.

She picked up a hairdryer and started work on the tresses. After fifteen minutes her hair was much lighter, in colour as well as substance. Her hair streamed away from her scalp, falling like a waterfall in front of her. Morgan raised himself carefully, lit her another ciggie and thrust it between her lips. She threw her head back and gave him one of those looks again.

Her head seemed to be exploding. Waves of hair mushrooming up and catching what little light there was. When her face tilted forward again, the fall-out from the drying blast settled around her shoulders and descended like nuclear fallout.

Paul stretched out a hand and flicked off the bedside-lamp. The room was now lit only by alternating red and white neon lights.

Morgan broke the silence. 'What sort of shape do you think those guys are in? Maybe we should call an ambulance.'

'They're OK,' Sara snapped, 'I didn't hit them that hard, just enough.'

'Pretty sure of yourself,' he said.

'Yes,' she snapped again, pulling a black silk wrap from her travel bag and reclining gracefully, bare legs uncovered.

Morgan again broke the silence, 'Where are you from Paul?'

'London.'

'London?'

'I've been over here about six months; took a few tapes to a few record companies, played a few gigs, talked to a few people, trying to make something happen.'

'How's it going?'

'Bad,' came the reply. 'I'm going back next week. I'll give my lady a ring tomorrow.'

'Six months is a long time to be away.' Morgan stated the obvious.

'There was nothing happening for me in England.'

'I can't understand that,' Morgan commiserated. 'You write some good stuff; you sound OK too. Have you done any recording?'

'Yeah, I've had about five albums out. UK and Germany mostly. I do OK in Germany, they like me there, but there's a strong club scene. In England you have to go into a pigeon-hole. You either have to be Jazz or Blues or Soul or Country and Western or Pop or Rock. You know. It goes on.'

Morgan sat up; he was becoming animated. 'Isn't that just crazy. People want to put a handle on you all the time, labels on everything and everyone. If you don't fit the slot, you can't get into the machine.'

'Right,' Paul agreed, 'it's a little freer over here.'

'Don't you believe it,' said Morgan. 'Maybe on the surface, but that's all. ... No hits?'

'No hits,' replied Paul. 'Small labels, no producer, low budgets, no marketing. Different managers that weren't too good for me. Publishers that weren't too good for me. Wrong place at the wrong time. Or the right place at the wrong time.'

'Who've you been playing with?'

'Oh, I've played with the old war-horses, Eric Burdon, Bert Jansch, Louisiana Red, Ralph McTell, Peter Thorup, Joanne Kelly, even supported Dave Crosby.'

'What, *the* Dave Crosby?'

'Yeah, it was in London. He was so out of it, the promoter had to pour coffee down him and strap him to a stool while he played guitar. Just him and an acoustic guitar. Do you know, he still blew away fifteen hundred people a show, two shows a night for three nights ... They loved him.'

'What about you?'

'Who ever loved a support act?' came the reply. 'It was all right'

' Ever been close to something?'

'Yeah, I had one of my tracks covered. A singer over there, Elkie Brooks, she put it on one of her albums. The album went platinum, and I did make a little money out of that.'

'Just the one?'

'Just the one.'

'Just need a little luck.'

'I think I've had my share of that, and it was all bad, or the luck was good and I was bad.'

'Like what?' Morgan asked.

'Like I was signed to Elton John's Rocket Label back in the early days.'

'Yeah.'

'I was signed as a singer-songwriter, but couldn't come up with a hit song. Elton's people grabbed me one day and said, "Take this home, listen to it. It's from the album." I said no, I only do my own stuff. They insisted and so I did. I came back the next day and they said, "What do you think?" I said it's beautiful, I love it, but it's *his* song not mine. I'm sorry ... "OK," they said, "but you're crazy."

'And what was it?'

'Candle in the Wind.' The room went quiet for a few seconds.

'Jesus,' sighed Sara.

Morgan seemed lost for words. Paul found some. 'I've tried my luck over here once before, and did a few spots at the Bottom Line in New York. I was doing just one song in my set that wasn't mine. It was Leonard Cohen's, *That's No Way to Say Good-bye*. Somebody took a copy to Cohen who reckoned it was the best version he'd heard. That was nice, but that was all. Let's get some sleep,' he said finally, bringing the conversation to a close.

After a while Morgan piped up again. 'Do you know, I'd hate to see you go the way of Tim Hardin. He wrote some amazing songs ... Reason to Believe ... If I Were a Carpenter ... I think he died without a penny.'

'Yes,' said Paul quietly, 'I interviewed him once, for a German mag.'

'No kidding'

'Yep, it was in a little club in London, Dingwall's. When he'd finished his set I went backstage with a small tape recorder and talked to him for about an hour. He died about two years later.'

Morgan was humming *Find the Cost of Freedom Buried in the Ground*.

'This time next week I'll be back in London. Things can't be any worse there.'

Sara piped up, 'Want a couple of roadies?'

Paul retorted, 'I thought you two only worked with bottles, one drinks them and the other throws them ... Why not?'

Virginia

Siemonsen was sitting behind his desk; there were no stripes of light across the room. Outside it was dark. A small table-lamp lit the room, highlighting the surface of his desk and the bottom surfaces of his face. He was perspiring, and his hands were sweating. He found holding the handset difficult.

With his free hand he mopped his face with a white handkerchief. He was agitated, and fielding the questions coming at him down the line with nervous jerking retorts.

'They were acting on their own initiative sir...Yes I can control my own Staff...It's taken care of. The Cleaners went in afterwards. No problem.'

This defence didn't seem to be working too well, so he turned to anger.

'There are certain ground rules allowing field staff to ...' He wasn't allowed to finish. Then in a quieter voice. 'Yes sir, yes sir ... It won't happen again.'

Virginia Golf Course

'What's up with Siemonsen?'

'Head's giving him a hard time.'

'Why?'

'I don't know. He's working on something sensitive enough to keep us all out of it. Only his inner-core of playmates are involved, and only some of those.'

'It's not the Escobar situation is it? I thought we'd straightened that out pretty effectively.'

'Yes, Gaviria's people did as instructed. They must have put about fifty bullets into him, but overkill was always the name of the game. If he'd only played it straight we could have had a nice thing going for a long time. Blowing up that airliner between Medellin and Bogota was just too much; we even got him out of jail *then*.'

'What did Gaviria say in that speech? "This is a vital step forward in Columbia's war on drug trafficking" ... He cannot be serious?'

'He should have taken a leaf out of Noriaga's book. Kept his mouth shut and taken a light rap. When are we letting *him* out by the way?'

'Well he's not really *in*, is he? We still let him get on with business.'

'I think Siemonsen's got Hudson acting as the co-ordinator. He takes instructions from old pineapple face and implements it. We'll probably need him back on the outside by ninety-five. There's some Liechtenstein accounts we want to get into and those tight bastards won't budge unless the man's there in person. They'll hold on to our money as long as they can.'

'We're putting all our muscle behind the Cali group now. They're not so crazy as Escobar was and we now seem to be the number one supplier of cocaine in the world.'

'Top of the Pops.'

'Yes, and the Cali cartel are going to make sure Cesar Gaviria is going to be re-elected. It looks like I'll be getting more involved in the South American side of the business. Carson screwed up letting customs seize that final shipment at Miami.'

'A thousand pounds of it, wasn't there? That's a hell of a lot to get through an airport.'

'Yeah, forty million dollars is a lot to lose in one hit.'

'Where's Carson now?'

'Don't ask, I think Siemonsen got one of the Ukrainian boys to come over and take care of him. None of us would have got close.'

'What about you?'

'Haiti ... we're taking off there, but Senator Moynihan is stirring things up. His bill will effectively end our role as a manipulator of events. No pro-active role any longer. That's why Head and Siemonsen have established this cell within Langley.

Moynihan's highlighted the fact that we've backed Noriega to prevent the threat of communism; and suppressed information on nuclear development in Pakistan because they helped the CIA fight the guerrilla war in Afghanistan.

The fact that we tried to depict Aristide as crazy, just as Clinton was claiming he was Haiti's best hope for democracy, didn't go down too well in the White House. The Haitian army officers, backed by us, were involved with the Columbian drug-dealers running coke into the States. So what? We took our cut.

We've moved from concentrating on the Soviets to monitoring third world countries under Woolsey. The fact that we *control* them as well is just a bonus.'

The last speaker drove off into the sunset, his ball just leaking off the fairway to the right.

Another location in Virginia

The fading day's copper light added highlights to the Cedarwood house.

Inside, the log fire did the same to the plastered walls as the night fell in Virginia.

'I think there's more to it than our group merely siphoning off massive chunks of somebody else's ill-gotten gains and using them, of course, for the ultimate good of our country. No ... something else is involved ... it goes deeper. There's another game being played, and I don't think you or I are in the same ball- park.'

The two men were in the den. One sat back deep in the leather. The other continued his delivery.

'There's a conspiracy, headed by Head in this country, and Siemonsen is his tool. There's a connection with sections of security services, politicians and people in powerful positions in all parts of the globe.'

'How do you know? ... What makes you so sure?'

'I'm not. It's a hunch, a feeling; I get on pretty well with Nancy, his PA. No, he doesn't know,' he said, in response to the raised eyebrows, 'it's just the odd thing that slips out ...'

'Really?' This time the raised eyebrows exposed a twinkling eye ... 'Like what?'

'Like his friend, Sir Anthony in London. I ran a check ... nobody knows what he does. It's rumoured he's close to the Queen. What's that all about?'

He went on. 'Large-scale movements of money, big money, but not to destabilise anyone. Nothing happens. She's been copying his paperwork for me ... before shredding. She thought one particular memo was about her transfer ... she applied to your group you know?' There was a little response from the formidable gentleman in the armchair. 'It linked Head's group with blue-chip companies from all over the world; the Monarchy in England, the Marcos family in Manila, various dictators, the Vatican, groups in Korea, Japan, Russia, Europe ... She didn't have time to register details, but it was never the government or rulers. Second and third strings only ... or sources of money. They seem to be structured like a large corporation, deciding who to elect, who to get rid of ... trading decisions, policy decisions ... They can get to anybody.

She found notes on the deliberate withholding of funds from disaster areas - and areas of special need ... something about not being able to sustain the whole population ... whole areas would be allowed to die. There's always a lot of stuff about keeping defence costs down ... stopping a spiral of waste ... something about a new system of defence.' He paused to finish his Malt. 'That's *our* job!'

'Are you talking about a new world order; with a cabal of powerful people taking over, and succeeding by stealth and string-pulling, not force of arms?'

The young man looked surprised. 'Yes, I suppose I am really.'

'I thought you meant something like that,' said the older man thoughtfully.

London

'Sir Anthony speaking ... So Yeltsin's on the piss again? Vlad's got him on the run or should that be runs! It seems to be working out very well. The mere threat of Zhirinovsky's imperialist stance has pushed Yeltsin into taking the same one. Clinton's a little worried, but he's got other things on his mind. A stable Russia restored to its former traditional glory is what we are seeking.'

Sir Anthony put down the receiver thus cutting off further communication from the East.

9

Reaching out for heaven

Sir Anthony's hand-made shoes were resting on the top of his rosewood desk. His feet were still in them, and the rest of his body was reclining. His telephone was jammed between cheek and shoulder, freeing his two hands to carefully pour a glass of Guinness. The glass was held at an acute angle in his left hand to minimise the amount of creamy head,

'Look Siemonsen,' exasperation obvious in his voice, 'the official line is that the plutonium produced at Thorp will be sold to a number of foreign governments, all of which we have good relations with. And, in fact, we intend to do just that ... with some of it ... You know damn well what we are going to do with the rest! We'll probably make about two hundred bombs for our own use, and it goes without saying that none of them will find their way into *your* neck of the woods ... you have my word.' Sir Anthony sipped at his drink, wiping away the cream moustache with his sleeve. 'Yes, I know your people are worried, but as always, you will receive up to date location plans ... one for your masters, and a real one for the *dame* ... yes, I'm sorry, I couldn't resist it. As far as the Pentagon is concerned, I will be able to prove to them that none of the material will end up in the hands of countries that are likely to use it against you ... bye for now.'

Virginia

Siemonsen turned to three colleagues. 'He assures me nothing has changed. The only people who can control our little enterprise are all holding.' He sat back and touched his fingers together.

'His government doesn't have a clue, of course ... only certain military people, some in the civil service, and advisors to the Royals, are in on it. He's got the Soviets sorted out and North Korea will be zapped by us if they try to flex their muscles independently, but they'll be supplying us with some of our needs - as they won't be allowed to use it themselves.'

'What about the Middle East?'

'Well, Saddam will play ball ... that was the deal ... and at the moment he's sticking to it.'

'It's his cousin I don't trust.'

'Which one?'

'All of them.'

'He's keeping the Iranian fanatics in check, and fully taking up Israel's attention. We're keeping the missile sales to a minimum, but the control of plutonium is more important. I think we've more or less cornered the market now.'

'Armenia?'

'Zhirinovsky wants a new Russian Empire. Clinton thinks he'll go away and that the upsurge in his popularity is only a protest vote against Yeltsin. Yeltsin himself is making noises about not being totally against the new Russian imperialist thinking, although he might fall short of Zhirinovsky's zeal to extend through India and open up a fleet base in the Indian ocean.' Siemonsen gave out the satisfied air of a man on top of his work.

'McLean's got Zhirinovsky in his pocket. I think he's promised him Hitler's other ball. He was toying with a jar of pickles at the time if I remember; something about being able to prove he was a two-ball man all along and any other rumour was only wicked Allied propaganda. Zhirinovsky went for this in a big way.

'McLean also provided lots of loot of course, enough to buy a good show in the elections. He won't topple Yeltsin, but we don't want him to. Influence without accountability, that's what we aspire to.

We wanted Aristide out of Haiti. I know he was democratically elected, but we wanted our man in there. The problems have been difficult to conceal ... bodies everywhere ... but at least we're in control and can protect our interests. The drugs come in from Columbia and we can distribute them easily from there. Mainly to the States, but also the Pacific Rim and Europe; the money of course keeping democracy in shape.'

'Moynihan still making waves?'

'Afraid so, but I think we can handle it.'

Siemonsen's expression was thoughtful, and he went off on another tack.

'Sir Anthony is an expert on ethnic mafias in the Soviet Union. There's a hell of a lot of them, apart from the Armenians. Azerbaijanis, Chechens, Caucasians, Ukrainians and most importantly, the Georgians, because *they* straddle the isthmus between Asia and Russia's Muslim south ... yes, the Caucasus Mountains are *very* strategically important.

Sir Anthony stepped in when Yeltsin tried to force Georgia to join the CIS. They ended up in possession of the Russian tanks instead of being obliterated by them and Yeltsin has given them a place at the conference table.

In return for McLean's help he has the use of them as hit men around the world, together with his Ukrainians ... it's very cost effective, and they can't compromise us ... they also tend our property interests and look after the *Placements*. Our regular operatives won't go near these installations; they're too worried about the consequences, although I've assured them they are perfectly safe.'

We have regular conference calls. Our own satellite of course, and a scrambler system second to none. We control the big decisions this way; give things a nudge in the right direction.'

Desert

They were heading west, towards Los Angeles on Route 15. Barstow was up ahead and the ghost town of Calico lay to the north; beyond that and even further to the North, lay the Mojave Desert, Edwards Air Base, Death Valley and Zabriskie Point.

Morgan had passed on the driving duties. Sara had insisted. Driving pissed on the road in the desert was one thing, wandering around on the freeway was not such a good idea. She couldn't work him out. She understood the practical mess he was in. She had solutions to those problems ... It was something deeper. She felt that lifting the lid was probably not a good move as what might come out could be something she couldn't handle. She knew she would anyway ... it just wasn't going to happen *yet*.

He was getting possessive about that damn tape. Little things ... pushing it deep into the right hand pocket of his leather jacket, wedging it with his ciggies or a wad of tissue. At night, he slipped it under his pillow and he'd started to talk in his sleep. He knew the lyrics ... not always in the right order. But they kept recurring ... his dreams, he sometimes talked in them ... She shrugged ... who knows why? ... and why didn't he play the whole tape straight through ... Only one track at a time ... ? She went over it in her mind. The lyrics tended to have a certain relevance, tended to echo their predicament. She dismissed it as mildly interesting, a chance sequence of events, his mind emphasising passages to fit in with certain situations. Could be true of any number of songs. As Morgan kept telling her... nothing is real, or did somebody else say that? She'd heard it before, couldn't place it. He was putting an emphasis on it which it didn't deserve. His blue blanket ... that should be Blues blanket. It was no surprise that he was cracking up and if the tape helped to keep him together, then so what ...? And then bumping into this guy, the songwriter, hell ... fate or what?

She was feeling it, this madness. 'What's it all about'... she spoke out loud. 'Eh!'

'Nothing.'

He was a man. She felt this was a bad start. Men belonged in a zoo, and this one was definitely circus material. Why was she falling for him? ... And she was ... despite her mental gymnastics, despite her deep resentment of all aspects of the male, she *was*. They were valueless, except for procreation and the time was rapidly approaching when that function would never again need a man to perform it. Perform ... Jesus! *that* was a joke. It was all right with *him*. With him it was ... all right. The act of union usually had most of the characteristics of a Union *Meeting*. Noisy, farcical, egotistical and the sudden ejaculated cry of triumph at unsuitable moments. The result was usually the same ... motion carried and mass abstentions; no one being satisfied by the result.

Only women could love, really love; truly, madly, deeply ... and express that physically. With another woman all aspects of her sexuality and therefore her spirituality, could be explored. She had only found satisfaction with another woman ... until this man. It wasn't the same, it wasn't as good ... but she was stuck on the same road as him and for the first time in her life she didn't want to know where it was leading.

The three were pushing west towards L.A. Morgan was smoking and drinking in equal amounts, lots. He was also feeling the back of his neck. Sara had hacked away at the locks when he had passed out and he looked cleaner and younger. He was not a happy man.

'When did you start smoking?' she asked, lighting up, 'At high school?'

'Two years ago.'

'You're kidding me?'

'No.'

'Why the shit did you get into this? Everybody was giving up then. In a big way.'

'That's probably why. Couldn't stand all that righteous indignation. I never thought about it until they were all telling me not to. What the hell, screw it.'

She shook her head. 'You're a funny guy, and I don't mean ha ha.'

'What about you?'

'Me? I just love it. I got hooked a long time ago.' She threw the half-finished cigarette into the wind.

'So you love it? ... Love ... not heard that word for a while, but words come with no price on their heads.'

'You must have used it often enough.'

'The word, Love, exists, but I'm not sure that *Love* does. I do believe in a loving relationship, and this is more of a practical matter than people like to think. All successful relationships are made up of the three F's.' She looked at him with that look that said, 'Go on, I know you're going to tell me anyway.'

'Physical, Philosophical and Financial.'

'That's only one F.'

'You know what I mean.' He wasn't to be put off. 'If all three elements are present in a relationship, then it's a fair bet that it will be successful. Physical; they get on well in the sack. Philosophical; they're of like minds, no arguing over the TV channels, or which newspaper to buy. And Financial? Well, that underpins the lot. When money goes out the door, love flies out the window.'

'That's nonsense. If you love someone, then that's it ... nothing left to say.'

He lit up again, but didn't let it pass. 'You need money, in varying degrees, to facilitate everything else; to build the nest, to feed the family, and to get drunk once in a while. It's like a three-stranded rope. As long as all the strands are present, then the rope is strong. Of course, as time goes by the strands will vary in thickness, but as long as an element of all three is present, the rope should hold.'

The traffic was thickening and her mirrored eyes were on the lanes either side of her. Her concentration was on the road, not on him. It made no difference, he was away.

'As a couple grow old together, the physical side thins out, but the financial side is usually getting stronger. They might start to have different interests, but it's important that one partner should always involve the other in some way.'

He looked at her. 'She could always come to ball games with me if she wanted ... and I let her caddie for me when I played golf.'

'You're all heart Morgan.'

'Keep that needle on fifty-five.'

She was.

'If one strand breaks completely, then the whole rope breaks. No relationship can survive on any two strands alone. The three F's mean no divorce.' He wasn't finished.

'There's another way to cut the divorce rate ... No ceremony. Sure, they can have a short legal document drawn up, but that's it ... they're allowed the full works after seven years. Guess how many girls would pull out if they couldn't have that one day in the church and all the trimmings? ... About fifty percent ... cut the divorce rate in half.'

'Romantic bastard, aren't you?'

Paul was slumped across the rear seat and well asleep. Morgan was reclining in the front passenger seat and ripping the tab off yet another can of beer. She looked across at him. 'How are your ribs?'

He grimaced, and rubbed them with his free hand. 'Not so good.'

'You're out of shape.'

'Maybe you're right.'

She twisted her head and looked at Paul, 'Didn't he say he was playing tonight?'

'Yeah. Some club on the west side that's got a good reputation for R 'n B and Country. Most clubs are disco now ... we've lost it, the energy of the live moment.'

Morgan regretted its passing. There was a strong dichotomy in the music business, partly due to the high spending by the bulge offspring created in the wake of the Second World War and now in their forties, who brought with them the sounds of the sixties and seventies.

The sale of back catalogue to this section of the record buying public was given a boost by the advent of CD. This lot all went out and bought the players, then duplicated their scruffy vinyl with CD versions. That leap in sales, a bonus for the record companies, was now tailing off.

Morgan wasn't a CD man anyway. CD was for wimps. He liked his vinyl stained with liquor and the prints of a thousand thumbs ... gave the sound a warm and personalised feel, each scratch, jump and warp an instant memory. A record of stages in his life, as well documented as the scratches etched on the desert rocks by the ancient peoples. The newest peoples, the

160

teenage market, which historically had been the largest, was now shunning the records made by committee.

In its search for something produced by an individual, for something from the soul, however flawed, it turned to the DJ's creating their own sounds by mixing singles on their turntables, scratching them in reverse through the stylus, destroying the sanitised and paralleling what Hendrix did with the guitar. Adding their own voices to the microphone was another option.

Every dance record they played was an event. Every track was different. The kids took to the sounds from the dance halls. House music took over and it was something the record companies couldn't package; it was live and it was unique. Inevitably, house bands followed. The music was dance orientated and therefore the lyrics were redundant.

Different ways of making the body jump up and down were created using different forms of beat and rhythm.

These sounds were unplayable on radio and were never meant to be, although many stations persisted in doing so. Any rare record success the record companies had in packaging these bands was short-lived, as the fashion moved faster than the labels' turnaround.

The music business, which had become all business and no music, was now becoming no music, no business. It was dying in ecstasy riddled pools of sweat on the floors of crowded sheds.

He could understand their anger, the kids' that is. A generation or two destroyed by his own peer group. The opportunity to develop the impulse created in the alternative era had been largely spurned. The wealth creation process handed to this group on a plate had been geared towards self-gratification. In doing so, greater barriers than ever before were placed between individuals; between those who benefited and those who did not. Whole continents were cut off, then countries, then ethnic groups, then communities, then their own children.

The *haves* communicated by television and telephone. The telepathy of the collective soul had ceased and the result was the imminent destruction of the world organism.

When individual parts of a machine are not integrated properly, when the spaces between constituent parts are not kept oiled, then the whole overheats, then explodes.

It was getting hotter.

'I don't think we should hang around in this town too much longer,' she said. 'We'll get our heads down tonight and get the first flight out in the morning.'

'Look, I've got a bit of a problem.'

She looked at him sideways with a look that said, 'Bit of one!'

'Money ... I just don't have that sort of money laying around in my account right now; I need to work a bit first.'

'You don't have any choice.' she said. 'If you hang around here any longer, well, you just won't *be* around to hang around if you know what I mean.' She looked down at the Speedo, checking she was on the fifty-five limit. They were keen on this route.

'I'll bankroll you,' she offered. 'You can pay me back.' She looked around again, 'Him too. I'll use cash, cards leave a trail.'

Morgan looked at her sideways. 'So how come you've got all this money?'

'My daddy was rich and my mummy's good-looking ... at least he was; he's dead now.'

Morgan went quiet for a moment, then settled back. 'And your mother?'

'Lives in Virginia ... get to see her about three times a year. Daddy's insurance has left her quite comfortably off. She puts her money and energy into me.'

Morgan was thoughtful. 'Look, I just can't take off like that. I've got a few things to do.'

'Like what?' she said sharply.

'Well, there's the funeral for one thing.'

'Funeral?'

'Yeah, Freddy. It's about now. I'd put it out of my mind for a couple of days, but the funeral will have to be about now ... and there's my wife ... ex-wife; she's probably freaking out and wondering why I haven't been in touch.'

'You feel you owe her something?'

'I owe her nothing,' he replied quickly, 'but she'll be falling apart about now.'

'And you're gonna put her together again?'

'Me, and all the King's men.'

Morgan lobbed the empty can into a roadside trash-can. It bounced once on the rim, then settled inside. Sara took this in, fixed her eyes back on the road and said nothing.

'Strange girl, strange girl my wife. She was English. Used to go back to see her folks every couple of years.'

'Thought you were only married a couple of years?'

'Yeah, but we lived together for about four years before that.'

'So what went wrong?'

'I don't know! I really don't know. I guess a lot of people say that when it happens to them. We seemed to get on fine for the first few years, then she had this thing about getting married before she was thirty. She pushed and pushed for it. We were getting on fine, but marriage never seemed to be an option. And then suddenly it was really important to her. I was happy to go along with that, in fact on paper everything was just fine.

Soon as we were married, it changed. There was a definite change in her; she was colder, more distant, more secretive. I probably spent more time in bars, more time at the gym, and more time just not being at home because there was no point. We just moved further and further apart. It was only during the divorce that I found out she had started screwing Freddy just before we married. I mean, can you believe that? What a dumb broad!'

'Sounds pretty sharp to me.'

Morgan leaned back as if he'd been shot.

'She had you ... *and* the best man. Can't have been *that* dumb.'

He looked straight ahead at the road and said nothing.

'But why go through with the marriage?' He said at last. 'What a crazy thing to do.'

'Maybe she wanted to hurt you.' Morgan lit a cigarette and looked at her. The question 'Why' was written on his face.

'People sometimes need to do that.' Morgan blew out the smoke and looked at the side of the road, across the scrub and rocky desert and towards the lower hills.

'Maybe women do,' he said to himself. He reached into his pocket and pulled out the tape.

Sara turned her head to him, 'And where are *you* going in life? What are you trying to do, to achieve?'

'Achieve?' he looked across at her, then started ... 'We are on this earth an average of seventy years or so. Most of us who are thinking hard about our lives are about halfway through them. A third of our lives we spend in sleep; a third we spend in work. The first third of our life, we are too young to know what it's all about, and the last third, we are too old to do anything about it. That gives us a third of a third of not very much. It doesn't leave very much time to LIVE.'

'So you're living,' she said sarcastically. 'Getting smashed, sucking cigarette smoke down into your lungs, screwing anything with two legs and a short skirt and throwing a football around and ...'

'And riding my bike,' said Morgan with a grin. The expression on his face indicated that he thought this was a pretty good definition of living.

Sara took a cigarette from the pack and beckoned to Morgan to light it for her. He did.

'You *are* disgusting you know,' she said. 'No, on reflection, not disgusting, just sad. What a waste.'

He narrowed his eyes and looked at her, 'And *you?*'

'I want to learn about things ... people, countries. I want to learn about things and then use my knowledge to make things happen. And I want to create a life for myself in which I can feel good about myself. Where I can be happy with my friends and my family,' she was groping for the words,

'I ... I want to be more than just happy. I want to feel that I'm contributing, you know what I mean?'

'I'd just like to make sense of it all ... I'm just reaching out for a reason.' He pressed *play*. An electric piano began to chime out a repetitive riff.

Don't promise me the earth promise me heaven instead

Give me wings to fly, where I might fear to tread.
I've been holding on, to this lifeline far too long.
My mind was in control, I believed my heart was wrong
Now I'm reaching out for heaven, in my life it's overdue
Now I'm reaching out for heaven, as I'm reaching out for you,
But I don't know, what on earth can one man do.
When the heaven in my heart is only you
Moments of meeting, now my life has changed
I was a ship that ran aground, now I'm in the outer lane.
Now the wind's behind me, I'm unchained and running free
And with you there beside me, I'm ready for the open sea
Now I'm reaching out for heaven, in my life it's overdue.
Now I'm reaching out for heaven, as I'm reaching out for you.
And these moments of our lives catch fire and brightly burn
Take hold of them before our pages' turn.
Now I'm reaching out for heaven, in my life it's overdue
Now I'm reaching out for heaven, as I'm reaching out for you,
But I don't know, what on earth can one man do
When the heaven in my heart is only you

'He reached for something golden that was hanging from a tree ... and his hand came down empty.'

Rich and royal hues hung all around them, gold stretching out on either side, rising to pink, then blue and in the distance, purple. The royal blue sky behind them was turning to crystal violet overhead and to the west, above Los Angeles, the sun was setting fire to the smog as evening caught fire.

'Come on baby, light my fire,' sang Morgan, looking first at the sun, and then at Sara. She had more practical matters on her mind.

'We'll stay at the Cadillac tonight, on Ocean-Front Walk. It's cheap, and there's usually lots of fun people about. It's on the beach at Venice. If Paul's playing late, we'll all get a little high; the management are pretty cool about that sort of thing.'

'I didn't think you were the partying type,' said Morgan. She didn't reply.

Morgan looked back at Paul. 'I think he's supporting at the Palomino

165

tonight.'

'We'll go straight to the hotel,' said Sara. 'We can clean up and get some sleep before tonight. I'll spend the evening trying to get our trip organised for tomorrow. I shouldn't have any problem getting seats. Any airline will do.'

She was concentrating on the traffic. It was bunching up. 'Look, I'll spend a few days with you in London, then I really have to move on ... to the rest of Europe. I'm supposed to be doing quite a bit of research and quite frankly I haven't got the time to get tied up with you two.'

Morgan's face clouded. He looked hurt.

'*Hey!*' she shouted, 'We've had a good time, OK? I think you're a nice guy. But I'm young. I know the line I'm going down. I don't want any distractions. Nothing that could become permanent.'

'Hell,' said Morgan, 'why do you have to plan everything so carefully? Chill out a little.'

'For God's sake Morgan, grow up. You're too old to be hip. The world is turning around you, but you're just not getting on the ride. You're not part of it.'

'Although the circle's turning, the centre still remains,' said Morgan.

'Yes, something like that.'

Desert

The Rat and his companion, their heads heavily bandaged, blinked furiously as they adjusted their eyes to the light of the midday sun. They rubbed their wrists in unison where the metal cuffs had bruised the skin. Squinting across the street, their joint focus was drawn to the black Caddy with heavily tinted windows. They straightened up and marched to the rear door which opened as they reached it. They stepped inside.

'What happened?' The questioner was sitting in the far corner. The Rat spoke first.

'The girl ... she got in the way.'

'Took you *both* out?'

'Took us from behind ... we weren't expected to allow for that.'

'No.' The questioner agreed flatly. They drove on in silence for some time.

'What happens now?' The Rat was squinting through the window, but all he could see was sand.

'Siemonsen is not a happy man,' said the questioner, adjusting his white cuffs under the dark suit. Behind the black glasses, the eyes could give nothing away. In the front seats, the driver and his passenger wore identical suits and peaked caps. They could alternate the driving on a long journey.

'Where are we headed?' The Rat was asking too many questions and his companion was getting nervous. He was also missing two teeth.

The questioner used the flat monotone again. 'We're getting you out of here.'

The car was moving at a constant speed. It did not vary its pace ... at slip roads, junctions, around the few stray vehicles and rare bends. The air-conditioning enhanced the feeling of unreality, together with the filtered light. They were moving North-West towards Death Valley, and what was visible grew paler and lost its form. The landscape became almost lunar as they climbed towards Zabriskie Point.

The rat's companion slipped his hand towards the recessed door handle, and gently fingered its resistance. He knew it would be locked from the front, and it was. He knew what was going to happen, but could do nothing. He wasn't armed and these men obviously were. There were a number of mirrors above the front windshield and the eyes of both front riders were in all of them. The rabbit caught in bright headlights, the man on Death Row, the Jews herded into wagons ... All knew, and all could have resisted, even if futile; but none did.

The calm inevitability of death, when recognised, rendered all physical action redundant. The inertia produced was of an almost spiritual quality. He reached out with his other hand and curled the little finger around that of his companion. The pressure he exerted was returned.

They turned off to the left, about five miles from the Point and after a further two miles of dusty driving, the car slid to a halt, swaying on its springs.

The front riders were out before the car subsided and the rear doors opened crisply. They were all outside in five seconds and stood in silence while the white dust settled around them. The Rat and colleague moved more than the others, who were as cool under the undiluted sun as they had been in the car. They weren't the ones who were going to die.

The car had come to rest against a sheer crust of rock, which cut out a third of the view. The rest of the terrain fell away in a gentle sweep and flattened into the white and salty horizon. The two men loosened their ties and unbuttoned the top of their shirts. The other three didn't. All stood waiting.

It was very still. So still, the faint breath of earth could barely rise. Pale white on pale sand. So still ... its beat so faint, it could not move its breath. Lying still and pale and heavy.

No thing moved, not for a while. Then a clatter, then nothing; a scrape, then no more. In the imagined shadow of the rock the pale grew darker and the light less.

'Good day gentlemen.' Siemonsen was standing on the summit of the outcrop, a black sentinel, hands clasped in front of him as if waiting in line to take the communion wine. 'Thank you for joining me.' He was holding a small two-way radio which caught the sun's light; it was the only indication of movement. 'I'm afraid that your services are no longer required and I am forced to let you go.'

He pointed past them and down into the shallow valley. The Rat and his friend followed the finger and now became aware of a chunky, four-wheel drive, off-roader. It was about three hundred yards away and partly hidden by the folding scree.

They looked at each other and back up to Siemonsen.

'Take it and take off ... I never want to set eyes on you again.' They looked at each other.

'Move!' The order came from the questioner.

This time they turned and walked. They didn't speak for a hundred yards. They were waiting for the hit. The Rat turned his head back to the ridge.

Siemonsen's silhouette was clearly visible and the three subordinates hadn't moved.

'Why don't they shoot?' 'Said the Rat.

'They would have done that by now,' said the other.

'Think it's OK then? ... Think they mean it? ... We can go?' They were halfway to the vehicle.

'No, they're waiting for something. One of his little events. He must have gotten the military to fly him down to the Edwards Base for this.' They held hands.

'I've never really been sure why he always insisted on a sense of theatre.'

'It's more like ritual. I've always likened it to the way the Indian regarded the hunt ... and then the kill.' They stumbled closer to the vehicle, a black Toyota. 'Never without reason, never taken for granted and always with thanks to the gods, or the *flag* in his case.'

'What about us, why us? ... One slip-up, and we couldn't have been expected to allow for that.'

'Just remember the good work we've done. We've done well. We'll go well.'

'It must be the car. It must be wired.'

They reached it. The doors were unlocked and the keys were in the ignition. They looked back one last time to see the group unmoved, stepped inside and clasped hands.

The Rat had taken the driving seat. He kissed his friend once on the lips and turned the key. The crashing roar which followed was only the engine bursting into life. The sweat on their brows ran down into their eyes and mingled with another salty flow.

The Rat threw it into first and put his foot down. The Toyota jerked forward and bounced over the brittle wasteland.

Rat's companion craned his neck and checked on the four figures, stark and black against the light. They were well out of gunshot range and he was starting to feel as if they might just be off the hook.

The Rat kept his eyes on the disappearing group more than on the faintly marked track. He saw the black cross appear over Siemonsen's head just before his companion heard the roar.

The cross moved with increasing speed, vertically through the rear view mirror and over the Toyota. The sun was almost directly overhead, but throwing their shadow in front of them. The shadow of the black cross emerged from the front of the vehicle and moved away directly ahead. The noise was deafening.

It passed overhead, very low. The ugly, stubby, carrier of death was taking its time. It made a gentle turn, low above the ground about five miles ahead, and came back towards them, its snout defiled by the instrument of appalling destruction.

The Rat jammed on the brakes. 'Run!' he screamed, but didn't move. They didn't even have time to hold hands. The Gatling gun in the nose made a noise like a spouting fax and the cannon shells ripped into the black metal coffin at the rate of six thousand a minute. The burst from the A10 Tankbuster didn't last for more than three seconds, but in that age, the Toyota evaporated in a pyrotechnic display of metallic fragments, flesh, bone and blood and wrapped in veils of white shroud kicked up from the desert's whitened crust. The billowing cloud flashed bright with yellow, then orange, as the evaporated petrol ignited and completed the cremation. Only the black smoke remained, drifting softly over the white, in the warm air.

The A10 moved away steadily; above Siemonsen's watching group, and back to the north. All that remained below the smudge of smoke was a circle of blackened fragments fifty yards in diameter, and the faint smell of burnt rubber ... or was it flesh.

Los Angeles

They headed south-west from Barstow still on Route 15 through Victorville, Cajon Junction and Verdemont. On the edge of the San Bernardino forest, west of Silverwood Lake, at the junction with Route 10, Rancho Cucamonga, they turned west into the eastern suburbs of L.A. Then on through Alhambra and Culver City to Venice and handily placed for the following day's flight from L.A. International Airport. 'LAX,' to the locals and 'Laxative' to those with a fear of flying.

The three booked themselves into and paid for, a twin room; the management didn't seem to mind. Morgan picked up the 'phone. It wasn't working.

'Don't complain,' said Sara. 'They turned a blind eye to a third person in this room. Let's not push it.'

'I've got to call England,' said Paul.

She looked at the two of them. 'Both going off to ring the women you left behind. That's really touching.'

Morgan looked at Paul. 'Why do women see everything in terms of black and white?'

'Maybe it's because that's the way things are,' she said. They left for the 'phone booths in reception. Morgan got through first.

'Hi, how are you ... well who the hell do you think it is ... what's it to you where I've been? ... Yes I know it's tomorrow ... I can't make it ... 1 just can't. Freddy was my best friend ... yours too huh? ... So there's no need to be like this. Well I think there's a need to be like that ... I just can't OK! I'm sure Freddy won't mind ... so don't bite my head off ... Sorry ... Sorry ... See you ...Yes!, you will get a cheque this month.' Click, went the receiver.

Morgan slumped against the booth and shook his head. He moved to the bar, passing Paul on the way.

Paul was banging at the 'phone-box with his fist, Morgan ignored it and kept walking towards where he hoped the bar would be. He turned around at the sound of louder crashes. Paul was kicking out at a drinks-dispenser.

'What's up?' Morgan shouted.

Paul joined him. 'The 'phone box has taken the last of my money without giving me anything in return, and I've just got a shock from that machine.'

'What are you drinking?'

'I'll have a beer.'

Virginia

171

The car was a black Cadillac, not stretched like the one occupied by the Director of Central Intelligence up ahead, but it still looked the part, having blacked-out windows and a variety of communication aerials sprouting from the roof and boot.

The drive had taken them to the other side of the Potomac via the Roosevelt Bridge and now they were heading north. They turned off the road towards the woods; through the guarded break in the wire and along the long drive into the flat oasis beyond the tree line.

The massive car-park was like an airport complex, the huge off-white terminal-like building brooding beyond it. As they drew nearer, the seven floors of sharply rectangular glass and concrete aggregate reminded Siemonsen of his student days. The same campus atmosphere, same rules, same committees, the lodges and fraternities, same departmentalisation, same politics. It wasn't even grown-up here. If anything, it was more juvenile.

The two cars swept into the underground tunnelled entrance reserved for the star players. When they pulled up and the doors were opened by silent men in quiet suits, the only thing missing were the cheerleaders.

This was the nest of the WASP. This was the home they'd built to fulfill the Yankee dream; to extend the debating societies and institutionalised political structures of their Ivy League days. Their beliefs and values were enshrined in this building. From here, they would fly out and sting their enemies; to death if need be.

This nest housed nearly twenty thousand of them, supporting a hundred thousand worldwide with a budget of thirty billion dollars. The Central Intelligence Agency took itself seriously.

Since Kissinger had been appointed Nixon's Special Assistant for National Security Affairs, and all the problems *that* had caused, the agency had rearranged itself into many sub-groups. Never again would all its resources and power be controlled by one individual. This, of course, was in the interests of democracy. The devolution and dissipation of decision-making being a prerequisite for a bulwark against megalomania.

The result was an inevitable plethora of megalomaniacs.

Siemonsen was adamant that his group would come out on top, the only sadness being the fact that they could never be recognised and lauded for their achievements.

Siemonsen waited politely for the chief to take the lift first.

'Poor bastard,' he thought. 'All those controls, all those meetings, all that lying to the President, the condescension. God, I could never put up with all that.'

He took the next lift and stopped at the fourth floor. He turned left out of the lift and flashed his card and a stiff smile at the girl on the first desk. At the second door past the fire door, he swiped another card and entered the corridor. At the fourth door on the left he inserted a third card and placed the palm of his right hand over the metal plate to the right of the wooden architrave.

Once inside, he threw his lightweight raincoat over the back of the nearest chair and reached inside the bottom drawer of the grey glossed desk and drew out a bottle of English gin. McLean's note of greeting was still tied to its neck.

Siemonsen poured himself three fingers and added a mixer of carbonated water. He drank greedily at first, then finished more slowly.

He poured another and hit the telephone. 'Get me Roberts ... yes now!'

He replaced the receiver and hit another button. 'Siemonsen here ... Can you tell me when we're going to offload the Trident onto the Brits ... Yes I know that, but when are the trials in Florida? ... Fine ... They're taking seventy aren't they ... and using their own warheads? ... Good ... Thank you.' The smirk had returned and coincided with a knock on the door.

Roberts was a very tall man possessing a permanent stoop, which at least prevented him from hitting his head on low slung obstructions. He was the team leader of the cipher section and his intellect could not be brought into question. This was mainly because nobody had enough intellect to ask any. His word was enough to terminate missions, missiles and men. He was regarded as a genius by those who were not, and were therefore in no position to judge.

He was wearing a white antistatic lab coat, sparkling white to match his sparkling skin, hair and nails. Sparkling wit, he did not possess, but that was not regarded as a deficiency in this organisation. This serious man, with receding hairline and bones so thin they creaked as he moved, had a strange intensity; intensified when faced with a particularly difficult problem. Siemonsen had given him one.

Gratitude shone out of the face of the keeper of the ciphers in the hall of bright computings.

Siemonsen poured himself another drink and offered one to Roberts, who declined. 'Do you have anything for me?' he inquired of the tall figure who was stooping even lower than normal as Siemonsen refused to rise to meet him.

The mania in the eyes would have been apparent to any normal person, but as Roberts was talking to a CIA man, it went unnoticed. 'As a matter of fact sir, I believe we're onto something.'

'Onto something,' said Simonsen flatly. 'What's the answer? ... Is it a code?'

'Well of course it's a code,' Roberts said shirtily. 'But it's not that simple.'

'Ah, not a simple code'

'No ... just not that simple.'

'Can you take me through it? ... In your own time?'

Roberts did the exasperated, speaking-to-a-child bit. 'We have to establish rhythms in the sequences, the parameters of the problem. We made some assumptions to cut corners, inspired guesses, based on experience of course. We felt that any information would be contained in the titles of the tracks only.

It's obviously an anagram, but there are so many options. We've tried the usual sequences, and the net result after four days of continuous running on two machines is this; There *is* a message in the tape. It is broken down into SEVEN lines and the recipient is meant to be MORGAN!'

Siemonsen put his glass down hard on the table. 'Well?'

Roberts was not to be rushed, 'And the sender is PAUL MILLNS.'

'And the message, what is it?'

Roberts bowed down even lower, 'It's in the MUSIC!'

174

'The MUSIC!'

'Right!' He beamed through glinting eyes. 'It took us a while to get to it ... very clever ... never been done before. They've used the note sequences to define the position of the letters, and key-changes to group them into words.

The order of the individual words is defined by the certain type of emphasis the vocalist puts into a phrase.

We've used a music sequencer reprogrammed to pick up on a number of variations, and this has proved to be the key.'

Roberts produced three CD's from a pocket and placed them on the desk. 'I've dug up all previously released material by this artist and these are the most recent ones. You'll see that some of the tracks on this tape have been recorded before. There is one significant change in the titles assigned to them.

The fourth track on side two, *Far Out There Tonight*. This has been changed from the original title on this CD ..."Secret Operations," released in Germany. On the album it's called *Far Out To Sea*.

They altered the words for no reason! It must have been to incorporate a message of some kind, either for Morgan, or someone else. I've been going over some of the stuff this Millns has been writing ... I've gone back ten years ... In my opinion this artist has left-wing tendencies. I believe the Curtis girl could have conspired with him to expose some of our activities.'

Siemonsen's face was twitching. 'Are you sure about this? ... Every rock singer in the world is anti-establishment ... Goes with the territory.'

'Well I *have* come up with a message.'

'My congratulations.' Siemonsen was gushing gratitude and admiration.

Roberts blushed and held up his hands. 'Well it *was* a nice piece of work and a real team effort of course.'

'Of course. I'll see your budgets are revised in the usual direction.'

'It was the change in title that started me off on the right track. If we remove *Far Out* from both titles, we are left with twelve letters in one version and five in the other, the difference is Seven!

This is the number of lines in the message. I've seen this used before ...

very crude, but the Soviet New York mafia have used this type of code for years, a hangover from the internal Georgian wars.

Then comes the signature letter. Of the remaining letters in the two titles, only ONE is common to both, and appears only ONCE.' Roberts placed a scrap of paper in front of his superior.

THERE TONIGHT - TO SEA

'It's the O ... Do you see?'

'So?'

'So we know that we are looking for seven separate lines and one signature line, the latter being denoted by an O.

What demarks the other lines?... We look for an excess of letters ... Out of their normal proportions. In this case it's the letter E.

There's far too many of them for normal speech. We now remove seven E's and one O and set the computers to work on the rest of the letters. We then match up them up with the analysis of the musical sequences and individual notes. Just a big anagram really.'

Roberts turned to leave.

'Haven't you forgotten something?'

'Pardon?'

'The message! ... What is it?'

'Ah ... yes ... Well we don't know yet.'

'What!'

'Your 'phone call interrupted us. We should have it in a few days.'

'Few days! ... I thought you had it cracked?' Siemonsen wasn't happy.

'The general principles yes; but exactly which of those principles have been selected for this code has not yet been finalised.'

'Two days! Two days, or, or ... It'll be the abacus for you ... I'll start hanging *pictures* on your wall.'

Roberts looked aghast, and moved out backwards, bowing nearly to the floor, the backs of his hands scraping the carpet.

10

Don't wait too long

The room had a cosy shabbiness. The crowd was light at eleven, but thickened towards midnight. The Palomino was L.A.'s Country music show-case, but a number of R'n B and Blues bands also played there. The crowds were warm and knowledgeable and the place went through till 2.00am. It was on Lankershim Boulevard, North Hollywood and the trio had made it there by cab, Sara having returned the car earlier in the evening. Morgan, as usual, was leaning on the bar drinking heavily and Sara was teasing a couple of ice cubes with her cocktail stick.

'When's he coming on?' She was becoming impatient.

'Midnight.' came the reply. Then, looking at his watch, 'About now.'

The lights around the stage got brighter and Paul's voice came over the microphone.

'I'd like to apologise before I start,' he said, 'for not being a Country and Western singer. I'm English, and I don't think I should be trying to bring coals to Newcastle.' The punters looked at each other, not grasping this particular point. 'I'll be doing some of my own stuff, and maybe some R'n B and maybe a little Blues later on, but as a token of my regard for Country Music, I would like to kick off with a song I wrote which has leanings in that direction.'

This brought one or two cheers from the crowd. The others clapped politely.

I called you today, long-distance telephone.
Two thousand miles babe, really made you feel alone.
And your voice came clear, full of sunshine and full of wine.
Oh it seems so long since I've seen that distant ocean shine
You say you've been sweeping up, all the dust of our affair
No crumbs of comfort there, no tasty crusts of love to spare
And the wind whistles around my hat, the rain aims arrows at my back
And all my bad, sad dreams re-arm and plan another dawn attack
Don't wait too long, Crazy time is rushing on.
Downhill it rolls, a train out of control. Hold on to love, don't let it go,
Don't wait too long
Now the city rides on my shoulder, 'neath a sky that's grey as lead
Human warmth is on the run, there's a price upon its head
If I had money in my pocket, instead of songs inside my mind,
I'd catch the next plane out of here just to see those dark eyes shine
Now I'm investing all my money in this yellow hotel telephone
But I can't seem to negotiate a normal dialling tone
And the management's on holiday, room service is off tonight
And the drinks machine gave me an electric shock
As my last coins dropped from sight
Don't wait too long
Crazy time is rushing on
Downhill it rolls, a train out of control
Hold on to love, don't let it go
Don't wait too long

He got more than the usual cheer reserved for support acts, and carried on happily into his short set.

Morgan had emptied half a bottle of Bushmills and was trying to persuade Sara to help him with the other half. Her hand kept trying to cover her glass, and the whiskey spilled partly into the glass, partly over her hand, but mostly over the table. She sucked it off the back of her hand, cursing

178

quietly. Paul sat down next to them.

'They seemed to like that.' Morgan held out a beer as he spoke.

'Yes.' Paul agreed, slightly surprised. 'When are we leaving?'

'What's the hurry?'

'Come on,' Sara said, standing up and picking up her bag. 'We've got a big day tomorrow.'

'Have a drink,' said Morgan. Paul and Sara looked at him without pity.

'Look, I want to go back to the hotel and put in a call to England.' Paul started to walk out. Morgan looked lost. 'My lady,' Paul explained, 'doesn't know I'm coming home tomorrow.'

'Fine' said Sara. 'Let's go now.' Morgan picked up the remains of the bottle and ambled towards the exit with the others.

The two raps were redundant, because the shadow behind the frosted glass that made them was already coming through the door. In its three-dimensional form it spoke.

'You'd better take a look at this, John,' said Weller. Big John looked up sharply.

'What is it?'

The clean cut young man was excited. 'It's a report from an Officer Wilson, about the death up in San Gabriel.'

'The headless biker?'

'That's right. I've been looking through this report and something strikes me as interesting.' He leaned over the desk. 'Apparently Wilson had gone back to the cabin the following day to interview John Morgan and he'd disappeared, but as the door was open Wilson went in. Smart boy that. He looked around and spotted an ansaphone. He had the good sense to listen to the tapes. Now I've highlighted an interesting message.'

Big John read aloud the highlighted section. Jackie's seductive voice was inviting Morgan round to her place. When he'd finished reading John looked up. 'So?'

'So?' said Weller. 'From the previous conversations on that tape, some of which had times left by the callers, it would seem this message was left a couple of days before the wire incident.'

'So?' said John again.

The young officer had a self-satisfied smile on his face. 'There are messages on either side of that one, and like I said, quite a few of them had given dates and times. It would seem that this message came through on the day of our other mysterious death.'

'Ah,' said John, his face brightening. 'The rich bitch with bizarre ideas.'

'You got it.' said Weller.

'How do you know it's her?' said John, eyes narrowing. The young detective slammed a ten dollar bill on the desk with one hand and waved the micro-cassette with the other.

'I'm going 'round to the maid's house now. I'll give you ten-to-one she'll confirm it's Jackie's voice.'

'Off you go,' said John, and then, looking at the ten-dollar bill, 'and I'm not taking the bet.'

Maria was sobbing and speaking through a large handkerchief cut from the white linen cloth that used to cover her mother's table. Most of the remainder now covered *her* dining table and protected it from the heat of Robert's plate. The rest cased their pillows.

She was nodding as well as speaking, the widening of the eyes told Weller the answer was affirmative before the words became clear. 'Yes that's her voice – and that's his photo .... I seen him around ... once, maybe twice. In the mornings ... leaving.' Maria blew her nose and wiped both cheeks. Robert stopped eating and waited until she'd completed her facial cleansing. He started again when she did.

'I saw his car ... once ... old and red ... noisy with no roof. Left marks in the drive when he took off... no respect.'

'Did you see it? Did you see anything on the day ... you know ... the day...'

'The day Miss Jackie died? .... No, I never seen nothing.'

'But this is the man Miss Curtis was seeing, yes?'

'Yes, that's him.' she sniffed again. 'Not the usual ... He was different ... From the usual ...' fingering the 'photo with shaking hands ... 'Didn't dress nice.'

London

'We've got the bloody Sportsmen arrivin' next week. That, I can do without, got enough on my plate as it is.'

'Oo the fuck are they, Tone?' The heavy slopped two dimpled pints of what used to be called ale on to the small round wooden table. Lunch time was ending and the pub in Westminster was emptying.

'From the Ukraine. Started as common smugglers, but they're getting a bit tasty now. Their leader, or *Captain*, as they like to call 'Im, lives in Budapest. I've set up a bank account for 'im offshore ... Guernsey.' Sir Anthony sipped his beer.

'Why?'

The second pint became a half in two gulps. 'Why are they cummin,' or why am I lookin after 'em?'

'Yeah.'

Another sip. 'There's a lot of dosh freein' up now that the Soviets 'ave seen the light, an' the power is always with the money. They brought over about four million dollars last year, an' much more to come. Got a friendly little solicitor in the City to smooth the way so to speak.'

'That's big numbers Tone.'

'Peanuts. I reckon we've got about fifteen percent of the world's cash in our offshore banks.'

The heavy's eyes narrowed. He was thinking. It took time. 'Nice little float that ... geddit? ... offshore, float... see?' Sir Anthony nodded wearily.

'Oo owns it then?'

'We do, the consortium, the defenders of the free world – No name, that would be too easy to trace. Order, Gerald, that's what makes the system tick over. Order. Can't 'ave people making lots of decisions that bugger everything up. Do you know that there's four thousand meetin's per second, every second goin' on in the civilised world. Nobody does nuthin' anymore. They just meet to talk about doin' somethin.' Now just imagine the damage people could do if they actually got on and *did* it? ... Jesus, talk about 'eadless chickens.'

'Another one Tone?' Gerald was keen to get to the bar. He returned with two more pints.

'Structure, that's what you want. Tradition. The certainty and rhythm of ritual.'

'Eh?' Gerald's face contorted to comprehend.

'Takes money though, not cheap. If the money's in the right 'ands, then we can control the bigger political fluctuations around the globe. Keep it sweet.'

'Oo's we?'

'*We*, Gerald,' Sir Anthony deliberated, 'have no name. You may think of us as a club if you like, quite informal of course, and very discreet. All major countries and most minor ones, are represented. We tend to wield our influence in the corridors of power and not in the spotlight. Gets out of 'and sometimes, and we end up running the show from the front. Columbia, Indonesia, Chile, the Ukraine, North Korea, they all went a bit silly and came out in the open. It never really works, because you're there to be shot at. Doesn't last.'

He emptied his jug and nodded for another. Gerald obliged. The second pint loosened up the narrator even more. 'You can't influence events from the front ... got to keep explainin' yourself, gettin' permission. We just get on with it. We have the money, therefore we have the power. We can do what we want. It's all for the good of course, to look after society, keeping it clean. Too many of them dissidents, troublemakers, bankers, politicians, lawyers an' types like that. Westminster's full of kiddie-fiddlers and bum-bandits, same as the Palace.'

Gerald's head bobbed in agreement. 'Yeah, they're gettin' down our way now. Brixton used to be alright, but we 'ad three social workers move into our street at Christmas. Them an' the wasters on the 'ousing committee ... an' their mates ... 'anging round the town 'all, givin' the area a bad name.'

'The Sportsmen are here to be briefed. They've got to understand they're part of a team. No point in playin' solo. They had to get rid of Odinvsov ...

started freelance drug smugglin'. You remember 'im?'

'Yeah, real jerk.'

'Right.'

Los Angeles

They had been at the airport for three hours and Paul and Morgan were into some serious drinking. Sara was doing her best to keep up.

'At least we had no problems with the passports'

'Why should we?'

'You may have forgotten, but there are four dead bodies out there ... all acquaintances of yours.' He started to sober up. 'At the moment there's no official call out on you. That could change. The sooner we're out of here the better. Bye the way, what have you done with the gun?'

'Got rid of it,' said Morgan quickly.

'Where?'

'Err ... Out in the desert.'

The flight was on time. Morgan had the window-seat in the smoking section. Sara sat next to him, the third seat was empty. Paul was asleep with the non-smokers. Two hours into the flight and the couple's trays were overflowing with plastic debris. The cabin staff were doing their best.

Morgan stared at the mess with eyes sloping under heavy lids. 'It always gets me; they bring us a nice neat plastic box the size of a ciggy carton and as soon as you touch it, it explodes to cover an area the size of Texas.'

Morgan picked up a fork and prodded at the centre of his tray. 'What are those bits of plastic?'

'Boeuf Bourguignon?' Sara suggested. A stewardess came to the rescue and piled everything into a bag.

'What can we have that's free?' Morgan was giving her his best side and best grin.

She smiled fixedly through gritted teeth. 'Half a bottle of wine sir ... but I do believe you've had your allocation.' She picked up three empty bottles.

'Any going spare?' He looked around, turning his long frame about its long axis. 'You're not full.'

'I'll check sir ... anything else?' She stared at the mess.

'Bin-liner?'

She turned away. She was American and the vowels were hard. 'How about a trough.' It wasn't a question.

Sara looked at him. 'We have four hours of peace ahead and we're going to use this time to go over your life history.' She produced a ball-point and several sheets of paper. 'We're going to try to pinpoint just what you've done to upset someone ... you talk, I'll write.'

'I was born in ...'

'Stop ... I'll ask questions.'

The five sheets of paper were covered in neatly written paragraphs. Sara was flicking them over and scanning the contents. Morgan's head was buried in a newspaper. It was a UK broadsheet and the article was making him smile. His elbow caught her in the ribs. 'Listen to this ... The Brits haven't a clue about organisation on a large scale. They're great in little committees, but government ... forget it! They've managed to lose enough plutonium to make four hundred nuclear bombs ... can you believe that ... four HUNDRED!'

'How do you know?'

Morgan peered closer, 'Some clever guy has worked out that the tonnage of plutonium ore imported, when matched against the number of declared warheads ... leads to four hundred extra bombs lying around somewhere! Could only happen in England.'

'We'll be there soon.'

'They'll probably lose the luggage.'

'We haven't got any ... not much anyway. I'm going to the Rest-Room.'

'Me too.'

They made their way towards the rear toilets. Just before they reached them, Morgan threw his arm around her shoulders and pulled her towards him. She tried to cry out, but his hand was over her mouth. He shouted at the nearest stewardess. 'Feeling sick ... she'll be OK in a minute.' He opened a toilet door and bundled her inside, following closely in one movement.

Her eyes were wide-open in question. He put a finger to his lips and released his grip. There wasn't much room.

'What the hell are you up to?'

'Mile-High Club.'

'I'm not a member.'

'I'm about to process your application.'

London

Quentin Fairchild took the moist flesh in his lips and slipped his tongue expertly underneath, guiding it to the back of his throat. The juices followed almost immediately. He had performed this feat five times already. Only one now remained, firm upon its shell.

'Late in the afternoon is the best time for these my dear chap,' he said, waving his delicate digits over the white starched linen. 'Any earlier is vulgar, and in the evening it's positively obscene.'

Sir Anthony looked at him closely, deciding this man was insane. A perfect example of generations of inbreeding.

'We need some triggers Quent; the Heathrow seizure didn't help.'

'At least it looked as if they were meant for Hussein, Anthony.' The wine was a Grand Cru Chablis and Quentin held it in his mouth for as long as possible before succumbing and swallowing.

'Yes, I always insist on a cover, should things go wrong.'

'You're a good man Anthony. Her Majesty really does appreciate your err ... *commitment*. She wants you to pop in sometime; I'll arrange it for Sandringham. By the way, her mum would like to see a little more of you.'

'Trouble with the horses?'

Quentin looked embarrassed 'I believe so. She finds it difficult to accept that other horses sometimes run faster than hers.'

The two cigarettes were sucked and blown in unison, then two long streams of smoke exhaled in parallel. The stewardess with the synchronised grin leaned over Sara and spoke sweetly. 'Are you feeling better now, madam?'

Sara's mouth opened to reply, but Morgan butted in, 'She just had a little something stuck in her throat.'

The grin was still fixed and she spoke without moving her lips. 'Yes I guessed it was only little.'

Morgan went quiet as the stewardess turned away.

'I've been going over your CV, and it sure does make depressing reading.' Sara was shuffling the sheets of paper like a deck of cards. 'I've narrowed the area of interest, down to the period immediately before the demise of your last girlfriend ... Jacqueline the Bondage Queen. Nothing else seems relevant ... if you've been telling the truth, that is?'

'Scout's honour.' Morgan was drinking from yet another bottle of wine and the fierce air-conditioning was struggling to cope with the fog around his head.

'I want you to go over your time with her in detail ... every day if you can, then every hour of every day.' She handed him the pen and paper again and he reluctantly went to work.

Her head was buried deep in thought and in his scrawl. 'Tell me about her house?' She spoke without raising her head and in that monotone beloved of schoolteachers when holding a child in suspense as to whether they are in favour or not. Morgan remembered it well, and began a guarded response.

'Only went there a couple of times ... Big, well kept, expensive furniture, but no taste.'

'And you'd know about that would you?' He said nothing and took another drink.

'Go on.'

'Walled, electronic gates, security video, beautiful gardens, lawns like Augusta National.' He lit up again. 'Big pool, two lousy fountains, stone figures people like to call figurines, God knows why. Cherubs spouting water from their mouths and holding trumpets, what's that all about?' He took another drink. 'Couple of big lounges, four, maybe five bedrooms.'

'What was *her* bedroom like?'

'Does it matter?'

'Does it to you?'

'No ... no, not anymore.'

'Anything odd about the place?' she went on quietly.

'Not that I can remember.'

'Try.'

'I was not that sober when I was there. Things were confused. I even got lost fetching a bottle of wine from her kitchen ... ended up in the cellar one night ... We'd run out, of booze, that is ... Went to the wrong door. I smashed in it and fell down a flight of steps. That was weird. The place was like a ... I don't know what it was like. Strange pipes and containers, like a distillery.'

'What do you mean?'

'Forget it, probably the air-con unit.'

'What sort of containers?'

'Hard to describe.'

She passed him a sheaf of paper and a pencil. 'Draw it ... All of it ... as much as you can remember.'

Sir Anthony picked up the receiver again and flicked a switch. 'Ah, Doris, can you get me Zhirinovsky.' After two minutes a Russian voice boomed down the line. Sir Anthony replied in perfect Russian.

'Hello Vlad, did you get the ciggies ... Marlboro as requested ... oh, I see, for the ladies, not you ... ah, you enjoyed them too ... Vlad the inhaler ... nothing, just a little joke ... anyway, are my people being useful Vlad? ... Good, good ... so you now have plenty of dollars in the kitty ... good, good. Yes it wasn't easy to get that much to you, but that lot should be able to buy you a good show at the elections. Yes I know the Yanks don't understand Vlad ... only authoritarian rule can work in that great wasteland of yours. Mind you,' he said thoughtfully, 'that's probably true of most countries. Look, it will take some time to shift Yeltsin completely and it's probably not a good idea anyway, you never know who's going to fill the void, but if we just get you up there in a strong pressure position then I think we'll probably achieve all we need to ... thank you Vlad, cheerio.'

Virginia

Siemonsen was sitting up in bed and was talking to someone in the bathroom. 'Sir Anthony is setting it all up, but I want you to be there to make sure nothing goes wrong.'

'Thank you,' said a male voice. The shower came on, The male voice had to shout through the sound of slapping water. 'This is going to be a really good one, I won't let you down.'

'I know you won't,' said Siemonsen. 'You're a true artist. You've done some beautiful jobs for us.'

'It's a shame it's not always appreciated,' came the wet voice. It went on, 'I mean, any fool can take somebody out without any ... *style*, but when you really believe in something and believe that what you're doing is important, then a sense of ritual must come into play.'

'Exactly,' Siemonsen agreed enthusiastically. 'The importance of our work cannot be overestimated. We are responsible for the well-being of our fellow citizens. Just because our work is regarded as the *grubby* end of the business we must make a stand and show Langley that the importance of our work needs a memorial.'

The shower was turned off abruptly, and the man padded into the room, towel around his waist. 'I believe,' said the towelled figure, 'that the more of an *event* we make our assignment, then the more respect we shall receive.'

'Right,' said Siemonsen. 'The American people would not tolerate our services declining to the standards of common criminals. Each piece of work we carry out has a dramatic effect on the lives of our fellow citizens and the event should be enshrined as such.'

'What's Sir Anthony got planned?' said the towelled figure sitting on the bed. Siemonsen reached out and took his hand.

'Now there's a man I can respect.' said Siemonsen. 'He understands the important of ritual. England has understood its importance for centuries.'

'The Charge of the Light Brigade,' said the towelled figure, eyes gleaming.

'Wonderful example. They weren't even doing it to the opposition. Ritual kamikaze at its most glorious ... and the effect it had on the country for hundreds of years afterwards.' Siemonsen was beaming. 'The moral written into that event kept England going through the last two world wars and kept their society on a relatively even keel. "We're all going to die because the situation is hopeless, therefore we will die gloriously and with a stiff upper lip." It's reflected in their society today.' He had decided to expand. 'Most of their citizens walk around, no weapons, no guns, and no questions. Criminals, crack dealers and their politicians surround them on all sides, armed to the teeth. They all go down gloriously, questioning nothing.'

'It sure is a wonderful thing,' nodded his companion in agreement.

Moscow

The black Zil turned off Gorky Street and pulled up outside the Irmotova Theatre. It used to be a theatre, but it was now a sad and empty building, the citizens of Moscow having been forced to embrace western systems had also followed in their footsteps by turning their backs on the Arts. It was being touted to western businessmen as a perfect site for a much needed hotel, all rooms in Moscow being permanently full. The plaster-work, intricate and in good order, deserved better. Its blue-washed walls contrasted with the more general washes of yellows, browns and ochres of the adjacent buildings. The centre of Russia's capital city reflected the summer sunlight from its wide roadways and even wider river. The lack of traffic ensured the light was not impeded on its journey around the great squares. The bull's-eye within the greater inner ring road was defined by the four great Gotham-City skyscrapers, their Gothic summits glaring down, daring any Gostbusters to advance at their peril.

Nikolai Golushko stepped out of the nearside rear door, wiped the thick lenses of his glasses on the loose folds of his shirt; they always gathered at his thickening waistline. His predecessors would have waited for the front-riders to open it, but Golushko was a 'Hands-on' man, his time in the Ukraine as head of the KGB's Fifth Directorate had taught him the value of doing everything for himself. Unfortunately, the KGB did not now exist and the political subtleties and nuances of the reformed Russia, supported and guarded by the newly formed Counter Intelligence Service did not lend itself to his more direct skills. He had many enemies ... powerful enemies.

Perspiration had been soaked up by his thick eyelashes and deposited on the inside of his lenses.

Russians Khasbulatov and Alexander Rutskoi were just such men. Sir Anthony had warned him about these two. They would have to be watched. Something was in the air. They had been in contact with Morris, the CIA man at the American Embassy. He didn't mind James going about his routine spying. It was mainly industrial stuff and mainly to assess how much the Soviets had managed to glean from the West ... but this was different. This was political interference and no reason for it. Yeltsin was in place, and although a stubborn and bombastic man, not exactly a threat to the West. They should be doing all they could to help. He smelled trouble. In the Ukraine his job was well defined. He had order then. He imposed it. Dissidents were dealt with ruthlessly and accountability was simply a body count.

He was not in control here. He needed his minders, but they were in London contributing to the new relationship and would stand out a mile in the new Moscow.

The American was glad to get out. He stood at the front of the Hotel Russia pleased to escape the odour of boiled cabbage and the scrutiny of the ladies who sat stone-faced at cheap desks on each floor. He cursed. A wall of official taxis were parked in front of him, the drivers asleep behind their wheel or standing in conspiratorial groups. It was impossible to get a cab in Moscow after midday. The driver's quota was fifty roubles a day. When they made that, they stopped. If they made sixty, then this time next year their target would rise to this amount.

Behind the official ranks of tired box-like cars a number of enterprising citizens parked their even more tired Trabants while they pestered the punters for trade. He took one gratefully, but was not impressed with the badly cracked windscreen or the fact that the driver kept switching off the engine at every set of lights.

The meeting had not gone well. He'd been stationed in Moscow for three years and his junior status at the American Embassy did not look as if it was going to improve. The shift of emphasis away from the Soviet bloc and towards the emerging countries had left him largely forgotten. His boss, Morris, was highly respected, but no reflected glory came his way.

He was worried. Golushko had hinted at a conspiracy, a guarded warning ... A group of powerful people in the West ... And here in Moscow ... They were already controlling events of global proportions. Golushko may have been drinking. There was probably nothing to it and he wouldn't mention it to Morris ... He'd think he was mad.

Inevitably the car ran out of petrol. The driver nonchalantly took a piece of tubing from the boot and flagged down one of the few passing motorists.

They moved away from the dignified centre and chugged through a Monument Valley of massive housing blocks. These were not carved by the wind of nature, but the wind of change.

The overall colour was grey, light grey in the sunshine. Although there was plenty of open, flat space, the grass did not come through the hard soil to give a stroke of colour.

These great estates were not depressing, as their western counterparts were. The lack of applied garish colour, wrongly thought to brighten up the grey monoliths in the west, was apparent. A uniformity which brought a different dignity to that of the centre, but dignity there was.

He wouldn't have known, but the ancestral home of Golushko's latest target, a Mr. Morgan, had retained a similar dignity.

The Welsh valleys had that communal colour still, despite being in a phase of transition. A phase forced upon them by a short-sighted national government. The mining valleys of South Wales were steeped in the rich traditions of integrity and social comradeship which were echoed in the homes. Leaning on each other for support, which was given willingly, the houses integrated with the land. The natural stone blocks were carved with a passion born of love for the *precision* of the work and not a chore of necessity. The people of the valley had created a habitat with their bare hands and it was not to be given away lightly.

A generation or two earlier in the Valleys, and the energy of the young

191

would have been directed up and around the surrounding hills. Climbing, tumbling, scuffling, scratching knees, wetting socks; clothes muddied by mine-workings and greened by the sap of the fern. Home to boxed-ears and loving scolds. Hot soup, three days good, the loaf standing bare on the table, its sides providing crusty scoops for the broth. Red-faced, red-eared and tingling. Eyes bright with remembered adventure.

Now the same hills contained different challenges for the youths, but only in that they were free of the dangerous mines and coal and slag. The earth had yielded its black treasure and now the reward was a tree-clad green.

The housing flowed along the bottom of the valley, like lead poured into an olive mould twelve miles long and one mile wide.

The homes in this valley grew together. Long strings of organic houses climbed the steep hillsides and twined around the remains of the mines. Stone-built and naturally coloured they existed in symbiosis with the mountains. There was no tree line, only a house line. It stopped when it was too steep to build, but the community didn't end there. The mountains were still an extension it.

Now that the mines had gone the demarcation was clearer, but the unity was not weaker. The hills were green and clean and the way forward was bright with the sight.

Moscow had not yet gone down this road and the collective will had fragmented with the new freedoms, not coalesced as it had in the valleys. Here, there were no hills to hold the souls in the palms of their hands.

11

Desperate heart

A second wave of food and drink seemed to have hit the plane. Morgan's table was again strewn with fresh debris, the usual drinks and cigarettes. Sheets of paper covered with sketches and notes lay in the mess. Sara was pretending to sleep, but occasionally opened one eye monitoring his progress. He finally put the pen down and leaned back in his seat. She opened both eyes.

'Well done!' She gathered together the sheets and glanced at them. A voice came over the speakers.

'This is your Captain speaking. Please fasten your seat-belts and observe the No-Smoking signs. We will shortly be beginning our descent to London Heathrow. I hope you have all enjoyed your flight.'

'They've gone,' said the glass door and Weller's voice. The door met Weller's shoulder on the way back, but the glass didn't break. Big John's voice did.

'What do you mean, *gone*?'

'Flew out this morning ... there's three of them. They flew to Heathrow from LAX.'

'Three of them?'

'Yep. John Morgan, Sara Beckman, a student, and the busker, Paul Millns.

He's English by the way.'

'When do they touch down?'

'They have' replied Weller.

'Right, get on to Scotland Yard,' John barked. 'You know the form.'

'Yes sir. Shall I issue a warrant?'

'No,' said John, 'not yet ... we've got nothing on him. Just get the guys over there to pull him in, then maybe we'd better get over there and have a chat with him.'

Weller turned and disappeared through the door.

England

England was a sad little country. A sense of order and rightness had disappeared along with the empire. Britain was an island with little or no natural resources. The coalmines had disappeared ... nothing wrong with the coal, just the management's ability to get it out of the ground as cheaply as its competitors. The North Sea oil revenues had been spent as fast as they had come in, and income from farm produce was negligible. The European Community legislators, dominated by the French and Germans, ensured the mainland took almost all the benefits.

An area with no natural resources to exploit can only do one thing ... buy in raw materials and make something with them, selling the product back for a profit. Britain had dismantled its manufacturing base. The heavy industries of steel and coal were almost gone. The car industry was in the hands of foreign owners and shipbuilding had been abandoned.

England was fading fast. The family silver had gone.

It was in the throes of the whirlpool-syndrome, desperately creating new small businesses selling to each other, trying to postpone the inevitable descent down the plug-hole. Hairdressers, financial consultants, commodity brokers, fashion designers, estate agents, stress counsellors and media types, ebbed and eddied and disappeared. Politicians focused on retaining their seat for another five years; once every five years. They did not push for power, just for a safe seat. It mattered not to which party flag-pole they pinned their rhetoric. Personal survival was what it was all about. The opportunities for making money once a seat had been acquired were immense, even for opposition parties.

It usually started by voting themselves a rise, days after winning an election by preaching about the need to draw in our belts. Then, how they would be honoured to humbly serve us. The servants then immediately became the masters. Then came the extra expenses. Then the researcher, long of leg and willing to serve. The directorships came next, together with the consultancies. Those individuals who had been particularly helpful to the party hierarchy were given one or two *quangos* to sit on. These were committees set up by the government to take control over specific areas normally handled by elected local authorities thus effectively bypassing the democratic process.

Even individuals who had lost out at the general election could find recompense and a nice little earner sitting on two or three Quangos.

This 'Trough for the boys' mentality percolated downwards through the population who wore permanent expressions of resignation. The fight had been drained from them. A triple-strata society was now well defined, the upper and lower layers feeding off the filling of the sandwich. Only two sections of the population did well ... the underclass and the overclassed. The middle class supported both these groups, but its contribution was now wearing thin. The society was going into a spiral of depression.

One section of the community who reaped the benefits, and the crates of wrath provided by the hard pressed population, were the pen-pushing yes-men in the utility services. The new patronage had decided that water, electricity, gas and coal were to be privatised and their running costs should no longer be a burden on the state. The responsibility for the work-force also disappeared, along with large chunks of it. All this could be described as good business sense, except for the avarice present in human nature.

The new heads of these private monopolies, who two years earlier were on forty to eighty grand a year, now awarded themselves rises bringing their salaries up to around two hundred thousand a year, plus lucrative share options providing risk-free amounts of loot which were in the region of hundreds of thousands in the first few years. Safe from competition, their only function was to provide their product for the cheapest manufacturing cost and to bring in the maximum amount of money. The only forces against were the ability of the population to pay for these vital services and the embarrassment of the government which occasionally limited the hike in charges. The Soviet model was working well in the UK.

A child of three could not fail to succeed. It was money for very old rope, but shame was not a current currency. If all the freeloading positions in the country were taken up there was always the trough on the mainland. Brussels and Strasbourg provided about a hundred grand a year in salary and expenses to individuals who were particularly useless or completely unknown.

All the lucky recipients had to do was to occasionally sign themselves into sessions of the European Community talking-shop. Nothing else was required or achieved. In Europe at least the inmates had finally got hold of the keys.

In a windy corner of Victoria, on the fifth floor of the New Scotland Yard offices, three men were sitting around a desk.

'The Los Angeles Police want to have a little chat with this character.' The senior officer threw the black and white, electronically composed likeness of John Morgan across the desk. 'They don't want any fuss, he's not been charged with anything, *yet.*'

'What do they want us to do?' enquired one of the others.

'They want us to persuade him to go back home again. Straight away. Firm, but gentle persuasion gentlemen.'

'What's he supposed to have done?' asked the third.

'He seems to have been wandering around Southern California leaving a trail of bodies.'

'Do we issue guns?'

'Definitely not.'

'But if he's dangerous?'

'They're not sure. Just find him and bring him in. This might help.' He put a magazine on the desk. It carried the picture of a man playing a piano. 'Start with this guy. His name is Paul Millns. M I L L N S. He plays the piano ... lives at this address in Putney. This John Morgan will probably be staying with him ... and you may find the girl there too.'

'What about *them?*'

'No, just this John Morgan. He's the only one they're interested in.' They turned and left the room. One, Detective Constable Daley, carrying the magazine. He was reading it as they walked down the corridor.

'What's it say?' inquired Detective Sergeant Regan.

'It's a review of this bloke playing at the Edinburgh Festival. He seems good. I'll ask him for a tape.'

Siemonsen's colleague and close friend walked through the *nothing to declare* section of customs and into the reception hall. The walk up the concourse behind the metal rail in full view of the lines of waiting relatives and friends always made him feel self-conscious. He found himself grinning inanely at the waiting faces. Once he had joined them, he started looking for his driver.

Well back from the crowd and half hidden by a pillar, a tall gentlemen with a black flat chauffeurs cap, dark glasses, black blazer, black trousers and black shoes, was standing holding a small, discreet placard bearing the legend, 'The Virginian.' Clive moved towards him. When he was within thirty feet of him, the man put away the card, turned and walked towards the exit. Clive followed behind, keeping at approximately the same distance. Outside, evening was falling and the temperature was markedly lower than that in the States. The chauffeur opened the rear door. Clive stepped in, putting his brief-case on the seat beside him. The chauffeur slid into the front seat and the black Daimler pulled away smoothly.

Once they had cleared the orange-lit neon tunnel and onto the M4 motorway, Clive spoke.

'Where to this time?'

'Maida Vale, sir.'

Clive thought back, he didn't think he'd been to a safe house in that particular area before. 'New, is it?'

'Afraid so, sir,' said the chauffeur. 'We've had squatters in two of the others.'

Clive was puzzled. 'Surely that's not a problem?'

'It is over here sir. We can get rid of most things, or people, but squatters! I'm afraid they've got better protection than most of the people we've had to deal with. At the end of the day sir, it's too much fuss, too much trouble and eventually, too many questions.'

The car was trapped in the motorway bottleneck at the Chiswick flyover, that valve which held back the eager London bound traffic from the West and Heathrow. The driver glared at the row of orange cones restricting the lanes even further and seemingly for no reason. He was wondering which faceless politician in the Department of Transport had shares in the company which manufactured them.

Clive shrugged his shoulders, sat back and admired the leather seats and walnut inlay. It was one of the things the English still did very well indeed. No American manufacturer could achieve this same sense of sheer class. The Japs had a good stab at it with the Lexus, but screwed it up with the plastic dashboard and if it wasn't plastic, it certainly looked like it. Mercedes got close to it, but would spoil it by ensuring their wood was so perfectly grained and polished it ended up looking like Formica. 'Why did they do it?' He thought. 'People have no sense of what is *right* anymore.'

The Daimler pulled up in the middle of a long elegant row of Victorian, bay-fronted terrace houses. They were about four stories high. The chauffeur opened Clive's door and handed over a key-ring with two keys. 'Main entrance sir and your flat's on the first floor.'

Without saying anything else he jumped back into the car and drove off. Clive looked up at the building and entered the front door.

The apartment was two-bedroomed, spacious and the bay window overlooked the street. A marble fireplace formed a centre piece in the room and was full of dried flowers. The 'fridge was well stocked, the day's papers were laid out on the table and new bedding had been placed on the bed. He opened the drinks-cabinet and made himself a martini, sat back and sipped contentedly.

Sir Anthony placed his coat on the stand, lifted his case and put it on the desk neatly. Picking up the telephone, he dialled an 081 number and waited.

'Hello Mr Trench,' said Sir Anthony, 'lovely day. That little piece of business I mentioned the other day, I do believe it's time we finalised the deal. Yes, the principals will be in town shortly ... I'll be getting word on the venue very soon and I'm looking forward to completion. You'll be working with the Sportsmen. I'll be in touch with you. Bye bye.'

He sipped his tea and grimaced. Picking up a small brass bell, he rang it. The mahogany door opened. 'Ah Doris ... the tea?'

'Sorry, Sir Anthony,' she replied, wiping her hands on her apron, 'I couldn't get no Earl Grey, it's PG Tips.'

'That's quite all right Doris, it really is very pleasant. It's just the shock you see ... to the taste buds.'

'I'll take it away right now Sir,' and she picked up the tray. After she had closed the door carefully behind her, Sir Anthony fished in his briefcase and took out a bottle of Newcastle Brown Ale, put the neck and metallic top against the cast-iron radiator and slapped the top with the palm of his hand. The metal grip-top flew off and tinkled down behind the radiator to join others that had passed that way before. He drank straight from the bottle.

The Tube was packed and the three had been standing for about forty minutes.

'We could have got a cab.' Morgan grumbled at Sara.

'Let's see the colour of your money.' He screwed up his face and said nothing.

'I'm changing at Earls Court and going down to Putney,' Paul said to them. 'I've got plenty of room, come and stay with me.'

'Great, thanks.' Morgan looked relieved.

'No,' cut in Sara, jerking on the end of her strap. 'Look Paul, this guy's in a bit of trouble, I think it's best for everybody if we just split.'

'How do we keep in touch?' Morgan was speaking to Paul.

'Doesn't seem to have been a problem so far.' The train jerked to a halt and the doors hissed open. Paul threw out a large soft holdall and a rucksack.

'This is where I change,' he shouted. He raised his hand to say goodbye, but the doors were closing and his words were lost as they collided together with a thump. He was still standing there with one hand raised in farewell as the train slid off. Morgan turned to her.

'Where to now?'

'We'll get off at Piccadilly.' She was looking at her map, 'And take a cab to Paddington.'

'Paddington?'

'Yes, lots of little cheap hotels around there that don't ask any questions.'

'Know it well?'

'I've been over here a couple of times, but only the usual tourist haunts.'

They got out at Piccadilly and threw their bags on the elevator, leaving just enough room for people to squeeze past. At the top of the first flight Morgan started to stride off towards the second and Sara pulled him back.

'We're going back down again.' Before he had time to argue she had thrown the bags onto the down elevator and he had to jump on after her.

'What are you doing?'

'Shut up,' she responded. When they reached the bottom she repeated the process by going up again. They made this vertical circuit about three or four times. She nudged him in the ribs.

'Do you recognise anybody?'

'What do you mean?'

'Just look at the faces, Morgan. If there was anybody following us we would have picked them up by now.'

'Ah.' Realisation dawned. 'Right. Well, I haven't been looking.'

'I have,' she replied, 'and it's OK.' They eventually left the tube station and caught a cab.

'Haven't been in one of these for years,' he said, sitting back, and gazing out of the window.

'Aren't they wonderful?' Sara was grinning broadly. 'Stability in an ever changing world.'

The cab dropped them at Paddington station and they started to walk the streets, choosing a hotel at random from the multitude available.

Morgan looked around at the faded flowered curtains, the striped bed linen and the polka dot linoleum. The worst of the cracks were covered by a scattering of bare rugs.

'Wherever I lay my hat, that's my home,' he said to himself and crashed on top the bed. Sara sat cross-legged in a corner of the room and shuffled through Morgan's scribblings.

'Do you think we'll catch anything in here?'

She replied without looking up. 'Do you know what rooms cost in this town? Be grateful.' Morgan leapt across towards her, but she shrugged him off. 'Not that grateful. Down boy! I'm trying to make some sense of this.'

Morgan placed his hands behind his head. 'What are we going to do now?'

'Well I know what *I'm* going to do. I'm going out to make some calls and get organised. Some old college friends of mine are based over here and they may be able to make some sense of your doodles.' He sat up and looked up at her. 'They seem vaguely scientific, if you know what I mean.' He shook his head. 'A bit like the experiments we used to set up in physics and chemistry. This thing here,' she pointed to a large vertical cylinder with a dome on it like a giant tube of lipstick. 'What was that made of?'

'God knows,' said Morgan, then, 'It was hard, yes, it was metallic.' She shuffled on in silence making occasional notes. Morgan suddenly sat up again.

'Crack! How about that? Crack! What about a crack factory?'

She looked at him. 'Not exactly Watts.'

'Yes, I know,' Morgan agreed, 'but the sort of money that business brings in could buy that sort of class.'

She looked at him quizzically. 'That's quite a statement coming from somebody who appears to have no idea of what's going on ... You suddenly come out with *crack!*'

'It's something I've been thinking about for a while ... She took a lot of coke. I mean seriously, a *lot* of coke. The jump between coke and crack is nothing ... It makes sense doesn't it? ... That would account for the body count. Some rival dealers may have got it into their heads that I was involved in this. That would fit, wouldn't it?'

She tapped the pen on her teeth, 'Yes, yes that would fit. Maybe you're right.' She looked at her watch. I'm going to get a train to Cambridge. I'll be back last thing tonight. What are *you* going to do?'

He thought for a moment. 'I'm going to the Tate.'

'Are you interested in art?'

'No,' he said, 'that's why I'm going to the Tate.'

She smiled and dragged a holdall from out under the bed. She started throwing some bits into it.

'Keep this week free,' she commanded. 'It's the Queen's birthday in a few days, one of them anyway'

'I haven't got a thing to wear.'

Ignoring this she slapped a coloured leaflet on the bed next to him. 'Trooping of the Colour!' Morgan rolled his eyes upwards. 'You'll like it,' she insisted, 'when in Rome ...'

'But it's not the Romans who do it,' bleated Morgan. 'It's everybody else, tourists, visitors ...'

'And people like us,' she replied chirpily. She snapped her bag shut and reached for the door. She stopped, dug into a pocket and threw fifty pounds in English notes on the bed. 'Hang on to that.'

'Thanks.'

'There's an off-licence on the corner.' She gave him a quick and reassuring smile, waved, and was gone.

The doorbell chimed and then the knocker. It was an impatient rap. Paul stepped over the bicycle in the hall and opened the door.

'Mr Millns? ... Mr Paul Millns? Police. I am Detective Sergeant Regan and this is Detective Constable Daley.' Identification was proffered.

'Can I help you?' said Paul. 'If it's about the car-tax I've been away for a few months.'

'May we come in, sir?' Paul shrugged and led them through to the living-room. One sat on the piano stool, the other paced the room. Paul couldn't remember which was which.

'I'm just finishing my supper,' said Paul, attacking an egg and two slices of toast.

'We have reason to believe,' said Regan, 'that a Mr Morgan, Mr John Morgan is staying here with you.'

'No.' Paul said.

'Mind if we look around sir.' Daley was cheerful.

'Carry on.' Paul waved his fork in the general direction of the staircase. Daley disappeared, Regan kept on talking.

'Do you know this man, sir?'

'Yes I do.' Paul was chomping away.

'Look sir,' said the standing Regan, leaning into Paul's space. 'This could take all night, and I haven't got all night.'

Paul looked at him, 'What do you want to know?'

'You flew over with him from the States this morning. You travelled into London with him. You are sitting here now.' He leaned closer. 'Do you know where he is ?'

'No'

The detective stretched himself high and sighed. He pulled up a chair and sat next to Paul.

'Tea?' offered Paul.

'No thanks son. Look, it's very important we find this man. Have you any idea where he is? A 'phone number, an address, who he's with?'

'He'll probably be with Sara,' said Paul.

'Sara who?'

'Don't know, I never knew her surname.'

'Well, do you know where they are?'

Paul put the fork down. 'All I know is ... that they're probably still in London, but that's by no means certain. I knew them for a few days in the States, I flew over with them. I left them in the middle of London on a tube train and that's it.'

Daley had come back down the stairs. 'Nothing sir.'

'Did they mention any hotel to you?' said Regan, leaning back. 'Did they mention any other names. Did they talk about going to other countries, other towns, other cities, anything?'

Paul thought for a while. 'The girl said she was going on to Europe at some point. He just didn't seem to know what he was doing.'

'A bit like us really sir.' Daley had just come down the stairs, two albums under his arm. He stopped smiling when he saw the look on his superior's face. The man in the chair pulled out a card and placed it on the table.

'That's my name and number. If either of those two get in touch with you find out where they are and let me know immediately.' He leaned forward, his face two inches away from Paul's. 'It is very, very important,' he said slowly.'

'I've got the message.'

Daley hung back as Regan left the room. 'Can't spare these can you?' he said to Paul.

'You can have *one*.'

'Thanks ...' He handed Paul a pen. 'Can you make it out to Terry?'

The two detectives stopped outside the house, watching the door slam.

'Right,' said Regan. 'Talk to all the neighbours. Ask them who and what they've seen today. Tell them all to ring us as soon as they see anybody arrive. Did you check the garden?'

'Yes, sir.'

'Get somebody watching this door round the clock for the next twenty-four hours. And get somebody on the back too.'

Daley scratched his head. 'We can't do that. We just don't have the man-power.'

Regan thought, mumbled under this breath and then said, 'All right. Put one on it for the next twelve hours and get him to alternate back and front.'

'Right sir.' They got into their Cavalier and drove off.

Cambridge England

The train journey had been longer than advertised and her back was aching from sitting upright in the economically designed seats. The jumble of London had been relieved by the green, flat orderliness of the Cambridgeshire countryside.

Matt had offered to meet her at the station, but she preferred to walk and take in the feel of the town.

The last time she had seen him was up at Stanford where he was working with the linear accelerator. This was housed in a grey single-storey building built in a wooded valley. It was two miles long. Along a narrow tube protected within it, electrons were shot at the speed of light to smash into atoms and fragment. The resulting particles from the collisions were measured and thus more and more was being discovered about less and less.

She remembered his devotion to the work. The eighteen-hour working day, the nights spent waiting for him and the comforting arm of their flatmate.

She remembered the leaving, the letter of explanation, the little presents, the leather-bound diary - and the chained crucifix gleaming coldly in silver.

The divorce rate in Santa Clara County was higher than the marriage rate. All their friends were on methamphetamine, and the days sped by. She reached his place and walked straight in.

'Sara!' The young man sprang up from the sofa and gave her a hug. 'It's wonderful to see you.' He held her away from him. 'It's been a long time.'

Sara smiled. 'Five years?'

'As long as that? Sit down and tell me everything you've been up to.' He patted the sofa.

Outside the window willow trees dipped their fingers in the River Cam and the reflected sunlight from the water danced crazily on the ceilings and walls.

'I've come to talk about *you*,' she said. '*I've* done nothing.' She sat down. 'I'm still the eternal student, although I work part-time for a couple of publishing houses. I'm going on through Europe and when I've written up my research I'll get my doctorate.'

'And then?'

'I may stick with publishing, or I'll probably teach.'

'So you are going to feed your knowledge back into the system instead of using it?'

'It's a dirty job, but somebody's got to do it.'

'I must admit I nearly went that route myself, but the offer here was too good. My own labs, my own technicians and a relatively free hand. My name appears at the top of all papers and,' tapping his nose, 'a percentage of all consultancy fees and royalties from the manufacturers of products that are spin-offs from my research.'

'You always were a true capitalist.'

'And quite right too. Have a scone ... Tea?'

'Thank you,' and then, eyes looking around the room, 'I don't suppose you've got anything stronger?'

He turned sharply, 'You? Seeking out alcohol?'

'And what the hell's wrong with that?'

'Nothing, nothing at all.' He put the pot of tea down. 'But you were always so, so,' she looked at him, '*prim*, I suppose. I don't believe I ever saw you take a drink.'

She stood up and looked through the leaded windows at the water, 'It seems such a long time ago.' Outside on the bank, a swan was hissing at an angler who had strayed too close. She spread her wings and hissed again, protecting her growing youngsters.

She turned around and said laughing, 'I suppose I've been corrupted in recent years.'

He was already pouring a sherry. Stopped when he saw the look on her face and looked for a larger glass. She had half of it down her when he spoke again.

'So what do you want of me my dear?' She put the glass down and extracted an envelope from her bag. She laid out four or five sheets of white paper with black scribblings.

'You can tell me what *this* is,' giving a precise account of how the sketches were arrived at. He looked at them for ten minutes.

'Look Sara, my bag's chemistry ... mainly. I think a physicist should take a look at this. There is something familiar about certain items, but for the life of me I can't think why. Can you leave it with me for a couple of days and I'll give you a ring. Are you staying in Cambridge?'

'No,' Sara replied, 'I'm afraid I have to get back to London.'

'Do you have a number?'

'No. I'll ring you.'

'You can, at least, stay for dinner.'

She stretched and arched her back in feline fashion. 'That'll be nice.'

He stood up and fixed her eyes with his. 'I was rather hoping that it would be a little more than nice.'

'It's too late baby, it's too late'

'But didn't we nearly make it.' he replied.

'Yes,' she said wistfully, fingering the crucifix under her blouse 'we nearly did.'

She hadn't been out of his sight since they'd met. He found the space and the silence more than disquieting ... He was suddenly lonely. He hadn't realised what effect she'd had on him. He didn't want to admit that he needed her ... He refused to believe that.

Morgan lit a cigarette and pulled the tape from his jacket. He had packed the cassette recorder and an international adapter. Once he had fixed it up, he inserted the tape and looked out of the window.

Desperate heart, left stranded in the dark.

Desperate heart, 'bin falling from the start.

I know your story very well,

there's nothing you can tell That I don't know

Desperate heart, when love has flown away

Desperate heart, no resting place to stay.

It leaves a bitter price to pay

There's nothing you can say that I don't know

And when no lover wants your body any more

And the nights pile up like leaves outside your door

Even the flowers on your curtains

Weep sad tears of silk
And your life's like shattered petals on the floor
Desperate heart, far out on stormy seas
Desperate heart, no shores to bring relief
I know your story very well, there's nothing you can tell
That I don't know

When the track had finished, he left. He walked out into the small square and along the faded stuccoed buildings, each one of them bearing a neon hotel sign. A large number of the owners used to be Welsh, Paddington being the main receiving station from that annexed country, but most had now been taken over by owners of Mediterranean extraction. They played host to their transient occupants of backpackers and hookers. He strolled along happily, enjoying the sense of freedom that three thousand miles of water brought to him. He felt he had tied his troubles up in a neat package and left it on the banks of the river. Having swum the river and walked away on the opposite bank he had effectively ended them. He had not opposed his sea of troubles, he had just walked away from them. At the back of his mind he knew he would have to go back for them.

He decided to keep moving. He couldn't function when she wasn't with him, but he hadn't got around to admitting this to himself.

The gentlemen from Calcutta who owned the off-licence had pointed him in the direction of Hyde Park. With a bottle of Bushmills deeply snug in the pocket of his leather jacket he strolled down the Edgware Road. He amused himself for twenty minutes exchanging insults with the speakers on Hyde Park Corner and sauntered into the park.

The sunlight bounced hard off the Serpentine and the grass was pale with the heat. He lay his long frame down and unscrewed the top of the bottle. His tan and what was left of his physique was attracting the occasional appreciative glance from the English roses scattered along the banks of the lake. He stretched out and drank a little. Life was good. He was doing fine without her. He looked at his watch; she'd been gone three hours.

He wondered what time Sara would return. He was feeling randy. The sun and the alcohol usually did that to him. He spent a lazy hour there and started back.

Up ahead, on a piece of the park opposite the Hilton, two formations of young men were facing up to each other. He could just make out figures running in various directions, others blocking ... shouts and whistles and the brown, lemon-shaped missile flying through the air. His grin widened as he drew nearer.

The NFL was being broadcast over in England and had rapidly achieved a small, but fanatical following. 'Nice to see the old country has seen the light at last,' he thought. As he drew nearer, the ball was punted very high and towards his right. He ran instinctively, covering a lot of ground in a short time. He didn't take his eye of the ball and caught it easily. A ripple of applause broke out from amongst the players training and a number of the people sitting around watching. He grinned self-consciously and flicked the ball with very little shoulder movement about forty yards. It flew like a bullet on a low trajectory, eventually spearing the hapless individual who tried to catch it, knocking him over. The applause this time was replaced by a gasp and a whistle.

A large sweaty individual in trainers ran over to him. He spoke with an American accent.

'Gee fella, who the hell are you?'

Morgan looked down sheepishly. 'The name's Morgan.'

The large man was more than slightly overweight and red-faced. He was puffing heavily. 'Done this before, ain't ya boy?'

'Just a bit.'

The man was looking hard at him now. 'It's John Morgan, isn't it? You're still in good shape. I'm Ben Jacobs, I seen you play in Pasadena ...'

Morgan tried to wave goodbye, but his arm was held. 'I train these guys. There are a few clubs like us that just play for a bit of fun, nothing serious. Are you just visiting Mr Morgan ... Are you passing through? Or are you going to be around for a while? I mean ... err; we could do with a bit of help.'

Morgan put his hands up. 'No ... no, no, I'm strictly passing through.'

Morgan got his arm back and trotted off with a wave.

'Careful how you go now son.' Morgan heard his voice in the distance. 'Hey fellas, guess who that was?'

'Guess who that was?' reflected Morgan. 'Yeah right. I told you when I came I was a stranger.'

'What do you make of that, Mr Trench?' The large man in the shiny suit and a neck like a bull looked as if he'd been sparring with the wrong guys. He looked down on, but deferred to, a figure incongruously dressed in a trench coat and brown trilby hat. Trench's pinched face twisted under its small brown moustache.

'Got a good right arm.' Trench replied.

'I'll take great pleasure in breaking it for 'im,' said the large man.

'No you won't,' Trench was firm, 'we wait for orders. There's something special lined up for *him*.'

They walked on after Morgan, increasing their stride length to catch up.

'I can take him any time, Mr Trench.'

'Think so?'

A shadow of doubt crossed the big man's face. 'Well, I think I'll get Ron in on it, just for insurance, know what I mean?'

'You'll do nothing, Reggie 'till I give the word, got it?'

'Sure boss.'

Morgan was concentrating on one point, a small crack in the ceiling. He wasn't succeeding and the room kept spinning. He fought it, holding the crack in focus as long as he could, but failing in the end. His drinking was getting heavier and the bouts increasing in frequency.

Morgan was losing his grip. The swagger had gone. His shoulders sagged, He did not make eye-contact unless absolutely necessary. The tan was turning grey and stubble appeared along the jaw line. Morgan forced himself off the bed and lifted the cheap kettle sitting on the floor. It had enough water to make coffee.

He flicked a switch and shuffled off to find a cup. She had been away for two days and it had done him no good. He rummaged in her carrier bag of shopping which had not yet been emptied and found a jar of brown granules. The pain in his head was banging on his skull to get out. He broke the seal with his finger and thrust his nose in the jar and breathed in deeply.

The kettle was boiling, He tipped a mound of coffee into a mug and threw in the water. A carton of milk was to hand, but he could find no sugar. He sipped the hot brew anyway; it helped. 'Got to have some sugar.' He was speaking to the four walls. He looked through all the drawers, searching for the packets of sugar she always pocketed at cafes. He was starting to hate himself. He was fighting to regain control of his senses. He opened drawers, scrabbled and slammed them. He opened the wardrobe doors and went through her pockets.

His eyes settled on her carrying-case. He vaguely thought it was strange that she hadn't taken it with her. He threw it on the bed and unzipped it. Fumbling with the zips on the smaller side pockets like a nervous virgin ... no small brown paper packets here.

His fingers found a blue book. 'The Study of Man - Rudolf Steiner.' He flicked the pages absently and returned it. He dived in again. The main body of the case was packed with brown envelopes and he felt along the bottom. Nothing. He pulled some of the large brown envelopes out to create more space ... still nothing. One of the envelopes was open at the top and he could see it contained a wedge of closely typed A4 paper.

If he had been sober he wouldn't have done it, or perhaps he would, but curiosity had got the better of him. He took out the paper and started to scan it. The typed papers seemed to be personal notes, each paragraph having a reference date and number of the file from which it was taken.

Most of the references were dates from the eighties. There looked to be about twenty-five different sections, the majority of which were dated over a two year period between 1986 and 1988. Something was still hammering on the inside of his skull. He put the type-written sheets on the bed and dived back into her bag where other envelopes contained photographs of individuals, hand-written notes paper-clipped to the back of them. Morgan propped two pillows against the bed-head. He took one of her stockings from the bottom of the wardrobe and tied it around his throbbing head, securing it with a tight knot.

The pressure created was almost as good as someone massaging his temples. He lay back and forced himself to concentrate on her text.

Names, dates and coroners verdicts swam in front of his eyes. Between the type-written sheets was a mass of scribbled scraps of paper, these occasionally contained the names of people in the first set of references, officers involved in the cases, coroners' names, cross references, 'phone numbers, names of press reporters and researchers.

These were liberally interspersed with bracketed references beginning with PENT. The names GEC, Marconi and Ferranti, cropped up at regular intervals, and the word STARWARS appeared seven or eight times, as did SDI. He was losing track; he couldn't focus. He lit another cigarette and stalked the room. He dived back in.

Marconi Underwater Systems, Croxley Green, Watford. Computer Software (Guidance System) Tigerfish Torpedo

Dead under Clifton Suspension Bridge, Bristol. August 1986. Verdict open.

He took some time to find her notes on this, then he saw it, Vimal Dajivhai, 24, alcoholic poisoning - witness H. Shah. Claims he was a non-drinker - police forgo forensic on his car.

Marconi Defence Systems, Stanmore. October 1986.

Death in car, verdict suicide.

He again flicked through her rough notes and found

Ashad Sharif, 26. Tied rope to tree, other end around neck, drove off. Depressed over woman? (met Eric Deakins MP on same day re VISA for girlfriend - no particular problem).

ROYAL MILITARY COLLEGE OF SCIENCE

Shrivenham, Oxfordshire.

Dead under car, verdict open.

He was having difficulty in reading her notes now; he must get out and get some air.

Peter Peapell, 46 (top classification - no information available).

Found in his garage under the car, engine running, door closed, carbon dioxide poisoning.

In a different coloured pen, she had written. 'Been to dinner party with wife, put the car away in garage. She fell asleep, didn't find him until the following morning, no reason for suicide.'

MARCONI, Leicester

Dead in car, pipe from exhaust. Verdict, suicide.

Her notes referred to a MOD contract for flight simulation (lost). She had written in red ink ...' Probably suicide.'

MARCONI (Easams - subsidiary)

Drove into wall, 1987, verdict open.

Her notes were headed 'Satellite project.'

Drove car into disused cafe in Hampshire, very happy, no reason for suicide. Car loaded with two petrol cans causing it to explode.

All these references seemed to be related to inquests in England. What sort of research was this girl up to? Morgan went through the rest of her bag, finding other envelopes with similar type-written pages and hand-written notes. There were press cuttings from various parts of the world, photocopies of faxes, the headings having been torn off, but it was the hand-written pages that he found the most interesting. They were also the hardest to read, especially in his state. He gave up at that point, eased himself off the bed and left the room, locking it carefully after him.

It was good to get outside. His head was clearing and the evening air was sharp. He walked along Praed Street and passed the assortment of brightly lit, delightfully grubby little shops. The fast-food places were still open catering for the local community and passengers from all points west of London.

He found a shop selling candy, postcards and gifts; it also sold what he was looking for... a small pack of coloured crayons. He pocketed them, then entered the nearest pub for a pint or two of English beer.

An hour later Morgan was sifting through her notes, coloured pencils scattered across the bed. He was underlining various sections in a variety of colours, co-ordinating dates, times, personnel and incidents. He was gradually making sense of it.

PLESSEY DEFENCE SYSTEMS August 1988

Software

Verdict open

Morgan was working with a plain sheet of paper. This was his first entry. He brought her scattered notes together. He wrote ...

Naval systems - dead in garden shed - electric wires around his body connected to mains supply -rag / handkerchief stuffed in mouth - fuse bypassed with paperclip.

Underneath Morgan wrote ...

MARCONI - John Ferry 60 (defence systems) -electrocuted (electric leads in mouth).

Underneath he wrote ... Beckham. August Bank Holiday (Sunday) Ferry died previous Sunday.

Both open verdicts.

Both same coroner - Michael Burgess, Surrey.

After an hour, Morgan had distilled the information down to a simplicity with which his brain could cope ...

British Aerospace - Sept 88, engineering, tube from exhaust. Suicide.

Plessey Defence Systems. Aug 88. A. Beckham. Electrocuted, - open.

Marconi. Aug 88. J. Ferry. Communications. Electrocuted, -open

Marconi Space and Defence Systems. March 88. Tube from car exhaust. T. Knight. - suicide.

Atomic Energy Research Establishment (Harwell). Jan 88. R. Smith. Fell over cliff. (Cornwall), - suicide.

Plessey. June 87. Electronic weapons. F. Jennings. - no inquest.

Plessey. May 87. M. Baker.

Digital communications. Car crash. (Dorset), - misadventure.

Bristol Poly. G. Koutis. April 87. Systems Analyst. Drowned in crashed car. (Liverpool), - misadventure.

Military College of Science. S. Gooding. Research. April 87. Car crash (Cyprus). - accident.

Marconi. D. Sands. Satellite projects. Car crash. - open.

Marconi. E. Skeels. Tube from exhaust. Feb 87. -suicide.

Military College of Science. P. Peapell. (Classified work). Feb 87. Exhaust fumes. - open.

Marconi Systems. Feb 87. T. Moore. Overdose, - suicide.

Military College of Science. Jan 87. J. Brittan. Exhaust fumes. - accident.

MoD. (Computers). Jan 87. Head and feet tied together, plastic bag over head. - accident.

MoD. M. Wisner. (Software Convert Aircraft). Plastic bag over head. Dec 86 - accident.

Marconi Defence Systems. Oct 86. A. Sharif. (Computers). Neck tied to tree, drove car. - suicide.

Marconi. V. Dajibha. (Software). Found dead, drink? Aug 86. -open.

Marconi. J. Wash. (Communications). Nov 85. Fall from hotel room. - still awaiting verdict.

Marconi. R. Hill. (Radar). Shotgun. March 85. - suicide.

Military College of Science. April 83. A. Godley. Vanished. - presumed dead...

Morgan gazed at this list and then at the ceiling. A number of other cases in England could have been put on this list,but these were the cases to which she had always referred in red ink. She had also made notes on both the type-written pages and her hand-written ones in green ink, but these seem to refer to another set of documents that were nowhere to be found.

They seemed to refer to similar incidents in the States. Taken individually, these were examples of personal and family tragedies and of little interest to people outside a close circle of friends. Taken together, however, the similarities in fields of work and projects, together with the recurrence of the same few company names, spelled out a more sinister connection. In Sara's notes he found confirmation that at least some of these scientists were working on the American SDI or Starwars project; or software and systems related to it.

Strange kind of research work, he thought. This wasn't so much European History as European Mystery and what tutor set her off on this course? It was certainly modern history, but modern-mystery may have been a better title for this work.

Cambridge England

'Making a fission weapon is simple.' Dr Weinstein sipped his coffee and leaned back into the deep corduroy armchair with a contented and self-satisfied smile on his lips.

He was known to his students, for obvious reasons, as 'Winestain,' but always with affection. 'One just has to create a supercritical mass of fissile material and a chain reaction will grow rapidly as each generation of neutrons generates more and more additional fission.'

'Easy,' said Sara, drawing on her cigarette, 'Just tell me how.'

Two sub-critical lumps have to be brought together very quickly. Too slow, and the initial energy released will force the lumps apart and the reaction will cease.

The most common method is the Gun which fires a uranium-235 bullet into a target of identical material. If one can hold the exploding mass together for an instant then the chain reaction will begin. A steel container would do the trick. We call it a tamper. It destroyed Hiroshima, but was not particularly efficient. The total weight was nine thousand pounds, but it only contained one hundred and five pounds of uranium.

This was about seventy percent enriched with U-235, but only about two pounds actually underwent fission.

The main problem with this type of bomb is finding enough enriched uranium, it's so inefficient you see.'

'I do understand,' said Sara in her most comforting manner. 'It must be quite disconcerting.'

'Quite.' He was warming to his theme now. 'The size of the uranium ball would be approximately the size of an orange.' She sneaked an involuntary glance at the fruit bowl.

'Of course the big danger in using this type of device is the fact that it could go off before you want it to.'

'I can see that would be a problem.' Sara agreed

'Pre-ignition is the thing to avoid.'

'Like the plague.' She nodded her head in vigorous agreement.

'It can be caused by stray neutrons you see, from cosmic rays or even spontaneous fission. Getting the thing to go off when one wants it to is a case of precise timing. Not enough neutrons ... damp squib. Too many, too early ... nasty shock although the final bang will be much reduced.

Uranium is not really a problem as its available neutrons are relatively few, but plutonium on the other hand needs careful handling. In a fission reactor the plutonium is a mix of Pu-239 and smaller quantities of Pu-240. The trouble is Pu-240 undergoes spontaneous fission at the drop of a hat.

We have to assemble a critical mass much faster than in a gun-type bomb. Almost every nuclear weapon around today uses the implosion technique. Instead of firing one piece into another, we surround the plutonium with explosive ... plastic's fine ... and when fired, this compresses the core making the mass supercritical and off she goes. It must be compressed uniformly and the only way to do this is to have a spherical core of the sensitive fissile material and an outer spherical coat of the plastic.'

'Like a condom I suppose,' she said. He missed this remark.

'The recent generation of bombs are very reliable and much more efficient.'

'That's nice.'

'They have an initiator to supply extra neutrons at the precise moment of detonation.'

'What's the difference between fission and fusion?'

'The former breaks up the nucleus of the atom, and the latter merges nuclei. The fusion of light nuclei at high temperatures produces heavier nuclei and energy ... that's the bang of course.'

He sipped his wine, but it didn't stop the flow. 'A deuterium-tritium fusion reaction produces helium, energy and a neutron ... and these neutrons can sustain a fission reaction. In a fusion boosted fission weapon, a small quantity of deuterium-tritium mixture at the centre of the imploding plutonium reaches such a high temperature that it undergoes fusion.

The neutrons released help a more complete fission process and we get more bang for our bucks. We get a thirty percent utilization of the plutonium, whereas the Hiroshima bomb used only one percent. Fission-fusion hybrid bombs ... that's the future.'

'Can't see how we ever lived without it.' Sara agreed. 'Didn't we have a problem with tritium production in the States?'

'No problem producing it, just cutting through the red tape and politics. The wimps would like all nuclear activity to cease. That's like asking the citizens of L.A. to park their cars and walk. There was a lot of talk about being politically correct whereas most of our Presidents would rather have been politically *erect*.'

'Why do we need so much? If we're limiting our nuclear arsenal ... and so is everyone else, haven't we got enough?'

'Small problem ... Tritium has a half-life of twelve years, which means the tritium in our bombs must be replaced every few years. We need a steady supply. Tritium is a radioactive isotope of hydrogen and occurs naturally in very small quantities. It boosts the warhead's explosive power and just a few grams of it is needed. Reagan ordered the Nuclear Regulatory Commission to draw up plans for seizing civilian nuclear power plants to produce Tritium in the event of a national security emergency. He was that worried.'

The silver hair caught the light as he leaned forward to replenish both their glasses. 'It's produced easily in nuclear reactors by bombarding lithium with neutrons. Most of it in the States is produced at the Savannah River nuclear facility in South Carolina, but the reactors were shut down for safety reasons in the late eighties. They're still not fully back on stream.'

'Isn't this a good opportunity to stop?'

'Some people think that twelve years is a good time scale for global nuclear disarmament ... yes'

'Is it feasible?'

'The answer my dear is pissing in the wind.'

They both looked up as Matt joined them. 'Is he being of any use to you Sara?' Matt slid easily into the empty chair next to her and poured a glass for himself.

'I don't know yet,' she replied. 'I don't know where this conversation's going.' Weinstein was about to open his mouth again when she jumped in.

'What sort of damage could this bomb cause and over what area?'

'What bomb? I meant no bomb. I was only posing a little academic accounting, I mean theory.'

'Worlds are destroyed by such theories.'

He put down his wine. 'Shall we take something stronger? ... It all depends on what sort of bomb we are talking about. I've covered two major types, but there are one or two more'

There are fusion weapons which use a fission bomb to instigate a thermonuclear fusion. It's complicated, because blowing up a fission bomb in the middle of fusion fuel would just disperse it. We have to separate the fission and fusion elements physically. X-ray and gamma-ray energy, which travels from the fission explosion at the speed of light, could then ignite fusion before the slower moving fission blast arrives.

Therefore we have a fission trigger which is a fusion-boosted, fission bomb... which is about the size of a football. This alone is about the size of the Hiroshima bomb. When it explodes, it sets off the little goody adjacent to it.'

He took a large gulp of the single malt Matt had got from the bar. 'This consists of a U-238 tamper surrounding a cylinder of solid lithium deuteride, and that in turn surrounds a rod of plutonium or uranium 235. The two separate bombs are kept apart by a plastic foam which compresses this second structure initiating a fission chain reaction.

Neutrons from this reaction convert lithium to tritium in the lithium deuteride fusion fuel, then ... the high temperature from the fission ignites the deuterium tritium fusion. The neutrons produced convert more lithium to tritium and D/T fusion engulfs the mass of fusion fuel ... But, the bang isn't over yet.' He looked around for another drink.

'High energy neutrons from D/T fusion now induce fission in the surrounding U- 238 tamper.

This hydrogen bomb is really a fission-fusion-fission bomb. Fission initiates fusion, and fusion-produced neutrons cause additional fission ... Does that clarify the situation?'

Sara put down her glass and looked up. 'Have you heard the one about In and Out ?'

'Pardon?'

'Never mind.'

'These bombs, can be designer bombs in that we can make them "Dirty" by incorporating materials that become highly radioactive when they absorb neutrons. This would produce an abundance of lethal fallout. By replacing the U- 238 tamper with a non-fissionable material we can produce a "Clean" bomb.

The neutron bomb, or enhanced-radiation weapon, is a thermonuclear device designed to minimise the blast and maximise the lethal effects of high energy neutrons produced in fission.

We can have variable yield by turning a dial on the weapon, a bit like setting the oven for a roast.'

He finished the drink, and Matt was on his way to the bar again. 'Third-generation bombs include enhanced-radiation devices aimed at destroying electronic systems in attacking missiles or aircraft, and nuclear powered X-ray lasers for missile defence.

The new generation of weapons can wipe out an area the size of our largest cities in one hit, and their effects would be felt over a hundred mile radius.'

'How big would these bombs be?' Sara swallowed the last of her wine.

'About the size of the vessels in these sketches ... and identical in shape.'

There was silence for three seconds, then Sara's drink slipped from her fingers, the glass shattering on the black lacquer table.

Weinstein and Matt cleared up the fragments. Sara sucked the blood off her finger.

When they had settled, Weinstein resumed. 'It's the two shapes together you see ... that's what triggered my thought process. It looks as if they had a basic Gun device in place and are replacing it with a thermonuclear device. See here ... This thing like a yard of ale, the long tube with a ball on the end ...That's the classic Gun configuration. And this ... this cylinder with a domed end. That's the big one.'

Outside, the river Cam flowed thoughtfully, soaking up the knowledge that centuries of learning had deposited on its banks. The holy trinity strolled in the June sunshine and reflected, along with the surface of the water.

Weinstein's face had taken on the pallor of yellow sandstone. The fourth malt had probably done it. He wasn't looking at the others as he talked. 'Decades of neglect have seen the virtual collapse of the entire US nuclear weapons' industry ... The Rocky Flats plant near Denver has been closed pending numerous safety and environmental improvements ... Rocky Flats was the sole manufacturer of plutonium triggers for thermonuclear weapons.

We used to produce five warheads a day ... now there's a lack of a permanent repository for the plutonium waste ... now that the reactor at Hanford, Washington has been closed ... and that's since 1987... It was too similar to the Chernobyl reactor. Fernald, Ohio was another to be closed, the State sued for violation of its clean air act, and of course, the vamp from Savannah.

The nuclear weapons business is spread over thirteen states and involves research labs, uranium enrichment and fuel-processing plants, reactors for the production of nuclear materials and factories manufacturing parts for weapons, a final assembly-plant and a test-site ... and do you know ... they're all hanging around waiting for some sort of direction ... people in the industry don't know what the hell's going on ...

The facilities are operated by well-known corporations under government contract. General Electric, Westinghouse, AT and T ... and even the University of California.'

'Seems like a lot of people are tied up in this business?' Sara stared down at the towpath.

'The industry employs a hundred thousand people,' Weinstein replied, 'and has an annual budget of ten billion dollars. The government agency overseeing this is not the Department of Defence, but the Department of Energy. Only when the weapons leave the final assembly plant are they turned over to the DOD.

In 1984 a federal judge ruled that nuclear weapons' plants must comply with federal anti-pollution laws and that, effectively, was the death knell for the industry... it's dying slowly.'

'Yes, it has that effect,' she said quietly.

'Sorry? ... Think you said effects?' said Weinstein, and carried on. 'The immediate effect of a nuclear explosion is an intense burst of radiation, primarily gamma rays and neutrons. This direct radiation is produced in the nuclear reactions themselves and lasts well under a second. It extends for a mile from a ten kiloton explosion. With most weapons this direct radiation is of little significance because other lethal effects encompass greater distances. The exception is the neutron bomb.'

'I've got to get back to London.' Interrupted Sara, 'When's the next train?' The other two appeared not to have heard.

'In microseconds the vaporisation forms a gas hotter than the Sun's twenty-million degree core ... this hot gas radiates away its energy in the form of X-rays which quickly heat the surrounding air. It could turn all the sand in the California deserts to glass.'

Matt was listening with intent and Sara was looking at her watch. Weinstein was becoming agitated; there was that gleam in the eye.

'A fireball of superheated air forms and grows rapidly ...Ten seconds after a one megaton explosion the fireball is one mile in diameter and glows visibly from its own heat and is many times brighter than the Sun ... the heat is radiated as a thermal flash ... it lasts for many seconds and accounts for one third of the weapon's explosive energy. It can cause severe burns on exposed flesh twenty miles away. The rapidly expanding fireball pushes into the surrounding air and creates a blast wave moving initially at ... at well, thousands of miles per hour ... It's man's ultimate miracle!'

'I think there's a train at three' said Sara.

'Don't worry,' said Matt. 'It doesn't usually leave on time.'

When Sara arrived at the station she walked straight past it. She had decided that going back to London was not a good idea. She wanted time to think. She had to contact someone urgently and with Morgan around that would not have been possible.

12

Rescue operation

Clive was a small man with rounded cherubic features and a sweet mouth. Unfortunately, the eyes were dark, small and hard. He softened these with just the slightest touch of make-up, softly brushed up into the eyebrows and away to the sides. He had spent the last of the afternoon in the Bond Street area and had returned to his apartment kitted out in Aquascutum and Gieves & Hawkes. The visit to the latter at Number One Savile Row had produced the country version of the English gentleman. Aquascutum had provided him with the stronger, sharper image.

When he stepped from the black taxi into Brewer Street, the long dark slim- cut blazer, grey flannel trousers and black shoes gave his figure a slightly more athletic appearance. These dark colours were offset by the pink and white striped shirt, pink carnation and an old school tie; he wasn't sure which school. He walked to the entrance of Madam JoJo's, the black of the evening broken violently by the neon signs of that establishment and others in its vicinity.

This was the heart of London's Soho, once the naughty red-light district, but now those delights appeared tired and tawdry, being replaced, generally, by a return to a village community led by specialist delicatessens, patisseries, wine shops and cafe-bars supporting the media industry.

The faint odour of refuse that used to predominate in the area had been replaced in recent years by the smell of pasta sauces and freshly ground coffee. This area of Brewer Street represented the last quaint reference to its less salubrious past.

JoJo's catered for transvestites, trans-sexuals, gays and a smattering of straights. Clive nodded at the doorman and descended the red-lit staircase into the red-lit room.

'Ullo Dad.'

'Ullo Lizzie luv,' said Tony, without stirring from his chair or putting down his paper. Lizzie, a good looking girl of about nineteen, with bubbly blond hair and a large chest, bounced through the living room, dropping two shopping bags in the middle of it as she went and pounded up the staircase.

'An' take those bags with you.' shouted Tony's wife from the kitchen, without looking up from her pastry board.

'I'm in a 'nurry Mum,' came the voice from above. Bedroom and bathroom doors slammed alternately.

Tony looked up. 'Bloody teenagers,' he spoke in the direction of the kitchen. 'Good thing we've only got the one, eh Mum?' But his eyes smiled as he said it.

'At least she gives us no trouble Dad,' said the voice from the kitchen, accompanied by the sound of freshly rolled pastry being slapped on wood.

'Naw, she's a pretty good 'un that.'

Wet hair appeared above the staircase, followed by an upside down face. 'Where's the towels Mum?'

'Why? where you going?' Tony answered the question with a question. Mum ignored the voice.

'Where's the towels?'

'Airing-cupboard luv,' came the voice from the kitchen, 'where they always are.' The face and hair disappeared and the feet pounded up the remainder of the stairs. Tony carried on reading. Five minutes later the feet came pounding down again and Lizzie disappeared into the kitchen where the sound of a hairdryer now formed a duet with that of a boiling kettle.

'Mind that ironing board, girl!' Shouted Mum.

'Got to get a sandwich, I'm late now.'

'You're not working tonight?' Shouted Tony through the door.

'Naw Dad, jus' goin' out with the girls. 'Though they may want me for an hour or so if they're busy.'

Tony shook his head and carried on reading. The hairdryer stopped and Lizzie bounded into the living- room and up the stairs, a sandwich stuffed into her mouth and crumbs trailing her.

'I don't know' said his wife. 'I don't know what gets into them ... rushing here, rushing there.'

'Without ever doing anything when they get there,' said Tony. 'At least when I put in a day's work I get things done.'

'I know luv,' said his wife. 'You got any more nights coming up this week?'

'Dunno, have to ring the Guv'nor. They're having a bit of trouble with their daughter-in-law now.'

'What sort of trouble?' said the shadow behind the glass door.

'Well she hasn't been getting on with their son for ages, and the regulars are noticing it.'

'She's a right little madam ... never works behind the bar, spends her time chatting up the regulars, like Lady Muck, putting on 'err airs and graces. The rest of the family get stuck in, but not 'err, an' now she's taken to disappearin' with one or two of the younger lads. People are talking. Their son's sure she's been seein' somebody regular.'

'How can she luv? I mean, it's obvious if she's gone missing, isn't it? They all live in that pub together.'

'Well she goes shopping, doesn't she? Got expensive tastes, that one.'

'Still luv,' said his wife, 'that pub seems to be making an awful lot of money. I'm sure they can afford it.'

'Oh yeah, right, and the Guvnor doesn't begrudge her spending it, not as long as she's part of the team that is.'

'Why? Do you think they'll split up or something luv?'

'They more or less 'ave, but things got nasty the other night. She slipped out of the bar to use the payphone in the corner. She was on the 'phone for hours, then the DJ got a bit naughty, tiptoed up quiet like and held the microphone just behind her head where she couldn't see it. Then he switched on the pub speaker system. Took her ages to realise that the whole conversation was 'eard around the pub, and very embarrassin' it was too.'

'Embarrassin' for their son, I should say.' His wife spoke with concern in her voice.

'He wasn't there luckily ... down the cellar changing the barrel, 'an parkin' the bowls, but the Guv'nor and his wife heard it, so did half the pub.'

'What's gonna happen now luv?' She had an anxious note in her voice. Tony put the paper down, folded his arms and stared at the picture of the Queen.

'Not sure luv, but the whisper is, that the daughter-in-law is thinkin' of taking another pub just down the road from her in-laws.'

'The brewery would never let her do that,' said the wife.

'Might be a different brewery, luv. Talk is, that the daughter-in-law thinks she'll pull most of the regulars with her.'

'Do you think she could?'

'Oh, she'll get one or two of the younger ones over there for a while, 'till the novelty wears off, but they'll be back. There's something about certain pubs you see luv, it's 'ard to define. It's a sort of ... *comfort* level, and that doesn't mean service with a smile, it means service with an 'eart. You know what I mean ... when you feel one of the family. That stuck-up skinny bitch could never achieve that.'

He turned over a noisy page. 'Oh, she'll have flowers on the bar an' clean glasses an' lots of smiles and leg, but the 'eart won't be there. Not bred for it you see. A hard game, the pub game. Got to get your hands dirty... and them hours; twenty-five hours a day, eight days a week. There's no rest, even at Christmas.'

Morgan stubbed out his cigarette in the battered tin ashtray next to the orange plastic table lamp and the just-started bottle of Jack Daniel's. His tape was playing. Morgan started to think about the singer. He must have been writing songs for over twenty years. How do people do that? ... how can they carry on believing in themselves when others do not appear to believe in *them*?

Morgan felt uncomfortable faced with such intensity; the lyrics seemed to be holding up a mirror to so many facets of his own life. He looked at his watch, he was expecting Sara back around midnight.

Life had moved very fast since he had met her. He was catching his breath for the first time in a long time. She was special. He thought of her and smiled inside. What was it about her? She looked good. Well ... maybe not the face that launched a thousand ships, but a face that could have haunted quite a few of the sailors. The eyes, maybe that was it. Those, now what colour were they? ... He made a mental note to look properly next time. Those eyes ... they could see right through him. He could never lie to her. Like the suspect being grilled by the cops, finally losing carefully created cockiness when one of the questions hits the bull's-eye. The body loses rigidity and tension, especially behind the knees and a point is reached when the suspect readily spouts the truth, relieving the guilty tension. She had that effect on him. He was starting to miss her. He took another drink. No, he thought, she wasn't a real beauty; her figure was a bit on the thin side, her face was too sharp ... he couldn't now be sure if her hair was light or dark, probably somewhere in between.

There was no one feature that he could pinpoint and say, 'My baby's got great whatever ...' except those eyes. He must remember to check on the colour. .

He paced the room. He always thought better when he was on the hoof. He didn't like losing control. He was feeling pushed along by events. The more he tried to reach out with his thoughts and establish some semblance of order the more transient were the images he was trying to make sense of.

He had lost two good friends, and two others who had come into his life had also died. The only relationship between them all was that they had come into contact with *him*. He needed to slow down, he needed time to think. He poured another drink and lit another cigarette.

It all started when he was given the tape. He looked at it, flipping the case over on the back of his knuckles. He took the paper insert out, looked at both sides and looked at the cassette itself. There must have been a dozen of these knocking about. He could find nothing unusual about the package.

He thought back again. Jackie. He had just met Jackie when all this started. He had met her in Downtown L.A., in that red sandstone block at California Plaza. The Museum of Contemporary Art had proved a regular bolt hole for Morgan since it opened in the late eighties. The Japanese architect Isozaki's contribution to Downtown's vertical slab architecture was a welcome relief, although in reality, it was only its colour and the eccentric tracing of pyramid skylights on top of a rectangular structure that gave this building its distinction.

Morgan had been slumped in front of a Liechtenstein when he was zapped by the long pair of legs encased thinly in black stockings. It was the seams that did it for him, so unusual in the heat of the Los Angeles day. Both were perfectly straight, from the back of the stiletto heel, through the middle of the back of the knee and upward and beyond a black hem-line. The wide brimmed dark hat sat low across her face covering her eyes; she had to tilt her head slightly in order to see. When the cream chin and nose peeked from out of the gloom Morgan was a gonna.

If he didn't start thinking, he'd be a *real* gonna. He needed help. The tape was leading him on, dictating his life, or was it? ... Was he just reacting to it? ... Was his life a blank tape, first recording, then playing back events and images? ... Was it to fail as the singer had ... And where was Paul now?

He placed the tape in the player and hit the button.

Hold on for a rescue operation, on your heart, on your soul
I heard that you 're in trouble, I heard you need a friend.
The world and all its problems got you down on your knees again.
I'm not a knight in shining armour, but I'll do the best I can.
We 'll talk the night till morning and find a better plan
What you need, is a rescue operation .On your heart and on your soul.
What you need, is a rescue operation.
Throw away the pain, all that hurt and blame.
Open up those chains, and let you go

228

I know you'll build defences and make them high and strong
'Cos your heart has been a prisoner, to another, far too long
But there's a harbour for the sailor, there's a calm before the storm
And there's one thing to remember, there must be dark before the dawn
What you need, is a rescue operation. On your heart, on your soul
What you need, is a rescue operation
Throw away the pain, all that hurt and blame
Open up those chains, and let you go
What you need, is a rescue operation on your heart and on your soul
What you need, is a rescue operation. On your heart and on your soul.
What you need, is a rescue operation
Open up those chains and let you go
He was in need of help.

It was 3.30am when Clive stepped out of the taxi. He rooted around in the deep pockets of his new overcoat and came up with some crumpled bank notes. The taxi-driver's fingers were drumming impatiently on the side of his cab. Clive squinted at the numbers on the notes in the poor street lighting, cursing the newly designed notes and the imbecilic designer who had made the variously valued notes all look the same. He gave up and handed two to the cabby. It was obviously a mistake because the cabby grinned cheerfully, waved goodnight and sped off, but not before Clive's companion had stepped languidly out of the rear door. She seemed about seven foot tall standing next to Clive, but was probably a foot shorter than that.

Her beautiful and flawless face glowed under a mass of curly red hair. Her long legs were exposed by the shortest of miniskirts. She took Clive's arm and together they mounted the steps to his flat. She balanced precariously on a pair of red stiletto shoes, the colour of which matched her lipstick. Clive scratched around at the lock for a while before gaining entry.

They climbed the flight of stairs to the first floor arm in arm and Clive repeated the process with the second lock. Once inside and the door shut tight, Clive threw off his coat and invited his companion to do the same.

'I'm not wearing one,' she replied.

Clive was looking at her legs. 'I hadn't noticed' he slurred, but he grinned broadly while he made these comments. She was not offended.

'What do you think of the place?'

She stood up and paced the room, looking around. 'Well,' she answered in a deep voice, 'It's not exactly my style, although you could call it neat. In fact,' she observed, 'it hasn't got any style. I suppose that's one thing in its favour.'

'Drink?' Clive had thrown open the doors of the drinks cabinet. 'Or would you prefer coffee?'

'Oh no,' she said deeply, 'I'll take a Bloody Mary.'

'How long have you been going to the club?' Clive inquired politely.

'Absolutely ages.' Clive brought the drinks over; he had joined her in the blood red liquid.

'And what do you do for a living?' He asked.

'I'm a plasterer, but things are a bit rough at the moment. The work is drying up.'

Clive reached out and touched her knee. 'Is it hard work?'

'Oh yes' she said, 'it takes me about four hours to get everything right before I go out looking like this. The worst bit is getting rid of the hair. There's no real answer to it but plucking it out. I hate that bit.' Clive nodded in sympathy. 'The rest of it is pretty straightforward really ... good diet, keeping in shape and lots and lots of makeup. 'Course, you have to know how to use it.'

'Of course,' said Clive in agreement. 'By the way, what's your name?'

'I call myself April.'

'Would you like a shower?' Clive nodded towards the bathroom. April considered this. 'I don't usually do this you know ... go home with somebody the first time.'

'I'm sure you don't,' said Clive, reaching for the vodka bottle and topping up her drink. The 'phone rang.

'Excuse me.' Clive picked it up and stiffened in response to the voice on the line. '... It's good to speak to you too.' He tried to make it sound sincere.

'Oh you haven't, have you?' said Clive. 'I didn't hear it ring ... well I have been in the bath and I was listening to the radio ...Yes I know it's only a two bedroom flat, but they build the walls thicker over here ... of course not ... I've been here all alone, all evening ...' He brought a finger up to his lips, opened his eyes wide and nodded towards April. She got the message, but looked a little put out. '...Yes, it's a big day tomorrow.' Clive said proudly, '... Everything is under control. I talked to Trench this evening. It'll be really beautiful ... bye bye ... bye luv.' The last two words were spoken in a guilty whisper.

'Having boyfriend troubles?' said April.

'Nothing I can't handle ... Especially as he's more than three thousand miles away.'

She uncrossed her legs and stood up. 'I think I'll take that shower now.' She growled huskily. Clive grinned.

'I'll run the bath for you, if you like?'

'Oh no, don't do that,' she said. 'I'll never get out again.'

'This is my bedroom.' Clive pushed the door open. 'There's another one here. You sleep where you want.' She leaned over and kissed him on his forehead.

'See you in a little while.'

Clive felt a warm heat rising through his body as he shut his bedroom door behind him. He heard the shower being switched on. He threw off his clothes, but folded them neatly on a chair at the side of the bed. He lay there, contemplating the delights to come. For him, this was to be the ultimate pleasure. To behave as a man can towards a man and as a man does towards a woman. This called for something special.

He leapt off the bed and threw open the wardrobe doors, together with his caution to the wind.

April was having trouble. She had made sure that the water hit her body from the neck down. She could never rebuild that face in the time available, besides, she didn't have all her equipment with her. Her wig was wet at the ends, but that was not a problem. Stopping it sliding off her head was more of one.

She dried herself off and wrapped the large white bathrobe around her. One last check in the mirror and she switched off the light and swayed towards his bedroom.

He was a nice clean man and she liked him - and she was sure he would be giving her a large tip in the morning. She needed the money. She knocked gently and provocatively twice on the bedroom door.

'Is that the postman?' came a voice from within. She opened the door wider and stood there transfixed. She had come across more bizarre things in her time, but not many.

Clive stood on the bed, bolt upright, with his chest puffed out. He was wearing a silver and gold helmet with white plumage, a magnificent red tunic and black riding boots, the sexy thigh-length ones. Apart from these garments, and a large ceremonial sabre in his right hand, he was stark naked.

He was having trouble with the chin strap because he didn't have much of a chin, or rather, too many of them. Despite this, he did look rather magnificent. He swished the sabre in the grand manner.

'Is this my knight in shining armour?' April said admiringly when she had recovered.

'Sure is honey,' mocked Clive. 'Show me a dragon and I'll slay it,' he bellowed, his sabre narrowly missing the electric light.

'I must say, it does something for you,' she observed. 'Where did you get it?'

'Theatrical costumiers sadly, but I aim to get hold of some genuine stuff pretty soon,' crowed Clive proudly and strutted the length and breadth of the bed using the sabre to steady himself by sticking it, either in the mattress, or into the walls. He eventually fell back into a sitting position on the bed and looked at her in triumph.

'It's a good thing you've stopped ... the room would have been cut to ribbons!'

'I'm sorry if I freaked you out honey, but I'm so excited about being over in England ...' She sat on the bed next to him, crossing her legs and exposing a length of thigh.

'And what is it you like most about England?' She was looking at him hungrily. He put the sword down.

'Your regard for tradition,' he replied with a lopsided grin.

She stood up and dropped her bathrobe. Clive eyed her body.

'And what traditions are those?' She said. 'Parliament? ... the Queen? ... Number Ten?'

He stared into her eyes. 'I was thinking more of number sixty-nine ...'

It was a beautiful morning and Hyde Park shimmered in sap green. Sara and Morgan were kicking up the dust in Rotten Row which stretched in a wide brown line away from them and into the hazy distance. On one side of this track, the park opened up and stretched away as far as the eye could see. A couple of riders cantered past giving them a wide berth and some harsh stares.

'Let's walk on the grass,' Sara suggested, 'we shouldn't linger on the horse track.' They sat with their backs to the open space and facing London's Knightsbridge. There were a number of people out riding and the park was beginning to fill up with ice-cream eaters.

'So your friends in Cambridge couldn't come up with anything?'

She picked at the grass and let the green shoots fall away through her fingers. 'No, not really, could be anything.' She was looking away from him.

'So how come it took you two days to figure that out?'

'Lot to catch up on, OK?' She displayed defensive anger.

Morgan let it pass, happy to have her around again. The light in his eyes had faded, along with his tan since she'd been away and here was a man just hanging on.

'It feels good to be alive. On a day like this everything is right.' he stated defiantly.

In the distance, half a dozen magnificently clad troopers of the Household Cavalry could be seen. The heroic figures on horseback were lazily heading their way.

'Wow, would you take a look at that!' Her eyes were as bright as the metalwork on the troopers. Morgan stood up and narrowed his eyes. They were full of admiration.

'I can just see two hundred of those flying at the guns now. If you gotta go, then why go quietly? I think the blaze of glory method is probably the best.'

'You being cynical?'

'Nope, I mean it.'

The small group was coming nearer now; they could hear the harness jangle. The horses' heads were down, nodding in unison, their riders likewise. As they came even nearer, five of the riders were seen to be bolt upright and at one with their steeds. The sixth lagged slightly behind the group and seemed to be having a little trouble with the horse. He didn't look as sharp as the others. He was leaning over the neck of the horse and rolling slightly from side to side.

'I think that last one's having a bit of trouble,' Said Morgan.

They were coming alongside now. The last horse appeared to be very restless, the trooper fighting to bring him into line. It suddenly kicked forward and headed straight for them. Morgan threw Sara to the ground as the horse reared above them, the trooper wrestling with the reins. Sara stayed down, Morgan rolled away from her. The horse followed, lashing out at him with its hooves.

The trooper had drawn his sword. As he wrestled for control he seemed to be slashing at Morgan at the same time. Morgan moved away fast, initially on all fours and then starting to get up and run. The horseman followed.

Morgan broke into a sprint. This time the horse was under control, but still bearing down on him. The trooper's face was a study in cherubic concentration. He drew the horse to one side of Morgan and brought the slashing sabre down towards his head. Morgan jerked back and the sword slashed his jacket, drawing blood across his neck and chest. He staggered away. The horse wheeled and raised its forelocks, coming in for another charge.

Sara had got to her feet and was half cowering behind a tree trunk. She was biting her lip and seemed to be coming to a decision. She sprinted towards the charging beast and threw herself at the horse and rider. She made no physical impression, but the horse was startled and reared up suddenly.

Unfortunately for the rider, but not for Morgan, this happened under the lowest branches of a spreading chestnut tree, smashing the rider's head on a branch and knocking him off the horse. The horse pranced and screamed and bolted off across the park.

Morgan was sprawled at the foot of the tree and raising himself on one knee. The fallen trooper lay very still, the other troopers had raced to the spot and two of them dismounted. One strode towards Morgan, the other to his fallen colleague. Morgan raised himself on both legs and leaned back on the tree trunk.

'Are you all right, sir?' The trooper inquired, producing a mobile 'phone from somewhere and dialling a number.

Morgan looked down at the neat slashes through his jacket. 'Do you always treat the tourists like this?'

'Can't understand it sir. It just doesn't happen ... err ... normally.'

The doors of the rosewood cabinet in a corner of Sir Anthony's office were wide open. It was purpose-built to house a twenty seven inch television set. The 2.45 at Kempton Park was just finishing and Sir Anthony's horse was lying third. As they crossed the line he smashed his fist on the top of his desk and swore.

He picked up the newspaper and stared at the form, licking the stub of a pencil and scoring heavily against the name of a particular jockey.

The telephone rang and he flicked the sound off with the remote.

'Yes!'

'Sorry to disturb you, Sir Anthony,' said Doris, but I've got the head-mistress for you and it seems pretty urgent.'

'Very well, Doris,' He replied sharply.

'Putting you through now Sir,' she said as she wrestled with the controls of her mini-switchboard.

'How are you my dear,' Sir Anthony had turned on the charm. 'What can I do for you, dear lady?'

The response from the caller was harsh enough to yank his heels off the desk and make him sit bolt upright. 'I am sorry, my dear, but there is no way I'm going to that bloody abortion in Vauxhall. It's the wrong side of the river for a start and how can anyone who chooses to work in a place like that ever be taken seriously? It's an embarrassment. Even the Yanks think it's in bad taste... and they built Eurodisney ... What do you mean, "What do I do anyway?" You know you have no right to ask that question ... You have no jurisdiction over me madam ... Who does? ... Go and bloody well find out for yourself.' He slammed the 'phone down.

After a few moments there was a knock on the door and Doris entered.

'I'm sorry Sir Anthony, but I couldn't help overhearing the shouting. I've just come to tell you I've put the kettle on.' It seemed to calm him down.

'Thank you Doris' he said, adjusting his tie and stretching his neck and pulling his waistcoat down. These little readjustments completed, he sat back.

'She sounds more like Delia Smith with each day that passes ... Do you know Doris ... Lager-Lass,' that was how he always referred to her, 'is trying to get us to move to the new building.'

Doris blanched. 'Oh no Sir.' She sounded disgusted. 'Not a man like you. How could YOU ever be seen dead in a place like that?'

'That will probably be the way I will be seen there one day,' he replied, 'but I don't intend it to be in the very near future.'

'And them colours Sir ... green and cream, it looks like somebody's vomited over a birthday cake.'

'Quite Doris, quite,' he agreed.

'If you pardon my language Sir,' she said, reddening.

'Not at all Doris, not at all ... quite understandable.'

'Right Sir,' she said, brightening up, 'I'll get on with the tea,' and she left.

He took a silver key out of his waistcoat pocket and opened the bottom drawer of his bureau. He carefully lifted out a telephone. This line did not go through any of the main switchboards in the block, in fact, not many people knew it existed. Sir Anthony had fixed it up quietly after taking up residence about ten years earlier. He pressed one of the pre-coded buttons. After some time the 'phone was answered.

'Quentin? ... Sir Anthony McLean here. How are you? ... Stella's been giving me a hard time ... Yes she is, isn't she ... No nothing I can't handle ... But maybe the Guv'nor can put a little pressure on ... Good, good ... Oh really? Well I thought everything was relatively under control? ... Yes, she is a pain in the arse isn't she ... What would you like me to do? ... Well we've done that already and I'm afraid those tapes seem to have rebounded on us ... Yes I know there's plenty more dirt to dig up, but I don't think the great unwashed would wear it a second time. Look Quentin, you lot got yourselves into this hole ... taking on the pea- brained lamp-post... and then you go and do it again with the fat one! I warned you about both of them. You should have gone for class, not crass ... Look, you can get rid of the fat one with money; she'll probably bugger off to Miami and become Queen of Florida ... or she could become a ride in Disney World, but your real problem is the brain-dead coat-hanger ... If *she* breaks loose she'll take Joe Public with her. Never underestimate the stupidity of a herd of humans. I may have to speak to Trench if things don't improve. Don't worry, I'll make sure any little accident will take place outside these shores ... The Cousins tend to do it that way and it works for them. Anyway; you'll be delighted to know that I have been giving it a lot of thought recently. If we come down on her any harder her popularity will increase in direct proportion. What we need Quentin, is a diversion ... That's right. We need something to take their minds off her ... and what better than a duplicate? ... No, no. I'm not suggesting another wife for him, people just wouldn't wear that at the moment, but I am suggesting that another member of the family should take centre stage, together with suitable supporting cast ... Yes I am suggesting that ... Leave it to me, Quentin, I guarantee that he can be persuaded ... Ah,' Sir Anthony touched his nose, 'that's my little secret ... and I think this newcomer should look as close to the real thing as possible ... I do have somebody in mind funnily enough ... Yes, she'll be livid, and an angry woman is a dangerous woman. I have even managed to maintain the Welsh connection. That will really wind her up. Just read the papers Quentin ... or better still, the colour supplements ... Bye Quentin.' Sir Anthony replaced the receiver and permitted himself a smile.

D.S. Regan sat at the back of the small cafe. He was mechanically dropping lumps of sugar into a large mug of tea and stirring slowly with his other hand. His elbows rested on the plastic table, soaking up the drops of tea that come with the territory.

The rain slashed at the glass panes, straight down, long slashes and wide apart. The kind of rain that falls on the English capital only in summer.

Regan pushed the remains of his third cup of tea to the far side of the table. A quick glance from the girl at the counter recognised and registered the gesture. She moved from behind her barricade and removed the cup and assorted debris, swishing back to her sanctuary in one, well-practised, and oft-repeated manoeuvre. The cup, saucer and spoon clinked and spat into the sink. Water swished abruptly and stopped with a loud silence. Cafes always sound the same when you're alone.

The door opened and Daley came through it. He swept the water out of his hair, looked around and went straight for Regan's table.

'Hello Guv, I was hoping to meet you here. This has just come through.' He placed a sheet of paper on the table. Regan picked it up.

'Well I'll be damned,' he said rhetorically.

'Morgan nearly was,' said Daley.

'Where is he now?'

'Dunno Guv.'

'What do you mean, you don't know?'

'He wouldn't accept no help. The paramedics just bunged some bandages on... and a bit of antiseptic and he just sodded off.'

'What about the girl?'

Daley shrugged. 'She disappeared too.'

'Where are the troopers now?'

'They're back at the barracks Guv, in Knightsbridge.'

'Right, let's go.' They both jumped up and rushed through the door.

'Hey!' screeched the voice behind them. Regan stopped in the doorway.

'That'll be £1.80,' said the waitress.

Regan screwed his face up, stuck his hand in his pocket and shouted to Daley. 'Have you got a couple of quid?'

Daley wasn't pleased, but dug deep and came up with the two coins. Regan slapped them on her glass display unit and followed Daley down the road.

Virginia

'Head's a fool' ... Siemonsen was standing in a 'phone box. 'He's passed these uncontrolled shipments and the buck stops with him ... What did we make out of that last delivery? ... The one out of Caracas. I paid out for three thousand pounds of Colombian ...' Siemonsen whistled at the response.

'So we siphoned off two thousand pounds ... I reckon that's about eighty million dollars, and where is it now? ... Good ... I'll use our Ukrainians in New York on this one. If we use the Mafia again then our Italian friends will be getting complacent. Besides, I want to break the routine up as much as possible.

Look what happened to the Haitian Intelligence Agency, they've gone into business for themselves ... Yes, I know we're still getting a cut, but I figure the percentages are on the low side. We may have to get the military involved in this one and give them a little shake-up.' He pumped more coins into the box.

'Senator Moynihan has been making waves again. Woolsey's getting a lot of flack and he, in turn, is putting pressure on Head ... Unfortunately for them, they have no control over events. It's guys like us who put the deals together, and it's the guys like us who know what has to be done.'

He checked his change.

'Getting back to Haiti ... Aristide has to go ... permanently! Our friends in the army can't afford to have him back in power. Your attempts to make him look like a loony just don't wash any more. I think the action has to be more direct. What's that? ... Oh, Clive's gone over to the UK. He's helping me sort something out for the Brits ...' Siemonsen became irate. 'So you heard that did you?' He was shouting. 'Well that's a load of bull, my team are the best! The crème de la crème ... And remember, *you* are one of them ... OK, OK, I'm sorry.' Siemonsen was calming down. 'I'm just not the same when Clive's not around ... Tonight?' Siemonsen paused for thought. 'Yes, I may be able to make that ... Yes, that could be really nice ... Come round about eight, I'll get some Cantonese sent up. See you later.'

London

Sir Anthony pressed another button on his telephone.

'Is that you George? Sir Anthony here. Tell me, how is Pindar getting on? ... Yes George, I know it's technically completed, but what's the real state of play ..?' Sir Anthony listened patiently for a couple of minutes. 'So after spending eighty million pounds, you're telling me it's not quite ready. Yes, I know you are working two hundred feet underground George and I will also jump in now and say it's nothing to do with me anyway, but it doesn't say much for British technology does it?... So let me sum up; you've spent twice as much money as based on your original estimate ... you've gone down four floors under the MOD ... you have completed the links between the bunker and Number Ten, and the bunker and the Houses of Parliament ... and you claim it will survive a direct hit by a nuclear weapon. Our key people are therefore safe.

Of course George, all of this is subject to a reasonable warning time. I can't see you getting a thousand people into the place in two minutes ... Now, the real reason for my call is to ensure that you've incorporated access for the *other* tunnel ...' Sir Anthony suddenly exploded. 'Are you mad? ... Are you telling me it cannot be done?... Do you realise what I could do to you ... and your company ...?' Sir Anthony sat back in his chair. 'Go on then, what have you done?'

The voice at the other end was high pitched and babbling. 'Calm down,' said Sir Anthony, 'and tell me again slowly ... Ah, so you're coming into Downing Street ... Ah umm, and you're linking up with Number Eleven ...? Yes, I can see it's a shorter and easier route, but will that still guarantee me direct access to the bunker ... Good, good.' Sir Anthony was breathing a little steadier now. 'And this weakness in the wall, it cannot be detected? ... Good, good ... No, no. Take the tunnel from under the Mall about seven feet away from the access point. We will make the breakthrough in our own time and in our own way; should ever the need arise of course,' Sir Anthony laughed out loud. 'You've done well George. I'll see to it that those contracts in the Middle East keep coming your way. Now about payment. I take it you've shifted the costs onto the Treasury? ... Good, good. We'll be paying you our bit in gold dear boy ... Yes the usual place and this time when you pop over to Luxembourg to confirm the arrival of funds, please take the boat-train ... Yes I know you have to slum it, but it really is the safest route you know. Far too unfashionable for any of the MI6 boys to cover it ... Cheerio for now.'

Sir Anthony replaced the receiver and rang the little brass bell on his desk.

Doris entered the room while stuffing a yellow duster into the pocket of her pinafore. She smelt of lavender.

'Another pot please Doris,' beamed Sir Anthony.

'Of course Sir,' she replied, 'but before I forget Sir, Lager-Lass was calling for you.'

'And what did she want?' frowned Sir Anthony.

'Don't know Sir, but she was saying something about, that if you had nothing to do, and had time on your hands, then perhaps you should get yourself to thinking about *Ireland.*'

Sir Anthony paled. 'Bitch ... Sit down Doris.' Doris waddled over to a leather captain's chair and sat bolt upright on the edge of it, crossing her hands and giving Sir Anthony her full attention.

'What would you do about Ireland Doris?'

'Oh, I don't know Sir. I mean, it's been going on a long time, hasn't it? It strikes me, that they don't know why they're killing each other anymore.'

'Do you think we should pull out of there Doris?'

'Well, are we actually *in* there Sir?'

Sir Anthony looked at her. 'Go on.'

'Well Sir, the way I see it ... that either Northern Ireland is part of Britain, or it isn't.'

'Yes.' He nodded.

'But haven't they got their own Parliament over there? ... Storming, or

241

something?'

'Stormont, Doris.'

'Yes, that's the one. If they really were a part of Britain Sir, like the West Country for example, well, if all them bombings and shootings were going on down there we'd soon put a stop to it, wouldn't we?'

'Would we Doris?'

'Of course Sir ... we can't have that going on. I mean, it's not right, is it?'

'Why is it right over there, Doris?'

'Exactly my point Sir, they can't be part of us, can they?'

Sir Anthony screwed his face up and stared out of the window.

'You see Sir, there's either a war going on, or there isn't. If there isn't, all those bombers and murderers would be lined up in court and banged away in prison... and they'd never come out. Or it's a war, and we just go in and shoot them all. Either way Sir, it would stop.'

'What about a political solution, Doris?'

'I don't think politics are involved Sir. Come to think of it, I don't think religion is anymore, either. If you got those two things sorted out, they'd probably be shooting each other if they had ginger hair, dark hair or blond hair ... Probably divide up three ways.'

'So let's simplify this, Doris. Number one ... We could regard all this activity as criminal... and try to apprehend the murderers individually, put them on trial and put them in prison. No good, because most of the villains jump over the border where they don't come under our jurisdiction. Number two ... It's a war situation then. Run over the borders with our troops and shoot. Problem here is, identification of the enemy. It's not as if they were wearing uniforms, Doris.'

'But,' she interjected, 'we do know who they are don't we Sir.'

'True Doris, true. So yes, it's a possibility, we could go to war. Of course, Doris, the problem is, the villains don't have a definitive country. Therefore we will be going to war with them in a country that we are not at war *with*. Number three, political solution ... that's out, because politics aren't involved; is that what you're saying?'

'That's right Sir.'

As Sir Anthony paced up and down, changing direction with each change of emphasis, Doris's head moved from side to side as if she was watching a slow rally at Wimbledon.

'Well, that's the answer then, Doris,' he said at last.

'Is it Sir?'

'Yes, I think you've solved it.'

She sat back looking very pleased with herself and a little puzzled.

'Can you tell me what it is then, Sir?'

'You've said it yourself Doris. This is our plan of action. Number one, we propose a political solution,'

'But that won't work Sir.'

'Correct Doris. So in this political solution, we hint that if the solution does not work because certain parties involved break their commitment, which we know they will ... then the full force of the law of all countries involved will be brought to bear upon the transgressors.'

'What does that mean Sir?'

'It means Doris, that when this political solution breaks down we can go in and zap them without upsetting the sensibilities of our allies. Especially the Yanks and our pinko friends in Europe.'

'But what about the government of the Republic Sir? Are they going to let you do that?'

'They'll be a party to the agreement Doris ... a third party, so they can't complain, can they?' Sir Anthony widened his arms towards her. 'Besides, they can take over the protection, money-laundering and drug-rackets ... although they're honourable people and aren't likely to do *that*. But, we can give some of the militant leaders some form of 'Get-out-of-jail' card and let them extend their influence into Northern Ireland and more or less take it off our hands.

Thus, we shall be seen to be strong in our crushing use of force... and also magnanimous in handing over what we don't really want anyway.'

'Brilliant, Sir Anthony,' she nodded.

'Most of the credit is down to you, my dear.' He opened his drinks-cabinet and brought out a bottle of sherry and two glasses. He handed one to her and poured from the bottle.

'British, Doris,' he said, studying the label ... 'We've taken the spirit of another country, blended it with the harvest from different regions and then after we've used our unique ability to ferment the whole, we screw it up and give it a label.'

She beamed and touched his glass in a toast.

Extremely Private Mayfair Club.

'Hello Stella.' The man threw the greeting over his shoulder and his coat over the club chair. 'Sorry I'm late, took ages to get a cab.'

The smart, twin set and pearled lady speared him with a withering look and he sat rapidly, sitting to attention and reaching for the gin.

'Not yet, Toby,' she commanded. 'I want answers, Now!'

'Err, of course.' He retracted his hand, but stared at the gin.

'What the fuck is going on?'

'Err, not quite sure to be absolutely honest ... not easy you know ... getting the info as it were ...' He tailed off lamely. 'Talked to Treasury, and they don't seem to own him. Hinted that he's funded, err, off the books.'

The lady's face was stone and Toby couldn't get a read. He stumbled on trying to muster a degree of competence. 'Damn it, Stella, the bloody place is so compartmentalised, right hand, left hand, and all that.'

'Slowly from the top please Toby. We've all afternoon. I want to know all there is to know about that horrible little man. I just can't believe that he's ensconced within one of my offices, having no file, no brief, no status, no elder, no fucking nothing!'

'Well now, that part about your offices. Think you'll find that particular lease is not held by HM Government.' She raised her eyebrows. 'Seems to be just HM.'

The Knightsbridge barracks was a tall modern block on the south side of Hyde Park. It stood tall and straight, just like its inhabitants. As Regan and Daley walked the corridors, they looked and felt out of place. They were going to interview somebody and yet they felt as if they were on the receiving end.

The smart young man striding ahead of them opened the door and ushered them in.

'Captain Clarke will be with you shortly gentlemen.'

They sat down and waited. A minute later the door opened smartly and three tall men marched in. They all wore immaculately pressed slacks and shirts and their ties bore the honourable colours. The first through the door had a neat bandage around the top of his head. They pulled up chairs and stared intently at the two CID men.

'How can we help you?' Clarke's voice was full of reason.

Regan shuffled in his seat. 'Tell me in your own words sir, exactly what happened.'

The blue eyes twinkled with amusement.

'Whose words *should* I be using?' His lips twitched into a smile, but he brought them back into line fairly smartly. 'I'm sorry Mr Regan, I know this is a serious matter.'

'Detective Sergeant ... and you're damned right it is,' puffed Regan, trying to exert some form of authority.

Clarke sat back. 'Well actually, there's not very much I can tell you. I was in full uniform ... it was the last minute before mounting up. We all try to go at the last minute,' he explained. Regan nodded sagely. 'I had taken my helmet off for a second to wash my face, and quite simply, somebody hit me over the head. Think they call it *Blunt Force Trauma*. When I came round I was sitting in one of the cubicles ... vest and pants only I'm afraid.'

'Are you telling me,' said Regan, 'that somebody could just walk in here, bash you over the head, strip you of your uniform, presumably put it on himself, mount your horse and take off without arousing any suspicion.'

Clarke coloured slightly. 'Well it's just not the sort of thing you would expect, is it sir?'

Regan looked at the other two. 'We were with Captain Clarke's section,' said one.

'And you noticed nothing odd?'

'We keep our eyes fixed ahead at all times,' said the other.

'Yes, I've seen them do that.' interjected Daley, receiving a swift dark look from Regan.

'I've got your detailed statements here.' Regan was trying not to explode and was looking down at his sheaf of papers. 'But what happened to this character ... this impostor, after the incident.'

All three looked at each other.

'He just seemed to melt away sir. We were busy with the injured party,' said one.

'And I was still in the loo.' Clarke said helpfully.

'But you just can't disappear in the middle of London dressed like a bloody, bloody ...' Regan left the sentence unfinished, as he received the gaze from three pairs of piercing blue eyes.

Daley rescued him. 'And what about the man who got injured?'

Two of them began to look uncomfortable. 'He insisted he was all right sir,' said one.

'He did receive rather a nasty slash,' The other one said, 'and it was bleeding quite a lot.'

'Wouldn't accept any help,' said the first.

'Getting back to the impostor,' Regan was tapping a pencil, butt end down on the table. 'he was knocked out, wasn't he? How the hell did he disappear when he was unconscious?'

'We just turned around and he was gone,' they chorused.

Daley looked at the ceiling and rolled his eyes.

13

Half way home

Sir Anthony opened his brown paper bag and scattered some of the contents over the pond. He walked slowly, a flotilla of ducks following at a respectable distance. Two large gentlemen were also following in Sir Anthony's wake. The one without the hat was talking earnestly.

'He's under observation now, Tony ... not been out of our sight for twenty-four hours. We can take him any time.'

'Good, good.' replied Sir Anthony. 'Better get on with it then, mustn't keep our American cousins waiting. By the way, where did the beggar doss down last night?'

The hatless heavy replied. 'He did all right Sir ... Dying man's last wish you might say ... picked up a barmaid and spent the night at her place.'

Sir Anthony scattered more bread on the water. 'I like to see 'em go with a smile on their face,' he said. The heavy in the hat handed Sir Anthony a piece of paper.

'Exes' Tony, things are a bit tight at the moment ... If you could sort of ...' He broke off. Sir Anthony's face was turning purple with rage. 'Everything all right Tone? You look a bit ...' He broke off again. 'We only drank halves.'

Sir Anthony sat down on the park bench. He was dumbstruck; he could hardly speak. Eventually he did.

'The Green Man! ... He picked her up in The Green Man! Where did she take him?'

'It's on the back Tone.'

Sir Anthony flipped over the paper. His face was almost black with rage. He was shaking with anger. '39 Acacia Avenue! ... He took her to 39 Acacia Avenue!?' The two heavies were looking at each other in trepidation.

'Yeah, Tone, spent the whole night there, he did,' said the second. 'Nipped out the back across the shed roof, dirty beggar.' Sir Anthony crunched up the paper in a tight fist and flung it across the water. The two heavies watched their expenses spread out, then gradually sink below the surface. Sir Anthony smashed his right fist into his left hand.

'I want 'im. I want 'im alive.' He whirled around and grabbed the hatless one by the collar. '*Alive!*' he shouted, 'Do you hear me? It's personal you see, *personal*, got it?'

'We got it, Tone, we got it.' They nodded their heads in unison. Sir Anthony wheeled and stalked off, throwing the brown bag and its contents into the pond. This action was greeted with a loud quack.

There were too many tourist boats on the Thames and it was late in the afternoon. The evening wind was lifting a chill off the water and Morgan and Sara were the only two people sitting in the cold sunlight on the upper deck. The boat was buffeting against the tide, hacking downstream.

It had passed under Blackfriars and was heading for London Bridge. To the left St Paul's was trying to shoulder itself into the skyline, above or between grey slabs of more recent architecture. Behind St Paul's and stretching to the east, lay the City of London, the financial hub of the empire and possibly the world. Behind them and to the west yellow clouds bore down on the sun, forcing evening on the water.

The filtered light painted a Pissarro Parliament and the river reflected it. The prow of the boat flicked flecks of the brown Thames high into the air and into Morgan's face. He wiped it away and turned to her.

'How did you find me?'

'Instinct.' She replied.

The lowering sun gilded her face. The violet bruising on which provided a contrast which would have pleased Van Gogh. Morgan strolled to the centre of the deck and turned three hundred and sixty degrees.

'Colourful isn't it?' he shouted, raising his arms in salute. The throb of the engine in sync with the gentle thud of prow on wave was not doing Sara's aching head much good. Morgan stopped rotating and grabbed her by the shoulders.

'Oh God,' she thought. 'He's looking serious again.'

'Give me one good reason why I shouldn't throw you over the side?'

'Because, big boy, I'll take your balls with me if you do.' At this point Morgan let out a scream and clutched at his groin.

'For God's sake let go,' he shouted. She had him tight and her eyes were glinting.

'Down boy, down,' she growled. He sank to his knees and she followed him down. He drew his arm back.

'If you hit me again, I swear I'll tear them off.' He thought better of it. His eyes were watering and he was gripping her wrist tightly. She suddenly let go and stood up. He stayed on his knees holding his tender parts. She looked down at him.

'Come a long way haven't you, cowboy? From L.A. to your knees.' He got to his feet slowly and clutched the rail. The pain was subsiding and he was getting things back in focus.

'You're out of your depth Morgan. I guess you have been most of your life. You're all bulge and no spunk ... Do you know what really pisses me off? I really thought you had something, it wasn't much, but you had it. It was a long time ago. You've just gone through life without touching the sides. You keep your head down behind a wall of clichés, it's safe there. Why don't you take a peek out now and again? Open your eyes and see what's going on? You think you're a man, but you don't know the meaning of the word.'

Morgan wasn't really taking all of this in; he was trying not to vomit. They were sliding past one of the river pubs at Wapping. Beer glasses were glinting orange on the wooden balcony. He looked at her from beneath lowered eyebrows.

TEARS OF GLASS

'You haven't got a drink on you, have you?' He pulled a crumpled pack of cigarettes out of his jacket pocket. Sara took a step forward, tore them from his grasp and then yanked out a fistful of the little white tubes. Morgan opened his mouth to protest and she jammed them in, clamping her arm around the back of his neck and forcing his jaw shut with the other. She twisted him to the deck and held him there. Morgan was not a weak man, but the leverage she put on his neck was so expertly done, he found he was unable to move.

He was gagging. After a minute she released her grip, allowing him to vomit the contents of the packet over the side. It wasn't appreciated by a number of passengers on the lower deck. Morgan was white with rage and more probably, sickness. He advanced and she retreated.

'Right you big ape, you asked for that. You've come down just about as far as I'm going to let you. I'm sure with your talents you could descend even further, but I'm not going to be around to see it happen.'

Morgan wiped dribbles of vomit from the sides of his mouth and chin. He felt ill. He stopped moving forward and sat down heavily on a bench, then placed his head between his legs. She looked down at him. A number of emotions battled to settle on her face. Disgust came out the winner.

'What's happened to you? A week ago you were riding high, cracking jokes amongst the falling bodies. Look at you now, you're a wreck, physically and mentally a wreck. So you've had a bit of a hard time ... haven't we all? So a few of your friends are dead, well, we all gotta go sometime. So somebody doesn't like you, and you now know who, so what? Are you going to cry about it for the rest of your life? Are you going to bury yourself in alcohol and cigarettes? Your mind's been wrecked so you decided to do the same thing to your body ... It's not yourself you should take revenge on!'

He looked up at her, forcing his head back just far enough for his eyes to get her into frame. As an example of a human being he didn't rate too highly. Unshaven, unhealthy, uncoordinated and unhygienic. He was also unbalanced.

She didn't seem to be getting any response from this tirade, so she kicked him in the head and he fell the floor.

250

'Hit the deck sucker,' she quipped the cliché tight.

Morgan dragged himself up to his knees. She stood over him, her short thin dress pinned to her slight frame by the wind off the water. The boat throbbed on.

Virginia

'When did Westinghouse start up in Savannah?'

Siemonsen pushed the remains of his meal to the side of the table, but not before taking the one remaining king-size prawn and dipping it into a small bowl of soy sauce. He took it by the tail and chewed on it for a while before answering.

'Westinghouse started there in eighty nine.'

'And what have we paid them since?' His companion had finished eating, and wanted to talk.

'The deal is worth two billion dollars a year to them,' replied Siemonsen, 'and we've given them about fifty million dollars in bonuses over that period.'

'What about the cost overruns?'

Siemonsen took the last bite and wiped his lips with a napkin. 'There are no cost overruns,' he replied. His companion was about to interject, when Siemonsen held up his hand.

'Sure, officially there are, but unofficially, that money is being well spent.'

'What do you mean?'

'Look, we officially give DuPont and Westinghouse contracts worth hundreds of billions of dollars. This is spent at atomic reprocessing plants all over the States. The nuclear industry is a relatively young one. It's impossible to predict accurate costs on this scale over a period of time, especially when you are dealing with material that has the potential of wiping out the planet.'

'But how come we can pay bonuses and still admit cost overruns?'

Siemonsen smiled. 'The Government contracts with these companies allow for a degree of self-reporting. Their costs may not meet our predicted figures, but the system of self-assessment and self-regulation allows for internal adjustments to ongoing costs.'

'What the hell does that mean?'

'It means, we give them a target and if they can't meet it, they come up with good reasons why not. And a new target.'

'And that's it?'

'Yes, that's it.'

'Why are you so happy about it?'

'Well officially it's none of my business.' Siemonsen poured his companion a glass of Chablis. 'Room temperature,' said Siemonsen. 'Chilling it can kill the flavour.'

'Fine,' said his companion.

'One of the advantages the nuclear industry offers organisations like ours is the fact that they have to be so incredibly secure. These plants have the highest possible security, both in terms of physical access and, of course, access to the accounts. The activities within each plant may also vary from the perception the general public has of them, but if that is the case... and I'm not saying that it is, then that variation of activity would be impossible to prove.'

'What sort of variation?'

'Maybe none at all,' said Siemonsen. 'On the other hand, maybe instead of reprocessing material, they could be *processing* it ... in small amounts of course.'

'Are you implying that we could be making more nuclear bombs then we are declaring?'

'Of course not,' said Siemonsen. 'Such a thing would be quite absurd. Such a thing, of course, would be purely whimsical fantasy ... and impossible to prove.' Siemonsen sipped his wine. 'Temperature all right?'

'A little hot,' said his companion.

Siemonsen smiled again and rose. 'Bring your drink into the lounge Peter, and we'll expand on the fantasy.'

London

The river boat had made a U-turn at Greenwich, picked up half a dozen passengers and was now heading back to Embankment. Sara was staring straight ahead at the low sun bloodying the sky. Morgan was slumped and hunched. She turned to him.

'I've seen bag-ladies in New York, beggars in Nicaragua, junkies in L.A. I've seen men on Death Row and my father told me about the look on Nixon's face when Watergate finished him. But I've never seen anyone looking so desolate.'

She was looking at him hard. His eyes were still fixed on the deck. 'Why don't you jump over the rails, Morgan and do us all a favour.' He didn't look up. 'It's the self-pity I can't stand ... you've no reason to be like this, not like this.'

Morgan ignored her, but got to his feet and walked to the rail. Nobody had joined them on the upper deck.

'How did you get into this?' he said to her.

She stared straight ahead at the gold leaf dancing on the water. 'My father,' she replied. 'He was head of station in Singapore ... ended up at a desk in Langley. He took me under his wing and the progression was a natural one.'

'And your mother?'

'I think dad drove her away. She never knew I got into this. She thinks I'm still a student. I guess I am in a way. This is only my second field placement.'

He looked at her, trying to comprehend. 'My job was to lead you into situations where the operatives could deal with you. Accidents are favourite. Covering up a murder is harder than you may think.'

'What about the details of those *accidents* I found in your file.'

She turned on him quickly. 'I never thought you'd have the energy to go snooping.'

'Well?'

'Just a little bit of private research,' she said. 'I don't think it's leading anywhere. They're just snippets from various files at Langley and most of it is straight out of the British press. I was researching the electronics industry in the UK, Aviation Electronics, that is. I was simply collating published data and relating that to what I knew was happening in Silicon

Valley. I was also making reality-spread assessments.'

'What the hell's that?'

'We know exactly what's going on in each division and in each laboratory at sensitive industries. The difference between what a company publishes, and what they're actually working on, is the spread I'm talking about. There's always a gap, both in terms of data and the timing of its release. However, if both those gaps get too big, alarm bells start to ring in my department. We want to know why.'

'What's that got to do with those notes I found?'

'Nothing directly. But when the information comes back from our moles, we encourage them to stick in as much anecdotal material as possible. Most of this is junk, but we do hold everything on file. I noticed that certain people in parallel lines of research were starting to meet with unfortunate accidents. There were a hell of a lot of them in a short period of time ... and it wasn't *our* guys.'

'Maybe they really were accidents?'

'You are probably right,' she said. 'In fact, I'm certain you are.'

'Tell me about this bomb?'

'There's not much doubt about it. I've talked to the right people. It's a thermonuclear device, probably replacing an older type... and could vaporize Downtown L.A. No bad thing perhaps?'

'If this thing existed... and your people knew about it, why didn't the cops find it?'

'Perhaps they did, or perhaps the cleaners got there first.'

'Cleaners?'

'Special section, they take care of loose ends. Look Morgan, you're out of your depth. Only one thing we can do.'

'We?'

'I'm in the shit too ... up to my neck.'

He took her by the shoulders and turned her face towards him. 'Because of the dumb animal?'

She looked up into the childlike face of this hunched hunk of a man and into his sad grey eyes. Then she threw her arms around him and held him tightly. She pushed herself away.

'We're going back to the States. To the smallest town we can find. We're going to forget and be forgotten. We'll go out though Dublin. If we leave now we just might make it. They'll pick us up at the other end, but I think we can wing it.'

'Aren't you forgetting one little thing? ... L.A. is about to disappear.'

'No way. My people weren't bothered about that little installation. Don't know why; they obviously had the situation under control ... until you barged in.'

Morgan stared ahead, London was lighting up. 'You're right, I'm a mess,' he said eventually. 'Maybe I'd better do something about it.'

'Like what?'

'I'm not letting this go. They've been trying to wipe us out. I don't like that. I'm not going gently into that good night. I'm going to get even, and stand on their graves till I'm sure that they're dead.'

Sara looked unimpressed. ' Miss-quoting both Dylans won't help.'

'We've got to tell someone.'

'Forget it,' she said. 'Who are you going to tell? ... THEY ALL KNOW! At least anyone who's anyone. People like you don't count. Not many of us do. We're the little people. Just stick your head back in the sand and keep it there until the next life. It'll all be revealed then, unless God's in on it too.' They were both silent for a while.

Sara stared at the water sluicing by. 'Don't look for justice. You won't see Saddam get what's coming to him. Or Noriega. And Mrs Marcos isn't exactly having a hard time.'

'Your boss,' said Morgan. 'Who is he? Where can I find him?' His eyes were glinting now.

'Siemonsen,' said Sara, 'and you don't find him, he ...'

'Finds you.' Morgan finished the sentence for her.

'Listen,' she placed a finger on his cheek. 'I think I can get him off our backs. I'm going to call him. I can do a deal. I ...' Sara broke off suddenly. She was looking past Morgan to the head of the staircase from the lower deck. Two large men in tight fitting suits had just come up and were moving with purpose towards them.

'We've got company.'

Morgan turned around and stiffened, moving in front of Sara and facing the men. He felt himself moving his weight over the balls of his feet. It was instinctive. The two stopped about three yards away. They were both well over six feet tall, and their tailor had obviously had trouble getting enough of the shiny material. They fitted tightly in all the right and wrong places. 'Mr Morgan is it?' said one in a boxer's accent. 'Been lookin' for you sir.' He looked at Sara. 'You too Ma'am.' The second man was wearing a small, pork-pie hat, which he doffed at Sara. The first one grinned. 'A gentleman friend of ours would like to 'ave a quiet word. Ever such a nice man sir ... won't take a minute.'

'On the other 'and,' said the other ... 'might take quite a while.' He grinned sadistically.

Most of the seating on this deck was fixed, but there were one or two heavy wooden stacking-chairs dotted about. One of these was convenient for Morgan's hand. He picked it up and hurled it at the two thugs. The hatless one caught it one handed, smiled again, and pulled it apart. Morgan's face clouded over; the word 'Shit' came softly to his lips. The two men advanced. They expected Morgan to back away and were more than surprised when he let out a cry, took a step forward and kicked the one with the hat in the face, sending him backwards. Unfortunately, this also sent Morgan backwards and flat on the deck.

He did have one piece of luck, however, in that when he came to rest, it was next to a piece of broken chair about the size of a sword, its shattered end forming a sharp point. Morgan grasped it and rolled just as the hatless heavy's foot crashed down at the spot where Morgan's head once lay.

He was quickly on his feet and bounded cat-like onto a nearby hatch cover, thus giving himself a slight height advantage. This first man had recovered and the two of them circled Morgan carefully.

Sara had moved to the other end of the deck and was shouting at the group. Morgan couldn't quite catch all the words, but one line sounded like, 'Come on Arthur ... stick it to them.'

'Bloody women,' he thought to himself. The first heavy had picked up the idea from Morgan, as well as another piece of the wrecked chair; it happened to be a bigger piece than the one Morgan was holding. 'Why do I always draw the short straw?' was another thought that went through his mind. Both the heavies were grinning even more now; it seemed to be the in expression.

'Right Gerald,' said the pork-pie to his companion. 'I think we've got 'im now, wants to play soldiers does he?' They moved around him, hatless was trying to get behind. Morgan was thrashing out at both. They kept their distance. Sara was still jumping up and down like a demented cheerleader. 'Go get 'em Morgan,' was one useful piece of advice. The hatted heavy's stick crashed against his right knee cap. The searing pain broke Morgan's concentration and almost his knee. The second heavy rushed in and knocked Morgan to the deck. Morgan had lost his grip mentally, but not his grip on his manufactured sword.

As the man who had rushed him followed through, Morgan had just about enough presence of mind to present the sharp end to this gentleman's throat. Luckily for Morgan, but unluckily for his opponent, the sharp wooden point cleanly severed the wind pipe and almost the spinal cord. Blood spurted like strands of dark rope and the heavy hit the deck, gurgling loudly.

Sara had stopped shouting. The boat throbbed on and the blood throbbed out. The pain in Morgan's knee had disappeared. The standing heavy threw down his stick and took a step forward, reaching out for Morgan's throat with two plate-like hands. Morgan grabbed the wrists but couldn't budge them. The thumbs were gouging into his windpipe. He tried to bring his knee up into the man's groin, but pork-pie was too streetwise for that. He easily foiled these attempts by shifting his body position. Morgan was getting desperate. 'Where's that bloody girl?' The oxygen levels in his brain were sinking. He had dropped his piece of wood and he couldn't even reach around the man's shoulders with his hands. The man was too big, the man was too strong.

The more Morgan struggled, the more futile he realised his resistance was. Morgan was fighting for consciousness, but the moments of dreamlike darkness were increasing. Suddenly the light came on again, as the attacker's right foot suddenly gave way under him. The pool of blood spreading from his companion's throat had worked its way under his feet. The sudden loss of friction resulted in the man losing his balance and collapsing forward suddenly. It was just the edge Morgan had been praying for. As the heavy released the pressure on his throat and used his hands to retain his balance, Morgan rolled away, lashing out wildly with his legs as he did so.

The second bit of luck saw one of Morgan's legs catch his assailant behind the knee, bringing him down on the deck and covering himself with even more of his colleague's blood.

They both got to their feet at the same time, but the heavy was now standing in the ever expanding bloody pool. He slipped again, this time falling backwards against the rail of the boat. Morgan did not need a second invitation and immediately lunged for the man's legs, putting both his arms around them behind the knees and yanking him off his feet. The rail of the boat formed a fulcrum in the middle of the man's back and when Morgan raised his legs in the air, his upper body weight ensured that the only way he was going to come down was on the watery side of the rail.

Morgan tossed the legs, caber-style, into the air and the man disappeared over the side.

The falling body must have alarmed the passengers on the lower deck, for within seconds the ticket collector's head popped up out of the stairwell. He was greeted with the sight of a blood soaked individual picking up a wooden sword and standing over a throatless body. He allowed the scene to sink in for a few moments, mumbled something about damages being extra and disappeared below stairs again.

Morgan looked back to the water in time to see the large floating body with flailing arms disappear under the cutting edge of a following tourist boat.

Looking back along the deck, he saw Sara was leaning nonchalantly against the far rail and clapping her hands slowly in mock salute.

'Thanks a lot,' he shouted.

'You were doing fine,' she retorted. 'Anyway, this is my last change of clothing, and you two weren't being careful about where you sloshed that claret.' She walked towards him and took the stick gently from his hand. He was breathing heavily. 'Sit down.' He did so, looking towards the small crowd gathered on the jetty. The boat had been thrown into reverse gear and was idling slowly towards its berth.

They spotted two uniformed police officers, arms folded, watching the boat come in.

'The reception committee,' she pointed out, needlessly.

'Must have radioed ahead,' he agreed.

D.S. Regan was absent-mindedly unwrapping the foil around his home-made sandwiches. Across the rest of the surface of his desk were spread various sections of that morning's newspaper. He had made a beeline for the Waterhouse column as he always did, twice a week. As London sunk into a moral decay all around him this column was a beacon of sanity in a world where the lunatics had not only taken over the asylum, but were now busily setting fire to it. He chuckled to himself, his eyes on the print while the tomato from his badly constructed sandwiches slid over the slippery cheese slices and over the trousers of his newly-cleaned suit. When his wife used to make them the bread wasn't stale and crumbly and the cheese was a more absorbent Wenslydale. Those sandwiches always remained intact, irrespective of what he was doing with his eyes and other hand.

A creature of habit, he still behaved as if this was still the case. The disintegrating mess in his right hand and the increasing mess on his trousers indicated that he had still not come to terms with the fact that she had left him over three years ago now. The lot of a policeman's wife is not a happy one. There was a polite knock on the door.

'Come!' He shouted absently.

Daley walked in. 'Just got this through, sir.'

Regan looked up.

'They've just picked up our man down at Charing Cross.'

'What's that?'

'John Morgan, sir,' said Daley.

'Shit!' Regan was staring down at his right trouser leg. He looked around for a tissue. There weren't any.

'Get you some bog paper, sir,' said Daley and dashed out.

Regan sat there with his right hand held away from his body allowing the contents of the sandwich to drip onto the carpet. Daley returned with sheets of toilet paper from the gents' dispenser. Regan grabbed them with his left hand and started to rub his right trouser leg. Unfortunately this Government-issue toilet paper was designed to spread, not absorb. The result was that the navy blue suit was covered in a tomato spread. He gave up and brushed off the remains with his hand.

'Morgan, sir,' Daley reminded him.

'Why did they pick him up?' Regan was looking at the sheet of paper.

'Seems he was involved in a brawl on a boat, sir. Two men dead,' he added.

'Bloody hell!'

'Yes, I believe it was,' said Daley.

Three men were sitting in the room lit by the horizontal stripes. Siemonsen had his telephone jammed in his ear. He was shouting.

'Don't talk to me like that you little hussy ... You've made me look an idiot ... Really? ... Consider yourself extinct... and that drunken loony. Don't be stupid, who's going to listen to you ... Oh.' Siemonsen switched the 'phone from one ear to another, he was looking concerned. He was becoming more obsequious now. 'Maybe we can work something out ... Yes ... OK ... Yes ... I'll do that ... If you get him over here I'll get someone to speak to him, put him straight, but if we tell him everything he's not to breathe a word ... You guarantee it?... OK, it's a deal ... When are you coming over?' He smiled grimly. 'OK, I'll wait to hear from you ...' He put the telephone down and turned to his colleagues. 'The bitch is putting the screws on me ... I'm going to play it her way ... mostly.'

'Say that again, slowly.' Regan's voice carried a calm menace. It was deliberate and slow and distinct. The uniformed officer felt his temperature rise. He adjusted his tie, which was like a piece of string under a crumpled collar and tried in vain to lift his eyes to meet Regan's. They almost made it, but at crunch time would deviate to the side, or look over the top of his head.

The result was a sort of wild oscillation. The unfortunate recipient of the impending wrath managed to concentrate on Regan's tie. 'They escaped from custody ... they did a runner ... sir,' he stammered slightly. Nobody said a word. He blurted out more words to fill the gap. 'She puked up over the arresting officers who were in the back with them.' He wiped his forehead with his sleeve. He could feel Regan's eyes boring into his face. 'We get to Parliament Square and are travelling a bit around one of those right angle corners ... and the motor leans a bit and she's suddenly vomiting over Sergeant Blake ... and then she's screaming and going bonkers, shouting she was going to die. Then *he* joins in, wanting the car to stop.'

'Surprise me.' Daley spoke to no one in particular as he leaned over his plastic coffee.

The young uniform shot him a glance and carried on with more force, driven by anger now. 'It was dangerous, sick everywhere, legs and arms waving about, shouting ... I decided it was sensible to stop and sort it all out before we continued. She seemed really ill.'

'Got over it quick I suppose,' Daley quipped.

The uniform ignored Daley. 'Blake got out and tried to wipe the mess off his tunic, instinctive I suppose. He helped the lady out and ... and then all hell broke out. The male Cauc ... err Morgan, he was a bit ... well he was very fast. He hit officer Jupp in the throat and pulled me back over the driver's seat by my collar. I couldn't move. She kicked Blake in the ba ... groin, and was off.

Morgan knotted my tie to the seat belt, and went after her ... he can run that one. By the time I'd got out of the car, they'd disappeared.'

'In a puff of smoke.' Daley's voice had a touch of irony.

Regan walked slowly round the driver, who didn't know if he should rotate with him, or keep eyes front.

When Regan had made a complete circuit, he sat on the edge of his desk and folded his arms. The tea stains on his elbows were a testament to his unimproved domestic situation. 'You didn't think to handcuff them?'

'They weren't under arrest, sir! In fact, they had just been assaulted ... if the statement of the boat's skipper is to be believed. They were only being brought in under escort on a general bulletin. Nothing about, *approach with care* or, *could be dangerous*.' He was gaining confidence now. The self-justification was seeming reasonable.

Regan and Daley exchanged glances and silently acknowledged the cock-up. Regan was about to open his mouth again when there was a knock on his door. It was opened before Regan could shout, 'Stay,' and the doorway filled with a shiny double-breasted suit.

'Regan?' said the huge suit, extending a shovel of a hand. 'Nick Steadman, LAPD... I believe you've got my guy?'

Sir Anthony was on the 'phone. 'I'm afraid I shall have to insist... yes ... we lost them ... Siemonsen tells me they're coming back your way ... God knows, probably Ireland, but they're not exactly helpful over there ... We will have to solve our problem at your end and, as I have already intimated ... I SHALL BE THERE ... I *have* informed the President, he would like to squeeze in a round of golf ... I think I may just have time ... yes. Cheerio Head, don't let the bastards grind you down.'

Sir Anthony picked up the little brass bell and rang it. Doris put her head around the door.

'Book me on the next RAF flight to Washington please Doris, if you would be so kind.'

'Right Sir,' she said. 'How's your daughter? ... Heard she's been poorly.'

'On the mend Doris, on the mend ... fell down the stairs. Won't be going out for a while.'

'How did you manage to throw up?'

'Swallowed my earring.'

Morgan smiled and shook his head, 'Part of the training?'

'Initiative.'

They were cradling two glasses of Scottish whisky, about three fingers in each. The small room at the back of the pub was almost empty.

'Now you know what it feels like.'

'Smells like.'

'With you ... you feel it.' She knocked back the drink. 'I can feel your wretchedness when you retch.'

He shrugged. Sara stood up, 'We've got to get cleaned up. Stand in the doorway and grab the first cab that comes along.' He didn't argue.

Three cabs later, they were in Paddington, but a different dive. The three flights of stairs still smelled of boiled cabbage and the room of cheap soap.

'OK cowboy, this is what we're going to do.' She propped herself up on one elbow and looked at him from under her top eyelids. It was that look again. 'And you can get some clothes on.' She didn't sound as if she meant it.

Half an hour later she turned to him sleepily. 'Where are your ciggies?'

'Given up. No not really. Why, do you want one?'

'Damn it yes. I only took it up to get close to you - now I miss it.'

'Think of your body.'

'I'd rather think of yours.' Her finger traced his cheekbone, then the jawline. 'We're going to spend two days here. We're going to think, rest, bathe our wounds, especially the mental ones and we're going to sleep.'

'Anything else?'

'We might just squeeze something in.'

Virginia

'Budgets have been squeezed since we've had our alternative deterrent in place ... No, the President doesn't know about it, neither do the upper echelons of the service. Head's department, although officially working for and paid for by the CIA, has a sub-committee overseen by Head and chaired by myself. This has separate funding.'

'What's the source of the funding? The budgets are well defined and there are so many damn financial committees ... I can't see where it comes from.'

'Well we've often increased our resources by taking a cut of the drug traffic, but the rest of the service needs this money as well as us. It's accountable within Langley anyway.'

'Isn't your budget accountable also?'

'Langley doesn't know we exist.'

His companion put down his glass quickly, eyes widening as they made contact with Siemonsen's, then they darted round the room.

'Relax, this is the safest safe-house you're likely to find. Lead-lined, white noise and every electronic anti-bugging device we could think of.'

His companion seemed to doubt this statement.

'Yes it does seem unlikely. Small apartment three floors up, the cost of these measures could buy the block. Our people BUILT the block.

Most of the other apartments are let to straights, not all though. The two on either side, and those directly above and below have our people in them. An unnecessary precaution perhaps, but I feel happier about it.'

'You're kidding me?'

'No.' Siemonsen filled both glasses.

'And the money?'

'Private enterprise. After all, commercial interests fund the Presidency... isn't it logical that private money should be used to protect the industries that made it in the first place ... or individuals should put their money where it will do them the most good. It started in England when Cromwell overthrew the Royalists. Do you think centuries of power would be thrown away just like that?' He snapped his fingers. 'There was more private wealth hidden away by those of Royal blood than the total assets of the country. It was wealth without power. The Royalists realised that putting their heads over the parapet was not a sensible move. Instead they secreted their money, jewels and land-leases, moving the bulk of it overseas and setting up dummy ownerships.

They used it wisely, putting their supporters into key positions within the new government and on parish councils. The law-making areas of public life were targeted, giving them space to breathe. Same thing happened in France after the Revolution. There have always been pockets of monied resistance.'

His companion was becoming interested.

'So having lost the use of affluence, they turned to the benefits of influence?'

'Got it in one,' beamed Siemonsen.

'How does this affect the situation over here?'

'Exactly the same way. Here the elected bodies make decisions on behalf of the country and control the lives of the citizens. They don't always get it right. They need a nudge in certain directions sometimes. Is it right that corporations that invest huge sums, bringing enhanced quality of life to all our people, are ignored when trade agreements with Europe or South America are being negotiated? The word LOBBY shouldn't exist in a truly democratic society. The people elect and the elected make the rules, right? ... Wrong! Big Business puts their man up for election and the media it controls tell the people who to vote for. There are more lobby groups on Capitol Hill than senators in Congress. The annual budget of the Jewish lobby could build the New Jerusalem and the National Rifle Association could provide a gun for every man, woman and child in the world, in fact they're halfway there already.'

'Our decision makers are under too much pressure. They can't stand back from a situation and think through all the consequences. We can do that for them, even pre-empt problems. We can certainly solve them ... without having to account to some red-taped committee full of pinkos and do-gooders. Hard-nosed businessmen with years of commercial tradition have all the qualities necessary to get this country back on line ... and make the trains run on time.

Take the defence issue. First and foremost a government's duty is the security of the population it represents. With the arms race spiralling upwards, and the cost following it something had to be done before the two superpowers bankrupted themselves.

The Presidential advisors felt the opposition would break before we did and they were right ... in a purely gross national product comparison; but the Soviet Union doesn't have the infrastructure to support as we do and their people are the toughest. They will put up with anything. We were being drained. Something had to be done. My Team solved the problem, which was becoming a standard business one. Two corporations driving up each other's costs in order to put the other out of business.

We just brought the price of the product right down and agreed to call it quits. The product being a safety net against one country being able to overrun the other.'

'What did you do?'

'Until I know you better I'm not in a position to go into details, but let me put it this way ... *we brought down the cost of delivery.'*

'Why are you telling me this?'

'I'm recruiting, with Head's permission.'

'He knows about this meeting?'

'Sure, he trusts my judgement.' Siemonsen put down his glass and moved over to the sofa beside his companion. 'I'll be straight with you. Do you know some of the other guys on my committee?'

'I didn't know you had a committee, maybe the odd rumour.'

'Lewis, Jackson, Milligan, Dwight, Hudson, they're all with me ... strike a chord?'

His companion flushed.

'We're special people you know, we have to stick together.' Siemonsen patted his guest on the thigh. 'The general thinking at Langley is that until more enlightened times come along guys like us are a security threat. I bet you've felt the hot breath of the Feds at the back of your neck from time to time? Head's not one of us, but he appreciates our ... talents. He's also being practical. He knows we'll stick together and toe his line. When you've enjoyed the freedom and rewards of being on Head's team, you'll never want to go back to basics.'

London

The Harvard Bar on the ground floor of the Grosvenor Hotel was crowded. The clientele was mainly made up of commuters waiting for their evening trains to take them home to the counties south of London. This was the perfect watering hole after a hot day in the office, a haven accessed directly from the station concourse via the discreet rear entrance.

Regan was at the bar trying to remember the order, with Daley acting as backup to help carry the drinks. Big John had sent Weller to commandeer a table while he went to the bathroom for the first time since he had left the plane.

'Why this place guv.' said Daley, looking around and taking in the green and brown decor and the calm of deeply polished dark wood. The designer had chopped up an old timber racing scull and had hung it triumphantly from the ceiling. The walls sported shields and oars from what he presumed were past triumphs of that American institution of learning,

'Thought it would make them feel at home,' said Regan sourly, raising his eyebrows and checking his change.

They shouldered their way sideways to a table in a corner, bearing three scotches and a pint for Daley.

'So what's the score with this Morgan?' Daley was addressing Big John. Nobody had spoken until three rounds had been demolished. It would be Weller's turn at the bar next. 'What's he done?'

'Hard to say,' the big man growled, 'but he attracts big trouble. I think he's got something that somebody wants ... very badly.'

Regan leaned forward and became officious. 'In what capacity are you over here ... I wasn' t informed about your visit.'

The big man emptied his glass. 'We had some leave coming. I persuaded young Weller here to see the old country.' The big man grinned broadly. Weller's face turned to Daley's and registered resignation.

'Your shout, I think.' Daley winked at Weller who rose and fumbled for UK currency.

The big man reached up and slapped Weller on the back with one hand, handing him a cassette with the other. 'While you're getting them in, ask them to get rid of the musak and play this.' Before Weller could protest, John said, 'If they object, tell the head barman that the LAPD is convinced that Ireland will win the World Cup ...' Weller's face creased to a puzzle.

'His name's Patrick Flynn ...I think we're on a winner, and make it Bushmills this time.'

Four shots later, Daley and Big John were humming in harmony. 'So I'll see you there around nine?' The big man confirmed.

Daley nodded in affirmation. 'That'll be just right, I think the set starts half an hour later... and you've got directions?'

'Over Putney bridge and turn right?'

'That's it ... then stop and ask ... anyone will tell you where the Half Moon is.' They all downed the last of their drinks.

'Think Morgan will really turn up there?' Regan expressed doubt.

'Maybe' said John, 'but I feel I'm more than half-way home.'

Los Angeles

The four men and a girl were attracting more than their fair share of stares. LAX always contained more than a smattering of odd individuals ... having five in a row was unusual. The group seemed like a bad hangover from the sixties. The four men had beards and beads and hair down to their waists. The girl had the same, except for the beard. They all sported large dark glasses and multi-coloured bell bottom trousers.

They made their way shakily along the concourse, balancing precariously on four inch platform heels. They straggled out towards the cab-rank opposite the big white spider and its suspended restaurant, pushing trolleys containing guitars and drum-cases, battered suitcases and tapestry bags. The leading male was over six feet tall, nearer seven with the platform shoes. He leaned towards the girl.

'I feel bloody ridiculous.'

'Quit moaning' was the reply, 'comebacks are always tough.'

'I never went.'

'I know,' she said.

'How did you get the passports?'

'You can buy anything in the Irish Republic. The photographs were the trickiest bit. Took them when you were both asleep, then had them retouched.'

One of the others was hand-rolling a large cigarette. 'Who wants a spliff?'

The girl turned on him. 'Put that thing away you asshole!' She turned to the tall one. 'Where did you find these guys?'

He shrugged, 'You said to make it authentic.'

'Which one's Paul?' She whispered.

He looked at them and shook his head. 'Not sure.'

When their turn for a cab eventually came, the driver was not impressed. 'You're not putting all that stuff in my cab, in fact,' he looked at them dubiously, 'I don't think I want *any* of it in my cab.'

The tall one turned around and shouted, 'Paul!' One of the hippies reacted quickly and jumped in. The tall one and the girl followed, having flung their bags into the trunk. She turned to the remaining members of the band.

'Bye guys.' They didn't seem bothered. They just sat on their gear and started rolling some more large cigarettes.

She got in the back with the other two and gave an address to the driver. She turned to the tall one. 'They seem quite happy.'

He looked through the rear screen as the cab pulled away. 'By the time they come down from whatever they're on they won't even remember us.'

London

'Nice set.' Said Daly to the other three.

'Yeah,' replied the big man, 'didn't expect that. The band were good too.' Would have been nice if this Millns guy had been playing – pity he'd cried off.'

The four officers of the law were a little worse for wear, but were bonding in a big way. They had spent most of the evening complaining about their bosses in particular, and their lot in life in general.

'I'm getting out,' said Big John, 'No, not this place, the job, the force.

Done my twenty. Good pension to come. Can't take the bullshit anymore. Can't put the bad guys down without three weeks of paperwork. Then they walk.'

'Same over here,' Regan responded. 'Nobody goes to jail cos they're full and we can't afford to build anymore.'

'But we can't *say* that,' said Daley, 'we have to tell the citizens of this great nation that we are *rehabilitating* the poor, unloved, little toe-rags by letting them continue to walk the streets.'

Weller turned to Big John. 'You're not serious ... are you?'

'The States is not a country for the likes of me anymore. I'm an old man before my time. I'd like to live a bit before I go.'

'It's hard not to go gently.' Said Regan, staring into his beer.

Silence descended on the small group. It was broken by the big man. 'I'd love to run a bar.' They all stared.

'A pub.' Said Regan.

'With music,' Said Weller and Daley together.

' Wonder how much they'd want for this place?' said the big man rising. Nick Steadman stood above the others, looked around slowly taking stock of the surroundings. 'If we all chipped in ...'

Los Angeles

'We meet at Venice.' Morgan was speaking from a 'phone at the back of a local store.

'You sure about this?' The deep brown voice at the other end encouraged caution.

'I'm going to finish it right now.'

'I've only got a small crew man.'

'That's OK ... you got my parcel?'

'Yeah, and another couple boxes of hollowpoints. You going to war?'

'If they're playing on my field.'

Virginia

Siemonsen was sitting in his office facing two colleagues. He was sitting on the edge of his chair in an upright position and he was talking into the mouthpiece using his 'I'm-in-control-of-the-situation' voice.

'Let's be sensible about this ... I'm offering you ... and the cowboy ...

your lives. I call the shots, OK? Yes ... yes, yes ... OK ... yes ... where? .... when? ... right ... yes.' He put the 'phone down and looked up at his colleagues. 'That fixed *her.*' They looked at each other with that look again.

London

The Daimler turned out of the crawling traffic on the A40 and into RAF Northolt. The driver drove straight at the red and white pole barrier without losing speed. The operator stared at the oncoming car wondering when it would slow down and stop.

It didn't appear to be doing so. His nerve broke and he raised the barrier just before the Daimler swept through. He picked up the telephone and dialled one digit. 'It's just gone through now... SAMOO7 ... so that's all right then? ... Fine.' A soldier looked enquiringly at the operator.

'Problem?'

'No,' said the operator. 'They were expecting him.'

'Interesting number plate,' said the soldier.

'Yes,' said the operator. 'Apparently it was a present from his uncle in America.'

'The number plate?'

'No,' came the reply. 'The car.'

Sir Anthony stepped out and walked across the windy tarmac and into a small brick building.

'Ah, Sir Anthony, good to see you,' said the officer, rising. The two shook hands. Sir Anthony rubbed his sleeve on the dirty window and stared across the bleak, flat fields outside.

'My transport here yet?'

'Coming in now, sir. There's a lot of traffic circling Heathrow at the moment and we had to give the area a wider berth than usual.' The officer was drinking his strong brown liquid out of a tin mug; he remembered his manners. 'Tea, sir?'

Sir Anthony squinted at the brew. 'I don't think so, thank you.'

The noise of the powerful motorbike increased as it neared the building, and cut out and died just outside the door.

'Must be orders,' said the officer.

The messenger handed over a small envelope. It was addressed to 'Sir Tony.' The back was sealed with red wax, stamped with a form of heraldic crest.

'Royal seal,' said the officer, passing the letter to Sir Anthony.

'Oh Christ,' came the response. Sir Anthony sat down on the wooden chair and tore the envelope open. The scrap of blue paper inside was scrawled with fine black ink, Sir Anthony read out loud.

'Get your arse back here. I have a runner in the 3.30 at Cheltenham. I think he was got-at the last time out, either that, or the jockey was drunk. I want you there to make sure all's well. Back to the stalls, Post-Haste.'

'Shit!' He exclaimed loudly. The 'phone rang. The officer answered it quickly, listened and then said, 'Right,' and put the 'phone down again.

'Three minutes Sir and your flight will be here.'

'Forget it,' said Sir Anthony, 'it looks as if I'm baby-sitting.'

The officer looked confused.

'My employer's mother,' said Sir Anthony cryptically and stalked out the room.

Los Angeles

The cab moved down Harbour Freeway 110, turned off at Wilmington and made its way into the San Pedro docklands area via Western Avenue. Not the Western Avenue Sir Anthony had just driven down; this one was six thousand miles away. It turned into Nine Street.

The female said, 'This is fine, just drop us here.'

They got out and stretched their legs.

'Did we have to change cabs three times?' said the tall one.

'It's probably not enough,' she replied, 'but I was running out of money.'

'Did you make your call?' Sara quizzed Morgan.

' No, she wasn't in.' She gave him one of her 'Oh yeah' looks, but said nothing.

After they had retrieved their baggage and the cab had pulled away, the smaller man said. 'And where to now?'

'Follow me,' she replied firmly, and led them down a series of small back streets.

The tall one was staring into the mirror carefully peeling off the long dark beard. 'Ouch!'

'Don't be such a baby,' said Sara, lifting off her long wig. 'Where's Paul?'

'He's lying in the bath, soaking it off.' Morgan was gingerly rubbing his blotchy exposed cheeks. 'I'll be glad to get out of these clothes.' Morgan seemed bushed.

'Why? They suit you.'

Morgan wasn't sure that this was meant as a compliment and ignored it. 'I'm having trouble with the moustache. I'll need a lot of hot water and soap.'

They fussed with the contents of their travelling bags, searching for things they were never going to find again.

Morgan peeled himself away from her sleeping form and slid out from under the sheets. He dressed quietly and moved to the door, glancing back just once. He walked the narrow corridor in his socks, holding his boots in one hand. At 2.00 am he was unlikely to meet another tenant on the stairway down to the exit.

Out on the street at the first corner a figure emerged from the shadows and stood in front of him. The man was taller and bigger.

'Did you bring everything?' said Morgan.

'Yes ... and my guys.' Aaron raised his arm and a large black sedan put on its lights and moved towards them.

'My package?'

'In the car, let's get out of the city limits before we get set.'

'OK,' said Morgan, 'Let's do it.'

The desert night sky was velvet black, pinpricked with a million lights.

The car swung off an unmade road and bounced towards the faded wooden buildings and scrub picked-out by the headlights. The reason for these shacks was unknown to Morgan, but not to Aaron who had suggested this spot. Morgan stretched and breathed in the cold and the clean. He head was filled with 'Ohio' and 'Southern Man' which had been playing on a loop at a million decibels. 'Gimme Shelter' was now leaking out the car and providing a little mood music.

'When are they due to be here.' Aaron directed his question to Morgan.

'Dawn.' Came the reply. 'Whenever that is.' Morgan went on. 'I wanted to be in place well before they arrive. Don't think they could have beaten us to it ... they wouldn't have got the message until now. I left a note with the shopkeeper to deliver at the nearest cop shop. Addressed to a Mr. Siemonsen, C/O CIA, Langley telling him to come here alone. That should bring his guys out of the woodwork.'

'If they *are* here we'd also be dead by now.' Said Aaron squinting at the darkness.

Three other black guys eased out of the back seat and stretched their cramped muscles. Flashlights illuminated the trunk and all five went to work, checking weapons and ammunition.

'Sure you want to do this?' Aaron looked at Morgan.

'Too late now.' Morgan took Aaron's arm. 'It ends here.' He gripped the arm tighter. 'They've killed a lady who was very close to me, they've killed Freddie and a couple of innocents... and have been trying to take out me and someone who's been keeping me alive. All for no reason that I can get my head around. *Enough.*'

Aaron nodded and dived under the driver's seat. He handed a package to Morgan. The heavy revolver was wrapped in an oily polythene wrap, tightly taped up.

'I took it apart and checked it out. Well looked after, didn't need too much work.'

Morgan opened it up and felt the weight of the silver cannon.

'Thanks. Thanks for all this. You and your guys didn't need to do this for me.'

'It's not for you. It's for me.'

'Why?'

'Cos I asked them.'

'OK.'

Aaron handed Morgan a box of shells. '.44 Hollow-points. If you manage to hit anything, it won't exist afterwards.'

'Suits me fine.'

Aaron took the gun off Morgan, broke it open and spun the chamber. 'Full load of six and a box refill. Do you know how to handle this?'

'How hard can it be?'

'Hold it two hands, it'll break your wrist otherwise. Point it a foot below your target at ten feet cos it'll kick upwards. Oh, and don't point it at me or any of our guys, we're a little sensitive.'

Morgan practiced dropping in shells and removing them. It was getting lighter. He could see the other three shapes checking out their weapons. One had a semi like Aaron and the other two had pump-action shotguns.

Morgan signalled them to join him. 'Listen up. I don't know who you are, but I'll thank you now as I may never get another chance. The people who I think will turn up will be here to kill me and anybody else who gets in their way. This is not a street fight with gangbangers. These people will be almost certainly East-European muscle with a bit more in terms of heavy hardware. If they do it right they will approach carefully in numbers and will have a lot of firepower. I've tried to negate this by giving them a very short time-frame ... and the fact that they are expecting only me.

Their boss is almost frantic to get rid of me quickly and that is why I'm hoping they will make mistakes ... but I would imagine they would have the sense to place some long range weapons on our flanks and move in quickly with the short range stuff. So maybe two cars, stopping short, then spreading out around this area. Surveillance first. That's how *I'd* do it.

So, what have we got? Surprise and set-up. We are in place *first*. We can turn this into a streetfight out in the desert. We have to second guess their positions and be there *first*. First to everything, first to fire and fire to put them down, permanently. No second chance.' They all nodded and didn't seem fazed.

The desert was now offering up its landscape, the shacks were becoming defined. The immediate terrain was almost flat with only slight undulations.

'Hard for anybody to surprise anybody around here.' Aaron scanned the gloom. 'Where do you want us, you seem to have a handle on all this.'

'Yeah, well I've had a good teacher recently. Apparently I have a natural instinct for survival.'

'Well that Indian blood should come in useful now. Hope it's not in the sand when it's over.'

Morgan shrugged. He walked away from the group and peered down the track. He stalked around the site in a 200 yard deep crescent. After twenty minutes he returned. 'Ok guys, first we blend, Aaron you got the gear?' Aaron produced aerosol glue and started to spray the track-suited figures. They all rolled in the sand. Morgan beckoned two of the team to follow him down the track, talking as he walked. 'They will have parked up way back, but maybe they'll bring one vehicle up to the shacks. You guys dig in a hundred yards either side and wait until you have them all in front of you. You're my back-stop. Remember, they have finite numbers. Every one you put down will have a big impact. Don't hesitate, take them out, then Move.! Dig your shallow pits at the points I've marked and keep moving and keep flat. Become the earth.' Morgan looked at the stars.

'We're all set yeah? I call the plays.'

They spread out, the only sounds breaking the quiet were the clicks and ratchets of safeties and chambered rounds.

They lay in the sand and waited.

The sun was just lifting itself over the low horizon when they came. Two cars stopped on the highway and after a minute one turned onto the track and slowly swayed up to the killing ground.

Morgan reckoned on four men in each car and when the moving car stopped, unloading five, he squinted back down the track for the other three. He couldn't see anything, just hoped the back-stop's were picking them up. He listened hard for any sounds of a chopper and was happy not to hear any. No chance they would be outflanked or hit from behind.

The five men were professional and well armed, some with automatic rifles. The leader was wearing a full-length leather coat, unbuttoned and loose. He called out towards the crumbling cluster of wooden buildings. His voice was thickly Slavic.

'Good morning Mr Morgan, I believe you wished to talk to us?'

Morgan was squatting inside the largest shack, right at the back and just inside a hole he'd kicked in the rear wall. He hoped the additional two or three men he assumed were out there somewhere had not made their way to his rear. He was relying on Aaron's two guys riding shotgun, literally.

'Is Siemonsen with you.' shouted Morgan. 'He was told to come in person.'

'He has been slightly detained, but you can talk to us.'

Morgan hurled himself through the opening at the back and started to sprint directly away from the shack. They had established he was inside and there was no reason for them to hold off. He was right. The leader grinned as he extracted an AK 47 with a grenade launcher, shouldered it and sent a grenade into the shack blowing the whole structure to a burning wreck.

The five stood in a semi-circle and seemed content. Morgan was head down thirty yards behind the bonfire, arms over his head protecting himself from the falling and floating debris.

The five started to move forward, pointing handguns and AKs. Behind them, two loud barks simultaneously smashed the silence, quickly followed by three more. Before the heavies could react, Aaron, Morgan and one of the crew rose out of the ground and opened up at the five, felling two instantly. Three ran towards the shotguns and one was cut in half by two more quick blasts. Only the leader and one other were standing, firing wildly in all directions. One of the shotguns screamed and went down, but the firepower was now in favour of Morgan's team.

The leader and his one remaining gunman sprinted for the highway, but were pursued by four determined and seriously pissed citizens of L.A., reloading as they ran. It was now a no-contest as the return fire had ceased. The leader went all out for speed, but his companion stopped suddenly, turned and dropped to one knee. He let off the remainder of his clip at the pursuers, scattering them, but not getting any hits. As his last round hit the dirt, so did he, riddled by slugs and shotgun pellets.

Morgan was still sprinting after the leader, the silver revolver like a baton in his hand. The others stopped and watched.

Morgan was gaining rapidly, the leader was not going to make the car. He started to turn when Morgan was almost on him, bringing a 9mm out of his belt and trying to get a bead, but too late. The blast from the .44 took him in the gut and off his feet throwing him backwards and spread-eagled.

He looked up at Morgan towering over him, the shock and pain numbing his ability to know he was dying. He tried to speak as blood trickled from his mouth, but didn't know what to say. Morgan was checking the chambers. One left.

Morgan heard a number of single shots behind him. They were not grouped. The crew were making sure.

The leader made another effort to speak as Morgan leaned closer.

'They *will* get you Mr. Morgan. Others will come ... It would go well for you if you help me ... get me to a hospital.' He held his stomach with both hands. 'I can talk to them ... it's not too late.'

'It is for you.' Morgan aimed at the man's head. He couldn't do it.

Aaron appeared on his shoulder. ' Do it, Finish it.'

Morgan was saved from making a decision. The man died.

Morgan turned to Aaron. ' It's over.'

'It's never over.'

The crew silently gathered around the killing ground. The man down was struggling to get up on one elbow.

'Smashed shoulder- bone and flesh wound in the thigh, we'll get back and get him looked after.'

'No hospitals.' Said Morgan

'No hospitals.' Agreed Aaron.

They made their way to the car and made the wounded guy as comfortable as possible. Aaron passed a bottle around and they lapsed into silence as they hit the highway and turned west.

'I don't know your names,' Morgan turned to the three in the back.

'Right.' Said one and nothing more was said.

The light was on in the small living-room and Sara was pouring two glasses of amber liquid. Morgan slumped and downed one. She filled the glass.

'You're up early.' He said.

'No ... haven't been to sleep.'

They both lit up.

'Is it done?' Sara's eyes searched his face. He thought about pretending he didn't know what she was talking about, but didn't have the energy.

'How did you know?'

'Trying to slip sleeping pills into my drink, quietly leaving like a herd of elephants, gangsta car with heavy crew... and when I called Siemonsen he tried to cancel tomorrow's meet. Probably thought you wouldn't be around. I suspect he now knows you will be.

'Yeah. I will be.' Morgan poured another drink. 'I was hoping he would have been there. Still, he'll be short-handed now.'

'Good.' She lit another. 'He'll need to be ultra careful. How many did you take out?'

'Eight.'

'Christ.' She blew out a long stream, 'He won't be able to make up the numbers that quickly. If he knows you're alone, then he has to play ball. He knows I'm still out there.'

'Aren't you pissed that you've been working for a psychopath for all this time?

'I would be ... 'cept for the fact that I haven't.'

Morgan stopped in mid-pour.

'I work for NEST...Nuclear Emergency Search Team. It's an organisation set up to investigate nuclear accidents, threats, transport incidents... and the tracking down of any illicit nuclear material within our borders. We've been worried about some form of new terrorist threat for some time.'

She blew out more smoke, then crushed the filter carefully. Morgan just stared at the ceiling muttering to himself.

'But what we've been getting from intercepts and the occasional rumour has been very odd. It seems the agencies dedicated to prevention of such an attack have been on top of their game and report nothing of any consequence ... but there has been persistent spikes and nuggets of information indicating that some sort of mutual activity has been ongoing between sections of our services and those of the Soviet bloc.

Morgan spoke to the ceiling. 'Anything else I should know about you?' Sara ignored him.

'We had to get involved as this activity often had a nuclear facet. We eventually narrowed the source of the rumours to Simonsen's people. It came back to his department. We had to get someone in there. That's me. He thinks I'm working for him. Problem is I'm still not sure what he's up to. That's why I want you to go tomorrow. I don't think you'll get the full story, but close enough for us to second guess. You're my mole Morgan ... go get the intel!'

They both sat back. They both watched the dawn get stronger.

'You got the address?'

'Yes.' he replied.

'Time?'

'Yes ... how did you get him to agree?'

'I've got something on him.'

'What?'

Sara threw the last of her clothes on the bed. She was naked except for a black choker around her neck – and the silver cross. 'He's been screwing one of the two who tried to waste us in the desert. His people don't like that.'

'She *was* a tasty lady.'

'It wasn't the lady.'

'Ah!'

' I was screwing the lady.' She fingered the cross. ' I gave her this.'

Morgan was trying to compute, nodded, then squeesed her hand.

'I wonder how Paul's getting on?' Morgan said, still rubbing his chin.

Sara pushed open the door and peeped inside the bathroom. 'Fine, he's fallen asleep in the bath. Don't worry, there's not enough water in it.'

She walked back in the room and shut the door. She plumped up a pillow and sat on the bed. 'When it's over, I know just the place for us. Quiet, friendly, nice people and a good kindergarten.'

'Kindergarten?'

'Steiner kindergarten ... yes. Rudolf Steiner ... Ever read his stuff ... Great philosopher. He opened people's eyes to spiritual values and the importance of the observation of nature as an aid to man's self-discovery....Remember your drunken ramble...Meaning of Life and all that ... Lots of circles, going round and round? ...Well this guy's cracked it ... It's the ESSENCE of the individual, not what's on the SURFACE ... That's what counts ...The centre of your circle. The Steiner schools reflect this. They treat each child as an individual; each centre is surrounded by different layers ...Veils of artifice which the teaching gently removes over a period of time ... Modern civilisation has ...'

Morgan interrupted. 'Kindergarten ... you said kindergarten.'

'Well?'

'Kindergarten,' went on Morgan, 'that's where they put ... KIDS!'

'You should know,' she replied. He sat on the edge of the bed and looked at her.

'You're not?'

She smiled. 'Oh yes ... VERY.' Morgan rose again. He was having difficulty finding words. He gave up.

'Kids!'

'Only one,' she said. 'I think.'

He sat on the bed again. 'Mine?'

She grinned. 'Very.'

He got up again and turned away, then suddenly spun round leaping in the air and hitting the ceiling.

'Christ!'

'Don't think so'

He leapt on the bed, pulling her tightly to him. After a moment he held her away from him. 'This Steiner, will he sort my boy out?'

She put a finger on his mouth. 'It all depends on what you put in, my love;

you can't go through life without touching the sides.'

She dived into his bag and found the cassette. She found the player in another bag and plugged it in.

'I think we're nearly there now.' She spoke quietly with clarity. 'We'll build a home, not a house. We'll build it where we can see the horizon. A place where we can bring up our kids as children. They're up there, waiting to come down to us. I want to protect them from the crap we've created, for as long as possible ... till they've built their defences strong. We're halfway there.'

Morgan was lying back in the bed, arms behind his head staring at the ceiling and grinning like an idiot. She pressed a button on the machine.

I've been moving quietly, setting new plans in motion
And I've been stepping lightly, over land, sea and ocean
And if you find yourself in trouble
And your heart is sinking like stone
Look for me out on the skyline
Come and meet me if you have the mind
Cos I'm almost halfway home
And when the weather comes, and the air is bright and cold
I'm on the homeward run, these wheels, burning as they roll
I know your life is turning without me
Sometimes fast and sometimes slow
But look for me out on the sky line
Come and meet me if you have the time
Cos I'm almost half way home
Halfway home, I've got the wind in my eyes
Halfway home, I'm clear through the night
Moving as faster than light, Gonna reach you before the morning rise
And when you find yourself in trouble, and your heart is sinking like a stone
Look for me out on the skyline
Come and meet me if you have the time
Cos I'm almost halfway home
Look out for me on the skyline, Halfway home

I'll meet you before the morning rise, Halfway home

Virginia

'SDI is crap.' Siemonsen's nose was buried in a large goblet of white wine. He inhaled deeply and returned his eye to the label on the greenish glass bottle with sloping shoulders. The label was cream and the red script confirmed that the wine was a Chablis Premier Cru of 1987 vintage. 'I've killed it with cold' he admitted. 'I'm struggling to get any nose out of this.' He sipped, worked it round his mouth and sipped again. 'Too thin, fuck it. I've been talking too much, too long in the bucket. What should have been verdigris in the aftertaste has turned to copper.' He put the bottle on the table a ritualistic distance from the iced water. 'I'll leave it to grow,' he said.

His companion nodded sagely, without having a clue as to why.

'Why crap? Surely the only way to ensure maximum security is a maximum expenditure on a defensive shield. The Strategic Defence Initiative will give us that. From maximum defence we then have the option of any degree of *offence.*'

Siemonsen was in minimal defensive mode. This was mainly the wine, but with relaxing contributions from marijuana and excited rushes from coke. He luxuriated in the controlled spilling of confidences.

'Balls.' Siemonsen filled his companion's glass and cupped his own in long digits. He was in expansive mood and expanded on his theme.

'A one hundred percent defensive shield, that's what Reagan promised in 1983. This was based on laser weapons in space and anti-missile missiles on the ground ... Balls!' Siemonsen took a sip and smiled. It was fine.

'A layered defence against incoming missiles at boost, mid-course and terminal phases. Fine, in theory, but in practice ...'

Siemonsen waved the glass at the ceiling. 'If we nailed ninety seven percent we'd still be wiped out ... and the cost? Crazy figures ... The jewel in the crown, get this ... is an X-ray laser. This would sit in space, with a nuclear reactor as its power source and deliver bursts of energy, directed with pin-point accuracy at something moving at thousands of miles per hour! X-rays from nuclear explosions would be directed by systems we haven't even developed yet!'

'But we WILL do it!' His companion was very patriotic, perhaps idiotic.

'Rowed for Harvard didn't you?' Siemonsen mused.

'Well yes, as a matter of fact I ...'

'Still got some of that water behind your ears.' His companion looked hurt and a little confused.

'WE NEVER INTENDED TO!' Siemonsen suddenly shouted 'DON'T YOU UNDERSTAND? All those speeches, all that rhetoric ... the artist's impressions. They were cheap. Ideas are cheap ... we could afford *those*.' He was slurring slightly.

'We scared the Ruskies shitless. All that stuff we fed Ames. He convinced them we were for real, because he BELIEVED we were for real. What the fuck do you think brought the wall down? They thought the game was up ... for *them!*'

14

Late in the year

Los Angeles

It was late in the evening and the last of the light had left. To Morgan's right, and left ajar deliberately, was a rusting metal door. This led into a piece of waste ground which in turn led to a largely looming black mass, only discernible from its surroundings by its uniform blackness.

Its interface with the sky was apparent at various points along its length where the broken glass in its skylights gathered and then reflected what little luminosity the umbrella of smog had retained. Morgan groped his way forward, glass occasionally crunching under-foot and sharp pieces of discarded metal clutching at his ankles. Morgan felt that at any moment a bear-trap would snap around his foot. The metal staircase was exactly where Sara had described it as being.

'Good girl,' he muttered. His strong boots slowly made their way upwards, his right hand clutching the thin guard rail. One flight up the staircase ended and he pushed open a creaking metal door. He cursed his stupidity in leaving the torch behind. He allowed himself a moment for his eyes to become accustomed to what light there was, for light there *was*, much to his surprise.

It came from a point at the far end of the floor and as this warehouse probably had no electricity for at least five years, Morgan assumed the light had been rigged by the man he had come here to meet.

He made his way carefully towards the light. He walked two or three paces at a time and paused for a moment after each advance before moving on. It was amazing how much sound could be generated in such a dead place.

The shadows cast by the one small source of light divided up the vast space into a series of horizontal and vertical lines, for the bulk of the interior was made up of empty lines of metal racking. As he crunched his way towards the light source the overall effect was that of a black, white and grey Mondrian, but without the inert quality. This vision was virtual reality, each step changing the picture in front of him. The sound around him consisted of cracking metallic noises as the racking cooled after the day's heat, the tinkle of glass as rats scratched their way in search of scraps and the steady drip of water. The light reflected small pools of it in front of him and also small rivulets of it as it slid down the structural metal posts.

It only required the addition of a steam hose and Ridley Scott could have shot his next movie here. As he came within fifty paces of the light, he could see that it was a small overhanging single bulb, its flex having been slung over a water pipe. This flex dangled down to floor level, where it was connected to a small car battery. As he came nearer, he could make out a small metal shade on the bulb which directed most of the light into a concentrated pool, twelve feet down to the floor below.

Although the air was perfectly still, the lamp was swaying slightly, allowing the shadows to dance. Morgan guessed correctly that the bulb had not been in place very long. He stopped at the edge of the circle of light and waited, trying to regulate his breathing as his ears filtered the sounds for those he wanted to hear.

Out of the blackest of the shadows and directly across the pool of light, emerged a man in a light raincoat. Underneath he was wearing a neat, dark suit, white shirt and dark tie.

'Glad you made it, Morgan.'

Morgan stood still. 'Who are you?'

The man stood there, his hands deep in his pockets. 'I work for Siemonsen, I've been told to put you straight.'

'Well?'

The agent looked around, and dragged a box into the centre of the light. He sat down on it. 'Pull something up and sit down.'

'No thanks, I'll stand if you don't mind.'

The agent shrugged and pulled out a packet of Marlboro. He lit one up and offered the pack to Morgan. 'Cigarette?'

'No thanks, I've given up ... Mostly'

The agent coughed. 'Good for you, I don't think I could do that myself. Anyway, my wife smokes, and I reckon if I give them up, I'll be letting the side down ... not showing solidarity. You understand?'

'No,' replied Morgan.

The agent shrugged again, his exhaled smoke rising to the light above. Morgan watched it rise in a straight line.

'Can we get on with this?' Morgan was edgy.

'Sure, sure,' said the agent ... Now where shall I start.' He pulled again on the cigarette. 'That bomb you found? We knew about that one. There *are* others ... planted in this city...and in fact, all major cities throughout the States. They exist in most large towns in all major countries...and some minor ones.'

Morgan had stiffened and his jaw started to drop.

'Over here most are Eastern bloc installations, but some are Israeli, some are French and then there is the odd smattering of contributions from Libya, North Korea and of course, Iraq. Yes, the smaller nations are getting their act together now, even the Brits. In fact, *they* may have more *placements* around the world than we have allowed for.'

'What the hell are you talking about!' exclaimed Morgan.

The agent moved on smoothly. 'We've got ours in their countries of course, and not just in the cities. We try to get close to military sites, but that's more difficult.'

'Am I dreaming this?'

The agent stubbed out his cigarette and lit another. 'Look Morgan, you don't actually think that we put a nuclear warhead in a missile the size of a tower block ... get it to travel six thousand miles, burning up thousands of dollars' worth of fuel ... and hope it doesn't MISS! That's plain STUPID!' The smoke from the cigarette formed a slim vertical line before encasing the light bulb.

'It's so much easier to walk off a plane with one in a suitcase! ... Or at least several suitcases; diplomatic bags are getting so much larger these days. For the rental of a dozen houses and a bit of DIY in the basements we can take out half the Soviet Union. All we have to do is dial a number, and BANG!

We can beam the call off a satellite just like a normal telephone connection. The smaller nations have to rent time on existing communications satellites, but we have our own.'

'Can you call collect?'

'Why do you think the Cold War warmed up? We don't dial their numbers, if they don't dial ours. Easy. It's kept the peace for at least ten years; brought the wall down too. At least we like to think it contributed.'

'But the missiles!' said Morgan. 'They exist! They're in great silos!'

'Dummies! A lot of them ... Covered in foil ... Real turkeys.'

The dripping silence was becoming more oppressive. 'We have maintained a very delicate balance between the destructive powers of East and West. It only takes a small speck on the scales to tip things one way or the other and the human race will cease to exist. When you kicked that door in, Curtis's people had to act quickly. They couldn't take any chances. You were the speck that had to be wiped off. They took care of Curtis, but his daughter and you were *our* responsibility.'

'So you think you have the right to kill someone because *they kicked a door off its hinges!*'

'It's for the greater good Morgan. There's a great weight on all our shoulders. We don't do this lightly. Can't take any chances, these nuclear installations are the only way to guarantee parity ... and *peace.*'

The agent stood up and paced the floor, staying within the circle of light. 'Of course this development hasn't gone down too well with the armament industry. We give them a big conventional war now and again to keep them happy. The Gulf was a great one. Falklands wasn't bad ... got one coming up in Africa soon. Algeria's making the bomb you see, with China's help. We'll have to put a stop to that ... Have to keep the club exclusive ... Eh?'

'What about the people working on the missile systems? And Star Wars and all that stuff ... are they wasting their time?'

'Mostly ... but of course we can't let them know that, might start a panic.'

Morgan said nothing for a while; thoughts were racing through his head. 'What if some of them got too close? Realised what was happening? Like maybe, twenty-two Brits, and God knows how many more in the States?'

'Now you don't want to believe everything you read in the papers, what sort of people do you think we are?'

'The Brits can't account for four hundred warheads ...They wouldn't be sitting in somebody's basement would they?'

'I'm not an expert on the UK.'

'Defence budgets,' reasoned Morgan. 'You have to be accountable. Where does the money go? You must have a lot of spare cash floating about?'

The agent became angry. 'Do you know what it costs to run a decent Security Service? What with slush-funds, pay-offs, drug-rackets, and the odd dictator to finance ... not to mention the campaign to re-elect the President. It's not easy.'

'This is madness,' said Morgan. 'You can't think I'm going to keep something like this quiet?'

'No, I suppose not.'

'We're all living with Armageddon in the basement, just waiting for some mad mullah to bring it into the living-room.'

The agent answered thoughtfully. 'Naturally, that scenario does give cause for concern.'

'I'm off,' said Morgan. 'Every goddamn Newspaper and TV station is going to get this ... *I'm going to shout it from the roof tops!*' He turned to leave.

'Mr Morgan? Just hold on a minute.' Morgan stopped and turned. 'I'm glad we had this little chat. You see I just couldn't see you off without you knowing *why* ... call me old fashioned, I suppose.'

Morgan was staring at a nine millimetre, nickel-plated, automatic hand-gun. The agent flipped off the safety and the loud click echoed around the building. He raised the gun and lined up a head shot.

'Good-bye Mr Morgan. I promise you won't feel a thing.'

That last sentence was too long. Before he had finished it, Morgan had hurled himself to the floor and was beginning a roll. After three rolls, he was in pitch blackness. Two bullets had kicked up the concrete floor near his head, but Morgan had hit the shadows. The agent cursed, and walked cautiously out of his lighted circle and towards Morgan's hiding place.

'Nice one, Mr Morgan. They said you used to move well. Well these little bullets are not as large as the hunks of beefcake you've been used to, but they move a little faster and I'm afraid they do a lot more damage when they arrive.' The agent continued to move towards Morgan's resting place. Morgan retreated as quietly as he could, back through the shadows.

A slow macabre dance unfolded against the grey and black background. The music that accompanied it was a slow movement of dripping water, the crunch of glass and the clatter of metal.

'Come now, Mr Morgan, don't make this harder than it has to be. Just one clean shot and you can relax.' The dance continued. 'Look Morgan,' the agent was getting angry now, and possibly nervous. 'I'm only doing my job. There's no way out for you. Even my boss is around here somewhere, just to make sure.' If he could have seen Morgan's face he would have noticed a look of surprise and then determination as he registered the presence of Siemonsen. The agent fired a shot into the darkness, its ricochet sending sparks down the building and the noise of the shot reverberating through it.

The dance continued. Every time Morgan bumped into something the noise would re-direct the agent who would then blast off in that general direction. Morgan was counting the bullets. He'd got to six before he realised he had no idea how many there should have been in a clip anyway. Morgan was backing away from the light and with every step he took, the darker it was getting.

He didn't know it, but he was about thirty yards away from another metal staircase leading to the floor above. This floor did not extend the length of the building, but formed a gallery occupying a third of the floor space. Two hands clasped the guard-rail and the face above them looked down on the scene. They were very well manicured hands, pale with long digits. Immaculate white cuffs extended for half an inch from the sleeves of a dark suit.

From this vantage-point Siemonsen could gaze from the darkness at the two black shapes moving slowly through the tangled industrial collage.

The two black shapes moved steadily towards him, like wet drips on a Pollock canvas. Sometimes moving freely and sometimes merging with solids already in place. He turned his head slightly and whispered behind him.

'Go down there and give our man a hand.' Whoever his colleague was, the answer expressed some doubt.

'I can't see a fucking thing.'

'Keep your ears open,' came the reply. His next whisper was fiercer. 'Go!'

His colleague started slowly down the stairs. The man should have worn trainers. If Siemonsen had told him what they were getting into beforehand he would have been prepared. Unfortunately, the hard leather soles on the hand-made shoes made noises on the metal despite his attempts to soften their impact.

Morgan became aware of footsteps high on the iron staircase to his right. The agent in front of him fired another shot and pieces of brickwork hit Morgan in the face. 'At least I know where the wall is,' thought Morgan, and moved away towards the centre of the room. 'Mustn't get boxed in,' he said to himself. 'Must drop back and get some protection.'

Morgan's nervous system was stretched tight. The pumping adrenalin had sharpened his senses to the point of maximum efficiency. In the blackness, other senses came into play. Maybe the Indian blood helped, but as Morgan continued his cat-like retreat telepathic signals between his two foes were being picked up in his brain, or was it just his imagination running riot. Whatever it was, it kept him half a step ahead of the game.

As Morgan was threatened with death and his opponents were not, he was just that little more finely tuned than they. The problem was, there was no clock ticking on this play. It would go on until he was dead.

Morgan knew he had to make for the door which he had used to enter the building. He also knew that the second man would have placed himself between Morgan and that door... further back in the blackness. This second man was very quiet and Morgan knew he had to keep moving and that the other man didn't thus putting Morgan at an extreme disadvantage. A piece of metal racking to Morgan's left screamed thinly as a slug tore at it. Morgan registered the flash a micro-second later. It was about fifteen yards away from him. Then the noise echoed again and died slowly. Morgan was sure that the second man had taken up a position in the corner of the building near the door. He just sensed it. It was also the logical place for him to be. The first agent seemed to be sweeping laterally through the building, moving Morgan slowly back towards that door. The first agent suddenly shouted.

'I'm driving him towards the far end.' The second man's face nodded a silent assent.

'Did you hear me? ... The far end!'

The second man's face contorted with rage. 'Shut up!' Came the cry from the area near the door. Morgan grinned grimly and the first agent shrugged his shoulders. Morgan crouched, and looked around for another exit. There weren't any. He and the two agents were forming a triangle in the dark. Morgan wanted it to be a straight line and moved steadily to where he knew the second man would be waiting. He heard a click and then a clatter and then a metallic sliding and slapping sound. The first agent had fixed up a fresh clip. Two more shots rang out quickly. Concrete and metal were scattered in the darkness, but they weren't close to him.

'He's losing his feel,' thought Morgan. 'He's becoming jumpy.' Morgan was aware of the faint scrape of shoe on glass and a thump of shoulder on metal. 'Things that go bump in the night,' he said quietly to himself. These noises had come from a point just inside the door. The first agent had heard it too.

He whispered loudly, which would have been farcical under any other circumstances, 'That you Siemonsen?'

Morgan tensed. The agent by the door was furious and hissed quietly to himself, 'Stupid sod.'

Morgan moved on all fours like a cat and scurried close to where the second man lay in position. Both agents tensed hearing these rapid noises. Morgan felt he was directly between the two men now and he suddenly raised himself on two feet shouting. 'He's over there ... on the right!' And crouched back down again before rolling to one side.

The first agent stopped in his tracks, shouting, 'Whose right?'

The second agent was becoming alarmed and blurted out, 'That's not right, that's ...'

The first agent broke in quickly, 'What do you mean not right? I am ...'

'It's Morgan!' shouted the second man.

The first became puzzled. 'Of course it's bloody Morgan!' He shouted back.

Morgan shouted from the darkness, aping the second man, 'He's got a gun!' The first threw himself to the floor.

'Christ!' He was worried now.

The second man was becoming extremely irate. 'It's Morgan!' He shouted again.

'Where?' cried the first agent, still flat on the floor. Morgan leapt again from his hiding place between the two men. As the second man could see Morgan silhouetted in the light, he moved forward triumphantly, reducing the space between them quickly and raising his gun.

'There!' shouted Morgan, unseen by the first against the black background, and rolled to one side. His first agent, who was now flat on the floor in a firing position was aiming his gun directly at the point where Morgan had been standing, his eyes trying to get focused on that area. The first thing that came to light was moving rapidly towards him. He squeezed the trigger triumphantly, three times in rapid succession, targeting the glow in the gloom. Had he lived, the second agent would never have forgiven his valet-service for putting so much starch into his white shirt. The three small red holes that appeared in the centre of the shirt were not echoed at the back ... When the body pitched forward and hit the floor, the back of the jacket was a ragged mess of purple, although it was not visible in the darkness.

It took a while for the echoes to finally fade. The agent who fired the shots got up on to one knee and was still pointing at the inert mass on the floor. It was very quiet. Even the water had stopped dripping. He shouted into the blackness.

'Is he dead? ... Well?' Silence . He started to sweat.

'Where the fuck are you?' he shouted. The silence dripped on. He suddenly rolled to the side and crouched behind a large piece of machinery. 'Shit,' he was cursing himself, bitterly realising he'd been conned. Up in the gallery, Siemonsen's face twisted with anger. He slipped a slim automatic out of the neatly cut shoulder holster, slipped off his shoes and descended the staircase quietly. The first agent kept his gun trained on the body, for lying next to it was the small neat handgun. Morgan couldn't be far away. In fact he wasn't. Morgan was about two steps away from that gun and was contemplating going for it. The agent moved forward cautiously, keeping his gun out ahead of him and training it on the gun on the floor.

'Come on then, Morgan,' he shouted, 'let's see you try for it.' The light was directly behind the agent, and from his shadow Morgan was monitoring his progress. He knew the guy could shoot ... the fact that he had just shot Simonsen with a nice tight grouping testified to that. The man was coming closer now. Morgan either had to go for it or retreat.

The man's angle of vision would soon bring Morgan into the frame. The gun cracked two more shots into the darkness around him.

'Haven't you got the guts,' shouted the gunman. It was very tempting, two strides and he'd have it. The gunman came nearer.

'I mustn't do what he wants me to do,' thought Morgan, and retreated. As he backed away, he realised he would never be allowed to make the door, he had to take this man out. He was about twenty yards away now and the gunman was standing over the body. 'He's got to pick that gun up,' thought Morgan. 'I'll have a fraction of a second when his full attention won't be on me'

He groped around on the floor for something, anything. Nothing. Small metal shavings, paper, slivers of glass, small pieces of concrete; he cut his hand as it scrabbled through the light rubble. He was aware of the gunman about to snatch the second gun from the floor.

Morgan's hand found a piece of concrete. It was about the size of his hand and very heavy. Morgan juggled with it, gauging its weight. He looked towards the shadow. The light of the distant bulb formed a halo around the head. He could see light gleaming off the fallen gun. 'He's about to pick it up,' thought Morgan.

As he was thinking this, the gunman's free hand appeared in silhouette reaching for the second gun and at the same time the gunman's head disappeared and the shoulders lowered. Morgan gripped the piece of concrete, took a step forward and hurled it at a spot halfway between where the head had been and the gleaming gun on the floor. Morgan got his angle, distances and speed of throw right, because as the gunman's hand gripped the butt of the gun the lump of concrete connected with his head. It sounded like a mud pie hitting a brick wall. The man turned into a formless bundle and crashed down on his former colleague.

Morgan moved forward towards the two heaps and flicked the two guns away with the toe of his boot. The piece of concrete had caught the man at the side of his head. The hair was matted with blood, but it didn't seem to be flowing freely.

Morgan started to shake. He walked unsteadily towards the pool of light and sat on the box. He leaned forward putting his head in his hands and took deep breaths. The whole building seemed to be creaking now and the water had started to drip again.

Morgan shook his head and stood up. He had to get out of there. Before he could move, three loud ironic claps echoed around the building and a man emerged from the shadows. He was clapping his free hand against a gun hand.

'Well played, Mr Morgan,' and Siemonsen stepped into the light.

'Who the hell are you?'

'Siemonsen,' came the reply. Morgan said nothing. He just stood there and glared. 'It was a pity you weren't playing on my team,' said Siemonsen.

'Sorry, said Morgan, 'I've got a long term contract with the good guys.'

'And is that what you are?' Morgan was aware that the small automatic was rock steady... his adrenalin had left him. He was drained and too tired to care.

'You know I can't let you leave here.' Siemonsen was very calm.

'Frankly, my dear, I don't give a toss.' Morgan walked slowly past Siemonsen.

'I am going to have to shoot you, Mr Morgan.'

'Sure you do. But you won't. She's still out there.'

'Goodbye, Mr Morgan.'

The sudden noise in Morgan's head deafened and blinded him, then the pain came, then nothing. Siemonsen stared down at the lifeless body and shook his head sadly.

He sat on the box and pulled out a small mobile 'phone. He dialled quickly, then spoke.

'Siemonsen here, I want the Cleaners ... three takeaways.'

'Where's Morgan?' Paul was unwrapping the Chinese.

'How many did you buy for?' she said.

'Three,' Paul replied.

'Well, I hope you're hungry.' Paul continued to dish it out.

'Where is he then?'

'Out.'

Paul tucked in. 'What about you?'

'I'm not hungry.' Paul scooped even more food onto his plate.

'When's he coming back?'

'I think I need a cigarette,' she replied. He looked at her.

'You hate them?'

'Yeah, that's right, I hate them.' She fingered the cross. ' He's looking for redemption.'

'Will he find it ?'

'No, not immediately. Maybe some time down the road. Just looking for it is probably enough.'

'Are you going to stop pacing up and down?'

She stopped, and poured a large drink from a one litre, duty-free spirit bottle.

'What are you drinking?' She shrugged, so did Paul, who carried on eating.

'That cross, did he give that to you?'

'No, I gave it to a lover – a long time ago.' Paul's eyebrows raised in question. 'I took it back after I killed her.'

Paul stopped chewing and stared at the ceiling – for a long time.

'Is he getting back tonight?'

'Late,' she replied. She hit a switch.

I can see a highway just behind your eyes

Over mountains and rivers it winds

Sometimes I think I know where that highway leads

Sometimes I think I miss the signs

Snow blown days and wine bright nights

We were running, wild deer, from the storm

We were swallows left behind from the longest flight

Finding new ways to keep each other warm

Now the east wind cries, take me back

West wind cries, let it go

It's so late in the year to start a new love

But it's much too soon to know

There are too many highways in this world

Too many roads run east or west

Too many miles lie down between me and you

We can only wait till this winter melts

Now the east wind cries, take me back

West wind cries, let it go

So late in the year to start a new love And much too soon to know

So late in the year to start a new love And much too soon to know

'I think it's too late for all of us. The world is on fast forward and I think we're about to reach the end of the tape.'

'You may be right ... It might be too late for what passes for success, but at least I've got something completed. Each song is something that can exist in its own right ... and if just one person gets something out of it, then that's all right by me.'

'Morgan and I have nothing ... except the baby.'

She poured another drink and studied Paul thoughtfully. 'Do you know something? ... Every time we listen to a track, or you play something, the lyrics echo our situation ... and the music catches the mood of the moment. Morgan has never played the tape straight through ... he takes it one track at a time ... just when he needs a shot, or a sign. He seems to rely on it for direction ... or maybe just confirmation.'

'It's almost the end, there's only one track left,' said Paul.

'That's what frightens me.'

Paul didn't reply, but helped himself to a drink.

Sara started to walk the room. 'It's a form of Karma,' she said, after about a dozen paces, 'Our destiny ... to all meet up ... to share the etheric together, after having been in a spiritual phase ... for centuries probably.'

'Probably.' Paul agreed. This was not a good time for debate.

Her paces were quickening. 'For millions of years nature has balanced out the extremes, has enabled all species to live and evolve in a relative harmony. In the last fifty years the human race has learned to harness the basic power present in the universe. Nuclear fission and fusion, the body's natural defence mechanisms against disease, the replacement of lost limbs and organs BUT, the processes have gone too far! Nature always takes it easy ... slowly, keeps its shape. We've bludgeoned our discoveries into the fabric of the planet'

She took another shot.

'The first result of excess is triumph ... but it's so short lived. Did we honestly believe we could put a lid on all infectious diseases? ... OK, for twenty years maybe, then the reprisals. We've gone to war on our habitat and we can't win. There will be new forms of what we have believed to be eradicated diseases sweeping across continents. A bug can get from here to Europe in half a day. Aids has run riot ... the nuclear power of the sun, we've tried to harness it, but it's been most successful when allowed to go out control as in the bombs on the Japanese cities. When we confine it we get Chernobyl and waste we can't get rid of ... The oil under the earth is finite and will run out one day ... and the fossil fuels are taking away the ozone layer.

It's over. It's too late. Love of our country, love of each other, love of self ... it's not enough. To love the whole of the planet is to touch the collective soul of the planet. When we kill it, we are killing each other.'

'Right.' said Paul, and let her go on.

'We all know this, but why aren't we changing it? ... I'll tell you why.'

'I didn't ask.'

'Because we all think short term. Five years for a politician, ten years to retirement, three years of exams, twenty years to pay off the house, eighteen years until the kids are off our hands ... why bother having them?'

She picked the bottle up by the neck and took a swig.

'Love of our country? ... Have you ever heard of anything so bloody ridiculous? We were told to be patriotic and not impeach Nixon when he was screwing us all ... He tried to change the law of the land to get himself off the hook. When he couldn't, he sacked the men of the law ... And he thought he could get away with it!'

'He didn't.'

'His vice-president Spiro Agnew did. "I'll plead guilty if I don't go to jail." Plea-bargaining ... morally disgusting. Everything has a price. Our elected representatives now talk to paid lobbyists ... NOT the people. Our legislation is developed with *their* influence ... Clinton lied five times over Whitewater ... sorry, made *contradictions*.

The British government were *Economical with the truth* ... The world's gone mad!'

Nothing could stop her now.

'Taxation takes up about a third of the product of our labour. That's OK, but the cost of getting the tax of individuals and multinationals sorted out, and the collection of it ... uses up billions. Just look at the skyscrapers the *accountants* have built for themselves. The millions of people busy counting other people's money ... waste ... they could be out there earning a living, or making something. If the West passed one law which stated ... Twenty-five percent of all income goes to the state ... no exceptions, no tax breaks, no concessions. All those glass towers full of useless bean-counters would disappear overnight. There'd be more money to go around.'

'And a lot on Social Security.'

'They could make themselves useful ... digging trenches, growing rice, cleaning out nuclear reactors, feeding whales, planting trees ... And as for what to do with all the extra cash and manpower ... ban all governments and get some democracy back.'

She buried her head in a pillow and Paul finished his supper.

15

Far out there tonight

Morgan's jacket was slung over one shoulder. Blood seeped through his white slit shirt. It seeped into his Levi's, forming widening purple patches. He slung one arm across her shoulder and using her as a crutch they staggered off across the park together. She looked at his torn jacket and shirt.

'I'll be up all night sewing that lot.'

He breathed heavily and stared straight ahead, saying nothing.

Virginia

The five grey suited men seated around the oval table sat as still as chess pieces. Horizontal lines of light again broke up the shades of grey. Head sat at one apex and was addressing the others.

'I have to tell you gentlemen that we have had a little trouble at the London end.' Siemonsen smirked and did not try very hard to keep his lips straight. Head sipped from a glass of water. 'I am beginning to think that every incompetent in the western hemisphere has decided to join the security services. I've had enough. I don't care if they blast him away in the middle of Marble Arch with a Chieftain tank.'

He thumped the table and shouted. 'I want him taken out ... *now!*' He turned to the smirking man on his right.

'Siemonsen, the next time we meet, the pimple will have been squeezed ... or you'll be squashed!' He picked up his papers and left.

Once the door was safely closed, Siemonsen turned to his colleagues, his arms outstretched. 'Can you believe that? ... I'm three thousand miles away ...' A colleague chipped in.

'Life's a bitch ... It seems our friend has a protective wall around him.' Siemonsen sat back and stared at the ceiling.

'Yes ... I do believe you're right.'

London

The red, open-topped, double-decker London bus swept sedately around Parliament Square and on up the Embankment. It was a typical summer's day in London and the rain was falling gently. What tourists there were had taken to the lower deck, leaving just two hardy individuals sat together, open to the heavens. Sir Anthony surveyed the storm grey river as the incoming tide slid by on its oily way upstream. The man in the trilby hat sitting next to him pulled the collar of his dirty raincoat tight around his neck.

'We 'ad 'im, Tony, stone cold he was. That bloody girl screwed it up for us.'

Sir Anthony turned away from the river and looked into Tony's dismal face.

'This is all very embarrassing ... very, very embarrassing. I promised you see ... gave my word. And Golushko sent over a couple of his best Ukrainians to oversee the operation ... to see how it's done.' Two large, and not very pretty men, had made their way up the stairs and taken their seats behind them. Trench's voice was rising in pitch.

'I'll never let you down again Tony, 'onest, cross me 'art and 'ope to die.'

'I know you won't son,' said Sir Anthony patting him on the knee, 'I'm sure of that. Cheerio.' Sir Anthony rose and made his way towards the stairs, bracing himself on the seats as the bus jerked along. It had left its usual route and was approaching a very low bridge as Sir Tony descended below.

Just before the bus disappeared under the bridge, Trench was suddenly yanked off his feet and lifted into the air from behind. The two heavies were holding him by his thighs. Trench just had time to let out a loud scream before the bus passed under the first low girder.

The scream was replaced by a loud thud.

When the bus emerged, the only occupants of the upper deck were the two heavies, pointing out the sights to each other in a Russian dialect. Behind them and receding into the distance, two feet could be seen dangling and swaying gently. The bus and its miserable passengers travelled on, unknowing and uncaring.

The badly painted sign across the back of the bus read ... 'Mystery Tour -You never know where you might end up.'

Virginia

'You're just about to make my day aren't you Roberts?' Siemonsen was leaning on his desk. He beckoned Roberts to hand over the piece of paper.

'It's all there,' said the creaky individual ... 'As promised.' Siemonsen flattened it out and stared at the result.

E GO TO LONDON MORGAN

E THERMONUCLEAR ARMAGEDDON - LOS ANGELES

E DISCOVERED NEW SECRET FISSION-FUSION HYBRID WAR-HEAD

E HOT INITIATOR. STAR-WAR RADIATION

E HEED THEFT IN SAVANNAH REACTOR

E PHONE TO FIRE TARGET. WHY? WHEN?

E FETCH THE GOV. GO TO PAPER. GET EVEN

E PAUL MILLNS

'Are you sure about this?'

'Absolutely ... It proves that they're all in this together.'

London

Morgan lay back, propped by two pillows. He was stripped to the waist, exposing a long diagonal scar from his left clavicle, down through his left nipple and descending to the right hand side of his pelvis. Sara had done an excellent job of cleaning the wound. Bottles of antiseptic and small bowls of water, together with pink bowls of wet cotton-wool, lay strewn around the small table at the side of the bed.

She dabbed on a final coating of antiseptic. Morgan winced but kept his mouth shut. 'There!' She exclaimed with satisfaction, 'and now for the dressing.' She placed a strip of gauze bandage along the length of the wound, layered cotton wool on top of this and then a final wrapping of bandage. She held the sandwich in place with strips of Elastoplast. She scooped the pink and white debris into a small carrier bag. Morgan looked on saying nothing.

'You're very quiet,' she said, not looking at him and busying herself with the clearing-up. She walked to the window and looked out. 'You were lucky.' She didn't get a reply. She turned on him. 'What's the matter with you?... Can't you be a little civil? ... Can't you ...'

'I'm thinking,' He broke in.

'About time,' she snapped.

'Yes,' he said, 'it is.' He was staring at her intently. 'We have to talk.' He said it quietly.

Sara's cheeks were colouring. She turned away.

'We always talk.' She said hesitantly.

He eased himself up as far as he could. 'You know what I mean ... it's over.' She looked up quickly.

'The game, your game ... It's finished ... Ref's blown the whistle ... Are you going to tell me about it?'

'I don't know what you're talking about.'

Morgan raised himself up. 'Cut the crap lady.'

She looked at him and dropped her jaw, which had the effect of opening her mouth. Morgan moved up off the bed, took a stride towards her, grabbed her by the throat with one hand and held her up against a wall.

'Talk!'

Sara was clutching at his one hand with two of hers.

'Can't breathe.'

He threw her on the bed. 'Talk!'

Sara was holding her throat. Morgan took a step towards her and slapped her hard across the face. Sara's head hit the pillow and one hand came up to her mouth protectively. She was livid, with anger and with colour on one cheek.

'If you ever ...' She didn't get to finish.

He slapped her again, this time across the other cheek, jerking her head in the opposite direction and evening out the colour scheme on her face. He raised his hand again and she raised both of hers.

'OK ... OK ... just don't hit me again.' Morgan straightened his shoulders and Sara tried to compose herself. They were both breathing heavily.

She suddenly bolted for the door, got her hand to it and half opened it before Morgan caught up with her and threw her back on the bed. He repeated the blows to her head, kicking the door shut behind him in the same action. Sara buried her head in the sheets.

'Stop, stop!' She screamed. 'Enough.'

Morgan turned and locked the door. Sara was sobbing; her head buried deep in the pillows. She eventually sat up on the edge of the bed holding her face. He screamed at her.

'You set me up! ... Again! When did they get to you? ... After the stabbing? ... Before?' Sara said nothing. She was dabbing the blood from the side of her mouth with the bed sheet.

Morgan's breathing was more regular, his voice was quieter.

'They always knew our movements. You were always so ... so *competent.*' He stood between her and the door; the silence continued for a long time. Sara broke it, speaking between sobs.

'They targeted you when you started screwing Jacqueline ... when you went to her house.'

'What!' Morgan grabbed her by the shoulders and shook her violently.

'They! ... They! ... Who the hell are *they*!? Who the hell are *you?*' Sara buried her face in her hands. Morgan raised his arm again.

'No!' She cried out. He lowered it.

'CIA ... Special department. They look after sensitive security issues ... I work for them.' Morgan continued to lower his arm, he was finished. His shoulders sagged, and he suddenly looked very tired.

Sara kept talking, between sobs.

'I was going to pick you up in the bar, when we first met ... when that guy turned up who knew me ... that blew it.' She continued to wipe away the blood, talking haltingly. 'Worked out OK though. When I picked you up on the train, it was made easier.' She caught the expression on his face.

'Yes, I picked *you* up. Another operative sat in your seat until you turned up. He moved just as you came along. You're a push-over. If there was a hoop to jump though, I could make you do it ... Easy ... My job was to set you up ... accidents are favourite.' She wiped away some more blood. 'And to find out what you know. You know fuck-all ... all a bloody waste of time.'

'Bloody!' said Morgan, finding his voice with difficulty ...'Yes, very!'

'You don't understand, sometimes it's necessary. I was trying to drop hints, trying to open your eyes.' Morgan grabbed her and shook her again.

'Why ... Why? ... Bloody well tell me *Why?*'

'I don't *know!*' She shouted back ... 'They work on a need to know basis. I do as I'm told, I don't ask why ... I think your girlfriend was working for the opposition. She was probably passing information or storing something. Maybe harbouring an agent ... who cares?'

'I bloody care!' He picked her up, and hurled her across the room. She hit the floor hard. He straddled her and banged her head against the floor repeatedly. 'You-tried-to-kill-me-you-bitch!' He put his hands around her throat. Her mouth opened and her tongue protruded. She was gasping. She struck out with her right hand, poking him in the eyes with two fingers. Morgan fell back holding his face. She half-rose towards him, just as he recovered and laid her out cold with the back of his hand. There was a knock on the door. Three loud raps.

Morgan got to his feet breathing heavily and opened the door six inches.

The Mediterranean landlord was looking worried. He was trying to peer past Morgan and into the room.

'Everything OK? I heard some noise ...' Morgan was sweating, the bandages were beginning to bleed and his breathing was still heavy.

'Fine ... no problem.' He answered. The suspicious look in the landlord's eyes made him continue. 'It's the wife, haven't been married long. She gets a bit excited ... Must have been all those horses. Know what I mean?'

'No.'

'Never mind.'

Morgan slammed the door shut and turned back to her. She was still out. He went into the bathroom and returned with a jug of water. He poured it over her face.

Sara opened her eyes and held her jaw. It wasn't broken, but with the amount of pain, it might as well have been. He sat on the bed and looked down on her, no hint of pity in his eyes. She felt her teeth, confirming one was loose and pulled herself up to her knees, holding the praying position.

'You bastard!'

'You've been trying to *kill* me! ...' He shouted.

'I've been SAVING you... you asshole!'

He leaned forward and grabbed her shoulders, shaking them furiously.

'What the hell are you talking about?'

'Who do you think shot the guy between the eyes? ... It wasn't the stiff! ... Who whacked the two in the alley? ... Who stopped the horse? ...You weren't lucky ... *I* was your luck! ... Why did I bother?...'

She was still on her knees when he spoke again. 'Why did you do that? ... When you had gone to the trouble of setting me up ... Why?'

Sara was feeling her loose tooth. 'Maybe I like to be kind to dumb animals.' Morgan was silent.

'Getting into the sack with me ... Part of the job?'

'Well, I wouldn't do it from choice, would I? You're a loser, Morgan. They're going to get you... and without me, sooner than later.'

Morgan rose and started to throw some clothes into a bag. He picked her handbag up off the floor and turned the contents out. He raked through the items with his fingers and took any cash that he could find. He walked to the wardrobe and took a clean shirt. He had difficulty getting it on. When he had done so, he threw the remains of his leather jacket over his shoulders, gave her one more long hard look and left.

In the black liquid patina of the late London pavements, the scattered neon reflections danced. It was nearly midnight, but there were few cowboys on the streets.

She dived off Oxford Street, into a small orange-lit cellar. The Hundred Club still had a couple of hours of jazz left. She felt she might get lucky. After scouring the bearded faces for twenty minutes she realised she wasn't going to be and left. She had tried Ronnies and a dozen other clubs in the central London area. She was beginning to think this was a waste of time.

Most of them were one-nighters, specialising in some sort of rap or rave music, others were purely jazz. She didn't feel Morgan would be at home in any of them. On the other hand, he could equally be at home anywhere. She was getting hungry. Food had been the last thing on her mind for some hours. She was just realising how dead London was after midnight.

She tried the splashes of colour around Piccadilly Circus, but couldn't bring herself to face the dripping kebabs. She walked down Piccadilly not really knowing why. There weren't many people about and there weren't many cabs about for that matter. Her face was throbbing with pain, the one loose tooth had not settled down and one side of her mouth was so puffed up that her lips on that side were permanently closed.

She knew the bruising was coming up around her eyes. 'Stupid bastard,' she kept repeating to herself. She was referring to Morgan. She was nearing the Ritz and was crossing an intersection when a splash of light to her right caught her eye. It was a bar on Dover Street. She walked towards the light and was relieved to find the door open and music coming from the basement. She walked down to a small cloakroom at the foot of the stairs.

'Still doing food?'

The reply from the young man was affirmative and she entered the gloom. About half the tables were taken up. She moved to one in a dark corner, sat down and picked up the menu. She was starting to feel better. There was a nice jazz band playing and the atmosphere was warm. She ordered a chilli as that didn't take much chewing and a bottle of white wine. She looked around the crowd ... there was no familiar jacket.

When she had finished the chilli and about half the bottle, she sat back and lit a cigarette, stubbing it out after one draw and taking another drink.

Her eyes scanned the bar area and homed in on a solitary individual. There was something familiar about him. She made her way over. He was seated. She stood next to him.

'We can't go on meeting like this,' she said, talking out the side of her mouth.

Paul turned around and stared at her face.

'We should wait 'till the bruises go down?'

She ordered two large whiskies.

'Where is he then?'

'God knows,' said Sara, 'We had a difference of opinion.'

'I can see that.'

They swallowed the scotches. 'He thinks I've been trying to kill him.'

'He must have flipped.'

'Yes,' she said, 'it was the people I worked for that were trying to kill him.'

'That's all right then ...' said Paul, and she ordered some more drinks.

The band finished to loud clapping and the manager jumped on stage to announce that Mr Paul Millns would be playing a few songs before the band's next set.

'Excuse me, I've got to do my bit now.' She didn't look up from her glass, just nodded in assent. He slid off his stool and strolled to the piano. She drank some more.

He's far out there tonight, several drinks ahead of me already.
He's on fire with a different light, and his body's no longer steady
Sometimes I've been out there with him, but tonight I'm glad I'm not.
He's tangled up in strange emotions, and he can't untie the knot
And there's nowhere for him to hide, out there in the glare of the spotlights
He thinks no one will ever take his side, but there's some who would stand by

him tonight

He's far out to sea again, and his anchor's running free
I'd throw out a line to reach to him, but he's too far away from me
No one else can say, high or low tomorrow.
He's piling leaves upon the flames, he's burning up all his sorrows
Sometimes I've been out there with him, but tonight I'm glad I'm not.
He's tangled up in strange emotions, and he can't untie the knot

The cab lurched to a halt and Morgan lurched out of it. The cabby pulled a window down and stuck his head in its place.

'This is it Guv! That'll be seven quid. Take my word for it, lots of life, late licence, forget the West End, it all 'appens 'ere.'

Morgan thrust his hand into his back pocket and pulled out some notes, handing them over to the driver who returned three of them.

'Mind 'ow you go, Guv,' said the driver waving and pulling off. Morgan had been drinking heavily and had decided to continue doing so as far from the centre of London as possible; while the bars were still open that is. He was now staring at the brightly lit exterior of an East-End public house. It had a dance-hall extension to one side and Morgan headed for the door.

Two large gentlemen in penguin suits gazed disapprovingly at him as he made his way up the steps.

'We're only open for another hour, sir,' said one. 'So I think you'd better shove off, don't you.'

Morgan looked at both men in turn. The doorman was starting to feel uneasy. This bloke may have been a bit of a shambles, but he still looked a bit tasty.

'An' you 'ave to 'ave a tie,' The second doorman smiled as he said it. Morgan had just about had enough for one day.

'Look gentlemen,' he said, as clearly as he could, 'I would just like to go in there and have a quiet drink and then leave, quietly, OK?' He raised his arms, which had the effect of opening up the slit in his jacket, rendering his appearance even more disturbing.

'Sorry sir,' they said it together, 'you 'ave to 'ave a tie. We don't want no trouble.'

Morgan couldn't see the connection. He pulled out some notes instead. 'Emma Chisit?'

'She's not in tonight, sir.'

'How-much-is-it?' He really had to concentrate.

One of the doormen had had enough and was feeling lucky. He grabbed the front of Morgan's leather jacket. As he pulled, the zip opened up, exposing the long red slash seeping through the white shirt.

'Christ,' said the other, 'he's been cut.'

'Shaving,' said Morgan.

The two bouncers raised themselves to their full height and stood shoulder to shoulder.

'Piss off son,' said the first, who was about six foot tall, but not much less, wide.

'An' I'd get to 'ospital if I were you,' said the second, 'before we 'ave to put you there.' This one was smaller, but not by much.

Morgan grinned and turned away. However, only the upper half of his body turned. He whipped around and swung a right hand catching the second man flush on the jaw and sending him over the top of the steps. The other one stood back.

'Easy son.' Eyes moving to the right and left for help. Morgan walked back down the steps and down and around to where the stricken doorman lay.

He reached down and tore off his black bow tie. He came back up the steps, putting the tie on over his open-necked shirt.

'Right,' said Morgan. 'I'm wearing a tie ... Can I come in please?'

The doorman realised that no help was at hand and he had seen the effect of one punch from this man. For what they were paying him, he didn't really fancy mixing it with this nutter. He pushed the door open.

'That'll be a fiver guv, just pay at reception.'

Morgan entered, and the doorman ran down the steps to check on his mate who was just waking up.

The crowd inside was heaving to massed strobes, which Morgan tried to ignore as he made for the bar. He surveyed the optics and the pumps and decided to try an English beer. A large bust appeared in front of him, topped by a pretty face, which in turn was surrounded by a mop of tousled blonde hair.

'A pint of bitter please ... Mine's a large one.'

She gave him a strange look and then a lecherous one.

'Large one, eh,' she murmured as she pulled on the handle. 'I'll 'old you to that later if you like.' Morgan grinned and leaned forward.

'I'll look forward to that.'

She gave him her best, theatrically sexy, pout and pushed the pint towards him. It had obviously been a long day for Morgan. He was halfway to the floor before he was halfway down the glass. One of the crowd tripped over him.

'Oh Christ! Can't you get rid of your bloody drunks? Can't get to the bar without stepping on 'em.' The buxom barmaid elbowed a barman.

'Give us an 'and with this one. Get 'im round the back'

Three of the staff dragged Morgan to the rear of the bar, out through a side door and into the car park. The buxom barmaid was following them, putting on her coat as she tottered behind. As the staff were propping Morgan into a sitting position against a wall she grabbed one of the barmen.

'I'm jacking it in tonight meself ... tell the Guv'nor I've got an 'eadache. See you tomorrow ... 'elp me get him into my car, I'll drop 'im off.' Two of the staff exchanged knowing looks, shrugged and got on with the job.

They propped him in the front seat and strapped him in. She shooed the staff back into the pub and as she drove out of the car park her headlights picked out the pub sign ... THE GREEN MAN.

The car was a small British hatchback and Morgan's head was almost between his knees. Her jerky driving had caused him to slip forward until only his knees and feet were above the level of the dashboard. His head was down around her thighs, so the first thing he saw as he came round were her suspenders and stocking tops. His eyes started to regain focus.

'Is this heaven?'

'Soon,' she replied. They jerked on for some time.

'What's your name?' he mumbled.

'Liz ...' She chirped. 'Elizabeth.' They drove on in silence.

The car following them contained one driver and one passenger. They were both large individuals and they had to travel slightly hunched, their heads touching the roof of the car. They followed Elizabeth at a distance of about a hundred yards. The driver of the tailing car turned to his passenger.

'Looks like 'e's found a bed for the night.'

'Lucky sod,' came the reply.

Virginia

Siemonsen was back in his own office talking earnestly to two colleagues.

'My guy's gone over. We ... I ... have a problem. The Brits will have to take him out... without our help to set him up.'

'The sort of help we've been giving them, they could do without,' said a colleague. Siemonsen coughed, and poured himself a glass of water.

'I have to admit our plant has been more of a hindrance than a help.'

'What plant?'

'The girl.' said Siemonsen, 'She was one of ours ... one of mine. They've both got to go. I've told London, no restrictions, no accidents, just speed. At least any crap will be on their doorstep. We'll be clean ... pity about the girl though, I'll miss her ... stupid bitch.' He pressed a button on his intercom. 'Nancy? ... Get rid of all the females on my staff. Yes ... ah! No ... not you ... just the others.' He turned to his colleagues. 'Best to be on the safe side ... it's the hormones.' Two men exchanged looks again.

London

The strong mid-morning sun was forcing itself between the chinks in the curtain. Morgan was lying on the bed, face down, fully clothed and breathing deeply. Elizabeth was sitting up in the bed, cradling her boobs protectively with her elbows. She was not looking very pleased. She pulled her nylon night-dress around her and shook Morgan violently with one hand.

'Get up, for God's sake ... get up, you great big useless ...' She took a large glass of water from beside her bed, lifted his collar and poured it down his back. He woke up and shook his head.

'What the hell happened?'

'Nothing.' She still didn't look happy.

'Where am I?'

She sighed. 'Why do they all say that? Now get the hell out of here. You'll 'ave to go out the window and onto the shed roof. If my dad catches you, there'll be no tellin'...' Morgan stood up and stretched. Elizabeth picked up a copy of Hello and ignored him. He drew back the curtains, blinked, and lifted the sash window very gingerly. He turned to her.

'Are you sure I have to do this?'

'Get on with it,' she whispered loudly. As he turned, his elbow knocked a framed picture of her dad off the dressing-table. He replaced it, hardly sparing a glance at Sir Anthony's stern features staring out at him.

Morgan slipped through the window, sat on the stone sill, gauged the distance to the roof of the shed and took off. The loud bump coincided with the snip of Tony's secateurs as he clipped his roses in the front garden. Tony stopped clipping, listened, shrugged his shoulders and carried on pruning.

Morgan couldn't take his eyes of the detailed jewelled colours. The Impressionists had always been his period, but he had always felt uneasy that it was the bright light of Southern France and the paintings that it inspired that had produced the greatest works. He felt reassured that Monet could still do the business even in London. What had surprised him was the intensity of feeling generated by the Pre-Raphaelites.

The paintings in this room seemed to be a collage of precious stones, the whole producing a surprisingly emotional feel. Millais, Holman Hunt, Arthur Hughes and Rossetti gave Morgan a feeling of reassurance and well-being that passed all his understanding.

He took away the gems in his mind and looked for the coffee shop to clear his head and polish his thoughts.

Even after the third cup of coffee, the feeling of unreality would not go away. This was not helped by the circular, mirrored, smoking area. Its multiple reflections enabled him to see the front and back of his head at the same time. This served only to increase his sense of vulnerability. Perhaps the universe had already started to contract.

Sara stared across the Thames at the monstrous green and cream stage set. There were no high-stepping show girls on its ramparts, just the builder's sign that was still displayed. 'Not exactly a *Secret* service' she thought.

She turned away and crossed the road towards the steep stone steps leading up to the pillared entrance. She stopped inside the marble hall, her head moving like a chicken to get her bearings. She headed to the right and got it wrong. The first couple of rooms she walked through looked as if they were just being decorated. She stopped at a female uniformed attendant and asked where the paintings were. The lady indicated a couple of points on the wall where the paint seemed to be peeling off and Sara realised that this section was too contemporary for Morgan.

She smiled weakly and beat a retreat. She tried a number of rooms on the left. They were more promising. After half an hour she gave up and went back to the main hall. She was about to stalk out towards the revolving door when something caught her eye.

A smooth creamy monolith with an elliptical hole seemed to be taking on a life of its own. She stared at it. It was probably a Henry Moore, but the bare arm that protruded from one of the holes was not his work.

The hand was holding a cigarette and moved up to where the mouth of the statue should be, much to the amusement of a couple of au pairs. Sara knew exactly who the arm belonged to. She walked purposefully towards the statue. The arm was moving up and down. The statue seemed utterly bored and indifferent, sucking furiously on its cigarette through a lip-less mouth.

As Sara approached the girls were laughing more openly. She pushed them aside and grabbed the arm. Morgan's head appeared around the side of the statue. At first grinning, then alarmed. Sara whispered ferociously. 'You try to move ... just an inch ... and you'll need a very large dustpan and brush.'

Morgan tried to jerk his arm free and the monolith moved slightly. They both looked round; the staff hadn't noticed. Sara spoke louder.

'I'm not letting go ... ever!' Morgan stopped struggling and gave her a hard look. He was trying to work her out. He jerked his hand again without success. She was holding on with two hands now. He put his foot up on the side of the stone and pulled hard, smashing Sara up against its side. She let go and fell back, crying out as she did so.

Two security staff turned at the shout and ran towards the source of the disturbance. Sara was picking herself up and Morgan was running away up the marble hall. He was closely followed by two security men and Sara. She stopped and shouted after him.

'It's a bomb ... a nuclear bomb!' Morgan's head jerked 'round. Unfortunately, as it did so he tripped over a pile of cream coloured bricks two courses high, scattering some of them and falling to the polished floor. He narrowly failed to knock over a German couple who were seriously studying Andre's latest version of his homage to the building industry.

'Kinetic art,' explained the Germanic voice ... 'quite impressive.' His companion duly marked her guide.

As Morgan was frog-marched out of the building by four security men, Sara was helping a crying trustee put the bricks back in the right order.

'Don't worry,' she said to him. 'I'll buy you some more ... twice as many if you like?' she said helpfully. But judging by his face, it didn't seem to.

'I'm doing all I can Quentin ... nobody could have done more.' Sir Anthony had the 'phone jammed in his ear.

'The problems are all at your end ...Yes ... Just as I'm getting results and the plebs are beginning to stir, your end falls apart. I'm just that much ...' He snapped his fingers, 'away from a revolution that would put the Royals back in the driving seat... and what happens? There's no Royal Family for them to turn to! ... You've got to get a grip!'

He licked the head off the Guinness before continuing. 'Look here, I've turned the system of justice on its head so that it's all in favour of the criminal and against the victim ... I've taken the police off crime and onto the motorist ... I've taken away the free services, like Water and Health and made the plebs pay through the nose for it ... then rubbing that very nose in it by giving their money to a few individuals too useless to make it anywhere else ... I've annoyed the commuters by jacking up the cost of getting to what work there's still left and then spent the money on new toy-town graphics on the stations, but keeping the punters in the cattle trucks ... AND THEY STILL PUT UP WITH IT! ...What more can I do? ... They still keep voting!'

I have one more little scam. I haven't been able to persuade them to march on Parliament yet, they still think they can vote themselves to democracy once every five years, but having dumbed down the education system to levels of infancy, I think I can turn it to our advantage. We've got some Euro-elections coming up ... I've organised a test-run and put up a candidate representing a fictitious party ... but the name of that party is similar to one of the main ones. If Joe Public is as stupid and apathetic as I think it is, then we could get more than five thousand per ward voting for the Literal Democrats instead of the Liberal Democrats, which could give the result to one of the other parties. If it works, then we could cause havoc by introducing a Conservatory party and a Laborious party, or perhaps a Labia party ... that should pick up quite a few votes ... No Quentin, they can't legislate against it ... It wouldn't be democratic would it? ... Besides, it would be admitting that the population are too stupid to be trusted to put a cross in the right box ... Yes, I know it's down to the comprehensive system, but you can't blame me for that ... it was that bloody woman in the Labour party. The one who made sure her little darling was educated privately.'

Sir Anthony poured more of the black stuff down his throat. 'I truly believe, Quentin, that as long as we can put a stop to the Royals going into show business, then the time is not far off when they will be back up where they belong.'

16

Meaning of the word

London

When she heard the sound of footsteps approaching down the polished linoleum, Doris was given quite a turn. Sir Anthony had left for America and she was not expecting him back for a week. She was even more surprised when the familiar footsteps turned out to be someone quite different.

'Ullo lady, is the guv'nor in?'

Doris was half out of her chair, but sat down again, her mouth imitating a fish. When the sound came out the first words were, 'Who are you? How did you get in here?'

The man was wearing faded dungarees and the air of a tradesman. He reminded her of someone, but she couldn't quite place him.

He waved a key cheerily at her. 'I'm Tony, Sir Anthony asked me to take a look at the radiator ... bit of a leak.'

'Now you come to mention it, he was talking about leaks. You'd better go in and get on with it. I'll put the kettle on.' Tony went on through, whistling softly.

Doris busied herself in her little kitchenette, shaking her head and looking for the biscuits.

'It wasn't right, he should have told her about this. Lager-Lass would be foaming. He never took the security side seriously. She was always telling him.'

Tony's whistling had stopped and she was almost certain she could hear voices.

She went back to her desk and listened carefully, straining her ears at the office door. She had more manners than to listen directly at the keyhole and went back to her Woman's Own.

She was dunking the third biscuit when the voices started up again. There was no doubt about it, the voices were raised, and one of them sounded like Sir Anthony.

She pressed the Bakelite switch on her board and nearly fell off her chair when he answered.

'Yes Doris?'

'I ... I'm sorry sir, I didn't know you were back ... I didn't see you come in!'

'Trip cancelled at the last moment Doris ... I nipped back earlier'

'I'm sorry I showed that man in without asking, Sir'

'Don't worry, Doris, we're getting on fine ... But you know what these people are like ... If you want a job done properly, you've got to do it yourself.'

'Yes Sir, I'll put some extra water in the pot.'

She decided to give them ten minutes to sort out their differences and settled down to the Indoor-Garden section. She was deliberating on the special offer; a specially minted, limited edition, porcelain effect representation of a reproduction garden sundial, suitable for very small gardens, and toilets. The monthly payments were quite reasonable, but they did go on for some time.

The voices were getting louder and she felt sure they were having a row. She'd take the tea in now.

Doris advanced towards the heavily varnished slab of mahogany, holding the silver tray out in front of her. It carried double its usual load and she had to turn her backside to the horizontal brass handle and use its overhang to ease it downwards. She did not have a hand free to knock.

319

As she squeezed through, pushing the tray ahead of her, the voices were rising to a crescendo.

'How dare you try to tell me how to do my job, you little shit?'

'Now 'ang on guv, no need to be like that.'

'I'll have you scrubbing the Mall if you don't pull your finger out. Every job I give you is a cock-up.'

As the door swung wider, she stood transfixed. To her right and reflected clearly in the glass protecting a full-length portrait of the Queen was the image of Tony. He seemed shorter than she'd remembered. His mouth was open to reply, but had stopped as she entered.

In front of her and in profile, Sir Anthony was staring straight ahead open-mouthed. He was sitting down and wearing his three-piece suit, but holding Tony's dungarees up to his chest. She looked at the reflection and back to Sir Anthony, and once more at the reflection, before dropping the tray and its load. The noise of the crash seemed to distract Sir Anthony for a moment.

'Ah Doris, there you are. We won't be needing the second cup, Tony is just leaving.'

'Fairchild ... Quentin Fairchild.' The voice was soothing, 'And yes, a second sugar would be most kind ... dear lady.'

They were sitting in her little alcove, just in front of the kettle. Two men in white coats had just staggered past, bearing a heavily strapped figure prone on a stretcher.

'The shot we've given him, it's done the trick I think,' said Quentin.

'Yes he seems a lot calmer now ... it did give me a turn.'

'Understandable, dear lady ... understandable.'

She shifted slightly as his hand remained on her knee a fraction too long.

'It was right of you to ring me ... very good that'

She sniffed bravely. 'Sir Ant ... I mean Tone ..'

'I think Sir Anthony will do.' The voice was full of reason.

'Yes ... well ... he said to ring that number if I ever had ... you know ... a problem.'

'And you did well Doris ... I shall see to it that you will be ...ah ... looked after.'

He put down his tea. 'Did Sir Anthony say anything before he ... before he was taken away?'

Doris sniffed into a wet handkerchief. 'No sir, nothing ... well nothing you know ... sensible. He did mention something about finding somebody if it was the last thing he'd do. Then he started going on about an *organ* I think it was. This man he wanted ... I think he had his *organ*.'

'And you rang no one else? ... She shook her head ... 'Excellent! It's the strain you see. He'll be fine in a few weeks. In the meantime we shall just have to make do.

Live alone do you? I'll see you get home. My driver will take you.'

'Thank you sir.'

'Just a little thing, could you give him the directions ... very slowly? Better still, *point*. He doesn't speak much English ... he's from the Ukraine. Take him up for a cup of tea if you like.'

Virginia

Roberts was beaming. His stoop wasn't so pronounced and his hands shook in triumph as he waved the white piece of typewritten paper at the three heavily- built suits.

'I have in my hand, a piece of paper,' he declared, his eyes bright with the light of a thousand VDU's. 'It proves beyond doubt that our security has been breached, and that an attempt is being made to expose our incredibly ultimate deterrent ... our *placement thermonuclear devices!*'

The stony expressions on the stone-built suits didn't register on any scale with Roberts. Rictus met Rickets, and they were poles apart; the suits indicating increasing negativity to Roberts' positive assertions.

'I've explained it all to Siemonsen,' said Roberts, sensing the scepticism in the atmosphere. His lights were dimming and the power was fading.

'You won't be reporting to Siemonsen anymore,' said one of the three. Roberts started to open his mouth, but nothing came out. Through the door, came a trolley, attended by two seriously concerned men wearing short white coats over their dark clothing. The first carried a hypodermic needle in his right hand.

The Rockies

The group of wooden buildings nestled under the protective wings of the tall firs, which in turn were protected by the mountains. Some were built partly of stone and loving hands had crafted both materials. The community of buildings seemed to have grown organically out of their habitat; somewhere in Idaho.

Within and around this settlement, for that is what it looked like, were well tended, neat tracts of soil, each growing a variety of vegetables in well defined areas. A pentatonic flute was being played in one of the little cabins, its notes finding a harmony with those of the environment.

The buildings were grouped together around a small courtyard at the centre of which, a stocky, red faced, bearded individual sat on a wooden stool. He was bent over a wooden workbench and was carefully carving a piece of timber using a wooden mallet and curved chisel. His left elbow obscured part of his work, although the legend, 'A Rudolf Steiner School' was plainly visible.

He worked in short flurries of activity, sweeping or blowing away the chippings periodically. The piece of timber was approximately four foot long by three foot high and looked like new signage for this establishment.

Almost all of the buildings were single-storey and looked as if they were no more than two years old.

The first building to the right of the entrance had a steeply sloping roof with large glass panels set into it. Inside this building the light was caught and reflected around the roomy interior. The light in this shadowless space had a translucent quality.

In a far corner of the room a lady was sitting working on a large tapestry. It was nearly completed. She was bending close to it, working the red thread into the dragon's body. St Michael stood proudly above the slain dragon.

She was heavily pregnant and had difficulty getting close to her work. She leaned back and caressed her burden, tight as a drum skin and urgent under her smock.

The slim young man standing behind her and admiring the work put his arm around her shoulders.

'It's nearly finished.'

'Yes,' she said, rubbing her lump again. She gripped his hand and smiled up at him. He looked down at her.

'We've all got our dragons to slay.'

She closed her eyes. He put his hand on her head and squeezed.

'I'll see you later. We've got some new staff arriving and I don't think the rooms are ready yet.' She smiled quickly at him and he left.

She turned back to the tapestry, but put down her needle and closed her eyes again. She started to think. It was something she had trained herself not to do ... she wasn't always successful.

Could it really have been half a year since she sent him to his death ... ?

Sara's thoughts went back to that last night. How could she have let him go? 'I must have been crazy. Of course they were going to kill him.' She remembered thinking that, but too late in the night.

She remembered running out of the flat, running to the docks, scrabbling into the rotting warehouse ... making her way through the industrial nightmare, seeing the two main players in her life acting out the final scene. And then hearing, then watching the curtain come down on the father of her baby.

She remembered walking trance-like towards the pool of light, the crack of the shot still reverberating around the building and her head.

The father of her child, dispatched in this Kafkaesque abattoir. She remembered the two hand-pistols gleaming dully in what little light there was. She remembered picking them up, one in each hand and advancing on the figure under the light. She remembered stopping to look down at her lover, then walking past towards his executioner.

She remembered the look on Siemonsen's face, the surprise, the triumph, then the shock when realisation dawned that two guns were levelled directly at him. She remembered him backing away to the edge of the circle of light. She remembered him reaching for his gun ... his shoulder was shattered by her first bullet.

He spun, and clung on to some racking with his good arm. His gun hit the floor. Her second bullet took out his other shoulder. He spun again, bouncing off the metal and hitting the floor.

'You crazy bitch,' he screamed. She was too numb to say anything. He got to his feet, stepping slowly backwards and away from her, towards darkness, towards safety. She followed him silently, never taking her eyes from his.

'What do you want?' he cried. 'It's over, OK! Quits ... My people will be here in a minute ... We'll look after you.' The third and fourth bullets took out both knee caps. He was writhing in agony on the floor now, but wriggling and sliding ever closer to the blackness. He reached the outer wall and could go no further. She felt the wetness of his blood underfoot.

'We had to do it.' he tried to shout, but it was more of a gurgle. He was having difficulty in maintaining consciousness. 'Don't you see?' he gasped. 'It was our *DUTY*.' His elbow was clutching at a radiator casing. He hauled himself up to a semi-sitting position, his back resting against the dirt-encrusted glass of the first floor window. He sat on the ledge, breathing deeply and bleeding in the blackness. He stretched his arms high, reaching for something and hung there briefly. A crucifixion scene.

She remembered raising the two barrels, pointing them at his chest. She thought his last word was, '*Duty*.' She unloaded both magazines into him, but the force of the twin blasts had taken his body through the window and out of the building before the magazines were empty. The last few rounds just disintegrated what remaining metal and glass there was in the window.

She dropped the guns and turned away. She remembered bending over Morgan's body and kissing him for the last time - and her hand feeling the wetness at the back of his shoulder blade. She looked at the face again. The blood on the forehead was not from the bullet. It had slammed into his shoulder and rammed him into a rack.

She turned him over quickly. His eyes were flickering and his mouth was opening and closing slightly. Christ! he's still alive! Siemonsen's exit had allowed the wind to enter. The bulb was swinging in its draught, creating bizarre patterns and shadows. She didn't have much time. She had put her arms under his shoulders and dragged him the length of the building.

Where that strength had come from, she did not know, but she felt that she was now on a path which would lead her to the answer.

He had come round enough to help her. His central nervous system was probably on automatic. She had got him to the top of the iron staircase when she heard the metal gate creak open. There was no alternative but to lower him, feet first as far as possible - and then drop.

She had jumped down after him and crouched next to his body in the darkness under the stairs. She was aware of four men in dark overalls and hard hats entering the building in single file.

When they were safely inside she slapped Morgan around the face and was surprised to find his responses had improved since the fall. She remembered getting him out into to the street. She remembered flagging down a cab, 'Don't get blood on the seat lady.' She remembered fetching Paul to help him into the flat. She remembered stripping, bathing and bandaging him.

The bullet was still inside somewhere. He was very weak; she didn't think he could live. She remembered telling Paul ... 'I've got to get out ... They're not having the baby.' She remembered throwing money on the bed. 'If he makes it, get him to me ... He'll know where.'

She snapped out of it and re-focused on her work, 'That was a long time ago, this is reality. I'm alone, but not quite,' she thought, patting the lump. 'I still have a piece of him with me.' She took out the tissue, dabbed her eyes and blew her nose, then fingered the silver crucifix. She picked up the needle again.

The slim young man came back into the room, this time he was holding hands with a sweet young thing.

'Judy wanted to see what you've been up to, Sara.' The young lady bounced up to her. 'And you'll be needing some help in the next few weeks,' patting Sara's lump. 'I just want to say that we're all here for you. Anything we can do.'

Sara turned to her, 'Thanks.'

'I'll leave you to it,' said the young man. 'A few people have just arrived,' he shouted back as he was leaving. 'I think one of them's the music teacher.'

Sara worked away with her needle.

'How long did that take you?' Judy asked brightly.

'I've been working at it on and off over the last couple of months.'

'I don't think I'd have the patience'

'It's a labour of love,' replied Sara, and sat back.

'Richard and I want a baby.'

Sara's lips tightened. 'Really?'

Judy's eyes were shining; she was obviously truly, madly, deeply. 'What does *she* know?' Sara's thoughts were tinged with bitterness. 'Just a kid.' Her tears were falling freely now.

'You OK?' chirped Judy. Sara kept her head down.

'Sure, fine.'

Judy bounced to the window and threw it open. Sara was vaguely aware that she was talking to somebody. She came back.

'It's the new music teacher ... I told him the piano is next door.' Sara nodded absently. She reached out and held Judy's hand. She gave it reassuring squeeze.

The sound of the piano came clearly through the open window from the adjacent building. Sara picked up her needle in one last determined effort to finish her work.

The melancholic chords were familiar. The man was singing now. The needle worked in and out ... she was becoming more aware of the music. She tried to shut it out, furiously attacking her canvas. The music was becoming intrusive and her tears were falling freely again. She stood up suddenly, rocking slightly and holding on to the tapestry for support. Judy was staring at her ... Sara turned and walked towards the door. She opened it. The music was getting louder.

She walked across to the next building and threw open the door. Her eyes were streaming, her steps gathered pace as she walked the length of the building to the room at the far end. The words were burning into her mind as the music grew louder ... She knew this voice ... she knew this music.

She flung open the door of the music room.

In the middle of the room was an upright piano, the player had his back to her. She moved unsteadily towards him ... She stood next to the player. He didn't look up. He was wearing Morgan's jacket, but it was too big for Paul and didn't sit easily on his shoulders.

'That's his jacket,' she said. 'Yes,' he replied. 'He won't be needing it anymore.'

The welling tears had become a flood, her shoulders were shaking.

'At least, not until he can lift his arm.'

The word, 'What?' formed on her lips, but the sound didn't come out.

Paul nodded towards the window, he kept playing. She walked to it haltingly, and looked out.

Fifty yards away on the bank of the stream, a tall man in jeans and cowboy boots stared down at the fast flowing water. Dark hair spilt down over his white shirt, and when he turned around, his left arm nestled in a heavy sling. He looked straight towards her with eyes that she knew to be grey.

She said, Love, you don't know the meaning of the word
infidelities and all those games, or so I've heard
you come pleading extenuating circumstances
needing comfort now and just a few more chances
alcoholic pilot, with your vision blurred
poor love, don't knew the meaning of the word
And lies, they sometimes rise easier than the truth
slip gently around our lives, like a hangman's noose
needing one more drink to forget bad dreams
hanging helplessly there like a crucifixion scene
so why am I so shaken but hardly stirred
by love, that didn't know the meaning of the word
She said, Yes, I know we made those tracks so deep
but they melted away with the snows when we turned from sleep
you say let's show reason, let's show sense
so many good things for, so few to hold against

but these bills were long ago incurred
when love, you didn't know the meaning of the word
And yes we were flying, dying through those nights
but the ground far down below strayed from your sights
with your feathers bright and freshly painted
never needing the time to get acquainted
but now you fly down like a wounded bird
poor love, don't know the meaning of the word
poor, poor love, don't know the meaning of the word

Afganistan

The long brown finger was pressing the digits very carefully. It had dialled a long series, then began the final sequence ...

0101-213-62 ... It hovered uncertainly; its owner was coming to a decision ...

'Do it ... finish it,' a dark brown voice urged.

The finger hesitated.

'I may be just starting it ...' replied the dialler.

The End...or maybe not.

If you enjoyed Tears of Glass, then I would really appreciate your thoughts in the form of a review.

Thank you.

David Lake

Your link to the Amazon review page is here. Thanks again.

https://amzn.to/2lKyqvf

If you wish further information and background from David Lake with regard to Tears of Glass and future projects, then please subscribe here.

Suscribe for further information and future publications

Thanks to :

Eric Howard, Chris Jones, Uli Hetscher, Sally Lake Edwards and Paul Millns.

PAUL MILLNS
   RECORDINGS To Date
   PAUL MILLNS
   GIBBI WESTGERMANY
   [Re-Released on CD]
   HEARTBREAKING HIGHWAY
   TILL THE MORNING COMES
   FINALLY FALLS THE RAIN
   [Re-Released on CD]
   REACHING OUT
   SECRET OPERATIONS
   [LP and CD]
   SIMPLY BLUE
   [Compilation CD]
   AGAINST THE TIDE
   PHILLIPS 1975 TELEFUNKEN 1980 BELL RECORDS 1990 TELE-FUNKEN 1981 MAYS RECORDS 1982 JETON RECORDS 1985 BELL RECORDS 1990 PLANE RECORDS 19871 ARIOLA/SA MOUNTAIN 1991 HYPERTENSION RECORDS 1993 HYPERTENSION RECORDS 1994

   Just released in Europe to wide critical acclaim, Paul's new CD,
   AGAINST THE TIDE

Featuring thirteen new songs and superb contributions from Bert Jansch, Ralph McTell, Christine Collister, and members of Pentangle and Fairport Convention.

   'Supremely lyrical and melodic songs.' TIMEOUT
   'One of the most expressive voices you will ever hear' MUSIC WEEK
   For further information on PAUL MILLNS
   Contact www.paulmillns.com

Since this book was first published, Paul has recorded many more albums and Bonny Tyler covered a track.

TEARS OF GLASS

TRACK LIST

SIDE 1 TEARS OF GLASS, MAN OVERBOARD, DROWNING IN THE DEEP END, WHEN LOVE COME CALLING, DRIVE SHE SAID, SECRET OPERATIONS. REACHING OUT FOR HEAVEN

SIDE 2 DONT WAIT TOO LONG, DESPERATE HEART, RESCUE OPERATION, FAR OUT THERE TONIGHT, HALF WAY HOME, LATE IN THE YEAR, MEANING OF THE WORD

ALL WORDS AND MUSIC COMPOSED AND PERFORMED BY PAULMILLNS

MUSIC PUBLISHED BY PAUL MILLNS MUSIC

PAULMILLNS

Born in Norfolk, Paul Millns spent his early musical years playing piano in various blues and soul bands; Music which has remained a strong influence in his work.

Moving to London, he subsequently toured the world in the bands of Alexis Korner, Eric Burdon, Bert Jansch, Jo Ann Kelly and the Chicago blues singer Louisiana Red. Later, as a solo artist he worked at various times with John Mayall, Ralph McTell, John Martyn, Peter Thorup, David Crosby and Murray Head.

SOLO

In the mid-70's, the first solo album of his own songs was released on Phillips and for the next few years he alternated his solo work with his piano duties. In 1979 a trip to Germany to record the soundtrack of original songs for a German feature film 'Gibbi Westgermany' brought him recognition and a reputation in Europe which increased throughout the 80's with subsequent record and CD releases.

TOURS and TELEVISION

Appearances in European TV shows. Notably his solo shows on the biggest TV rock show of the 80's ... ROCK PALAST in Germany.

He has performed in the USA and CANADA and now tours regularly throughout Europe, both solo and with the backing of top British musicians, including critically acclaimed appearances in the main continental festivals and in Britain at the Edinburgh Arts and Cambridge Festivals.

Paul's songs have retained his soul and blues background, but range, unusually, across social, political and personal relationship subject matter, which sometimes shows a more European influence.

His songs have been translated into four other languages and have been performed and recorded by other artists: his 'Too much between us' was chosen by Elkie Brooks for her hit album 'Pearls 2'.

The soul quality of his vocal style has been compared with Ray Charles [One of his early heroes] and Joe Cocker and his piano style, from Memphis Slim to Lenny Tristano. Recently Paul has composed music and songs for other European film productions and music for Thames TV, Channel Four and BBC2. He won a BAFTA award for a Thames TV Production and he regularly contributes to various BBC and ILR radio programmes.

Bonnie Tyler has recorded ' Forget Her' since this book was first published in 1994

www.paulmillns.com

About the Author

David Lake's incarnations include -

Scientist, Marketing Director Virgin Records, Interior Architect, Rock Club Owner and Promotor of Concerts such as Tangerine Dream in three English Cathedrals, Vangelis at the Royal Albert Hall and six David Crosby concerts in London.

His production company made a number of Music Videos for MTV and Arts programmes for TV and Cinema.

David lives with his family in Sussex, England.

Printed in Poland
by Amazon Fulfillment
Poland Sp. z o.o., Wrocław